Sir Arthur Conan Doyle in his study at Hindhead, circa 1904.
(Photo from *Cassell's Magazine*, December, 1906.)

THE BEST SUPERNATURAL TALES OF

Arthur Conan Doyle

Selected and Introduced by

E. F. BLEILER

DOVER PUBLICATIONS, INC.
NEW YORK

This Dover edition, first published in 1979, is an unabridged republication of fifteen stories by Arthur Conan Doyle, all of which originally appeared in periodicals during the years 1880–1921. Detailed bibliographical information is contained in the introduction written especially for this Dover edition by E. F. Bleiler.

International Standard Book Number

ISBN-13: 978-0-486-23725-1
ISBN-10: 0-486-23725-7

Library of Congress Catalog Card Number: 78-66710

Manufactured in the United States by RR Donnelley
23725713 2016
www.doverpublications.com

CONTENTS

ARTHUR CONAN DOYLE AND HIS SUPERNATURAL FICTION

ABOUT the life of Arthur Conan Doyle there is little need to say much, since most readers know something about him. Born in Edinburgh in 1859 into the gifted and influential Irish Doyle family, he took degrees in medicine at Edinburgh University, hoping eventually to specialize in ophthalmology. He was not successful as a practitioner, however, and was forced to various expediencies to make a living. He acted as an assistant to a strange medical charlatan in Plymouth, and served as a ship's doctor on a freighter up and down the coast of West Africa, where he contracted a tropical fever. (In his student days, between his M.B. and M.D., he had previously held the same position on a whaler, where he doubled as apprentice harpooner.) Doyle wrote when medical practice was slack, which meant very often, and bombarded the periodicals with fiction.

Doyle's first published story, "The Mystery of Sasassa Valley" (*Chambers's Journal*, 1879) was a fantasy based on the fluorescence of diamonds. This was followed by a succession of isolated stories, culminating in "A Study in Scarlet" (*Beeton's Christmas Annual* #29, 1887), for which he received a total payment of £25. This was the first Sherlock Holmes story. By 1891, however, Doyle finally realized that he was a writer and not a physician; as Hesketh Pearson put it, "He perceived that it was silly to finance himself as an ophthalmologist, whom no one wanted to consult out of earnings as a writer whom everyone wanted to read." The impetus to success was double: the appearance of *The White Company* in book form and the explosion of popularity when *The Adventures of Sherlock Holmes* appeared serially in 1891 in *The Strand Magazine.*

Doyle soon became the most popular writer in England. For Doyle and for Doyle alone was the print run of *The Strand Magazine* increased when a new story appeared. Today we think of Doyle primarily as the foremost writer of detective stories since Poe, but he was also preëminent in historical fiction, science fiction, adventure and sports stories, topical stories, historical works and journalism. In his own opinion, with which I concur, his best work was the fascinating novel of events in the 13th-century Europe of the Black Prince, *The White Company.*

Doyle also moved much in public life and had opinions, often worth listening to, on many contemporary matters, including military science, in which he was a generation ahead of his day. A staunch supporter of the Establishment in most things, he received a knighthood for his work as an apologist for the British side in the Boer War. In World War I he was semi-official chronicler of the British Army. A remarkably generous man, sincerely moved by abuses of power, he also devoted much time to correcting two judicial injustices, the famous Slater and Edalji cases.

In later life, around 1915–6, Doyle became converted to Spiritualism, and most of his activity thereafter was concerned with missionary work. He travelled and lectured, wrote pamphlets and books, and considered himself bound to defend every aspect of his creed against all comers. In his old age his gullibility was pathetic. He died in 1930.

II

Doyle wrote only fourteen supernatural short stories and four supernatural novels, three of which are short. This is not a large production, especially when one compares it with his writings in other areas. He wrote some sixty stories about Sherlock Holmes and sixteen about Brigadier Gerard of the Napoleonic Army, while his literary corpus comes to more than four hundred works, not counting individual poems and minor journalism.

Yet these few stories reflect his inner personality and interests, just as his sports stories reflect his bouncing athleticism. While his earlier supernatural stories were journalistic, they did not fall into the easy path of the conventional Victorian ghost story, but introduced ideas that he had picked up during his serious reading. His later stories, on the other hand, were often frankly propaganda for the Spiritualist cause.

Doyle left an enormous mass of personal documents, letters, diaries and reading notes (since he apparently was unable to throw such things away), and these reveal that his final conversion to Spiritualism during World War I was not a trauma on the road to Damascus, but a logical development within one channel of his oddly segmented, compartmentalized mind.

After receiving his baccalaureate in medicine Doyle found himself an agnostic. This situation caused great consternation and resentment in his larger family, the Doyles of national importance, since they were all religious to the point of fanaticism. A complete estrangement was the result. But his agnosticism and materialism were only temporary positions, for Doyle, like many others who have been unable to accept traditional religion, soon was unwittingly undertaking a quest for a new Something to take the place of the former absolutism. Strange though it may seem to us today, it was quite possible in the late 19th century to work into a new religious position through the sciences.

When Doyle was a young man science was seriously investigating the phenomena of the supersensual world. On the historical-clinical side, the Society for Psychical Research and the American Society for Psychical Research were conducting investigations into anecdotes of survival and clairvoyance, while the scientists Wallace,

Brewster and Crookes came out in support of mediumistic phenomena.

At this time D. D. Home, the Scottish-American medium, probably the most skilled practitioner of all time, since he was never caught out, was dazzling St. Petersburg and London society with remarkable feats, including daylight levitations. On one famous occasion, it is claimed, Home floated out a window of Ashley House, Buckingham Gate, London, and into another, in the presence of witnesses. William Crookes, the renowned chemist and physicist, investigated Home in his laboratory, and reported that Home could play an accordion fastened under a table while his hands were secured above. Home, it is also reported, could increase or decrease his height at will, and could vary his weight.

Even more spectacular, however, was the case of Katie King. Crookes undertook a laboratory investigation of the medium Florence King, who specialized in materializations. Out of her cabinet, as Crookes reported, there stepped a flesh and blood girl, one Katie King; she was revealed to be a materialization from the spirit world of a West Indian girl who had been dead for two hundred years. Crookes took her photograph and embraced her, stroking her skin, to be sure she was real, as she was. (About a year later a young lady named Eliza White failed to convince the faithful—including Doyle, years later—that she had played the part of Katie King.)

As can be seen, psychical events were exciting in the 1870's and 1880's, far more so than today, where the best that can be done is slide razor blades under a plastic pyramid or bend spoons.

Doyle watched all this attentively. While living at Portsmouth in the 1880's (as reported by John Dickson Carr in his *Life of Sir Arthur Conan Doyle*) he avidly followed psychical research. In 1887 he read more than seventy books dealing with the topic, and in the same year he attended seances and kept detailed notes of what had occurred at each. At an early date Doyle came to the conclusion that Spiritualistic phenomena were genuine—the levitations of tables, the raps, the horn blowing, the messages from the dead—but he was baffled that such trivialities could be associated with a topic so important as survival, and refused to accept the total Spiritualist position. He was caught, to paraphrase Paul, between "Greeks seeking science and Jews demanding miracles." Eventually he came to the position that one need not demand significant evidence; evidence of any sort was sufficient. (It is not appropriate here to tell about the embarrassments of his old age, since his supernatural fiction is mostly from his youth.)

Against this background it is disappointing that Doyle, while in his prime as a writer, say 1890–1905, did not devote more of his abundant energy to supernatural fiction.

III

Most of the stories in this collection originated in ideas that can be traced without too much difficulty either in Doyle's life or in the cultural atmosphere of the day. The earlier stories show an apt journalistic versatility that was able to seize on concepts that were already fairly familiar and channel them into new stories.

"The American's Tale" (*London Society*, 1880), Doyle's second published story, is probably based on the wonderful man-eating plant of Madagascar. This was a traveller's tale familiar to Victorian readers and often retold in popular articles about natural wonders, true or otherwise. Based largely upon an account by William Ellis in his *Three Trips to Madagascar*, it tells of a gigantic plant (perhaps a unique specimen) that grew in a secret jungle glade. From a curiously shaped trunk, long, tentacle-like leaves swirled and trailed onto the ground surrounding it. Should an animal or human be unwary enough to tread on one, he would be whipped aloft into the heart of the plant and eaten, much as a fly is eaten by the Venus fly-trap.

According to the legend, the natives used it for human sacrifices. (Unfortunately, the plant has never been found!) Doyle's approach to this, as he would have frankly admitted, was colored by the popularity of Bret Harte in Great Britain.

More personal to Doyle is the pellucid horror of "The Captain of the *Polestar*" (*Temple Bar*, 1883), with the darkless brilliance of endless day and the horrors of night. It obviously draws on Doyle's experiences in the whaler *Hope*, even to the personalities of the Scottish crew members, who are recorded in Doyle's papers. As for the ghost that pursues and lures, is there perhaps an echo of *Frankenstein*?

"The Silver Hatchet" (*London Society*, 1883) and "The Leather Funnel" (*McClure's Magazine*, 1900) share an idea that probably emerged from Doyle's serious reading in the literature of Spiritualism. This was psychometry, or the concept that inanimate objects may retain a certain latent memory, as it were, which can be re-experienced by suitable sensitive persons. Many a medium during Doyle's youth pressed old rags, stones or artifacts against his or her forehead, hoping to emerge with a vision of the past. I remember one American volume of psychometric readings from the 1860's in which a medium constructed a Carboniferous forest from a lump of coal and after handling a meteorite fragment described a wonderful utopia on another planet. Doyle turned this concept around into thriller situations, much as he did with the contagious magic implicit in "The Brown Hand" (*The Strand Magazine*, 1899).

Doyle's other reading may have provided the ideas for two stories. *Vice Versa* by Doyle's friend F. Anstey was very popular in the early 1880's. It was a humorous novel about a personality exchange between a Victorian schoolboy and his domineering heavy father, caused by an ill-considered wish made on a magical stone. In "The Great Keinplatz Experiment" (*Belgravia*, 1885) the exchange of personalities is caused by hypnosis, which was very much in the air at the time, what with Bramwell's experiments with medical hypnosis in India. Similarly "John Barrington Cowles" (*Cassell's Saturday Journal*, 1886) is derivative from Oliver Wendell Holmes's *Elsie Venner*. Doyle admired Holmes greatly, and many years later he headed a delegation to lay a wreath on Holmes's grave.

"J. Habakuk Jephson's Statement," which appeared in the January 1884 issue of the prestigious *Cornhill Magazine*, is in a class by itself as a fantasy of history. Like Arthur Machen's "Angels of Mons" or Meinhold's *Amber Witch*, it is one of the few pieces of fiction that have been taken seriously as fact and have been hotly refuted or defended by persons who should have known better.

This story, which appeared anonymously, was based on the historical incident of the *Mary Celeste*, one of the great mysteries of the sea. In December, 1872, a brig under full sail was seen working its way erratically through the seas about 250 miles west of Portugal. It did not respond to signals, and when boarded revealed a strange situation: the ship was derelict, unmanned; perfectly sound in all respects; cargo untouched. Yet it bore evidence of having been abandoned in the greatest of haste. The sails were set, personal effects (including jewelry) were still on board the ship, food was exposed in the galley, and the log, in the last entry, placed the ship almost 900 miles farther west, about ten days earlier. What had happened to the crew, the captain, his wife and baby daughter? Today, one might invoke an Azorean Triangle in explanation, but the 19th century had no such explanation. The mystery remains unsolved today, although there have been many reasonable and unreasonable attempts at solutions.

While most of Doyle's readers probably had enough sense to recognize that Mr. J. Habakuk Jephson was a Yankee of literature and that his adventures on board the *Marie Celeste* (Doyle's spelling) were unlikely, Mr. Solly Flood, Her Majesty's Advocate-General and Proctor at

Gibraltar, who had handled the salvage of the *Mary Celeste*, sent public telegrams denouncing the story as untrue. He followed this with an official report to the Admiralty proclaiming Jephson to be a hoaxer. Needless to say, the press, when details emerged, was delighted, as was Dr. Doyle.

Less likely to be taken for current events are Doyle's two Egyptological stories, "The Ring of Thoth" (*The Cornhill Magazine*, 1890) and "Lot No. 249" (*Harpers Magazine*, 1892). Both good thrillers, they show the intense interest in ancient Egypt that arose during the last part of the 19th century after the findings of the Egypt Exploration Society. It is interesting to compare Doyle's low-keyed development of the mummy theme with the sensationalism of E. and H. Heron's "Story of Baelbrow" (*Pearson's Magazine*, 1898), where occult detective Flaxman Low encounters a similar entity.

"Playing with Fire" (*The Strand Magazine*, 1900) might have some autobiographical interest if it could be taken as marking a stage in Doyle's religious development. The narrator makes points that Doyle would have accepted: that there may be fraud in the occult, that there are genuine phenomena, that the explanations are not wholly satisfactory. Readers who are interested in a story more sophisticated in idea, if more primitive in telling, might compare Doyle's story with Charles Williams's novel *The Place of the Lion*, where the Archetypes, through a similar breaking of bonds, flash loose.

Not until late in his career, when he was 60, did Doyle write a conventional ghost story with Victorian values. This is "The Bully of Brocas Court" (*The Strand Magazine*, 1921), in which the ghost is a traditional personal fragment of a dead person, earthbound until its crimes are expiated. But it must be noted that the background of the story is very unusual, since the Bully is tied in with Doyle's earlier Regency sporting stories, like *Rodney Stone*, rather than with conventional settings.

Not surprisingly, since it strikes a sports note that Doyle delighted in, it is one of Doyle's best stories.

There is little that can be said of the remaining stories in this collection. The "Los Amigos Fiasco" (*The Idler Magazine*, 1892) is an amusing fantasy in the mode of Bret Harte. "Selecting a Ghost" (*London Society*, 1883), also known as "The Secret of Goresthorpe Grange," and "A Literary Mosaic" (*The Boy's Own Paper*, 1886), also known as "Cyprian Overbeck Wells," are pleasant tours de force, notable only in that they are not as dull as most comparable stories.

In addition to the stories in this collection Doyle wrote six other works that involve supernaturalism. *The Land of Mist* (1926) is a fairly long novel which is avowedly propaganda for the Spiritualist cause. In it the arrogant but brilliant Professor Challenger is forced to grovel before the spirits when his daughter becomes a medium and he attains contact with his dead wife. It was not well received when it appeared. The three shorter novels are also supernatural. These are *The Mystery of Cloomber* (1889), a restirring of motifs from *The Moonstone* plummed out with a little Stevenson; *The Parasite* (1894), which deals with psychological bondage and hypnotism; and "The Maracot Deep" (*The Strand Magazine*, 1927–8). The last story tells of a group of scientists who accidently drop into Atlantis, via a bathysphere, and there take part in a cosmic battle between Good and Evil. There are also two short stories, "How It Happened" (*The Strand Magazine*, 1913) and "The Silver Mirror" (*The Strand Magazine*, 1908), which are not significant.

IV

Arthur Conan Doyle, it must be admitted, was not the towering figure in supernatural fiction that he was in the detective story or the historical novel. No one places his name with those of his contemporaries Bram Stoker, M. R. James, Algernon Blackwood, Arthur Machen or

Ambrose Bierce. His was not a new vision, as was theirs; his was merely respectable accomplishment.

This is not to say that his supernatural stories are not worth reading. Doyle was one of the finest storytellers in modern English literature, and the dynamism of his better work often appeared in his lesser writings. If his weak area is idea, the zest and vitality with which his stories are told, the clear and forceful expression outweigh deficiencies. The situation in "The Great Keinplatz Experiment" is farcical, yet the reader is likely to remember Professor von Baumgarten, while the strange, immortal Egyptian of "The Ring of Thoth" may haunt the memory corridors of our mind-museums long after Doyle's "better" stories are forgotten.

E. F. Bleiler

THE BULLY OF BROCAS COURT

THAT year—it was in 1878—the South Midland Yeomanry were out near Luton, and the real question which appealed to every man in the great camp was not how to prepare for a possible European war, but the far more vital one how to get a man who could stand up for ten rounds to Farrier-Sergeant Burton. Slogger Burton was a fine upstanding fourteen stone of bone and brawn, with a smack in either hand which would leave any ordinary mortal senseless. A match must be found for him somewhere or his head would outgrow his dragoon helmet. Therefore Sir Fred. Milburn, better known as Mumbles, was dispatched to London to find if among the fancy there was no one who would make a journey in order to take down the number of the bold dragoon.

They were bad days, those, in the prize-ring. The old knuckle-fighting had died out in scandal and disgrace, smothered by the pestilent crowd of betting men and ruffians of all sorts who hung upon the edge of the movement and brought disgrace and ruin upon the decent fighting men, who were often humble heroes whose gallantry has never been surpassed. An honest sportsman who desired to see a fight was usually set upon by villains, against whom he had no redress, since he was himself engaged on what was technically an illegal action. He was stripped in the open street, his purse taken, and his head split open if he ventured to resist. The ringside could only be reached by men who were prepared to fight their way there with cudgels and hunting-crops. No wonder that the classic sport was attended now by those only who had nothing to lose.

On the other hand, the era of the reserved building and the legal glove-fight had not yet arisen, and the cult was in a strange intermediate condition. It was impossible to regulate it, and equally impossible to abolish it, since nothing appeals more directly and powerfully to the average Briton. Therefore there were scrambling contests in stableyards and barns, hurried visits to France, secret meetings at dawn in wild parts of the country, and all manner of evasions and experiments. The men themselves became as unsatisfactory as their surroundings. There could be no honest open contest, and the loudest bragger talked his way to the top of the list. Only across the Atlantic had the huge figure of John Lawrence Sullivan appeared, who was destined to be the last of the earlier system and the first of the later one.

Things being in this condition, the sporting Yeomanry Captain found it no easy matter among the boxing saloons and sporting pubs of London to find a man who could be relied upon to give a good account of the huge Farrier-Sergeant. Heavy-weights were at a premium. Finally his choice fell upon Alf Stevens of Kentish Town, an excellent rising middle-weight who had never yet known defeat and had indeed some claims to the championship. His professional experience and craft would surely make up for the three stone of weight which separated him from the formidable dragoon. It was in this hope that Sir Fred. Milburn engaged him, and proceeded to convey him in his dog-cart behind a pair of spanking greys to the camp of the Yeomen. They were to start one evening, drive up the Great North Road, sleep at St. Albans, and finish their journey next day.

The prize-fighter met the sporting Baronet at the Golden Cross, where Bates, the little groom, was standing at the head of the spirited horses. Stevens, a pale-faced, clean-cut young fellow, mounted beside his employer and waved his hand to a little knot of fighting men, rough, collarless, reefer-coated fellows who had gathered to bid their comrade good-bye. " Good luck, Alf ! " came in a hoarse chorus as the boy released the horses' heads and sprang in behind, while the high dog-cart swung swiftly round the curve into Trafalgar Square.

Sir Frederick was so busy steering among the traffic in Oxford Street and the Edgware Road that he had little thought for anything else, but when he got into the edges of the country near Hendon, and the hedges had at last taken the place of that endless panorama of brick dwellings, he let his horses go easy with a loose rein while he turned his attention to the young man at his side. He had found him by correspondence and recommendation, so that he had some curiosity now in looking him over. Twilight was already falling and the light dim, but what the Baronet saw pleased him well. The man was a fighter every inch, clean-cut, deep-chested, with the long straight cheek and deep-set eye which goes with an obstinate courage. Above all, he was a man who had never yet met his master and was still upheld by the deep sustaining confidence which is never quite the same after a single defeat. The Baronet chuckled as he realized what a surprise packet was being carried north for the Farrier-Sergeant.

" I suppose you are in some sort of training, Stevens ? " he remarked, turning to his companion.

" Yes, sir ; I am fit to fight for my life."

" So I should judge by the look of you."

" I live regular all the time, sir, but I was matched against Mike Connor for this last week-end and scaled down to eleven four. Then he paid forfeit, and here I am at the top of my form."

" That's lucky. You'll need it all against a man who has a pull of three stone and four inches."

The young man smiled.

"I have given greater odds than that, sir."

"I dare say. But he's a game man as well."

"Well, sir, one can but do one's best."

The Baronet liked the modest but assured tone of the young pugilist. Suddenly an amusing thought struck him, and he burst out laughing.

"By Jove!" he cried. "What a lark if the Bully is out to-night!"

Alf Stevens pricked up his ears.

"Who might he be, sir?"

"Well, that's what the folk are asking. Some say they've seen him, and some say he's a fairy-tale, but there's good evidence that he is a real man with a pair of rare good fists that leave their marks behind him."

"And where might he live?"

"On this very road. It's between Finchley and Elstree, as I've heard. There are two chaps, and they come out on nights when the moon is at full and challenge the passers-by to fight in the old style. One fights and the other picks up. By George! the fellow *can* fight, too, by all accounts. Chaps have been found in the morning with their faces all cut to ribbons to show that the Bully had been at work upon them."

Alf Stevens was full of interest.

"I've always wanted to try an old-style battle, sir, but it never chanced to come my way. I believe it would suit me better than the gloves."

"Then you won't refuse the Bully?"

"Refuse him! I'd go ten mile to meet him."

"By George! it would be great!" cried the Baronet. "Well, the moon is at the full, and the place should be about here."

"If he's as good as you say," Stevens remarked, "he should be known in the ring, unless he is just an amateur who amuses himself like that."

"Some think he's an ostler, or maybe a racing man from the training stables over yonder. Where there are horses there is boxing. If you can believe the accounts, there is something a bit queer and outlandish about the fellow. Hi! Look out, damn you, look out!"

The Baronet's voice had risen to a sudden screech of surprise and of anger. At this point the road dips down into a hollow, heavily shaded by trees, so that at night it arches across like the mouth of a tunnel. At the foot of the slope there stand two great stone pillars, which, as viewed by daylight, are lichen-stained and weathered, with heraldic devices on each which are so mutilated by time that they are mere protuberances of stone. An iron gate of elegant design, hanging loosely upon rusted hinges, proclaims both the past glories and the present decay of Brocas Old Hall, which lies at the end of the weed-encumbered avenue. It was from the shadow of this ancient gateway that an active figure had sprung suddenly into the centre of the road and had, with great dexterity, held up the horses, who ramped and pawed as they were forced back upon their haunches.

"Here, Rowe, you 'old the tits, will ye?" cried a high strident voice. "I've a little word to say to this 'ere slap-up Corinthian before 'e goes any farther."

A second man had emerged from the shadows and without a word took hold of the horses' heads. He was a short, thick fellow, dressed in a curious brown many-caped overcoat, which came to his knees, with gaiters and boots beneath it. He wore no hat, and those in the dog-cart had a view, as he came in front of the side-lamps, of a surly red face with an ill-fitting lower lip clean shaven, and a high black cravat swathed tightly under the chin. As he gripped the leathers his more active comrade sprang forward and rested a bony hand upon the side of the splashboard while he looked keenly up with a pair of fierce blue eyes at the faces of the two travellers, the light beating full upon his own features. He wore a hat low upon his brow, but in spite of its shadow both the Baronet and the pugilist could see enough to shrink from him, for it was an evil face, evil but very formidable, stern, craggy, high-nosed, and fierce, with an inexorable mouth which bespoke a nature which would neither ask for mercy nor grant it. As to his age, one could only say for certain that a man with such a face was young enough to have all his virility and old enough to have experienced all the wickedness of life. The cold, savage eyes took a deliberate survey, first of the Baronet and then of the young man beside him.

"Aye, Rowe, it's a slap-up Corinthian, same as I said," he remarked over his shoulder to his companion. "But this other is a likely chap. If 'e isn't a millin' cove 'e ought to be. Any'ow, we'll try 'im out."

"Look here," said the Baronet, "I don't know who you are, except that you are a damned impertinent fellow. I'd put the lash of my whip across your face for two pins!"

"Stow that gammon, gov'nor! It ain't safe to speak to me like that."

"I've heard of you and your ways!" cried the angry soldier. "I'll teach you to stop my horses on the Queen's high road! You've got the wrong men this time, my fine fellow, as you will soon learn."

"That's as it may be," said the stranger. "May'ap, master, we may all learn something before we part. One or other of you 'as got to get down and put up your 'ands before you get any farther."

Stevens had instantly sprung down into the road.

"If you want a fight you've come to the right shop," said he; "it's my trade, so don't say I took you unawares."

The stranger gave a cry of satisfaction.

"Blow my dickey!" he shouted. "It *is* a millin' cove, Joe, same as I said. No more chaw-bacons for us, but the real thing. Well, young man, you've met your master to-night. Happen you never 'eard what Lord Longmore said o' me? 'A man must be made special to beat you,' says 'e. That's wot Lord Longmore said."

"That was before the Bull came along," growled the man in front, speaking for the first time.

" Stow your chaffing, Joe ! A little more about the Bull and you and me will quarrel. 'E bested me once, but it's all betters and no takers that I glut 'im if ever we meet again. Well, young man, what d'ye think of me ? "

" I think you've got your share of cheek."

" Cheek. Wot's that ? "

" Impudence, bluff—gas, if you like."

The last word had a surprising effect upon the stranger. He smote his leg with his hand and broke out into a high neighing laugh, in which he was joined by his gruff companion.

" You've said the right word, my beauty," cried the latter, " ' Gas ' is the word and no error. Well, there's a good moon, but the clouds are comin' up. We had best use the light while we can."

Whilst this conversation had been going on the Baronet had been looking with an ever-growing amazement at the attire of the stranger. A good deal of it confirmed his belief that he was connected with some stables, though making every allowance for this his appearance was very eccentric and old-fashioned. Upon his head he wore a yellowish-white top-hat of long-haired beaver, such as is still affected by some drivers of four-in-hands, with a bell crown and a curling brim. His dress consisted of a short-waisted swallow-tail coat, snuff-coloured, with steel buttons. It opened in front to show a vest of striped silk, while his legs were encased in buff knee-breeches with blue stockings and low shoes. The figure was angular and hard, with a great suggestion of wiry activity. This Bully of Brocas was clearly a very great character, and the young dragoon officer chuckled as he thought what a glorious story he would carry back to the mess of this queer old-world figure and the thrashing which he was about to receive from the famous London boxer.

Billy, the little groom, had taken charge of the horses, who were shivering and sweating.

" This way ! " said the stout man, turning towards

the gate. It was a sinister place, black and weird, with the crumbling pillars and the heavy arching trees. Neither the Baronet nor the pugilist liked the look of it.

"Where are you going, then?"

"This is no place for a fight," said the stout man. "We've got as pretty a place as ever you saw inside the gate here. You couldn't beat it on Molesey Hurst."

"The road is good enough for me," said Stevens.

"The road is good enough for two Johnny Raws," said the man with the beaver hat. "It ain't good enough for two slap-up millin' coves like you an' me. You ain't afeard, are you?"

"Not of you or ten like you," said Stevens, stoutly.

"Well, then, come with me and do it as it ought to be done."

Sir Frederic and Stevens exchanged glances.

"I'm game," said the pugilist.

"Come on, then."

The little party of four passed through the gateway. Behind them in the darkness the horses stamped and reared, while the voice of the boy could be heard as he vainly tried to soothe them. After walking fifty yards up the grass-grown drive the guide turned to the right through a thick belt of trees, and they came out upon a circular plot of grass, white and clear in the moonlight. It had a raised bank, and on the farther side was one of those little pillared stone summer-houses beloved by the early Georgians.

"What did I tell you?" cried the stout man, triumphantly. "Could you do better than this within twenty mile of town? It was made for it. Now, Tom, get to work upon him, and show us what you can do."

It had all become like an extraordinary dream. The strange men, their odd dress, their queer speech, the moonlit circle of grass, and the pillared summer-house all wove themselves into one fantastic whole. It was only the sight of Alf Stevens's ill-fitting tweed suit, and his homely English face surmounting it, which brought the Baronet back to the workaday world. The thin stranger had taken off his beaver hat, his swallow-tailed coat, his silk waistcoat, and finally his shirt had been drawn over his head by his second. Stevens in a cool and leisurely fashion kept pace with the preparations of his antagonist. Then the two fighting men turned upon each other.

But as they did so Stevens gave an exclamation of surprise and horror. The removal of the beaver hat had disclosed a horrible mutilation of the head of his antagonist. The whole upper forehead had fallen in, and there seemed to be a broad red weal between his close-cropped hair and his heavy brows.

"Good Lord," cried the young pugilist. "What's amiss with the man?"

The question seemed to rouse a cold fury in his antagonist.

"You look out for your own head, master," said he. "You'll find enough to do, I'm thinkin', without talkin' about mine."

This retort drew a shout of hoarse laughter from his second. "Well said, my Tommy!" he cried. "It's Lombard Street to a China orange on the one and only."

The man whom he called Tom was standing with his hands up in the centre of the natural ring. He looked a big man in his clothes, but he seemed bigger in the buff, and his barrel chest, sloping shoulders, and loosely-slung muscular arms were all ideal for the game. His grim eyes gleamed fiercely beneath his misshapen brows, and his lips were set in a fixed hard smile, more menacing than a scowl. The pugilist confessed, as he approached him, that he had never seen a more formidable figure. But his bold heart rose to the fact that he had never yet found the man who could master him, and that it was hardly credible that he would appear as an old-fashioned stranger on a country road. Therefore, with an answering smile, he took up his position and raised his hands.

But what followed was entirely beyond his experience.

The stranger feinted quickly with his left, and sent in a swinging hit with his right, so quick and hard that Stevens had barely time to avoid it and to counter with a short jab as his opponent rushed in upon him. Next instant the man's bony arms were round him, and the pugilist was hurled into the air in a whirling cross-buttock, coming down with a heavy thud upon the grass. The stranger stood back and folded his arms while Stevens scrambled to his feet with a red flush of anger upon his cheeks.

"Look here," he cried. "What sort of game is this?"

"We claim foul!" the Baronet shouted.

"Foul be damned! As clean a throw as ever I saw!" said the stout man. "What rules do you fight under?"

"Queensberry, of course."

"I never heard of it. It's London prize-ring with us."

"Come on, then!" cried Stevens, furiously. "I can wrestle as well as another. You won't get me napping again."

Nor did he. The next time that the stranger rushed in Stevens caught him in as strong a grip, and after swinging and swaying they came down together in a dog-fall. Three times this occurred, and each time the stranger walked across to his friend and seated himself upon the grassy bank before he recommenced.

"What d'ye make of him?" the Baronet asked, in one of these pauses.

Stevens was bleeding from the ear, but otherwise showed no sign of damage.

"He knows a lot," said the pugilist. "I don't know where he learned it, but he's had a deal of practice somewhere. He's as strong as a lion and as hard as a board, for all his queer face."

"Keep him at out-fighting. I think you are his master there."

"I'm not so sure that I'm his master anywhere, but I'll try my best."

It was a desperate fight, and as round followed round it became clear, even to the amazed Baronet, that the middle-weight champion had met his match. The stranger had a clever draw and a rush which, with his springing hits, made him a most dangerous foe. His head and body seemed insensible to blows, and the horribly malignant smile never for one instant flickered from his lips. He hit very hard with fists like flints, and his blows whizzed up from every angle. He had one particularly deadly lead, an uppercut at the jaw, which again and again nearly came home, until at last it did actually fly past the guard and brought Stevens to the ground. The stout man gave a whoop of triumph. " The whisker hit, by George !. It's a horse to a hen on my Tommy ! Another like that, lad, and you have him beat."

" I say, Stevens, this is going too far," said the Baronet, as he supported his weary man. " What will the regiment say if I bring you up all knocked to pieces in a bye-battle ! Shake hands with this fellow and give him best, or you'll not be fit for your job."

" Give him best? Not I !" cried Stevens, angrily. " I'll knock that damned smile off his ugly mug before I've done."

" What about the Sergeant ? "

" I'd rather go back to London and never see the Sergeant than have my number taken down by this chap."

" Well, 'ad enough ? " his opponent asked, in a sneering voice, as he moved from his seat on the bank.

For answer young Stevens sprang forward and rushed at his man with all the strength that was left to him. By the fury of his onset he drove him back, and for a long minute had all the better of the exchanges. But this iron fighter seemed never to tire. His step was as quick and his blow as hard as ever when this long rally had ended. Stevens had eased up from pure exhaustion. But his opponent did not ease up. He came back on him with a shower of furious blows which beat down the weary guard of the pugilist. Alf Stevens was at the end of his strength and would in another instant have sunk to the ground but for a singular intervention.

It has been said that in their approach to the ring the party had passed through a grove of trees. Out of these there came a peculiar shrill cry, a cry of agony, which might be from a child or from some small woodland creature in distress. It was inarticulate, high-pitched, and inexpressibly melancholy. At the sound the stranger, who had knocked Stevens on to his knees, staggered back and looked round him with an expression of helpless horror upon his face. The smile had left his lips and there only remained the loose-lipped weakness of a man in the last extremity of terror.

" It's after me again, mate ! " he cried.

" Stick it out, Tom ! You have him nearly beat ! It can't hurt you."

" It can 'urt me ! It will 'urt me ! " screamed the fighting man. " My God ! I can't face it ! Ah, I see it ! I see it ! "

With a scream of fear he turned and bounded off into the brushwood. His companion, swearing loudly, picked up the pile of clothes and darted after him, the dark shadows swallowing up their flying figures.

Stevens, half-senselessly, had staggered back and lay upon the grassy bank, his head pillowed upon the chest of the young Baronet, who was holding his flask of brandy to his lips. As they sat there they were both aware that the cries had become louder and shriller. Then from among the bushes there ran a small white terrier, nosing about as if following a trail and yelping most piteously. It squattered across the grassy sward, taking no notice of the two young men. Then it also vanished into the shadows. As it did so the two spectators sprang to their feet and ran as hard as they could tear for the gateway and the trap. Terror had seized them—a panic terror far above reason or control. Shivering and shaking, they threw themselves into the dog-cart, and it was not until the willing horses had put two good miles between that ill-omened hollow and themselves that they at last ventured to speak.

"Did you ever see such a dog?" asked the Baronet.

"No," cried Stevens. "And, please God, I never may again."

Late that night the two travellers broke their journey at the Swan Inn, near Harpenden Common. The landlord was an old acquaintance of the Baronet's, and gladly joined him in a glass of port after supper. A famous old sport was Mr. Joe Horner, of the Swan, and he would talk by the hour of the legends of the ring, whether new or old. The name of Alf Stevens was well known to him, and he looked at him with the deepest interest.

"Why, sir, you have surely been fighting," said he. "I hadn't read of any engagement in the papers."

"Enough said of that," Stevens answered, in a surly voice.

"Well, no offence! I suppose"—his smiling face became suddenly very serious—"I suppose you didn't, by chance, see anything of him they call the Bully of Brocas as you came north?"

"Well, what if we did?'

The landlord was tense with excitement.

"It was him that nearly killed Bob Meadows. It was at the very gate of Brocas Old Hall that he stopped him. Another man was with him. Bob was game to the marrow, but he was found hit to pieces on the lawn inside the gate where the summer-house stands."

The Baronet nodded.

"Ah, you've been there!" cried the landlord.

"Well, we may as well make a clean breast of it," said the Baronet, looking at Stevens. "We have been there, and we met the man you speak of—an ugly customer he is, too!"

"Tell me!" said the landlord, in a voice that sank

to a whisper. "Is it true what Bob Meadows says, that the men are dressed like our grandfathers, and that the fighting man has his head all caved in?"

"Well, he was old-fashioned, certainly, and his head was the queerest ever I saw."

"God in Heaven!" cried the landlord. "Do you know, sir, that Tom Hickman, the famous prize-fighter, together with his pal, Joe Rowe, a silversmith of the City, met his death at that very point in the year 1822, when he was drunk, and tried to drive on the wrong side of a wagon? Both were killed and the wheel of the wagon crushed in Hickman's forehead."

"Hickman! Hickman!" said the Baronet. "Not the gasman?"

"Yes, sir, they called him Gas. He won his fights with what they called the 'whisker hit,' and no one could stand against him until Neate—him that they called the Bristol Bull—brought him down."

Stevens had risen from the table as white as cheese. "Let's get out of this, sir. I want fresh air. Let us get on our way."

The landlord clapped him on the back.

"Cheer up, lad! You've held him off, anyhow, and that's more than anyone else has ever done. Sit down and have another glass of wine, for if a man in England has earned it this night it is you. There's many a debt you would pay if you gave the Gasman a welting, whether dead or alive. Do you know what he did in this very room?"

The two travellers looked round with startled eyes at the lofty room, stone-flagged and oak-panelled, with great open grate at the farther end.

"Yes, in this very room. I had it from old Squire Scotter, who was here that very night. It was the day when Shelton beat Josh Hudson out St. Albans way, and Gas had won a pocketful of money on the fight. He and his pal Rowe came in here upon their way, and he was mad-raging drunk. The folk fairly shrunk into the corners and under the tables, for he was stalkin' round with the great kitchen poker in his hand, and there was murder behind the smile upon his face. He was like that when the drink was in him—cruel, reckless, and a terror to the world. Well, what think you that he did at last with the poker? There was a little dog, a terrier as I've heard, coiled up before the fire, for it was a bitter December night. The Gasman broke its back with one blow of the poker. Then he burst out laughin', flung a curse or two at the folk that shrunk away from him, and so out to his high gig that was waiting outside. The next we heard was that he was carried down to Finchley with his head ground to a jelly by the wagon wheel. Yes, they do say the little dog with its bleeding skin and its broken back has been seen since then, crawlin' and yelpin' about Brocas Corner, as if it were lookin' for the swine that killed it. So you see, Mr. Stevens, you were fightin' for more than yourself when you put it across the Gasman."

"Maybe so," said the young prize-fighter, "but I want no more fights like that. The Farrier-Sergeant is good enough for me, sir, and if it is the same to you, we'll take a railway train back to town."

THE CAPTAIN OF THE *POLESTAR*

[Being an extract from the singular journal of John M'Alister Ray, student of medicine.]

SEPTEMBER 11*th*.—Lat. 81° 40′ N.; long. 2° E. Still lying-to amid enormous ice-fields. The one which stretches away to the north of us, and to which our ice-anchor is attached, cannot be smaller than an English county. To the right and left unbroken sheets extend to the horizon. This morning the mate reported that there were signs of pack ice to the southward. Should this form of sufficient thickness to bar our return, we shall be in a position of danger, as the food, I hear, is already running somewhat short. It is late in the season, and the nights are beginning to reappear. This morning I saw a star twinkling just over the fore-yard, the first since the beginning of May. There is considerable discontent among the crew, many of whom are anxious to get back home to be in time for the herring season, when labour always commands a high price upon the Scotch coast. As yet their displeasure is only signified by sullen countenances and black looks, but I heard from the second mate this afternoon that they contemplated sending a deputation to the captain to explain their grievance. I much doubt how he will receive it, as he is a man of fierce temper, and very sensitive about anything approaching to an infringement of his rights. I shall venture after dinner to say a few words to him upon the subject. I have always found that he will tolerate from me what he would resent from any other member of the crew. Amsterdam Island, at the north-west corner of Spitzbergen, is visible upon our starboard quarter—a rugged line of volcanic rocks, intersected by white seams, which represent glaciers. It is curious to think that at the present moment there is probably no human being nearer to us than the Danish settlements in the south of Greenland—a good nine hundred miles as the crow flies. A captain takes a great responsibility upon himself when he risks his vessel under such circumstances. No whaler has ever remained in these latitudes till so advanced a period of the year.

9 P.M.—I have spoken to Captain Craigie, and though the result has been hardly satisfactory, I am bound to say that he listened to what I had to say very quietly and even deferentially. When I had finished he put on that air of iron determination which I have frequently observed upon his face, and paced rapidly backwards and forwards across the narrow cabin for some minutes. At first I feared that I had seriously offended him, but he dispelled the idea by sitting down again, and putting his hand upon my arm with a gesture which almost amounted to a caress. There was a depth of tenderness too in his wild dark eyes which surprised me considerably. "Look here, Doctor," he said, "I'm sorry I ever took you—I am indeed—and I would give fifty pounds this

minute to see you standing safe upon the Dundee quay. It's hit or miss with me this time. There are fish to the north of us. How dare you shake your head, sir, when I tell you I saw them blowing from the masthead?"—this in a sudden burst of fury, though I was not conscious of having shown any signs of doubt. "Two-and-twenty fish in as many minutes as I am a living man, and not one under ten foot.[1] Now, Doctor, do you think I can leave the country when there is only one infernal strip of ice between me and my fortune? If it came on to blow from the north to-morrow we could fill the ship and be away before the frost could catch us. If it came on to blow from the south—well, I suppose the men are paid for risking their lives, and as for myself it matters but little to me, for I have more to bind me to the other world than to this one. I confess that I am sorry for *you*, though. I wish I had old Angus Tait who was with me last voyage, for he was a man that would never be missed, and you—you said once that you were engaged, did you not?"

"Yes," I answered, snapping the spring of the locket which hung from my watch-chain, and holding up the little vignette of Flora.

"Curse you!" he yelled, springing out of his seat, with his very beard bristling with passion. "What is your happiness to me? What have I to do with her that you must dangle her photograph before my eyes?" I almost thought that he was about to strike me in the frenzy of his rage, but with another imprecation he dashed open the door of the cabin and rushed out upon deck, leaving me considerably astonished at his extraordinary violence. It is the first time that he has ever shown me anything but courtesy and kindness. I can hear him pacing excitedly up and down overhead as I write these lines.

I should like to give a sketch of the character of this

[1] A whale is measured among whalers not by the length of its body, but by the length of its whalebone.

man, but it seems presumptuous to attempt such a thing upon paper, when the idea in my own mind is at best a vague and uncertain one. Several times I have thought that I grasped the clue which might explain it, but only to be disappointed by his presenting himself in some new light which would upset all my conclusions. It may be that no human eye but my own shall ever rest upon these lines, yet as a psychological study I shall attempt to leave some record of Captain Nicholas Craigie.

A man's outer case generally gives some indication of the soul within. The captain is tall and well-formed, with dark, handsome face, and a curious way of twitching his limbs, which may arise from nervousness, or be simply an outcome of his excessive energy. His jaw and whole cast of countenance is manly and resolute, but the eyes are the distinctive feature of his face. They are of the very darkest hazel, bright and eager, with a singular mixture of recklessness in their expression, and of something else which I have sometimes thought was more allied with horror than any other emotion. Generally the former predominated, but on occasions, and more particularly when he was thoughtfully inclined, the look of fear would spread and deepen until it imparted a new character to his whole countenance. It is at these times that he is most subject to tempestuous fits of anger, and he seems to be aware of it, for I have known him lock himself up so that no one might approach him until his dark hour was passed. He sleeps badly, and I have heard him shouting during the night, but his cabin is some little distance from mine, and I could never distinguish the words which he said.

This is one phase of his character, and the most disagreeable one. It is only through my close association with him, thrown together as we are day after day, that I have observed it. Otherwise he is an agreeable companion, well-read and entertaining, and as gallant a seaman as ever trod a deck. I shall not easily forget the way in which he handled the ship when we were caught by a gale among the loose ice at the beginning of April. I have never seen him so cheerful, and even hilarious, as he was that night, as he paced backwards and forwards upon the bridge amid the flashing of the lightning and the howling of the wind. He has told me several times that the thought of death was a pleasant one to him, which is a sad thing for a young man to say; he cannot be much more than thirty, though his hair and moustache are already slightly grizzled. Some great sorrow must have overtaken him and blighted his whole life. Perhaps I should be the same if I lost my Flora—God knows! I think if it were not for her that I should care very little whether the wind blew from the north or the south to-morrow. There, I hear him come down the companion, and he has locked himself up in his room, which shows that he is still in an unamiable mood. And so to bed, as old Pepys would say, for the candle is burning down (we have to use them now since the nights are closing in), and the steward has turned in, so there are no hopes of another one.

September 12th.—Calm, clear day, and still lying in the same position. What wind there is comes from the south-east, but it is very slight. Captain is in a better humour, and apologised to me at breakfast for his rudeness. He still looks somewhat distrait, however, and retains that wild look in his eyes which in a Highlander would mean that he was "fey"—at least so our chief engineer remarked to me, and he has some reputation among the Celtic portion of our crew as a seer and expounder of omens.

It is strange that superstition should have obtained such mastery over this hard-headed and practical race. I could not have believed to what an extent it is carried had I not observed it for myself. We have had a perfect epidemic of it this voyage, until I have felt inclined to serve out rations of sedatives and nerve-tonics with the Saturday allowance of grog. The first symptom of it was that shortly after leaving Shetland the men at the wheel used to complain that they heard plaintive cries and screams in the wake of the ship, as if something were following it and were unable to overtake it. This fiction has been kept up during the whole voyage, and on dark nights at the beginning of the seal-fishing it was only with great difficulty that men could be induced to do their spell. No doubt what they heard was either the creaking of the rudder-chains, or the cry of some passing sea-bird. I have been fetched out of bed several times to listen to it, but I need hardly say that I was never able to distinguish anything unnatural. The men, however, are so absurdly positive upon the subject that it is hopeless to argue with them. I mentioned the matter to the captain once, but to my surprise he took it very gravely, and indeed appeared to be considerably disturbed by what I told him. I should have thought that he at least would have been above such vulgar delusions.

All this disquisition upon superstition leads me up to the fact that Mr. Manson, our second mate, saw a ghost last night—or, at least, says that he did, which of course is the same thing. It is quite refreshing to have some new topic of conversation after the eternal routine of bears and whales which has served us for so many months. Manson swears the ship is haunted, and that he would not stay in her a day if he had any other place to go to. Indeed the fellow is honestly frightened, and I had to give him some chloral and bromide of potassium this morning to steady him down. He seemed quite indignant when I suggested that he had been having an extra glass the night before, and I was obliged to pacify him by keeping as grave a countenance as possible during his story, which he certainly narrated in a very straightforward and matter-of-fact way.

"I was on the bridge," he said, "about four bells in the middle watch, just when the night was at its darkest. There was a bit of a moon, but the clouds were blowing across it so that you couldn't see far from the ship. John M'Leod, the harpooner, came aft from the fo'c'sle-head and reported a strange noise on the starboard bow. I went forrard and we both heard it, sometimes like a bairn crying and sometimes like a wench in pain. I've been seventeen years to the country and I never heard seal, old or young, make a sound like that. As we were standing there on the fo'c'sle-head the moon came out from behind a cloud, and we both saw a sort of white figure moving across the ice-field in the same direction that we had heard the cries. We lost sight of it for a while, but it came back on the port bow, and we could just make it out like a shadow on the ice. I sent a hand aft for the rifles, and M'Leod and I went down on to the pack, thinking that maybe it might be a bear. When we got on the ice I lost sight of M'Leod, but I pushed on in the direction where I could still hear the cries. I followed them for a mile or maybe more, and then running round a hummock I came right on to the top of it standing and waiting for me seemingly. I don't know what it was. It wasn't a bear, anyway. It was tall and white and straight, and if it wasn't a man nor a woman, I'll stake my davy it was something worse. I made for the ship as hard as I could run, and precious glad I was to find myself aboard. I signed articles to do my duty by the ship, and on the ship I'll stay, but you don't catch me on the ice again after sundown."

That is his story, given as far as I can in his own words. I fancy what he saw must, in spite of his denial, have been a young bear erect upon its hind legs, an attitude which they often assume when alarmed. In the uncertain light this would bear a resemblance to a human figure, especially to a man whose nerves were already somewhat shaken. Whatever it may have been, the occurrence is unfortunate, for it has produced a most unpleasant effect upon the crew. Their looks are more sullen than before, and their discontent more open.

The double grievance of being debarred from the herring fishing and of being detained in what they choose to call a haunted vessel, may lead them to do something rash. Even the harpooners, who are the oldest and steadiest among them, are joining in the general agitation.

Apart from this absurd outbreak of superstition, things are looking rather more cheerful. The pack which was forming to the south of us has partly cleared away, and the water is so warm as to lead me to believe that we are lying in one of those branches of the gulf-stream which run up between Greenland and Spitzbergen. There are numerous small Medusæ and sea-lemons about the ship, with abundance of shrimps, so that there is every possibility of "fish" being sighted. Indeed one was seen blowing about dinner-time, but in such a position that it was impossible for the boats to follow it.

September 13th.—Had an interesting conversation with the chief mate, Mr. Milne, upon the bridge. It seems that our captain is as great an enigma to the seamen, and even to the owners of the vessel, as he has been to me. Mr. Milne tells me that when the ship is paid off, upon returning from a voyage, Captain Craigie disappears, and is not seen again until the approach of another season, when he walks quietly into the office of the company, and asks whether his services will be required. He has no friend in Dundee, nor does any-one pretend to be acquainted with his early history. His position depends entirely upon his skill as a seaman, and the name for courage and coolness which he had earned in the capacity of mate, before being entrusted with a separate command. The unanimous opinion seems to be that he is not a Scotchman, and that his name is an assumed one. Mr. Milne thinks that he has devoted himself to whaling simply for the reason that it is the most dangerous occupation which he could select, and that he courts death in every possible manner. He mentioned several instances of this, one of which is rather curious, if true. It seems that on one occasion he did not put in an appearance at the office, and a substitute had to be selected in his place. That was at the time of the last Russian and Turkish War. When he turned up again next spring he had a puckered wound in the side of his neck which he used to endeavour to conceal with his cravat. Whether the mate's inference that he had been engaged in the war is true or not I cannot say. It was certainly a strange coincidence.

The wind is veering round in an easterly direction, but is still very slight. I think the ice is lying closer than it did yesterday. As far as the eye can reach on every side there is one wide expanse of spotless white, only broken by an occasional rift or the dark shadow of a hummock. To the south there is the narrow lane of blue water which is our sole means of escape, and which is closing up every day. The captain is taking a heavy responsibility upon himself. I hear that the tank of potatoes has been finished, and even the biscuits are running short, but he preserves the same impassable countenance, and spends the greater part of the day at the crow's nest, sweeping the horizon with his glass. His manner is very variable, and he seems to avoid my society, but there has been no repetition of the violence which he showed the other night.

7.30 P.M.—My deliberate opinion is that we are commanded by a madman. Nothing else can account for the extraordinary vagaries of Captain Craigie. It is fortunate that I have kept this journal of our voyage, as it will serve to justify us in case we have to put him under any sort of restraint, a step which I should only consent to as a last resource. Curiously enough it was he himself who suggested lunacy and not mere eccentricity as the secret of his strange conduct. He was standing upon the bridge about an hour ago, peering as usual through his glass, while I was walking up and down the quarter-deck. The majority of the men were below at their tea, for the watches have not been regularly kept of late. Tired of walking, I leaned against the bulwarks, and admired the mellow glow cast by the sinking sun upon the great ice-fields which surround us. I was suddenly aroused from the reverie into which I had fallen by a hoarse voice at my elbow, and starting round I found that the captain had descended and was standing by my side. He was staring out over the ice with an expression in which horror, surprise, and something approaching to joy were contending for the mastery. In spite of the cold, great drops of perspiration were coursing down his forehead, and he was evidently fearfully excited. His limbs twitched like those of a man upon the verge of an epileptic fit, and the lines about his mouth were drawn and hard.

"Look!" he gasped, seizing me by the wrist, but still keeping his eyes upon the distant ice, and moving his head slowly in a horizontal direction, as if following some object which was moving across the field of vision. "Look! There, man, there! Between the hummocks! Now coming out from behind the far one! You see her—you *must* see her! There still! Flying from me, by God, flying from me—and gone!"

He uttered the last two words in a whisper of concentrated agony which shall never fade from my remembrance. Clinging to the ratlines he endeavoured to climb up upon the top of the bulwarks as if in the hope of obtaining a last glance at the departing object. His strength was not equal to the attempt, however, and he staggered back against the saloon skylights, where he leaned panting and exhausted. His face was so livid that I expected him to become unconscious, so lost no time in leading him down the companion, and stretching him upon one of the sofas in the cabin. I then poured him out some brandy, which I held to his lips, and which had a wonderful effect upon him, bringing the blood back into his white face and steadying his poor shaking limbs. He raised himself up upon his elbow, and looking round to see that we were alone, he beckoned to me to come and sit beside him.

"You saw it, didn't you?" he asked, still in the same subdued awesome tone so foreign to the nature of the man.

"No, I saw nothing."

His head sank back again upon the cushions. "No, he wouldn't without the glass," he murmured. "He couldn't. It was the glass that showed her to me, and then the eyes of love—the eyes of love. I say, Doc, don't let the steward in! He'll think I'm mad. Just bolt the door, will you!"

I rose and did what he had commanded.

He lay quiet for a while, lost in thought apparently, and then raised himself up upon his elbow again, and asked for some more brandy.

"You don't think I am, do you, Doc?" he asked, as I was putting the bottle back into the after-locker. "Tell me now, as man to man, do you think that I am mad?"

"I think you have something on your mind," I answered, "which is exciting you and doing you a good deal of harm."

"Right there, lad!" he cried, his eyes sparkling from the effects of the brandy. "Plenty on my mind—plenty! But I can work out the latitude and the longitude, and I can handle my sextant and manage my logarithms. You couldn't prove me mad in a court of law, could you, now?" It was curious to hear the man lying back and coolly arguing out the question of his own sanity.

"Perhaps not," I said; "but still I think you would be wise to get home as soon as you can, and settle down to a quiet life for a while."

"Get home, eh?" he muttered, with a sneer upon his face. "One word for me and two for yourself, lad. Settle down with Flora—pretty little Flora. Are bad dreams signs of madness?"

" Sometimes," I answered.

" What else ? What would be the first symptoms ? "

" Pains in the head, noises in the ears, flashes before the eyes, delusions——"

" Ah ! what about them ? " he interrupted. " What would you call a delusion ? "

" Seeing a thing which is not there is a delusion."

" But she *was* there ! " he groaned to himself. " She *was* there ! " and rising, he unbolted the door and walked with slow and uncertain steps to his own cabin, where I have no doubt that he will remain until to-morrow morning. His system seems to have received a terrible shock, whatever it may have been that he imagined himself to have seen. The man becomes a greater mystery every day, though I fear that the solution which he has himself suggested is the correct one, and that his reason is affected. I do not think that a guilty conscience has anything to do with his behaviour. The idea is a popular one among the officers, and, I believe, the crew ; but I have seen nothing to support it. He has not the air of a guilty man, but of one who has had terrible usage at the hands of fortune, and who should be regarded as a martyr rather than a criminal.

The wind is veering round to the south to-night. God help us if it blocks that narrow pass which is our only road to safety ! Situated as we are on the edge of the main Arctic pack, or the " barrier " as it is called by the whalers, any wind from the north has the effect of shredding out the ice around us and allowing our escape, while a wind from the south blows up all the loose ice behind us, and hems us in between two packs. God help us, I say again !

September 14th.—Sunday, and a day of rest. My fears have been confirmed, and the thin strip of blue water has disappeared from the southward. Nothing but the great motionless ice-fields around us, with their weird hummocks and fantastic pinnacles. There is a deathly silence over their wide expanse which is horrible.

No lapping of the waves now, no cries of seagulls or straining of sails, but one deep universal silence in which the murmurs of the seamen, and the creak of their boots upon the white shining deck, seem discordant and out of place. Our only visitor was an Arctic fox, a rare animal upon the pack, though common enough upon the land. He did not come near the ship, however, but after surveying us from a distance fled rapidly across the ice. This was curious conduct, as they generally know nothing of man, and being of an inquisitive nature, become so familiar that they are easily captured. Incredible as it may seem, even this little incident produced a bad effect upon the crew. "Yon puir beastie kens mair, ay, an' sees mair nor you nor me!" was the comment of one of the leading harpooners, and the others nodded their acquiescence. It is vain to attempt to argue against such puerile superstition. They have made up their minds that there is a curse upon the ship, and nothing will ever persuade them to the contrary.

The captain remained in seclusion all day except for about half an hour in the afternoon, when he came out upon the quarter-deck. I observed that he kept his eye fixed upon the spot where the vision of yesterday had appeared, and was quite prepared for another outburst, but none such came. He did not seem to see me, although I was standing close beside him. Divine service was read as usual by the chief engineer. It is a curious thing that in whaling vessels the Church of England Prayer-book is always employed, although there is never a member of that Church among either officers or crew. Our men are all Roman Catholics or Presbyterians, the former predominating. Since a ritual is used which is foreign to both, neither can complain that the other is preferred to them, and they listen with all attention and devotion, so that the system has something to recommend it.

A glorious sunset, which made the great fields of

ice look like a lake of blood. I have never seen a finer and at the same time more weird effect. Wind is veering round. If it will blow twenty-four hours from the north all will yet be well.

September 15th.—To-day is Flora's birthday. Dear lass! it is well that she cannot see her boy, as she used to call me, shut up among the ice-fields with a crazy captain and a few weeks' provisions. No doubt she scans the shipping list in the *Scotsman* every morning to see if we are reported from Shetland. I have to set an example to the men and look cheery and unconcerned; but God knows, my heart is very heavy at times.

The thermometer is at nineteen Fahrenheit to-day. There is but little wind, and what there is comes from an unfavourable quarter. Captain is in an excellent humour; I think he imagines he has seen some other omen or vision, poor fellow, during the night, for he came into my room early in the morning, and stooping down over my bunk, whispered, "It wasn't a delusion, Doc; it's all right!" After breakfast he asked me to find out how much food was left, which the second mate and I proceeded to do. It is even less than we had expected. Forward they have half a tank full of biscuits, three barrels of salt meat, and a very limited supply of coffee beans and sugar. In the after-hold and lockers there are a good many luxuries, such as tinned salmon, soups, haricot mutton, etc., but they will go a very short way among a crew of fifty men. There are two barrels of flour in the store-room, and an unlimited supply of tobacco. Altogether there is about enough to keep the men on half rations for eighteen or twenty days—certainly not more. When we reported the state of things to the captain, he ordered all hands to be piped, and addressed them from the quarter-deck. I never saw him to better advantage. With his tall, well-knit figure, and dark animated face, he seemed a man born to command, and he discussed the situation in a cool sailor-like way which showed that while appreciating the danger he had an eye for every loophole of escape.

"My lads," he said, "no doubt you think I brought you into this fix, if it is a fix, and maybe some of you feel bitter against me on account of it. But you must remember that for many a season no ship that comes to the country has brought in as much oil-money as the old *Polestar*, and every one of you has had his share of it. You can leave your wives behind you in comfort, while other poor fellows come back to find their lassies on the parish. If you have to thank me for the one you have to thank me for the other, and we may call it quits. We've tried a bold venture before this and succeeded, so now that we've tried one and failed we've no cause to cry out about it. If the worst comes to the worse, we can make the land across the ice and lay in a stock of seals which will keep us alive until the spring. It won't come to that, though, for you'll see the Scotch coast again before three weeks are out. At present every man must go on half rations, share and share alike, and no favour to any. Keep up your hearts and you'll pull through this as you've pulled through many a danger before." These few simple words of his had a wonderful effect upon the crew. His former unpopularity was forgotten, and the old harpooner whom I have already mentioned for his superstition, led off three cheers, which were heartily joined in by all hands.

September 16th.—The wind has veered round to the north during the night, and the ice shows some symptoms of opening out. The men are in a good humour in spite of the short allowance upon which they have been placed. Steam is kept up in the engine-room, that there may be no delay should an opportunity for escape present itself. The captain is in exuberant spirits, though he still retains that wild "fey" expression which I have already remarked upon. This burst of cheerfulness puzzles me more than his former gloom. I cannot understand it. I think I mentioned in an early part of this journal that one of his oddities is that he never permits any person to enter his cabin, but insists upon making his own bed, such as it is, and performing every other office for himself. To my surprise he handed me the key to-day and requested me to go down there and take the time by his chronometer while he measured the altitude of the sun at noon. It is a bare little room, containing a washing-stand and a few books, but little else in the way of luxury, except some pictures upon the walls. The majority of these are small cheap oleographs, but there was one water-colour sketch of the head of a young lady which arrested my attention. It was evidently a portrait, and not one of those fancy types of female beauty which sailors particularly affect. No artist could have evolved from his own mind such a curious mixture of character and weakness. The languid, dreamy eyes, with their drooping lashes, and the broad, low brow, unruffled by thought or care, were in strong contrast with the clean-cut, prominent jaw, and the resolute set of the lower lip. Underneath it in one of the corners was written, "M.B., æt. 19." That anyone in the short space of nineteen years of existence could develop such strength of will as was stamped upon her face seemed to me at the time to be well-nigh incredible. She must have been an extraordinary woman. Her features have thrown such a glamour over me that, though I had but a fleeting glance at them, I could, were I a draughtsman, reproduce them line for line upon this page of the journal. I wonder what part she has played in our captain's life. He has hung her picture at the end of his berth, so that his eyes continually rest upon it. Were he a less reserved man I should make some remark upon the subject. Of the other things in his cabin there was nothing worthy of mention—uniform coats, a camp-stool, small looking-glass, tobacco-box, and numerous pipes, including an oriental hookah—which, by the by, gives some colour to Mr. Milne's story about his participation in the war, though the connection may seem rather a distant one.

11.20 P.M.—Captain just gone to bed after a long and interesting conversation on general topics. When he chooses he can be a most fascinating companion, being remarkably well-read, and having the power of expressing his opinion forcibly without appearing to be dogmatic. I hate to have my intellectual toes trod upon. He spoke about the nature of the soul, and sketched out the views of Aristotle and Plato upon the subject in a masterly manner. He seems to have a leaning for metempsychosis and the doctrines of Pythagoras. In discussing them we touched upon modern spiritualism, and I made some joking allusion to the impostures of Slade, upon which, to my surprise, he warned me most impressively against confusing the innocent with the guilty, and argued that it would be as logical to brand Christianity as an error because Judas, who professed that religion, was a villain. He shortly afterwards bade me good night and retired to his room.

The wind is freshening up, and blows steadily from the north. The nights are as dark now as they are in England. I hope to-morrow may set us free from our frozen fetters.

September 17th.—The Bogie again. Thank Heaven that I have strong nerves! The superstition of these poor fellows, and the circumstantial accounts which they give, with the utmost earnestness and self-conviction, would horrify any man not accustomed to their ways. There are many versions of the matter, but the sum-total of them all is that something uncanny has been flitting round the ship all night, and that Sandie M'Donald of Peterhead and "lang" Peter Williamson of Shetland saw it, as also did Mr. Milne on the bridge —so, having three witnesses, they can make a better case of it than the second mate did. I spoke to Milne after breakfast, and told him that he should be above such nonsense, and that as an officer he ought to set the men a better example. He shook his weather-beaten head ominously, but answered with characteristic caution, "Mebbe, aye, mebbe na, Doctor," he said, "I didna ca' it a ghaist. I canna' say I preen my faith in sea-bogles an' the like, though there's a mony as claims to ha' seen a' that and waur. I'm no easy feared, but maybe your ain bluid would run a bit cauld, mun, if instead o' speerin' aboot it in daylicht ye were wi' me last night, an' seed an awfu' like shape, white an' gruesome, whiles here, whiles there, an' it greetin' and ca'ing in the darkness like a bit lambie that hae lost its mither. Ye would na' be sae ready to put it a' doon to auld wives' clavers then, I'm thinkin'." I saw it was hopeless to reason with him, so contented myself with begging him as a personal favour to call me up the next time the spectre appeared—a request to which he acceded with many ejaculations expressive of his hopes that such an opportunity might never arise.

As I had hoped, the white desert behind us has become broken by many thin streaks of water which intersect it in all directions. Our latitude to-day was 80° 52′ N., which shows that there is a strong southerly drift upon the pack. Should the wind continue favourable it will break up as rapidly as it formed. At present we can do nothing but smoke and wait and hope for the best. I am rapidly becoming a fatalist. When dealing with such uncertain factors as wind and ice a man can be nothing else. Perhaps it was the wind and sand of the Arabian deserts which gave the minds of the original followers of Mahomet their tendency to bow to kismet.

These spectral alarms have a very bad effect upon the captain. I feared that it might excite his sensitive mind, and endeavoured to conceal the absurd story from him, but unfortunately he overheard one of the men making an allusion to it, and insisted upon being informed about it. As I had expected, it brought out all his latent lunacy in an exaggerated form. I can hardly believe that this is the same man who discoursed philosophy last night with the most critical acumen and coolest judgment. He is pacing backwards and forwards upon the quarter-deck like a caged tiger, stopping now and again to throw out his hands with a yearning gesture, and stare impatiently out over the ice. He keeps up a continual mutter to himself, and once he called out, "But a little time, love—but a little time!" Poor fellow, it is sad to see a gallant seaman and accomplished gentleman reduced to such a pass, and to think that imagination and delusion can cow a mind to which real danger was but the salt of life. Was ever a man in such a position as I, between a demented captain and a ghost-seeing mate? I sometimes think I am the only really sane man aboard the vessel—except perhaps the second engineer, who is a kind of ruminant, and would care nothing for all the fiends in the Red Sea so long as they would leave him alone and not disarrange his tools.

The ice is still opening rapidly, and there is every probability of our being able to make a start to-morrow morning. They will think I am inventing when I tell them at home all the strange things that have befallen me.

12 P.M.—I have been a good deal startled, though I feel steadier now, thanks to a stiff glass of brandy. I am hardly myself yet, however, as this handwriting will testify. The fact is, that I have gone through a very strange experience, and am beginning to doubt whether I was justified in branding everyone on board as madmen because they professed to have seen things which did not seem reasonable to my understanding. Pshaw! I am a fool to let such a trifle unnerve me; and yet, coming as it does after all these alarms, it has an additional significance, for I cannot doubt either Mr. Manson's story or that of the mate, now that I have experienced that which I used formerly to scoff at.

After all it was nothing very alarming—a mere sound, and that was all. I cannot expect that anyone reading this, if anyone ever should read it, will sympathise with my feelings, or realize the effect which it produced upon me at the time. Supper was over, and I had gone on deck to have a quiet pipe before turning in. The night was very dark—so dark that, standing under the quarter-boat, I was unable to see the officer upon the bridge. I think I have already mentioned the extraordinary silence which prevails in these frozen seas. In other parts of the world, be they ever so barren, there is some slight vibration of the air—some faint hum, be it from the distant haunts of men, or from the leaves of the trees, or the wings of the birds, or even the faint rustle of the grass that covers the ground. One may not actively perceive the sound, and yet if it were withdrawn it would be missed. It is only here in these Arctic seas that stark, unfathomable stillness obtrudes itself upon you all in its gruesome reality. You find your tympanum straining to catch some little murmur, and dwelling eagerly upon every accidental sound within the vessel. In this state I was leaning against the bulwarks when there arose from the ice almost directly underneath me a cry, sharp and shrill, upon the silent air of the night, beginning, as it seemed to me, at a note such as prima donna never reached, and mounting from that ever higher and higher until it culminated in a long wail of agony, which might have been the last cry of a lost soul. The ghastly scream is still ringing in my ears. Grief, unutterable grief, seemed to be expressed in it, and a great longing, and yet through it all there was an occasional wild note of exultation. It shrilled out from close beside me, and yet as I glared into the darkness I could discern nothing. I waited some little time, but without hearing any repetition of the sound, so I came below, more shaken than I have ever been in my life before. As I came down the companion I met Mr. Milne coming up to relieve the watch. "Weel, Doctor," he said, "maybe that's auld wives' clavers tae? Did ye no hear it skirling? Maybe that's a supersteetion? What d'ye think o't noo?" I was obliged to apologise to the honest fellow, and acknowledge that I was as puzzled by it as he was. Perhaps to-morrow things may look different. At present I dare hardly write all that I think. Reading it again in days to come, when I have shaken off all these associations, I should despise myself for having been so weak.

September 18*th*.—Passed a restless and uneasy night, still haunted by that strange sound. The captain does not look as if he had had much repose either, for his face is haggard and his eyes bloodshot. I have not told him of my adventure of last night, nor shall I. He is already restless and excited, standing up, sitting down, and apparently utterly unable to keep still.

A fine lead appeared in the pack this morning, as I had expected, and we were able to cast off our ice-anchor, and steam about twelve miles in a west-sou'-westerly direction. We were then brought to a halt by a great floe as massive as any which we have left behind us. It bars our progress completely, so we can do nothing but anchor again and wait until it breaks up, which it will probably do within twenty-four hours, if the wind holds. Several bladder-nosed seals were seen swimming in the water, and one was shot, an immense creature more than eleven feet long. They are fierce, pugnacious animals, and are said to be more than a match for a bear. Fortunately they are slow and clumsy in their movements, so that there is little danger in attacking them upon the ice.

The captain evidently does not think we have seen the last of our troubles, though why he should take a gloomy view of the situation is more than I can fathom, since everyone else on board considers that we have had a miraculous escape, and are sure now to reach the open sea.

"I suppose you think it's all right now, Doctor?" he said, as we sat together after dinner.

"I hope so," I answered.

"We mustn't be too sure—and yet no doubt you are

right. We'll all be in the arms of our own true loves before long, lad, won't we? But we mustn't be too sure—we mustn't be too sure."

He sat silent a little, swinging his leg thoughtfully backwards and forwards. "Look here," he continued; "it's a dangerous place this, even at its best—a treacherous, dangerous place. I have known men cut off very suddenly in a land like this. A slip would do it sometimes—a single slip, and down you go through a crack, and only a bubble on the green water to show where it was that you sank. It's a queer thing," he continued with a nervous laugh, "but all the years I've been in this country I never once thought of making a will—not that I have anything to leave in particular, but still when a man is exposed to danger he should have everything arranged and ready—don't you think so?"

"Certainly," I answered, wondering what on earth he was driving at.

"He feels better for knowing it's all settled," he went on. "Now if anything should ever befall me, I hope that you will look after things for me. There is very little in the cabin, but such as it is I should like it to be sold, and the money divided in the same proportion as the oil-money among the crew. The chronometer I wish you to keep yourself as some slight remembrance of our voyage. Of course all this is a mere precaution, but I thought I would take the opportunity of speaking to you about it. I suppose I might rely upon you if there were any necessity?"

"Most assuredly," I answered; "and since you are taking this step, I may as well——"

"You! you!" he interrupted. "*You're* all right. What the devil is the matter with *you*? There, I didn't mean to be peppery, but I don't like to hear a young fellow, that has hardly began life, speculating about death. Go up on deck and get some fresh air into your lungs instead of talking nonsense in the cabin, and encouraging me to do the same."

The more I think of this conversation of ours the less do I like it. Why should the man be settling his affairs at the very time when we seem to be emerging from all danger? There must be some method in his madness. Can it be that he contemplates suicide? I remember that upon one occasion he spoke in a deeply reverent manner of the heinousness of the crime of self-destruction. I shall keep my eye upon him, however, and though I cannot obtrude upon the privacy of his cabin, I shall at least make a point of remaining on deck as long as he stays up.

Mr. Milne pooh-poohs my fears, and says it is only the "skipper's little way." He himself takes a very rosy view of the situation. According to him we shall be out of the ice by the day after to-morrow, pass Jan Meyen two days after that, and sight Shetland in little more than a week. I hope he may not be too sanguine. His opinion may be fairly balanced against the gloomy precautions of the captain, for he is an old and experienced seaman, and weighs his words well before uttering them.

* * * * *

The long-impending catastrophe has come at last. I hardly know what to write about it. The captain is gone. He may come back to us again alive, but I fear me—I fear me. It is now seven o'clock of the morning of the 19th of September. I have spent the whole night traversing the great ice-floe in front of us with a party of seamen in the hope of coming upon some trace of him, but in vain. I shall try to give some account of the circumstances which attended upon his disappearance. Should anyone ever chance to read the words which I put down, I trust they will remember that I do not write from conjecture or from hearsay, but that I, a sane and educated man, am describing accurately what actually occurred before my very eyes. My inferences are my own, but I shall be answerable for the facts.

The captain remained in excellent spirits after the

conversation which I have recorded. He appeared to be nervous and impatient, however, frequently changing his position, and moving his limbs in an aimless choreic way which is characteristic of him at times. In a quarter of an hour he went upon deck seven times, only to descend after a few hurried paces. I followed him each time, for there was something about his face which confirmed my resolution of not letting him out of my sight. He seemed to observe the effect which his movements had produced, for he endeavoured by an overdone hilarity, laughing boisterously at the very smallest of jokes, to quiet my apprehensions.

After supper he went on to the poop once more, and I with him. The night was dark and very still, save for the melancholy soughing of the wind among the spars. A thick cloud was coming up from the northwest, and the ragged tentacles which it threw out in front of it were drifting across the face of the moon, which only shone now and again through a rift in the wrack. The captain paced rapidly backwards and forwards, and then seeing me still dogging him, he came across and hinted that he thought I should be better below—which, I need hardly say, had the effect of strengthening my resolution to remain on deck.

I think he forgot about my presence after this, for he stood silently leaning over the taffrail and peering out across the great desert of snow, part of which lay in shadow, while part glittered mistily in the moonlight. Several times I could see by his movements that he was referring to his watch, and once he muttered a short sentence, of which I could only catch the one word "ready." I confess to having felt an eerie feeling creeping over me as I watched the loom of his tall figure through the darkness, and noted how completely he fulfilled the idea of a man who is keeping a tryst. A tryst with whom? Some vague perception began to dawn upon me as I pieced one fact with another, but I was utterly unprepared for the sequel.

By the sudden intensity of his attitude I felt that he saw something. I crept up behind him. He was staring with an eager questioning gaze at what seemed to be a wreath of mist, blown swiftly in a line with the ship. It was a dim nebulous body, devoid of shape, sometimes more, sometimes less apparent, as the light fell on it. The moon was dimmed in its brilliancy at the moment by a canopy of thinnest cloud, like the coating of an anemone.

"Coming, lass, coming," cried the skipper, in a voice of unfathomable tenderness and compassion, like one who soothes a beloved one by some favour long looked for, and as pleasant to bestow as to receive.

What followed happened in an instant. I had no power to interfere. He gave one spring to the top of the bulwarks, and another which took him on to the ice, almost to the feet of the pale misty figure. He held out his hands as if to clasp it, and so ran into the darkness with outstretched arms and loving words. I still stood rigid and motionless, straining my eyes after his retreating form, until his voice died away in the distance. I never thought to see him again, but at that moment the moon shone out brilliantly through a chink in the cloudy heaven, and illuminated the great field of ice. Then I saw his dark figure already a very long way off, running with prodigious speed across the frozen plain. That was the last glimpse which we caught of him—perhaps the last we ever shall. A party was organized to follow him, and I accompanied them, but the men's hearts were not in the work, and nothing was found. Another will be formed within a few hours. I can hardly believe I have not been dreaming, or suffering from some hideous nightmare, as I write these things down.

7.30 P.M.—Just returned dead beat and utterly tired out from a second unsuccessful search for the captain. The floe is of enormous extent, for though we have traversed at least twenty miles of its surface, there has been no sign of its coming to an end. The frost has been so severe of late that the overlying snow is frozen as hard as granite, otherwise we might have had the footsteps to guide us. The crew are anxious that we should cast off and steam round the floe and so to the southward, for the ice has opened up during the night, and the sea is visible upon the horizon. They argue that Captain Craigie is certainly dead, and that we are all risking our lives to no purpose by remaining when we have an opportunity of escape. Mr. Milne and I have had the greatest difficulty in persuading them to wait until to-morrow night, and have been compelled to promise that we will not under any circumstances delay our departure longer than that. We propose therefore to take a few hours' sleep, and then to start upon a final search.

September 20th, evening.—I crossed the ice this morning with a party of men exploring the southern part of the floe, while Mr. Milne went off in a northerly direction. We pushed on for ten or twelve miles without seeing a trace of any living thing except a single bird, which fluttered a great way over our heads, and which by its flight I should judge to have been a falcon. The southern extremity of the ice-field tapered away into a long narrow spit which projected out into the sea. When we came to the base of this promontory, the men halted, but I begged them to continue to the extreme end of it, that we might have the satisfaction of knowing that no possible chance had been neglected.

We had hardly gone a hundred yards before M'Donald of Peterhead cried out that he saw something in front of us, and began to run. We all got a glimpse of it and ran too. At first it was only a vague darkness against the white ice, but as we raced along together it took the shape of a man, and eventually of the man of whom we were in search. He was lying face downwards upon a frozen bank. Many little crystals of ice and feathers of snow had drifted on to him as he lay, and sparkled upon his dark seaman's jacket. As we came up some wandering puff of wind caught these tiny flakes in its vortex, and they whirled up into the air, partially descended again, and then, caught once more in the current, sped rapidly away in the direction of the sea. To my eyes it seemed but a snow-drift, but many of my companions averred that it started up in the shape of a woman, stooped over the corpse and kissed it, and then hurried away across the floe. I have learned never to ridicule any man's opinion, however strange it may seem. Sure it is that Captain Nicholas Craigie had met with no painful end, for there was a bright smile upon his blue pinched features, and his hands were still outstretched as though grasping at the strange visitor which had summoned him away into the dim world that lies beyond the grave.

We buried him the same afternoon with the ship's ensign around him, and a thirty-two pound shot at his feet. I read the burial service, while the rough sailors wept like children, for there were many who owed much to his kind heart, and who showed now the affection which his strange ways had repelled during his lifetime. He went off the grating with a dull, sullen splash, and as I looked into the green water I saw him go down, down, down until he was but a little flickering patch of white hanging upon the outskirts of eternal darkness. Then even that faded away, and he was gone. There he shall lie, with his secret and his sorrows and his mystery all still buried in his breast, until that great day when the sea shall give up its dead, and Nicholas Craigie come out from among the ice with the smile upon his face, and his stiffened arms outstretched in greeting. I pray that his lot may be a happier one in that life than it has been in this.

I shall not continue my journal. Our road to home lies plain and clear before us, and the great ice-field will soon be but a remembrance of the past. It will be some time before I get over the shock produced by recent events. When I began this record of our voyage

I little thought of how I should be compelled to finish it. I am writing these final words in the lonely cabin, still starting at times and fancying I hear the quick nervous step of the dead man upon the deck above me. I entered his cabin to-night, as was my duty, to make a list of his effects in order that they might be entered in the official log. All was as it had been upon my previous visit, save that the picture which I have described as having hung at the end of his bed had been cut out of its frame, as with a knife, and was gone. With this last link in a strange chain of evidence I close my diary of the voyage of the *Polestar*.

[NOTE by Dr. John M'Alister Ray, senior.—I have read over the strange events connected with the death of the captain of the *Polestar*, as narrated in the journal of my son. That everything occurred exactly as he describes it I have the fullest confidence, and, indeed, the most positive certainty, for I know him to be a strong-nerved and unimaginative man, with the strictest regard for veracity. Still, the story is, on the face of it, so vague and so improbable, that I was long opposed to its publication. Within the last few days, however, I have had independent testimony upon the subject which throws a new light upon it. I had run down to Edinburgh to attend a meeting of the British Medical Association, when I chanced to come across Dr. P——, an old college chum of mine, now practising at Saltash, in Devonshire. Upon my telling him of this experience of my son's, he declared to me that he was familiar with the man, and proceeded, to my no small surprise, to give me a description of him, which tallied remarkably well with that given in the journal, except that he depicted him as a younger man. According to his account, he had been engaged to a young lady of singular beauty residing upon the Cornish coast. During his absence at sea his betrothed had died under circumstances of peculiar horror.]

THE BROWN HAND

EVERYONE knows that Sir Dominick Holden, the famous Indian surgeon, made me his heir, and that his death changed me in an hour from a hard-working and impecunious medical man to a well-to-do landed proprietor. Many know also that there were at least five people between the inheritance and me, and that Sir Dominick's selection appeared to be altogether arbitrary and whimsical. I can assure them, however, that they are quite mistaken, and that, although I only knew Sir Dominick in the closing years of his life, there were, none the less, very real reasons why he should show his goodwill towards me. As a matter of fact, though I say it myself, no man ever did more for another than I did for my Indian uncle. I cannot expect the story to be believed, but it is so singular that I should feel that it was a breach of duty if I did not put it upon record—so here it is, and your belief or incredulity is your own affair.

Sir Dominick Holden, C.B., K.C.S.I., and I don't know what besides, was the most distinguished Indian surgeon of his day. In the Army originally, he afterwards settled down into civil practice in Bombay, and visited, as a consultant, every part of India. His name is best remembered in connection with the Oriental Hospital which he founded and supported. The time came, however, when his iron constitution began to show signs of the long strain to which he had subjected it, and his brother practitioners (who were not, perhaps, entirely disinterested upon the point) were unanimous in recommending him to return to England. He held on so long as he could, but at last he developed nervous symptoms of a very pronounced character, and so came back, a broken man, to his native county of Wiltshire. He bought a considerable estate with an ancient manor-house upon the edge of Salisbury Plain, and devoted his old age to the study of Comparative Pathology, which had been his learned hobby all his life, and in which he was a foremost authority.

We of the family were, as may be imagined, much excited by the news of the return of this rich and childless uncle to England. On his part, although by no means exuberant in his hospitality, he showed some sense of his duty to his relations, and each of us in turn had an invitation to visit him. From the accounts of my cousins it appeared to be a melancholy business, and it was with mixed feelings that I at last received my own summons to appear at Rodenhurst. My wife was so carefully excluded in the invitation that my first impulse was to refuse it, but the interests of the children had to be considered, and so, with her consent, I set out one October afternoon upon my visit to Wiltshire, with little thought of what that visit was to entail.

My uncle's estate was situated where the arable land of the plains begins to swell upwards into the rounded chalk hills which are characteristic of the county. As I drove from Dinton Station in the waning light of that autumn day, I was impressed by the weird nature of the scenery. The few scattered cottages of the peasants were so dwarfed by the huge evidences of prehistoric life, that the present appeared to be a dream and the past to be the obtrusive and masterful reality. The road wound through the valleys, formed by a succession of grassy hills, and the summit of each was cut and carved into the most elaborate fortifications, some circular, and some square, but all on a scale which has defied the winds and the rains of many centuries. Some call them Roman and some British, but their true origin and the reasons for this particular tract of country being so interlaced with entrenchments have never been finally made clear. Here and there on the long, smooth, olive-coloured slopes there rose small, rounded barrows or tumuli. Beneath them lie the cremated ashes of the race which cut so deeply into the hills, but their graves tell us nothing save that a jar full of dust represents the man who once laboured under the sun.

It was through this weird country that I approached my uncle's residence of Rodenhurst, and the house was, as I found, in due keeping with its surroundings. Two broken and weather-stained pillars, each surmounted by a mutilated heraldic emblem, flanked the entrance to a neglected drive. A cold wind whistled through the elms which lined it, and the air was full of the drifting leaves. At the far end, under the gloomy arch of trees, a single yellow lamp burned steadily. In the dim half-light of the coming night I saw a long, low building stretching out two irregular wings, with deep eaves, a sloping gambrel roof, and walls which were criss-crossed with timber balks in the fashion of the Tudors. The cheery light of a fire flickered in the broad, latticed window to the left of the low-porched door, and this, as it proved, marked the study of my uncle, for it was thither that I was led by his butler in order to make my host's acquaintance.

He was cowering over his fire, for the moist chill of an English autumn had set him shivering. His lamp was unlit, and I only saw the red glow of the embers beating upon a huge, craggy face, with a Red Indian nose and cheek, and deep furrows and seams from eye to chin, the sinister marks of hidden volcanic fires. He sprang up at my entrance with something of an old-world courtesy and welcomed me warmly to Rodenhurst. At the same time I was conscious, as the lamp was carried in, that it was a very critical pair of light-blue eyes which looked out at me from under shaggy eyebrows, like scouts beneath a bush, and that this outlandish uncle of mine was carefully reading off my character with all the ease of a practised observer and an experienced man of the world.

For my part I looked at him, and looked again, for I had never seen a man whose appearance was more fitted to hold one's attention. His figure was the framework of a giant, but he had fallen away until his coat dangled straight down in a shocking fashion from a pair of broad and bony shoulders. All his limbs were huge and yet emaciated, and I could not take my gaze from his knobby wrists, and long, gnarled hands. But his eyes—those peering, light-blue eyes—they were the most arrestive of any of his peculiarities. It was not their colour alone, nor was it the ambush of hair in which they lurked; but it was the expression which I read in them. For the appearance and bearing of the man were masterful, and one expected a certain corresponding arrogance in his eyes, but instead of that I read the look which tells of a spirit cowed and crushed, the furtive, expectant look of the dog whose master has taken the whip from the rack. I formed my own medical diagnosis upon one glance at those critical and yet appealing eyes. I believed that he was stricken with some mortal ailment, that he knew himself to be exposed to sudden death, and that he lived in terror of it. Such was my judgment—a false one, as the event showed; but I mention it that it may help you to realize the look which I read in his eyes.

My uncle's welcome was, as I have said, a courteous one, and in an hour or so I found myself seated between him and his wife at a comfortable dinner, with curious, pungent delicacies upon the table, and a stealthy, quick-eyed Oriental waiter behind his chair. The old couple had come round to that tragic imitation of the dawn of life when husband and wife, having lost or scattered all those who were their intimates, find themselves face to face and alone once more, their work done, and the end nearing fast. Those who have reached that stage in sweetness and love, who can change their winter into a gentle, Indian summer, have come as victors through the ordeal of life. Lady Holden was a small, alert woman with a kindly eye, and her expression as she glanced at him was a certificate of character to her husband. And yet, though I read a mutual love in their glances, I read also mutual horror, and recognized in her face some reflection of that stealthy fear which I had detected in his. Their talk was sometimes merry and sometimes sad, but there was a forced note in their merriment and a naturalness in their sadness which told me that a heavy heart beat upon either side of me.

We were sitting over our first glass of wine, and the servants had left the room, when the conversation took a turn which produced a remarkable effect upon my host and hostess. I cannot recall what it was which started the topic of the supernatural, but it ended in my showing them that the abnormal in psychical experiences was a subject to which I had, like many neurologists, devoted a great deal of attention. I concluded by narrating my experiences when, as a member of the Psychical Research Society, I had formed one of a committee of three who spent the night in a haunted house. Our adventures were neither exciting nor convincing, but, such as it was, the story appeared to interest my auditors in a remarkable degree. They listened with an eager silence, and I caught a look of intelligence between them which I could not understand. Lady Holden immediately afterwards rose and left the room.

Sir Dominick pushed the cigar-box over to me, and we smoked for some little time in silence. That huge, bony hand of his was twitching as he raised it with his cheroot to his lips, and I felt that the man's nerves were vibrating like fiddle-strings. My instincts told me that he was on the verge of some intimate confidence, and I feared to speak lest I should interrupt it. At last he turned towards me with a spasmodic gesture like a man who throws his last scruple to the winds.

" From the little that I have seen of you it appears to me, Dr. Hardacre," said he, " that you are the very man I have wanted to meet."

" I am delighted to hear it, sir."

" Your head seems to be cool and steady. You will acquit me of any desire to flatter you, for the circumstances are too serious to permit of insincerities. You have some special knowledge upon these subjects, and you evidently view them from that philosophical standpoint which robs them of all vulgar terror. I presume that the sight of an apparition would not seriously discompose you ? "

" I think not, sir."

" Would even interest you, perhaps ? "

" Most intensely."

" As a psychical observer, you would probably investigate it in as impersonal a fashion as an astronomer investigates a wandering comet ? "

" Precisely."

He gave a heavy sigh.

" Believe me, Dr. Hardacre, there was a time when I could have spoken as you do now. My nerve was a byword in India. Even the Mutiny never shook it for an instant. And yet you see what I am reduced to —the most timorous man, perhaps, in all this county of Wiltshire. Do not speak too bravely upon this subject, or you may find yourself subjected to as long-drawn a test as I am—a test which can only end in the madhouse or the grave."

I waited patiently until he should see fit to go farther in his confidence. His preamble had, I need not say, filled me with interest and expectation.

" For some years, Dr. Hardacre," he continued, " my life and that of my wife have been made miserable by a cause which is so grotesque that it borders upon the ludicrous. And yet familiarity has never made it more easy to bear—on the contrary, as time passes my nerves become more worn and shattered by the constant attrition.

If you have no physical fears, Dr. Hardacre, I should very much value your opinion upon this phenomenon which troubles us so."

"For what it is worth my opinion is entirely at your service. May I ask the nature of the phenomenon?"

"I think that your experiences will have a higher evidential value if you are not told in advance what you may expect to encounter. You are yourself aware of the quibbles of unconscious cerebration and subjective impressions with which a scientific sceptic may throw a doubt upon your statement. It would be as well to guard against them in advance."

"What shall I do, then?"

"I will tell you. Would you mind following me this way?" He led me out of the dining-room and down a long passage until we came to a terminal door. Inside there was a large, bare room fitted as a laboratory, with numerous scientific instruments and bottles. A shelf ran along one side, upon which there stood a long line of glass jars containing pathological and anatomical specimens.

"You see that I still dabble in some of my old studies," said Sir Dominick. "These jars are the remains of what was once a most excellent collection, but unfortunately I lost the greater part of them when my house was burned down in Bombay in '92. It was a most unfortunate affair for me—in more ways than one. I had examples of many rare conditions, and my splenic collection was probably unique. These are the survivors."

I glanced over them, and saw that they really were of a very great value and rarity from a pathological point of view: bloated organs, gaping cysts, distorted bones, odious parasites—a singular exhibition of the products of India.

"There is, as you see, a small settee here," said my host. "It was far from our intention to offer a guest so meagre an accommodation, but since affairs have taken this turn, it would be a great kindness upon your part if you would consent to spend the night in this apartment. I beg that you will not hesitate to let me know if the idea should be at all repugnant to you."

"On the contrary," I said, "it is most acceptable."

"My own room is the second on the left, so that if you should feel that you are in need of company a call would always bring me to your side."

"I trust that I shall not be compelled to disturb you."

"It is unlikely that I shall be asleep. I do not sleep much. Do not hesitate to summon me."

And so with this agreement we joined Lady Holden in the drawing-room and talked of lighter things.

It was no affectation upon my part to say that the prospect of my night's adventure was an agreeable one. I have no pretence to greater physical courage than my neighbours, but familiarity with a subject robs it of those vague and undefined terrors which are the most appalling to the imaginative mind. The human brain is capable of only one strong emotion at a time, and if it be filled with curiosity or scientific enthusiasm, there is no room for fear. It is true that I had my uncle's assurance that he had himself originally taken this point of view, but I reflected that the break-down of his nervous system might be due to his forty years in India as much as to any psychical experiences which had befallen him. I at least was sound in nerve and brain, and it was with something of the pleasurable thrill of anticipation with which the sportsman takes his position beside the haunt of his game that I shut the laboratory door behind me, and partially undressing, lay down upon the rug-covered settee.

It was not an ideal atmosphere for a bed-room. The air was heavy with many chemical odours, that of methylated spirit predominating. Nor were the decorations of my chamber very sedative. The odious line of glass jars with their relics of disease and suffering stretched in front of my very eyes. There was no blind to the window, and a three-quarter moon streamed its white light into the room, tracing a silver square with filigree lattices upon the opposite wall. When I had extinguished my candle this one bright patch in the midst of the general gloom had certainly an eerie and discomposing aspect. A rigid and absolute silence reigned throughout the old house, so that the low swish of the branches in the garden came softly and smoothly to my ears. It may have been the hypnotic lullaby of this gentle susurrus, or it may have been the result of my tiring day, but after many dozings and many efforts to regain my clearness of perception, I fell at last into a deep and dreamless sleep.

I was awakened by some sound in the room, and I instantly raised myself upon my elbow on the couch. Some hours had passed, for the square patch upon the wall had slid downwards and sideways until it lay obliquely at the end of my bed. The rest of the room was in deep shadow. At first I could see nothing, presently, as my eyes became accustomed to the faint light, I was aware, with a thrill which all my scientific absorption could not entirely prevent, that something was moving slowly along the line of the wall. A gentle, shuffling sound, as of soft slippers, came to my ears, and I dimly discerned a human figure walking stealthily from the direction of the door. As it emerged into the patch of moonlight I saw very clearly what it was and how it was employed. It was a man, short and squat, dressed in some sort of dark-grey gown, which hung straight from his shoulders to his feet. The moon shone upon the side of his face, and I saw that it was chocolate-brown in colour, with a ball of black hair like a woman's at the back of his head. He walked slowly, and his eyes were cast upwards towards the line of bottles which contained those gruesome remnants of humanity. He seemed to examine each jar with attention, and then to pass on to the next. When he had come to the end of the line, immediately opposite my bed, he stopped, faced me, threw up his hands with a gesture of despair, and vanished from my sight.

I have said that he threw up his hands, but I should have said his arms, for as he assumed that attitude of despair I observed a singular peculiarity about his appearance. He had only one hand! As the sleeves drooped down from the upflung arms I saw the left plainly, but the right ended in a knobby and unsightly stump. In every other way his appearance was so natural, and I had both seen and heard him so clearly, that I could easily have believed that he was an Indian servant of Sir Dominick's who had come into my room in search of something. It was only his sudden disappearance which suggested anything more sinister to me. As it was I sprang from my couch, lit a candle, and examined the whole room carefully. There were no signs of my visitor, and I was forced to conclude that there had really been something outside the normal laws of Nature in his appearance. I lay awake for the remainder of the night, but nothing else occurred to disturb me.

I am an early riser, but my uncle was an even earlier one, for I found him pacing up and down the lawn at the side of the house. He ran towards me in his eagerness when he saw me come out from the door.

"Well, well!" he cried. "Did you see him?"

"An Indian with one hand?"

"Precisely."

"Yes, I saw him"—and I told him all that occurred. When I had finished, he led the way into his study.

"We have a little time before breakfast," said he. "It will suffice to give you an explanation of this extraordinary affair—so far as I can explain that which is essentially inexplicable. In the first place, when I tell you that for four years I have never passed one single night, either in Bombay, aboard ship, or here in England without my sleep being broken by this fellow, you will understand why it is that I am a wreck of my former self. His programme is always the same. He appears by my bedside, shakes me roughly by the shoulder, passes from my room into the laboratory, walks slowly along the line of my bottles, and then vanishes. For more than a thousand times he has gone through the same routine."

"What does he want?"

"He wants his hand."

"His hand?"

"Yes, it came about in this way. I was summoned to Peshawur for a consultation some ten years ago, and while there I was asked to look at the hand of a native who was passing through with an Afghan caravan. The fellow came from some mountain tribe living away at the back of beyond somewhere on the other side of Kaffiristan. He talked a bastard Pushtoo, and it was all I could do to understand him. He was suffering from a soft sarcomatous swelling of one of the metacarpal joints, and I made him realize that it was only by losing his hand that he could hope to save his life. After much persuasion he consented to the operation, and he asked me, when it was over, what fee I demanded. The poor fellow was almost a beggar, so that the idea of a fee was absurd, but I answered in jest that my fee should be his hand, and that I proposed to add it to my pathological collection.

"To my surprise he demurred very much to the suggestion, and he explained that according to his religion it was an all-important matter that the body should be reunited after death, and so make a perfect dwelling for the spirit. The belief is, of course, an old one, and the mummies of the Egyptians arose from an analogous superstition. I answered him that his hand was already off, and asked him how he intended to preserve it. He replied that he would pickle it in salt and carry it about with him. I suggested that it might be safer in my keeping than his, and that I had better means than salt for preserving it. On realizing that I really intended to carefully keep it, his opposition vanished instantly. 'But remember, sahib,' said he, 'I shall want it back when I am dead.' I laughed at the remark, and so the matter ended. I returned to my practice, and he no doubt in the course of time was able to continue his journey to Afghanistan.

"Well, as I told you last night, I had a bad fire in my house at Bombay. Half of it was burned down, and, among other things, my pathological collection was largely destroyed. What you see are the poor remains of it. The hand of the hillman went with the rest, but I gave the matter no particular thought at the time. That was six years ago.

"Four years ago—two years after the fire—I was awakened one night by a furious tugging at my sleeve. I sat up under the impression that my favourite mastiff was trying to arouse me. Instead of this, I saw my Indian patient of long ago, dressed in the long, grey gown which was the badge of his people. He was holding up his stump and looking reproachfully at me. He then went over to my bottles, which at that time I kept in my room, and he examined them carefully, after which he gave a gesture of anger and vanished. I realized that he had just died, and that he had come to claim my promise that I should keep his limb in safety for him.

"Well, there you have it all, Dr. Hardacre. Every night at the same hour for four years this performance has been repeated. It is a simple thing in itself, but it has worn me out like water dropping on a stone. It has brought a vile insomnia with it, for I cannot sleep now for the expectation of his coming. It has poisoned my old age and that of my wife, who has been the sharer in this great trouble. But there is the breakfast gong, and she will be waiting impatiently to know how it fared with you last night. We are both much indebted to you for your gallantry, for it takes something from the weight of our misfortune when we share it, even for a single night, with a friend, and it reassures us to our sanity, which we are sometimes driven to question."

This was the curious narrative which Sir Dominick

confided to me—a story which to many would have appeared to be a grotesque impossibility, but which, after my experience of the night before, and my previous knowledge of such things, I was prepared to accept as an absolute fact. I thought deeply over the matter, and brought the whole range of my reading and experience to bear upon it. After breakfast, I surprised my host and hostess by announcing that I was returning to London by the next train.

"My dear doctor," cried Sir Dominick in great distress, "you make me feel that I have been guilty of a gross breach of hospitality in intruding this unfortunate matter upon you. I should have borne my own burden."

"It is, indeed, that matter which is taking me to London," I answered; "but you are mistaken, I assure you, if you think that my experience of last night was an unpleasant one to me. On the contrary, I am about to ask your permission to return in the evening and spend one more night in your laboratory. I am very eager to see this visitor once again."

My uncle was exceedingly anxious to know what I was about to do, but my fears of raising false hopes prevented me from telling him. I was back in my own consulting-room a little after luncheon, and was confirming my memory of a passage in a recent book upon occultism which had arrested my attention when I read it.

"In the case of earth-bound spirits," said my authority, "some one dominant idea obsessing them at the hour of death is sufficient to hold them in this material world. They are the amphibia of this life and of the next, capable of passing from one to the other as the turtle passes from land to water. The causes which may bind a soul so strongly to a life which its body has abandoned are any violent emotion. Avarice, revenge, anxiety, love and pity have all been known to have this effect. As a rule it springs from some unfulfilled wish, and when the wish has been fulfilled the material bond relaxes. There are many cases upon record which show the singular persistence of these visitors, and also their disappearance when their wishes have been fulfilled, or in some cases when a reasonable compromise has been effected."

"*A reasonable compromise effected*"—those were the words which I had brooded over all the morning, and which I now verified in the original. No actual atonement could be made here—but a reasonable compromise! I made my way as fast as a train could take me to the Shadwell Seamen's Hospital, where my old friend Jack Hewett was house-surgeon. Without explaining the situation I made him understand what it was that I wanted.

"A brown man's hand!" said he, in amazement. "What in the world do you want that for?"

"Never mind. I'll tell you some day. I know that your wards are full of Indians."

"I should think so. But a hand——" He thought a little and then struck a bell.

"Travers," said he to a student-dresser, "what became of the hands of the Lascar which we took off yesterday? I mean the fellow from the East India Dock who got caught in the steam winch."

"They are in the *post-mortem* room, sir."

"Just pack one of them in antiseptics and give it to Dr. Hardacre."

And so I found myself back at Rodenhurst before dinner with this curious outcome of my day in town. I still said nothing to Sir Dominick, but I slept that night in the laboratory, and I placed the Lascar's hand in one of the glass jars at the end of my couch.

So interested was I in the result of my experiment that sleep was out of the question. I sat with a shaded lamp beside me and waited patiently for my visitor. This time I saw him clearly from the first. He appeared beside the door, nebulous for an instant, and then hardening into as distinct an outline as any living man. The slippers beneath his grey gown were red and heelless, which accounted for the low, shuffling sound which he made as he walked. As on the previous night he passed slowly along the line of bottles until he paused before that which contained the hand. He reached up to it, his whole figure quivering with expectation, took it down, examined it eagerly, and then, with a face which was convulsed with fury and disappointment, he hurled it down on the floor. There was a crash which resounded through the house, and when I looked up the mutilated Indian had disappeared. A moment later my door flew open and Sir Dominick rushed in.

"You are not hurt?" he cried.

"No—but deeply disappointed."

He looked in astonishment at the splinters of glass, and the brown hand lying upon the floor.

"Good God!" he cried. "What is this?"

I told him my idea and its wretched sequel. He listened intently, but shook his head.

"It was well thought of," said he, "but I fear that there is no such easy end to my sufferings. But one thing I now insist upon. It is that you shall never again upon any pretext occupy this room. My fears that something might have happened to you—when I heard that crash—have been the most acute of all the agonies which I have undergone. I will not expose myself to a repetition of it."

He allowed me, however, to spend the remainder of that night where I was, and I lay there worrying over the problem and lamenting my own failure. With the first light of morning there was the Lascar's hand still lying upon the floor to remind me of my fiasco. I lay looking at it—and as I lay suddenly an idea flew like a bullet through my head and brought me quivering with excitement out of my couch. I raised the grim relic from where it had fallen. Yes, it was indeed so. The hand was the *left* hand of the Lascar.

By the first train I was on my way to town, and hurried at once to the Seamen's Hospital. I remembered that both hands of the Lascar had been amputated, but I was terrified lest the precious organ which I was in search of might have been already consumed in the crematory. My suspense was soon ended. It had still been preserved in the *post-mortem* room. And so I returned to Rodenhurst in the evening with my mission accomplished and the material for a fresh experiment.

But Sir Dominick Holden would not hear of my occupying the laboratory again. To all my entreaties he turned a deaf ear. It offended his sense of hospitality, and he could no longer permit it. I left the hand, therefore, as I had done its fellow the night before, and I occupied a comfortable bedroom in another portion of the house, some distance from the scene of my adventures.

But in spite of that my sleep was not destined to be uninterrupted. In the dead of night my host burst into my room, a lamp in his hand. His huge, gaunt figure was enveloped in a loose dressing-gown, and his whole appearance might certainly have seemed more formidable to a weak-nerved man than that of the Indian of the night before. But it was not his entrance so much as his expression which amazed me. He had turned suddenly younger by twenty years at the least. His eyes were shining, his features radiant, and he waved one hand in triumph over his head. I sat up astounded, staring sleepily at this extraordinary visitor. But his words soon drove the sleep from my eyes.

"We have done it! We have succeeded!" he shouted. "My dear Hardacre, how can I ever in this world repay you?"

"You don't mean to say that it is all right?"

"Indeed I do. I was sure that you would not mind being awakened to hear such blessed news."

"Mind! I should think not indeed. But is it really certain?"

"I have no doubt whatever upon the point. I owe you such a debt, my dear nephew, as I have never owed a man before, and never expected to. What can I possibly do for you that is commensurate ? Providence must have sent you to my rescue. You have saved both my reason and my life, for another six months of this must have seen me either in a cell or a coffin. And my wife—it was wearing her out before my eyes. Never could I have believed that any human being could have lifted this burden off me." He seized my hand and wrung it in his bony grip.

" It was only an experiment—a forlorn hope—but I am delighted from my heart that it has succeeded. But how do you know that it is all right ? Have you seen something ? "

He seated himself at the foot of my bed.

" I have seen enough," said he. " It satisfies me that I shall be troubled no more. What has passed is easily told. You know that at a certain hour this creature always comes to me. To-night he arrived at the usual time, and aroused me with even more violence than is his custom. I can only surmise that his disappointment of last night increased the bitterness of his anger against me. He looked angrily at me, and then went on his usual round. But in a few minutes I saw him, for the first time since this persecution began, return to my chamber. He was smiling. I saw the gleam of his white teeth through the dim light. He stood facing me at the end of my bed, and three times he made the low, Eastern salaam which is their solemn leave-taking. And the third time that he bowed he raised his arms over his head, and I saw his *two* hands outstretched in the air. So he vanished, and, as I believe, for ever."

So that is the curious experience which won me the affection and the gratitude of my celebrated uncle, the famous Indian surgeon. His anticipations were realised, and never again was he disturbed by the visits of the restless hillman in search of his lost member. Sir Dominick and Lady Holden spent a very happy old age, unclouded, so far as I know, by any trouble, and they finally died during the great influenza epidemic within a few weeks of each other. In his lifetime he always turned to me for advice in everything which concerned that English life of which he knew so little; and I aided him also in the purchase and development of his estates. It was no great surprise to me, therefore, that I found myself eventually promoted over the heads of five exasperated cousins, and changed in a single day from a hard-working country doctor into the head of an important Wiltshire family. I, at least, have reason to bless the memory of the man with the brown hand, and the day when I was fortunate enough to relieve Rodenhurst of his unwelcome presence.

THE LEATHER FUNNEL

MY friend, Lionel Dacre, lived in the Avenue de Wagram, Paris. His house was that small one, with the iron railings and grass plot in front of it, on the left-hand side as you pass down from the Arc de Triomphe. I fancy that it had been there long before the avenue was constructed, for the grey tiles were stained with lichens, and the walls were mildewed and discoloured with age. It looked a small house from the street, five windows in front, if I remember right, but it deepened into a single long chamber at the back. It was here that Dacre had that singular library of occult literature, and the fantastic curiosities which served as a hobby for himself, and an amusement for his friends. A wealthy man of refined and eccentric tastes, he had spent much of his life and fortune in gathering together what was said to be a unique private collection of Talmudic, cabalistic, and magical works, many of them of great rarity and value. His tastes leaned toward the marvellous and the monstrous, and I have heard that his experiments in the direction of the unknown have passed all the bounds of civilization and of decorum. To his English friends he never alluded to such matters, and took the tone of the student and *virtuoso*; but a Frenchman whose tastes were of the same nature has assured me that the worst excesses of the black mass have been perpetrated in that large and lofty hall, which is lined with the shelves of his books, and the cases of his museum.

Dacre's appearance was enough to show that his deep interest in these psychic matters was intellectual rather than spiritual. There was no trace of asceticism upon his heavy face, but there was much mental force in his huge, dome-like skull, which curved upward from amongst his thinning locks, like a snow-peak above its fringe of fir trees. His knowledge was greater than his wisdom, and his powers were far superior to his character. The small bright eyes, buried deeply in his fleshy face, twinkled with intelligence and an unabated curiosity of life, but they were the eyes of a sensualist and an egotist. Enough of the man, for he is dead now, poor devil, dead at the very time that he had made sure that he had at last discovered the elixir of life. It is not with his complex character that I have to deal, but with the very strange and inexplicable incident which had its rise in my visit to him in the early spring of the year '82.

I had known Dacre in England, for my researches in the Assyrian Room of the British Museum had been conducted at the time when he was endeavouring to establish a mystic and esoteric meaning in the Babylonian tablets, and this community of interests had brought us together. Chance remarks had led to daily conversation, and that to something verging upon friendship. I had promised him that on my next visit to Paris I would call upon him. At the time when I was able to fulfil my compact I was living in a cottage at Fontainebleau, and as the evening trains were inconvenient, he asked me to spend the night in his house.

"I have only that one spare couch," said he, pointing

to a broad sofa in his large salon ; " I hope that you will manage to be comfortable there."

It was a singular bedroom, with its high walls of brown volumes, but there could be no more agreeable furniture to a bookworm like myself, and there is no scent so pleasant to my nostrils as that faint, subtle reek which comes from an ancient book. I assured him that I could desire no more charming chamber, and no more congenial surroundings.

" If the fittings are neither convenient nor conventional, they are at least costly," said he, looking round at his shelves. " I have expended nearly a quarter of a million of money upon these objects which surround you. Books, weapons, gems, carvings, tapestries, images —there is hardly a thing here which has not its history, and it is generally one worth telling."

He was seated as he spoke at one side of the open fireplace, and I at the other. His reading-table was on his right, and the strong lamp above it ringed it with a very vivid circle of golden light. A half-rolled palimpsest lay in the centre, and around it were many quaint articles of bric-à-brac. One of these was a large funnel, such as is used for filling wine casks. It appeared to be made of black wood, and to be rimmed with discoloured brass.

" That is a curious thing," I remarked. " What is the history of that ? "

" Ah ! " said he, " it is the very question which I have had occasion to ask myself. I would give a good deal to know. Take it in your hands and examine it."

I did so, and found that what I had imagined to be wood was in reality leather, though age had dried it into an extreme hardness. It was a large funnel, and might hold a quart when full. The brass rim encircled the wide end, but the narrow was also tipped with metal.

" What do you make of it ? " asked Dacre.

" I should imagine that it belonged to some vintner or maltster in the Middle Ages," said I. " I have seen in England leathern drinking flagons of the seventeenth century—' black jacks ' as they were called—which were of the same colour and hardness as this filler."

" I dare say the date would be about the same," said Dacre, " and, no doubt, also, it was used for filling a vessel with liquid. If my suspicions are correct, however, it was a queer vintner who used it, and a very singular cask which was filled. Do you observe nothing strange at the spout end of the funnel."

As I held it to the light I observed that at a spot some five inches above the brass tip the narrow neck of the leather funnel was all haggled and scored, as if someone had notched it round with a blunt knife. Only at that point was there any roughening of the dead black surface.

" Someone has tried to cut off the neck."

" Would you call it a cut ? "

" It is torn and lacerated. It must have taken some strength to leave these marks on such tough material, whatever the instrument may have been. But what do you think of it ? I can tell that you know more than you say."

Dacre smiled, and his little eyes twinkled with knowledge.

" Have you included the psychology of dreams among your learned studies ? " he asked.

" I did not even know that there was such a psychology."

" My dear sir, that shelf above the gem case is filled with volumes, from Albertus Magnus onward, which deal with no other subject. It is a science in itself."

" A science of charlatans."

" The charlatan is always the pioneer. From the astrologer came the astronomer, from the alchemist the chemist, from the mesmerist the experimental psychologist. The quack of yesterday is the professor of tomorrow. Even such subtle and elusive things as dreams will in time be reduced to system and order. When that time comes the researches of our friends on the bookshelf yonder will no longer be the amusement of the mystic, but the foundations of a science."

"Supposing that is so, what has the science of dreams to do with a large, black, brass-rimmed funnel?"

"I will tell you. You know that I have an agent who is always on the lookout for rarities and curiosities for my collection. Some days ago he heard of a dealer upon one of the Quais who had acquired some old rubbish found in a cupboard in an ancient house at the back of the Rue Mathurin, in the Quartier Latin. The dining-room of this old house is decorated with a coat of arms, chevrons, and bars rouge upon a field argent, which prove, upon inquiry, to be the shield of Nicholas de la Reynie, a high official of King Louis XIV. There can be no doubt that the other articles in the cupboard date back to the early days of that king. The inference is, therefore, that they were all the property of this Nicholas de la Reynie, who was, as I understand, the gentleman specially concerned with the maintenance and execution of the Draconic laws of that epoch."

"What then?"

"I would ask you now to take the funnel into your hands once more and to examine the upper brass rim. Can you make out any lettering upon it?"

There were certainly some scratches upon it, almost obliterated by time. The general effect was of several letters, the last of which bore some resemblance to a B.

"You make it a B?"

"Yes, I do."

"So do I. In fact, I have no doubt whatever that it is a B."

"But the nobleman you mentioned would have had R for his initial."

"Exactly! That's the beauty of it. He owned this curious object, and yet he had someone else's initials upon it. Why did he do this?"

"I can't imagine; can you?"

"Well, I might, perhaps, guess. Do you observe something drawn a little farther along the rim?"

"I should say it was a crown."

"It is undoubtedly a crown; but if you examine it in a good light, you will convince yourself that it is not an ordinary crown. It is a heraldic crown—a badge of rank, and it consists of an alternation of four pearls and strawberry leaves, the proper badge of a marquis. We may infer, therefore, that the person whose initials end in B was entitled to wear that coronet."

"Then this common leather filler belonged to a marquis?"

Dacre gave a peculiar smile.

"Or to some member of the family of a marquis," said he. "So much we have clearly gathered from this engraved rim."

"But what has all this to do with dreams?" I do not know whether it was from a look upon Dacre's face, or from some subtle suggestion in his manner, but a feeling of repulsion, of unreasoning horror, came upon me as I looked at the gnarled old lump of leather.

"I have more than once received important information through my dreams," said my companion in the didactic manner which he loved to affect. "I make it a rule now when I am in doubt upon any material point to place the article in question beside me as I sleep, and to hope for some enlightenment. The process does not appear to me to be very obscure, though it has not yet received the blessing of orthodox science. According to my theory, any object which has been intimately associated with any supreme paroxysm of human emotion, whether it be joy or pain, will retain a certain atmosphere or association which it is capable of communicating to a sensitive mind. By a sensitive mind I do not mean an abnormal one, but such a trained and educated mind as you or I possess."

"You mean, for example, that if I slept beside that old sword upon the wall, I might dream of some bloody incident in which that very sword took part?"

"An excellent example, for, as a matter of fact, that

sword was used in that fashion by me, and I saw in my sleep the death of its owner, who perished in a brisk skirmish, which I have been unable to identify, but which occurred at the time of the wars of the Frondists. If you think of it, some of our popular observances show that the fact has already been recognized by our ancestors, although we, in our wisdom, have classed it among superstitions."

"For example?"

"Well, the placing of the bride's cake beneath the pillow in order that the sleeper may have pleasant dreams. That is one of several instances which you will find set forth in a small *brochure* which I am myself writing upon the subject. But to come back to the point, I slept one night with this funnel beside me, and I had a dream which certainly throws a curious light upon its use and origin."

"What did you dream?"

"I dreamed——" He paused, and an intent look of interest came over his massive face. "By Jove, that's well thought of," said he. "This really will be an exceedingly interesting experiment. You are yourself a psychic subject—with nerves which respond readily to any impression."

"I have never tested myself in that direction."

"Then we shall test you to-night. Might I ask you as a very great favour, when you occupy that couch to-night, to sleep with this old funnel placed by the side of your pillow?"

The request seemed to me a grotesque one; but I have myself, in my complex nature, a hunger after all which is bizarre and fantastic. I had not the faintest belief in Dacre's theory, nor any hopes for success in such an experiment; yet it amused me that the experiment should be made. Dacre, with great gravity, drew a small stand to the head of my settee, and placed the funnel upon it. Then, after a short conversation, he wished me good night and left me.

* * * * *

I sat for some little time smoking by the smouldering fire, and turning over in my mind the curious incident which had occurred, and the strange experience which might lie before me. Sceptical as I was, there was something impressive in the assurance of Dacre's manner, and my extraordinary surroundings, the huge room with the strange and often sinister objects which were hung round it, struck solemnity into my soul. Finally I undressed, and turning out the lamp, I lay down. After long tossing I fell asleep. Let me try to describe as accurately as I can the scene which came to me in my dreams. It stands out now in my memory more clearly than anything which I have seen with my waking eyes.

There was a room which bore the appearance of a vault. Four spandrels from the corners ran up to join a sharp, cup-shaped roof. The architecture was rough, but very strong. It was evidently part of a great building.

Three men in black, with curious, top-heavy, black velvet hats, sat in a line upon a red-carpeted dais. Their faces were very solemn and sad. On the left stood two long-gowned men with portfolios in their hands, which seemed to be stuffed with papers. Upon the right, looking toward me, was a small woman with blonde hair and singular, light-blue eyes—the eyes of a child. She was past her first youth, but could not yet be called middle-aged. Her figure was inclined to stoutness and her bearing was proud and confident. Her face was pale, but serene. It was a curious face, comely and yet feline, with a subtle suggestion of cruelty about the straight, strong little mouth and chubby jaw. She was draped in some sort of loose, white gown. Beside her stood a thin, eager priest, who whispered in her ear, and continually raised a crucifix before her eyes. She turned her head and looked fixedly past the crucifix at the three men in black, who were, I felt, her judges.

As I gazed the three men stood up and said something, but I could distinguish no words, though I was aware that it was the central one who was speaking. They then swept out of the room, followed by the two men with the papers. At the same instant several rough-looking fellows in stout jerkins came bustling in and removed first the red carpet, and then the boards which formed the dais, so as to entirely clear the room. When this screen was removed I saw some singular articles of furniture behind it. One looked like a bed with wooden rollers at each end, and a winch handle to regulate its length. Another was a wooden horse. There were several other curious objects, and a number of swinging cords which played over pulleys. It was not unlike a modern gymnasium.

When the room had been cleared there appeared a new figure upon the scene. This was a tall, thin person clad in black, with a gaunt and austere face. The aspect of the man made me shudder. His clothes were all shining with grease and mottled with stains. He bore himself with a slow and impressive dignity, as if he took command of all things from the instant of his entrance. In spite of his rude appearance and sordid dress, it was now *his* business, *his* room, his to command. He carried a coil of light ropes over his left forearm. The lady looked him up and down with a searching glance, but her expression was unchanged. It was confident—even defiant. But it was very different with the priest. His face was ghastly white, and I saw the moisture glisten and run on his high, sloping forehead. He threw up his hands in prayer and he stooped continually to mutter frantic words in the lady's ear.

The man in black now advanced, and taking one of the cords from his left arm, he bound the woman's hands together. She held them meekly toward him as he did so. Then he took her arm with a rough grip and led her toward the wooden horse, which was little higher than her waist. On to this she was lifted and laid, with her back upon it, and her face to the ceiling, while the priest, quivering with horror, had rushed out of the room. The woman's lips were moving rapidly, and though I could hear nothing I knew that she was praying. Her feet hung down on either side of the horse, and I saw that the rough varlets in attendance had fastened cords to her ankles and secured the other ends to iron rings in the stone floor.

My heart sank within me as I saw these ominous preparations, and yet I was held by the fascination of horror, and I could not take my eyes from the strange spectacle. A man had entered the room with a bucket of water in either hand. Another followed with a third bucket. They were laid beside the wooden horse. The second man had a wooden dipper—a bowl with a straight handle—in his other hand. This he gave to the man in black. At the same moment one of the varlets approached with a dark object in his hand, which even in my dream filled me with a vague feeling of familiarity. It was a leathern filler. With horrible energy he thrust it—but I could stand no more. My hair stood on end with horror. I writhed, I struggled, I broke through the bonds of sleep, and I burst with a shriek into my own life, and found myself lying shivering with terror in the huge library, with the moonlight flooding through the window and throwing strange silver and black traceries upon the opposite wall. Oh, what a blessed relief to feel that I was back in the nineteenth century—back out of that mediæval vault into a world where men had human hearts within their bosoms. I sat up on my couch, trembling in every limb, my mind divided between thankfulness and horror. To think that such things were ever done—that they *could* be done without God striking the villains dead. Was it all a fantasy, or did it really stand for something which had happened in the black, cruel days of the world's history? I sank my throbbing head upon my shaking hands. And then, suddenly, my heart seemed to stand still in my bosom, and I could not even scream, so great was my terror. Something was advancing toward me through the darkness of the room.

It is a horror coming upon a horror which breaks a

man's spirit. I could not reason, I could not pray; I could only sit like a frozen image, and glare at the dark figure which was coming down the great room. And then it moved out into the white lane of moonlight, and I breathed once more. It was Dacre, and his face showed that he was as frightened as myself.

"Was that you? For God's sake what's the matter?" he asked in a husky voice.

"Oh, Dacre, I am glad to see you! I have been down into hell. It was dreadful."

"Then it was you who screamed?"

"I dare say it was."

"It rang through the house. The servants are all terrified." He struck a match and lit the lamp. "I think we may get the fire to burn up again," he added, throwing some logs upon the embers. "Good God, my dear chap, how white you are! You look as if you had seen a ghost."

"So I have—several ghosts."

"The leather funnel has acted, then?"

"I wouldn't sleep near the infernal thing again for all the money you could offer me."

Dacre chuckled.

"I expected that you would have a lively night of it," said he. "You took it out of me in return, for that scream of yours wasn't a very pleasant sound at two in the morning. I suppose from what you say that you have seen the whole dreadful business."

"What dreadful business?"

"The torture of the water—the 'Extraordinary Question,' as it was called in the genial days of 'Le Roi Soleil.' Did you stand it out to the end?"

"No, thank God, I awoke before it really began."

"Ah! it is just as well for you. I held out till the third bucket. Well, it is an old story, and they are all in their graves now anyhow, so what does it matter how they got there? I suppose that you have no idea what it was that you have seen?"

"The torture of some criminal. She must have been a terrible malefactor indeed if her crimes are in proportion to her penalty."

"Well, we have that small consolation," said Dacre, wrapping his dressing-gown round him and crouching closer to the fire. "They *were* in proportion to her penalty. That is to say, if I am correct in the lady's identity."

"How could you possibly know her identity?"

For answer Dacre took down an old vellum-covered volume from the shelf.

"Just listen to this," said he; "it is in the French of the seventeenth century, but I will give a rough translation as I go. You will judge for yourself whether I have solved the riddle or not."

"'The prisoner was brought before the Grand Chambers and Tournelles of Parliament, sitting as a court of justice, charged with the murder of Master Dreux d'Aubray, her father, and of her two brothers, MM. d'Aubray, one being civil lieutenant, and the other a counsellor of Parliament. In person it seemed hard to believe that she had really done such wicked deeds, for she was of a mild appearance, and of short stature, with a fair skin and blue eyes. Yet the Court, having found her guilty, condemned her to the ordinary and to the extraordinary question in order that she might be forced to name her accomplices, after which she should be carried in a cart to the Place de Grève, there to have her head cut off, her body being afterwards burned and her ashes scattered to the winds.'

The date of this entry is July 16, 1676."

"It is interesting," said I, "but not convincing. How do you prove the two women to be the same?"

"I am coming to that. The narrative goes on to tell of the woman's behaviour when questioned. 'When the executioner approached her she recognized him by the cords which he held in his hands, and she at once held out her own hands to him, looking at him from head to foot without uttering a word.' How's that?"

"Yes, it was so."

"'She gazed without wincing upon the wooden horse and rings which had twisted so many limbs and caused so many shrieks of agony. When her eyes fell upon the three pails of water, which were all ready for her, she said with a smile, "All that water must have been brought here for the purpose of drowning me, Monsieur. You have no idea, I trust, of making a person of my small stature swallow it all."' Shall I read the details of the torture?"

"No, for Heaven's sake, don't."

"Here is a sentence which must surely show you that what is here recorded is the very scene which you have gazed upon to-night: 'The good Abbé Pirot, unable to contemplate the agonies which were suffered by his penitent, had hurried from the room.' Does that convince you?"

"It does entirely. There can be no question that it is indeed the same event. But who, then, is this lady whose appearance was so attractive and whose end was so horrible?"

For answer Dacre came across to me, and placed the small lamp upon the table which stood by my bed. Lifting up the ill-omened filler, he turned the brass rim so that the light fell full upon it. Seen in this way the engraving seemed clearer than on the night before.

"We have already agreed that this is the badge of a marquis or of a marquise," said he. "We have also settled that the last letter is B."

"It is undoubtedly so."

"I now suggest to you that the other letters from left to right are, M, M, a small d, A, a small d, and then the final B."

"Yes, I am sure that you are right. I can make out the two small d's quite plainly."

"What I have read to you to-night," said Dacre, "is the official record of the trial of Marie Madeleine d'Aubray, Marquise de Brinvilliers, one of the most famous poisoners and murderers of all time."

I sat in silence, overwhelmed at the extraordinary nature of the incident, and at the completeness of the proof with which Dacre had exposed its real meaning. In a vague way I remembered some details of the woman's career, her unbridled debauchery, the cold-blooded and protracted torture of her sick father, the murder of her brothers for motives of petty gain. I recollected also that the bravery of her end had done something to atone for the horror of her life, and that all Paris had sympathised with her last moments, and blessed her as a martyr within a few days of the time when they had cursed her as a murderess. One objection, and one only, occurred to my mind.

"How came her initials and her badge of rank upon the filler? Surely they did not carry their mediæval homage to the nobility to the point of decorating instruments of torture with their titles?"

"I was puzzled with the same point," said Dacre, "but it admits of a simple explanation. The case excited extraordinary interest at the time, and nothing could be more natural than that La Reynie, the head of the police, should retain this filler as a grim souvenir. It was not often that a marchioness of France underwent the extraordinary question. That he should engrave her initials upon it for the information of others was surely a very ordinary proceeding upon his part."

"And this?" I asked, pointing to the marks upon the leathern neck.

"She was a cruel tigress," said Dacre, as he turned away. "I think it is evident that like other tigresses her teeth were both strong and sharp."

LOT NO. 249

OF the dealings of Edward Bellingham with William Monkhouse Lee, and of the cause of the great terror of Abercrombie Smith, it may be that no absolute and final judgment will ever be delivered. It is true that we have the full and clear narrative of Smith himself, and such corroboration as he could look for from Thomas Styles the servant, from the Reverend Plumptree Peterson, Fellow of Old's, and from such other people as chanced to gain some passing glance at this or that incident in a singular chain of events. Yet, in the main, the story must rest upon Smith alone, and the most will think that it is more likely that one brain, however outwardly sane, has some subtle warp in its texture, some strange flaw in its workings, than that the path of Nature has been overstepped in open day in so famed a centre of learning and light as the University of Oxford. Yet when we think how narrow and how devious this path of Nature is, how dimly we can trace it, for all our lamps of science, and how from the darkness which girds it round great and terrible possibilities loom ever shadowly upwards, it is a bold and confident man who will put a limit to the strange by-paths into which the human spirit may wander.

In a certain wing of what we will call Old College in Oxford there is a corner turret of an exceeding great age. The heavy arch which spans the open door has bent downwards in the centre under the weight of its years, and the grey, lichen-blotched blocks of stone are bound and knitted together with withes and strands of ivy, as though the old mother had set herself to brace them up against wind and weather. From the door a stone stair curves upward spirally, passing two landings, and terminating in a third one, its steps all shapeless and hollowed by the tread of so many generations of the seekers after knowledge. Life has flowed like water down this winding stair, and, waterlike, has left these smooth-worn grooves behind it. From the long-gowned, pedantic scholars of Plantagenet days down to the young bloods of a later age, how full and strong had been that tide of young, English life. And what was left now of all those hopes, those strivings, those fiery energies, save here and there in some old-world churchyard a few scratches upon a stone, and perchance a handful of dust in a mouldering coffin? Yet here were the silent stair and the grey, old wall, with bend and saltire and many another heraldic device still to be read upon its surface, like grotesque shadows thrown back from the days that had passed.

In the month of May, in the year 1884, three young men occupied the sets of rooms which opened on to the separate landings of the old stair. Each set consisted simply of a sitting-room and of a bedroom, while the two corresponding rooms upon the ground-floor were used, the one as a coal-cellar, and the other as the living-room of the servant, or scout, Thomas Styles, whose duty it was to wait upon the three men above him. To right and to left was a line of lecture-rooms and of offices, so that the dwellers in the old turret enjoyed a certain seclusion, which made the chambers popular among the more studious undergraduates. Such were the three who occupied them now—Abercrombie Smith above, Edward Bellingham beneath him, and William Monkhouse Lee upon the lowest storey.

It was ten o'clock on a bright, spring night, and Abercrombie Smith lay back in his arm-chair, his feet upon the fender, and his briar-root pipe between his lips. In a similar chair, and equally at his ease, there lounged on the other side of the fireplace his old school friend Jephro

Hastie. Both men were in flannels, for they had spent their evening upon the river, but apart from their dress no one could look at their hard-cut, alert faces without seeing that they were open-air men—men whose minds and tastes turned naturally to all that was manly and robust. Hastie, indeed, was stroke of his college boat, and Smith was an even better oar, but a coming examination had already cast its shadow over him and held him to his work, save for the few hours a week which health demanded. A litter of medical books upon the table, with scattered bones, models, and anatomical plates, pointed to the extent as well as the nature of his studies, while a couple of single-sticks and a set of boxing-gloves above the mantelpiece hinted at the means by which, with Hastie's help, he might take his exercise in its most compressed and least-distant form. They knew each other very well—so well that they could sit now in that soothing silence which is the very highest development of companionship.

"Have some whisky," said Abercrombie Smith at last between two cloudbursts. "Scotch in the jug and Irish in the bottle."

"No, thanks. I'm in for the sculls. I don't liquor when I'm training. How about you?"

"I'm reading hard. I think it best to leave it alone."

Hastie nodded, and they relapsed into a contented silence.

"By the way, Smith," asked Hastie, presently, "have you made the acquaintance of either of the fellows on your stair yet?"

"Just a nod when we pass. Nothing more."

"Hum! I should be inclined to let it stand at that. I know something of them both. Not much, but as much as I want. I don't think I should take them to my bosom if I were you. Not that there's much amiss with Monkhouse Lee."

"Meaning the thin one?"

"Precisely. He is a gentlemanly little fellow. I don't

think there is any vice in him. But then you can't know him without knowing Bellingham."

"Meaning the fat one?"

"Yes, the fat one. And he's a man whom I, for one, would rather not know."

Abercrombie Smith raised his eyebrows and glanced across at his companion.

"What's up, then?" he asked. "Drink? Cards? Cad? You used not to be censorious."

"Ah! you evidently don't know the man, or you wouldn't ask. There's something damnable about him—something reptilian. My gorge always rises at him. I should put him down as a man with secret vices—an evil liver. He's no fool, though. They say that he is one of the best men in his line that they have ever had in the college."

"Medicine or classics?"

"Eastern languages. He's a demon at them. Chillingworth met him somewhere above the second cataract last long, and he told me that he just prattled to the Arabs as if he had been born and nursed and weaned among them. He talked Coptic to the Copts, and Hebrew to the Jews, and Arabic to the Bedouins, and they were all ready to kiss the hem of his frock-coat. There are some old hermit Johnnies up in those parts who sit on rocks and scowl and spit at the casual stranger. Well, when they saw this chap Bellingham, before he had said five words they just lay down on their bellies and wriggled. Chillingworth said that he never saw anything like it. Bellingham seemed to take it as his right, too, and strutted about among them and talked down to them like a Dutch uncle. Pretty good for an undergrad. of Old's, wasn't it?"

"Why do you say you can't know Lee without knowing Bellingham?"

"Because Bellingham is engaged to his sister Eveline. Such a bright little girl, Smith! I know the whole family well. It's disgusting to see that brute with her.

A toad and a dove, that's what they always remind me of."

Abercrombie Smith grinned and knocked his ashes out against the side of the grate.

" You show every card in your hand, old chap," said he. " What a prejudiced, green-eyed, evil-thinking old man it is! You have really nothing against the fellow except that."

" Well, I've known her ever since she was as long as that cherry-wood pipe, and I don't like to see her taking risks. And it is a risk. He looks beastly. And he has a beastly temper, a venomous temper. You remember his row with Long Norton?"

" No; you always forget that I am a freshman."

" Ah, it was last winter. Of course. Well, you know the towpath along by the river. There were several fellows going along it, Bellingham in front, when they came on an old market-woman coming the other way. It had been raining—you know what those fields are like when it has rained—and the path ran between the river and a great puddle that was nearly as broad. Well, what does this swine do but keep the path, and push the old girl into the mud, where she and her marketings came to terrible grief. It was a blackguard thing to do, and Long Norton, who is as gentle a fellow as ever stepped, told him what he thought of it. One word led to another, and it ended in Norton laying his stick across the fellow's shoulders. There was the deuce of a fuss about it, and it's a treat to see the way in which Bellingham looks at Norton when they meet now. By Jove, Smith, it's nearly eleven o'clock!"

" No hurry. Light your pipe again."

" Not I. I'm supposed to be in training. Here I've been sitting gossiping when I ought to have been safely tucked up. I'll borrow your skull, if you can share it. Williams has had mine for a month. I'll take the little bones of your ear, too, if you are sure you won't need them. Thanks very much. Never mind a bag, I can carry them very well under my arm. Good night, my son, and take my tip as to your neighbour."

When Hastie, bearing his anatomical plunder, had clattered off down the winding stair, Abercrombie Smith hurled his pipe into the wastepaper basket, and drawing his chair nearer to the lamp, plunged into a formidable, green-covered volume, adorned with great, coloured maps of that strange, internal kingdom of which we are the hapless and helpless monarchs. Though a freshman at Oxford, the student was not so in medicine, for he had worked for four years at Glasgow and at Berlin, and this coming examination would place him finally as a member of his profession. With his firm mouth, broad forehead, and clear-cut, somewhat hard-featured face, he was a man who, if he had no brilliant talent, was yet so dogged, so patient, and so strong that he might in the end overtop a more showy genius. A man who can hold his own among Scotchmen and North Germans is not a man to be easily set back. Smith had left a name at Glasgow and at Berlin, and he was bent now upon doing as much at Oxford, if hard work and devotion could accomplish it.

He had sat reading for about an hour, and the hands of the noisy carriage clock upon the side-table were rapidly closing together upon the twelve, when a sudden sound fell upon the student's ear—a sharp, rather shrill sound, like the hissing intake of a man's breath who gasps under some strong emotion. Smith laid down his book and slanted his ear to listen. There was no one on either side or above him, so that the interruption came certainly from the neighbour beneath—the same neighbour of whom Hastie had given so unsavoury an account. Smith knew him only as a flabby, pale-faced man of silent and studious habits, a man whose lamp threw a golden bar from the old turret even after he had extinguished his own. This community in lateness had formed a certain silent bond between them. It was soothing to Smith when the hours stole on towards dawning to feel that there was another so close who set as small a value upon his sleep as he did. Even now, as his thoughts turned towards him, Smith's feelings were kindly. Hastie was a good fellow, but he was rough, strong-fibred, with no imagination or sympathy. He could not tolerate departures from what he looked upon as the model type of manliness. If a man could not be measured by a public-school standard, then he was beyond the pale with Hastie. Like so many who are themselves robust, he was apt to confuse the constitution with the character, to ascribe to want of principle what was really a want of circulation. Smith, with his stronger mind, knew his friend's habit, and made allowance for it now as his thoughts turned towards the man beneath him.

There was no return of the singular sound, and Smith was about to turn to his work once more, when suddenly there broke out in the silence of the night a hoarse cry, a positive scream—the call of a man who is moved and shaken beyond all control. Smith sprang out of his chair and dropped his book. He was a man of fairly firm fibre, but there was something in this sudden, uncontrollable shriek of horror which chilled his blood and pringled in his skin. Coming in such a place and at such an hour, it brought a thousand fantastic possibilities into his head. Should he rush down, or was it better to wait? He had all the national hatred of making a scene, and he knew so little of his neighbour that he would not lightly intrude upon his affairs. For a moment he stood in doubt and even as he balanced the matter there was a quick rattle of footsteps upon the stairs, and young Monkhouse Lee, half-dressed and as white as ashes, burst into his room.

"Come down!" he gasped. "Bellingham's ill."

Abercrombie Smith followed him closely downstairs into the sitting-room which was beneath his own, and intent as he was upon the matter in hand, he could not but take an amazed glance around him as he crossed the threshold. It was such a chamber as he had never seen before—a museum rather than a study. Walls and ceiling were thickly covered with a thousand strange relics from Egypt and the East. Tall, angular figures bearing burdens or weapons stalked in an uncouth frieze round the apartments. Above were bull-headed, stork-headed, cat-headed, owl-headed statues, with viper-crowned, almond-eyed monarchs, and strange, beetle-like deities cut out of the blue Egyptian lapis lazuli. Horus and Isis and Osiris peeped down from every niche and shelf, while across the ceiling a true son of Old Nile, a great, hanging-jawed crocodile, was slung in a double noose.

In the centre of this singular chamber was a large, square table, littered with papers, bottles, and the dried leaves of some graceful, palm-like plant. These varied objects had all been heaped together in order to make room for a mummy case, which had been conveyed from the wall, as was evident from the gap there, and laid across the front of the table. The mummy itself, a horrid, black, withered thing, like a charred head on a gnarled bush, was lying half out of the case, with its claw-like hand and bony forearm resting upon the table. Propped up against the sarcophagus was an old, yellow scroll of papyrus, and in front of it, in a wooden arm-chair, sat the owner of the room, his head thrown back, his widely opened eyes directed in a horrified stare to the crocodile above him, and his blue, thick lips puffing loudly with every expiration.

"My God! he's dying!" cried Monkhouse Lee, distractedly.

He was a slim, handsome young fellow, olive-skinned and dark-eyed, of a Spanish rather than of an English type, with a Celtic intensity of manner which contrasted with the Saxon phlegm of Abercrombie Smith.

"Only a faint, I think," said the medical student. "Just give me a hand with him. You take his feet. Now on to the sofa. Can you kick all those little wooden devils off? What a litter it is! Now he will be all right if we undo his collar and give him some water. What has he been up to at all ? "

" I don't know. I heard him cry out. I ran up. I know him pretty well, you know. It is very good of you to come down."

" His heart is going like a pair of castanets," said Smith, laying his hand on the breast of the unconscious man. " He seems to me to be frightened all to pieces. Chuck the water over him ! What a face he has got on him ! "

It was indeed a strange and most repellent face, for colour and outline were equally unnatural. It was white, not with the ordinary pallor of fear, but with an absolutely bloodless white, like the under side of a sole. He was very fat, but gave the impression of having at some time been considerably fatter, for his skin hung loosely in creases and folds, and was shot with a meshwork of wrinkles. Short, stubbly brown hair bristled up from his scalp, with a pair of thick, wrinkled ears protruding at the sides. His light-grey eyes were still open, the pupils dilated and the balls projecting in a fixed and horrid stare. It seemed to Smith as he looked down upon him that he had never seen Nature's danger signals flying so plainly upon a man's countenance, and his thoughts turned more seriously to the warning which Hastie had given him an hour before.

" What the deuce can have frightened him so ? " he asked.

" It's the mummy."

" The mummy ? How, then ? "

" I don't know. It's beastly and morbid. I wish he would drop it. It's the second fright he has given me. It was the same last winter. I found him just like this, with that horrid thing in front of him."

" What does he want with the mummy, then ? "

" Oh, he's a crank, you know. It's his hobby. He knows more about these things than any man in England. But I wish he wouldn't ! Ah, he's beginning to come to."

A faint tinge of colour had begun to steal back into Bellingham's ghastly cheeks, and his eyelids shivered like a sail after a calm. He clasped and unclasped his hands, drew a long, thin breath between his teeth, and suddenly jerking up his head, threw a glance of recognition around him. As his eyes fell upon the mummy, he sprang off the sofa, seized the roll of papyrus, thrust it into a drawer, turned the key, and then staggered back on to the sofa.

"What's up?" he asked. "What do you chaps want?"

"You've been shrieking out and making no end of a fuss," said Monkhouse Lee. "If our neighbour here from above hadn't come down, I'm sure I don't know what I should have done with you."

"Ah, it's Abercrombie Smith," said Bellingham, glancing up at him. "How very good of you to come in! What a fool I am! Oh, my God, what a fool I am!"

He sank his head on to his hands, and burst into peal after peal of hysterical laughter.

"Look here! Drop it!" cried Smith, shaking him roughly by the shoulder.

"Your nerves are all in a jangle. You must drop these little midnight games with mummies, or you'll be going off your chump. You're all on wires now."

"I wonder," said Bellingham, "whether you would be as cool as I am if you had seen——"

"What then?"

"Oh, nothing. I meant that I wonder if you could sit up at night with a mummy without trying your nerves. I have no doubt that you are quite right. I dare say that I have been taking it out of myself too much lately. But I am all right now. Please don't go, though. Just wait for a few minutes until I am quite myself."

"The room is very close," remarked Lee, throwing open the window and letting in the cool night air.

"It's balsamic resin," said Bellingham. He lifted

up one of the dried palmate leaves from the table and frizzled it over the chimney of the lamp. It broke away into heavy smoke wreaths, and a pungent, biting odour filled the chamber. "It's the sacred plant—the plant of the priests," he remarked. "Do you know anything of Eastern languages, Smith?"

"Nothing at all. Not a word."

The answer seemed to lift a weight from the Egyptologist's mind.

"By the way," he continued, "how long was it from the time that you ran down, until I came to my senses?"

"Not long. Some four or five minutes."

"I thought it could not be very long," said he, drawing a long breath. "But what a strange thing unconsciousness is! There is no measurement to it. I could not tell from my own sensations if it were seconds or weeks. Now that gentleman on the table was packed up in the days of the eleventh dynasty, some forty centuries ago, and yet if he could find his tongue, he would tell us that this lapse of time has been but a closing of the eyes and a reopening of them. He is a singularly fine mummy, Smith."

Smith stepped over to the table and looked down with a professional eye at the black and twisted form in front of him. The features, though horribly discoloured, were perfect, and two little nut-like eyes still lurked in the depths of the black, hollow sockets. The blotched skin was drawn tightly from bone to bone, and a tangled wrap of black, coarse hair fell over the ears. Two thin teeth, like those of a rat, overlay the shrivelled lower lip. In its crouching position, with bent joints and craned head, there was a suggestion of energy about the horrid thing which made Smith's gorge rise. The gaunt ribs, with their parchment-like covering, were exposed, and the sunken, leaden-hued abdomen, with the long slit where the embalmer had left his mark; but the lower limbs were wrapped round with coarse, yellow bandages. A number of little clove-like pieces of myrrh and of cassia were sprinkled over the body, and lay scattered on the inside of the case.

"I don't know his name," said Bellingham, passing his hand over the shrivelled head. "You see the outer sarcophagus with the inscriptions is missing. Lot 249 is all the title he has now. You see it printed on his case. That was his number in the auction at which I picked him up."

"He has been a very pretty sort of fellow in his day," remarked Abercrombie Smith.

"He has been a giant. His mummy is six feet seven in length, and that would be a giant over there, for they were never a very robust race. Feel these great, knotted bones, too. He would be a nasty fellow to tackle."

"Perhaps these very hands helped to build the stones into the pyramids," suggested Monkhouse Lee, looking down with disgust in his eyes at the crooked, unclean talons.

"No fear. This fellow has been pickled in natron, and looked after in the most approved style. They did not serve hodsmen in that fashion. Salt or bitumen was enough for them. It has been calculated that this sort of thing cost about seven hundred and thirty pounds in our money. Our friend was a noble at the least. What do you make of that small inscription near his feet, Smith?"

"I told you that I know no Eastern tongue."

"Ah, so you did. It is the name of the embalmer, I take it. A very conscientious worker he must have been. I wonder how many modern works will survive four thousand years?"

He kept on speaking lightly and rapidly, but it was evident to Abercrombie Smith that he was still palpitating with fear. His hands shook, his lower lip trembled, and look where he would, his eye always came sliding round to his gruesome companion. Through all his fear, however, there was a suspicion of triumph in his tone and manner. His eyes shone, and his footstep, as he paced the room, was brisk and jaunty. He gave the impression of a man who has gone through an ordeal, the marks of which he still bears upon him, but which has helped him to his end.

"You're not going yet?" he cried, as Smith rose from the sofa.

At the prospect of solitude, his fears seemed to crowd back upon him, and he stretched out a hand to detain him.

"Yes, I must go. I have my work to do. You are all right now. I think that with your nervous system you should take up some less morbid study."

"Oh, I am not nervous as a rule; and I have unwrapped mummies before."

"You fainted last time," observed Monkhouse Lee.

"Ah, yes, so I did. Well, I must have a nerve tonic or a course of electricity. You are not going, Lee?"

"I'll do whatever you wish, Ned."

"Then I'll come down with you and have a shake-down on your sofa. Good night, Smith. I am so sorry to have disturbed you with my foolishness."

They shook hands, and as the medical student stumbled up the spiral and irregular stair he heard a key turn in a door, and the steps of his two new acquaintances as they descended to the lower floor.

In this strange way began the acquaintance between Edward Bellingham and Abercrombie Smith, an acquaintance which the latter, at least, had no desire to push further. Bellingham, however, appeared to have taken a fancy to his rough-spoken neighbour, and made his advances in such a way that he could hardly be repulsed without absolute brutality. Twice he called to thank Smith for his assistance, and many times afterwards he looked in with books, papers and such other civilities as two bachelor neighbours can offer each other. He was, as Smith soon found, a man of wide reading, with catholic tastes and an extraordinary memory. His manner, too, was so pleasing and suave that one came, after a time, to overlook his repellent appearance. For a jaded and wearied man he was no unpleasant companion, and Smith found himself, after a time, looking forward to his visits, and even returning them.

Clever as he undoubtedly was, however, the medical student seemed to detect a dash of insanity in the man. He broke out at times into a high, inflated style of talk which was in contrast with the simplicity of his life.

"It is a wonderful thing," he cried, "to feel that one can command powers of good and of evil—a ministering angel or a demon of vengeance." And again, of Monkhouse Lee, he said,—"Lee is a good fellow, an honest fellow, but he is without strength or ambition. He would not make a fit partner for a man with a great enterprise. He would not make a fit partner for me."

At such hints and innuendoes stolid Smith, puffing solemnly at his pipe, would simply raise his eyebrows and shake his head, with little interjections of medical wisdom as to earlier hours and fresher air.

One habit Bellingham had developed of late which Smith knew to be a frequent herald of a weakening mind. He appeared to be for ever talking to himself. At late hours of the night, when there could be no visitor with him, Smith could still hear his voice beneath him in a low, muffled monologue, sunk almost to a whisper, and yet very audible in the silence. This solitary babbling annoyed and distracted the student, so that he spoke more than once to his neighbour about it. Bellingham, however, flushed up at the charge, and denied curtly that he had uttered a sound; indeed, he showed more annoyance over the matter than the occasion seemed to demand.

Had Abercrombie Smith had any doubt as to his own ears he had not to go far to find corroboration. Tom Styles, the little wrinkled man-servant who had attended to the wants of the lodgers in the turret for a longer time than any man's memory could carry him, was sorely put to it over the same matter.

" If you please, sir," said he, as he tidied down the top chamber one morning, " do you think Mr. Bellingham is all right, sir ? "

" All right, Styles ? "

" Yes, sir. Right in his head, sir."

" Why should he not be, then ? "

" Well, I don't know, sir. His habits has changed of late. He's not the same man he used to be, though I make free to say that he was never quite one of my gentlemen, like Mr. Hastie or yourself, sir. He's took to talkin' to himself something awful. I wonder it don't disturb you. I don't know what to make of him, sir."

" I don't know what business it is of yours, Styles."

" Well, I takes an interest, Mr. Smith. It may be forward of me, but I can't help it. I feel sometimes as if I was mother and father to my young gentlemen. It all falls on me when things go wrong and the relations come. But Mr. Bellingham, sir. I want to know what it is that walks about his room sometimes when he's out and when the door's locked on the outside."

" Eh ? you're talking nonsense, Styles."

" Maybe so, sir ; but I heard it more'n once with my own ears."

" Rubbish, Styles."

" Very good, sir. You'll ring the bell if you want me."

Abercrombie Smith gave little heed to the gossip of the old man-servant, but a small incident occurred a few days later which left an unpleasant effect upon his mind, and brought the words of Styles forcibly to his memory.

Bellingham had come up to see him late one night, and was entertaining him with an interesting account of the rock tombs of Beni Hassan in Upper Egypt, when Smith, whose hearing was remarkably acute, distinctly heard the sound of a door opening on the landing below.

" There's some fellow gone in or out of your room," he remarked.

Bellingham sprang up and stood helpless for a moment, with the expression of a man who is half-incredulous and half-afraid.

"I surely locked it. I am almost positive that I locked it," he stammered. "No one could have opened it."

"Why, I hear someone coming up the steps now," said Smith.

Bellingham rushed out through the door, slammed it loudly behind him, and hurried down the stairs. About half-way down Smith heard him stop, and thought he caught the sound of whispering. A moment later the door beneath him shut, a key creaked in a lock, and Bellingham, with beads of moisture upon his pale face, ascended the stairs once more, and re-entered the room.

"It's all right," he said, throwing himself down in a chair. "It was that fool of a dog. He had pushed the door open. I don't know how I came to forget to lock it."

"I didn't know you kept a dog," said Smith, looking very thoughtfully at the disturbed face of his companion.

"Yes, I haven't had him long. I must get rid of him. He's a great nuisance."

"He must be, if you find it so hard to shut him up. I should have thought that shutting the door would have been enough, without locking it."

"I want to prevent old Styles from letting him out. He's of some value, you know, and it would be awkward to lose him."

"I am a bit of a dog-fancier myself," said Smith, still gazing hard at his companion from the corner of his eyes. "Perhaps you'll let me have a look at it."

"Certainly. But I am afraid it cannot be to-night; I have an appointment. Is that clock right? Then I am a quarter of an hour late already. You'll excuse me, I am sure."

He picked up his cap and hurried from the room. In spite of his appointment, Smith heard him re-enter his own chamber and lock his door upon the inside.

This interview left a disagreeable impression upon the medical student's mind. Bellingham had lied to him, and lied so clumsily that it looked as if he had desperate reasons for concealing the truth. Smith knew that his neighbour had no dog. He knew, also, that the step which he had heard upon the stairs was not the step of an animal. But if it were not, then what could it be? There was old Style's statement about the something which used to pace the room at times when the owner was absent. Could it be a woman? Smith rather inclined to the view. If so, it would mean disgrace and expulsion to Bellingham if it were discovered by the authorities, so that his anxiety and falsehoods might be accounted for. And yet it was inconceivable that an undergraduate could keep a woman in his rooms without being instantly detected. Be the explanation what it might, there was something ugly about it, and Smith determined, as he turned to his books, to discourage all further attempts at intimacy on the part of his soft-spoken and ill-favoured neighbour.

But his work was destined to interruption that night. He had hardly caught up the broken threads when a firm, heavy footfall came three steps at a time from below, and Hastie, in blazer and flannels, burst into the room.

"Still at it!" said he, plumping down into his wonted arm-chair. "What a chap you are to stew! I believe an earthquake might come and knock Oxford into a cocked hat, and you would sit perfectly placid with your books among the ruins. However, I won't bore you long. Three whiffs of baccy, and I am off."

"What's the news, then?" asked Smith, cramming a plug of bird's-eye into his briar with his forefinger.

"Nothing very much. Wilson made 70 for the freshmen against the eleven. They say that they will play him instead of Buddicomb, for Buddicomb is clean off colour. He used to be able to bowl a little, but it's nothing but half-volleys and long hops now."

"Medium right," suggested Smith, with the intense

gravity which comes upon a 'varsity man when he speaks of athletics.

"Inclining to fast, with a work from leg. Comes with the arm about three inches or so. He used to be nasty on a wet wicket. Oh, by the way, have you heard about Long Norton?"

"What's that?"

"He's been attacked."

"Attacked?"

"Yes, just as he was turning out of the High Street, and within a hundred yards of the gate of Old's."

"But who——"

"Ah, that's the rub! If you said 'what,' you would be more grammatical. Norton swears that it was not human, and, indeed, from the scratches on his throat, I should be inclined to agree with him."

"What, then? Have we come down to spooks?"

Abercrombie Smith puffed his scientific contempt.

"Well, no; I don't think that is quite the idea, either. I am inclined to think that if any showman has lost a great ape lately, and the brute is in these parts, a jury would find a true bill against it. Norton passes that way every night, you know, about the same hour. There's a tree that hangs low over the path—the big elm from Rainy's garden. Norton thinks the thing dropped on him out of the tree. Anyhow, he was nearly strangled by two arms, which, he says, were as strong and as thin as steel bands. He saw nothing; only those beastly arms that tightened and tightened on him. He yelled his head nearly off, and a couple of chaps came running, and the thing went over the wall like a cat. He never got a fair sight of it the whole time. It gave Norton a shake up, I can tell you. I tell him it has been as good as a change at the seaside for him."

"A garrotter, most likely," said Smith.

"Very possibly. Norton says not; but we don't mind what he says. The garrotter had long nails, and was pretty smart at swinging himself over walls. By the way, your beautiful neighbour would be pleased if he heard about it. He had a grudge against Norton, and he's not a man, from what I know of him, to forget his little debts. But hallo, old chap, what have you got in your noddle ? "

" Nothing," Smith answered curtly.

He had started in his chair, and the look had flashed over his face which comes upon a man who is struck suddenly by some unpleasant idea.

" You looked as if something I had said had taken you on the raw. By the way, you have made the acquaintance of Master B. since I looked in last, have you not ? Young Monkhouse Lee told me something to that effect."

" Yes ; I know him slightly. He has been up here once or twice."

" Well, you're big enough and ugly enough to take care of yourself. He's not what I should call exactly a healthy sort of Johnny, though, no doubt, he's very clever, and all that. But you'll soon find out for yourself. Lee is all right ; he's a very decent little fellow. Well, so long, old chap ! I row Mullins for the Vice-Chancellor's pot on Wednesday week, so mind you come down, in case I don't see you before."

Bovine Smith laid down his pipe and turned stolidly to his books once more. But with all the will in the world, he found it very hard to keep his mind upon his work. It would slip away to brood upon the man beneath him, and upon the little mystery which hung round his chambers. Then his thoughts turned to this singular attack of which Hastie had spoken, and to the grudge which Bellingham was said to owe the object of it. The two ideas would persist in rising together in his mind, as though there were some close and intimate connection between them. And yet the suspicion was so dim and vague that it could not be put down in words.

" Confound the chap ! " cried Smith, as he shied his book on pathology across the room. " He has spoiled my night's reading, and that's reason enough, if there were no other, why I should steer clear of him in the future."

For ten days the medical student confined himself so closely to his studies that he neither saw nor heard anything of either of the men beneath him. At the hours when Bellingham had been accustomed to visit him, he took care to sport his oak, and though he more than once heard a knocking at his outer door, he resolutely refused to answer it. One afternoon, however, he was descending the stairs when, just as he was passing it, Bellingham's door flew open, and young Monkhouse Lee came out with his eyes sparkling and a dark flush of anger upon his olive cheeks. Close at his heels followed Bellingham, his fat, unhealthy face all quivering with malignant passion.

"You fool!" he hissed. "You'll be sorry."

"Very likely," cried the other. "Mind what I say. It's off! I won't hear of it!"

"You've promised, anyhow."

"Oh, I'll keep that! I won't speak. But I'd rather little Eva was in her grave. Once for all, it's off. She'll do what I say. We don't want to see you again."

So much Smith could not avoid hearing, but he hurried on, for he had no wish to be involved in their dispute. There had been a serious breach between them, that was clear enough, and Lee was going to cause the engagement with his sister to be broken off. Smith thought of Hastie's comparison of the toad and the dove, and was glad to think that the matter was at an end. Bellingham's face when he was in a passion was not pleasant to look upon. He was not a man to whom an innocent girl could be trusted for life. As he walked, Smith wondered languidly what could have caused the quarrel, and what the promise might be which Bellingham had been so anxious that Monkhouse Lee should keep.

It was the day of the sculling match between Hastie and Mullins, and a stream of men were making their way down to the banks of the Isis. A May sun was shining brightly, and the yellow path was barred with the black shadows of the tall elm-trees. On either side the grey colleges lay back from the road, the hoary old mothers of minds looking out from their high, mullioned windows at the tide of young life which swept so merrily past them. Black-clad tutors, prim officials, pale, reading men, brown-faced, straw-hatted young athletes in white sweaters or many-coloured blazers, all were hurrying towards the blue, winding river which curves through the Oxford meadows.

Abercrombie Smith, with the intuition of an old oarsman, chose his position at the point where he knew that the struggle, if there were a struggle, would come. Far off he heard the hum which announced the start, the gathering roar of the approach, the thunder of running feet, and the shouts of the men in the boats beneath him. A spray of half-clad, deep-breathing runners shot past him, and craning over their shoulders, he saw Hastie pulling a steady thirty-six, while his opponent, with a jerky forty, was a good boat's length behind him. Smith gave a cheer for his friend, and pulling out his watch, was starting off again for his chambers, when he felt a touch upon his shoulder, and found that young Monkhouse Lee was beside him.

"I saw you there," he said, in a timid, deprecating way. "I wanted to speak to you, if you could spare me a half-hour. This cottage is mine. I share it with Harrington of King's. Come in and have a cup of tea."

"I must be back presently," said Smith. "I am hard on the grind at present. But I'll come in for a few minutes with pleasure. I wouldn't have come out only Hastie is a friend of mine."

"So he is of mine. Hasn't he a beautiful style? Mullins wasn't in it. But come into the cottage. It's a little den of a place, but it is pleasant to work in during the summer months."

It was a small, square, white building, with green doors and shutters, and a rustic trellis-work porch, standing back some fifty yards from the river's bank. Inside, the main room was roughly fitted up as a study—deal table, unpainted shelves with books, and a few cheap oleographs upon the wall. A kettle sang upon a spirit-stove, and there were tea things upon a tray on the table.

" Try that chair and have a cigarette," said Lee. " Let me pour you out a cup of tea. It's so good of you to come in, for I know that your time is a good deal taken up. I wanted to say to you that, if I were you, I should change my rooms at once."

" Eh ? "

Smith sat staring with a lighted match in one hand and his unlit cigarette in the other.

" Yes ; it must seem very extraordinary, and the worst of it is that I cannot give my reasons, for I am under a solemn promise—a very solemn promise. But I may go so far as to say that I don't think Bellingham is a very safe man to live near. I intend to camp out here as much as I can for a time."

" Not safe ! What do you mean ? "

" Ah, that's what I mustn't say. But do take my advice and move your rooms. We had a grand row to-day. You must have heard us, for you came down the stairs."

" I saw that you had fallen out."

" He's a horrible chap, Smith. That is the only word for him. I have had doubts about him ever since that night when he fainted—you remember, when you came down. I taxed him to-day, and he told me things that made my hair rise, and wanted me to stand in with him. I'm not straight-laced, but I am a clergyman's son, you know, and I think there are some things which are quite beyond the pale. I only thank God that I found him out before it was too late, for he was to have married into my family."

" This is all very fine, Lee," said Abercrombie Smith curtly. " But either you are saying a great deal too much or a great deal too little."

" I give you a warning."

" If there is real reason for warning, no promise can bind you. If I see a rascal about to blow a place up with dynamite no pledge will stand in my way of preventing him."

" Ah, but I cannot prevent him, and I can do nothing but warn you."

" Without saying what you warn me against."

" Against Bellingham."

" But that is childish. Why should I fear him, or any man ? "

" I can't tell you. I can only entreat you to change your rooms. You are in danger where you are. I don't even say that Bellingham would wish to injure you. But it might happen, for he is a dangerous neighbour just now."

" Perhaps I know more than you think," said Smith, looking keenly at the young man's boyish, earnest face. " Suppose I tell you that someone else shares Bellingham's rooms."

Monkhouse Lee sprang from his chair in uncontrollable excitement.

" You know, then ?" he gasped.

" A woman."

Lee dropped back again with a groan.

" My lips are sealed," he said. " I must not speak."

" Well, anyhow," said Smith, rising, " it is not likely that I should allow myself to be frightened out of rooms which suit me very nicely. It would be a little too feeble for me to move out all my goods and chattels because you say that Bellingham might in some unexplained way do me an injury. I think that I'll just take my chance, and stay where I am, and as I see that it's nearly five o'clock, I must ask you to excuse me."

He bade the young student adieu in a few curt words, and made his way homeward through the sweet spring evening, feeling half-ruffled, half-amused, as any other strong, unimaginative man might who has been menaced by a vague and shadowy danger.

There was one little indulgence which Abercrombie Smith always allowed himself, however closely his work might press upon him. Twice a week, on the Tuesday and the Friday, it was his invariable custom to walk over to Farlingford, the residence of Doctor Plumptree Peterson, situated about a mile and a half out of Oxford. Peterson had been a close friend of Smith's elder brother, Francis, and as he was a bachelor, fairly well-to-do, with a good cellar and a better library, his house was a pleasant goal for a man who was in need of a brisk walk. Twice a week, then, the medical student would swing out there along the dark country roads and spend a pleasant hour in Peterson's comfortable study, discussing, over a glass of old port, the gossip of the 'varsity or the latest developments of medicine or of surgery.

On the day which followed his interview with Monkhouse Lee, Smith shut up his books at a quarter past eight, the hour when he usually started for his friend's house. As he was leaving his room, however, his eyes chanced to fall upon one of the books which Bellingham had lent him, and his conscience pricked him for not having returned it. However repellent the man might be, he should not be treated with discourtesy. Taking the book, he walked downstairs and knocked at his neighbour's door. There was no answer; but on turning the handle he found that it was unlocked. Pleased at the thought of avoiding an interview, he stepped inside, and placed the book with his card upon the table.

The lamp was turned half down, but Smith could see the details of the room plainly enough. It was all much as he had seen it before—the frieze, the animal-headed gods, the hanging crocodile, and the table littered over with papers and dried leaves. The mummy case stood upright against the wall, but the mummy itself was missing. There was no sign of any second occupant of the room, and he felt as he withdrew that he had probably done Bellingham an injustice. Had he a guilty secret to preserve, he would hardly leave his door open so that all the world might enter.

The spiral stair was as black as pitch, and Smith was slowly making his way down its irregular steps, when he was suddenly conscious that something had passed him in the darkness. There was a faint sound, a whiff of air, a light brushing past his elbow, but so slight that he could scarcely be certain of it. He stopped and listened, but the wind was rustling among the ivy outside, and he could hear nothing else.

"Is that you, Styles?" he shouted.

There was no answer, and all was still behind him. It must have been a sudden gust of air, for there were crannies and cracks in the old turret. And yet he could almost have sworn that he heard a footfall by his very side. He had emerged into the quadrangle, still turning the matter over in his head, when a man came running swiftly across the smooth-cropped lawn.

"Is that you, Smith?"

"Hullo, Hastie!"

"For God's sake come at once! Young Lee is drowned! Here's Harrington of King's with the news. The doctor is out. You'll do, but come along at once. There may be life in him."

"Have you brandy?"

"No."

"I'll bring some. There's a flask on my table."

Smith bounded up the stairs, taking three at a time, seized the flask, and was rushing down with it, when, as he passed Bellingham's room, his eyes fell upon something which left him gasping and staring upon the landing.

The door, which he had closed behind him, was now open, and right in front of him, with the lamp-light shining upon it, was the mummy case. Three minutes ago it had been empty. He could swear to that. Now it framed the lank body of its horrible occupant, who stood, grim and stark, with his black, shrivelled face towards the door. The form was lifeless and inert, but it seemed to Smith as he gazed that there still lingered a lurid spark of vitality, some faint sign of consciousness in the little eyes which lurked in the depths of the hollow sockets. So astounded and shaken was he that he had forgotten his errand, and was still staring at the lean, sunken figure when the voice of his friend below recalled him to himself.

"Come on, Smith!" he shouted. "It's life and death, you know. Hurry up! Now, then," he added, as the medical student reappeared, "let us do a sprint. It is well under a mile, and we should do it in five minutes. A human life is better worth running for than a pot."

Neck and neck they dashed through the darkness, and did not pull up until panting and spent, they had reached the little cottage by the river. Young Lee, limp and dripping like a broken water-plant, was stretched upon the sofa, the green scum of the river upon his black hair, and a fringe of white foam upon his leaden-hued lips. Beside him knelt his fellow-student, Harrington, endeavouring to chafe some warmth back into his rigid limbs.

"I think there's life in him," said Smith, with his hand to the lad's side. "Put your watch glass to his lips. Yes, there's dimming on it. You take one arm, Hastie. Now work it as I do, and we'll soon pull him round."

For ten minutes they worked in silence, inflating and depressing the chest of the unconscious man. At the end of that time a shiver ran through his body, his lips trembled, and he opened his eyes. The three students burst out into an irrepressible cheer.

"Wake up, old chap. You've frightened us quite enough."

"Have some brandy. Take a sip from the flask."

"He's all right now," said his companion Harrington. "Heavens, what a fright I got! I was reading here, and he had gone out for a stroll as far as the river, when heard a scream and a splash. Out I ran, and by the time I could find him and fish him out, all life seemed to have gone. Then Simpson couldn't get a doctor, for he has a game-leg, and I had to run, and I don't know what I'd have done without you fellows. That's right, old chap. Sit up."

Monkhouse Lee had raised himself on his hands, and looked wildly about him.

"What's up?" he asked. "I've been in the water. Ah, yes; I remember."

A look of fear came into his eyes, and he sank his face into his hands.

"How did you fall in?"

"I didn't fall in."

"How then?"

"I was thrown in. I was standing by the bank, and something from behind picked me up like a feather and hurled me in. I heard nothing, and I saw nothing. But I know what it was, for all that."

"And so do I," whispered Smith.

Lee looked up with a quick glance of surprise.

"You've learned, then?" he said. "You remember the advice I gave you?"

"Yes, and I begin to think that I shall take it."

"I don't know what the deuce you fellows are talking about," said Hastie, "but I think, if I were you, Harrington, I should get Lee to bed at once. It will be time enough to discuss the why and the wherefore when he is a little stronger. I think, Smith, you and I can leave him alone now. I am walking back to college; if you are coming in that direction, we can have a chat."

But it was little chat that they had upon their homeward path. Smith's mind was too full of the incidents of the evening, the absence of the mummy from his neighbour's rooms, the step that passed him on the stair, the reappearance—the extraordinary, inexplicable reappearance of the grisly thing—and then this attack upon Lee, corresponding so closely to the previous outrage upon another man against whom Bellingham bore a grudge. All this settled in his thoughts, together with the many little incidents which had previously turned him against his neighbour, and the singular circumstances under which he was first called in to him. What had been a dim suspicion, a vague, fantastic conjecture, had suddenly taken form, and stood out in his mind as a grim fact, a thing not to be denied. And yet, how monstrous it was! how unheard of! how entirely beyond all bounds of human experience. An impartial judge, or even the friend who walked by his side, would simply tell him that his eyes had deceived him, that the mummy had been there all the time, that young Lee had tumbled into the river as any other man tumbles into a river, and the blue pill was the best thing for a disordered liver. He felt that he would have said as much if the positions had been reversed. And yet he could swear that Bellingham was a murderer at heart, and that he wielded a weapon such as no man had ever used in all the grim history of crime.

Hastie had branched off to his rooms with a few crisp and emphatic comments upon his friend's unsociability, and Abercrombie Smith crossed the quadrangle to his corner turret with a strong feeling of repulsion for his chambers and their associations. He would take Lee's advice, and move his quarters as soon as possible, for how could a man study when his ear was ever straining for every murmur or footstep in the room below? He observed, as he crossed over the lawn, that the light was still shining in Bellingham's window, and as he passed up the staircase the door opened, and the man himself looked out at him. With his fat, evil face he was like some bloated spider fresh from the weaving of his poisonous web.

"Good evening," said he. "Won't you come in?"

"No," cried Smith fiercely.

"No? You are as busy as ever? I wanted to ask you about Lee. I was sorry to hear that there was a rumour that something was amiss with him."

His features were grave, but there was the gleam of a hidden laugh in his eyes as he spoke. Smith saw it, and he could have knocked him down for it.

"You'll be sorrier still to hear that Monkhouse Lee is doing very well, and is out of all danger," he answered. "Your hellish tricks have not come off this time. Oh, you needn't try to brazen it out. I know all about it."

Bellingham took a step back from the angry student, and half-closed the door as if to protect himself.

"You are mad," he said. "What do you mean? Do you assert that I had anything to do with Lee's accident?"

"Yes," thundered Smith. "You and that bag of bones behind you; you worked it between you. I tell you what it is, Master B., they have given up burning folk like you, but we still keep a hangman, and, by George! if any man in this college meets his death while you are here, I'll have you up, and if you don't swing for it, it won't be my fault. You'll find that your filthy Egyptian tricks won't answer in England."

"You're a raving lunatic," said Bellingham.

"All right. You just remember what I say, for you'll find that I'll be better than my word."

The door slammed, and Smith went fuming up to his chamber, where he locked the door upon the inside, and spent half the night in smoking his old briar and brooding over the strange events of the evening.

Next morning Abercrombie Smith heard nothing of his neighbour, but Harrington called upon him in the afternoon to say that Lee was almost himself again. All day Smith stuck fast to his work, but in the evening he determined to pay the visit to his friend Doctor Peterson upon which he had started the night before. A good walk and a friendly chat would be welcome to his jangled nerves.

Bellingham's door was shut as he passed, but glancing back when he was some distance from the turret, he saw his neighbour's head at the window outlined against the lamp-light, his face pressed apparently against the glass as he gazed out into the darkness. It was a blessing to be away from all contact with him, if but for a few hours, and Smith stepped out briskly, and breathed the soft spring air into his lungs. The half-moon lay in the west between two Gothic pinnacles, and threw upon the silvered street a dark tracery from the stone-work above. There was a brisk breeze, and light, fleecy clouds drifted swiftly across the sky. Old's was on the very border of the town, and in five minutes Smith found himself beyond the houses and between the hedges of a May-scented, Oxfordshire lane.

It was a lonely and little-frequented road which led to his friend's house. Early as it was, Smith did not meet a single soul upon his way. He walked briskly along until he came to the avenue gate, which opened into the long, gravel drive leading up to Farlingford. In front of him he could see the cosy, red light of the windows glimmering through the foliage. He stood with his hand upon the iron latch of the swinging gate, and he glanced back at the road along which he had come. Something was coming swiftly down it.

It moved in the shadow of the hedge, silently and furtively, a dark, crouching figure, dimly visible against the black background. Even as he gazed back at it, it had lessened its distance by twenty paces, and was fast closing upon him. Out of the darkness he had a glimpse of a scraggy neck, and of two eyes that will ever haunt him in his dreams. He turned, and with a cry of terror he ran for his life up the avenue. There were the red lights, the signals of safety, almost within a stone's-throw of him. He was a famous runner, but never had he run as he ran that night.

The heavy gate had swung into place behind him but he heard it dash open again before his pursuer. As he rushed madly and wildly through the night, he could hear a swift, dry patter behind him, and could see, as he threw back a glance, that this horror was bounding like a tiger at his heels, with blazing eyes and one stringy arm out-thrown. Thank God, the door was ajar. He could see the thin bar of light which shot from the lamp in the hall. Nearer yet sounded the clatter from behind. He heard a hoarse gurgling at his very shoulder. With a shriek he flung himself against the door, slammed and bolted it behind him, and sank half-fainting on to the hall chair.

" My goodness, Smith, what's the matter ? " asked Peterson, appearing at the door of his study.

" Give me some brandy."

Peterson disappeared, and came rushing out again with a glass and a decanter.

" You need it," he said, as his visitor drank off what he poured out for him. " Why, man, you are as white as a cheese."

Smith laid down his glass, rose up, and took a deep breath.

" I am my own man again now," said he. " I was never so unmanned before. But, with your leave, Peterson, I will sleep here to-night, for I don't think I could face that road again except by daylight. It's weak, I know, but I can't help it."

Peterson looked at his visitor with a very questioning eye.

" Of course you shall sleep here if you wish. I'll tell Mrs. Burney to make up the spare bed. Where are you off to now ? "

" Come up with me to the window that overlooks the door. I want you to see what I have seen."

They went up to the window of the upper hall whence they could look down upon the approach to the house. The drive and the fields on either side lay quiet and still, bathed in the peaceful moonlight.

" Well, really, Smith," remarked Peterson, " it is well that I know you to be an abstemious man. What in the world can have frightened you ? "

" I'll tell you presently. But where can it have gone ?

Ah, now, look, look! See the curve of the road just beyond your gate."

"Yes, I see; you needn't pinch my arm off. I saw someone pass. I should say a man, rather thin, apparently, and tall, very tall. But what of him? And what of yourself? You are still shaking like an aspen leaf."

"I have been within hand-grip of the devil, that's all. But come down to your study, and I shall tell you the whole story."

He did so. Under the cheery lamp-light with a glass of wine on the table beside him, and the portly form and florid face of his friend in front, he narrated, in their order, all the events, great and small, which had formed so singular a chain, from the night on which he had found Bellingham fainting in front of the mummy case until this horrid experience of an hour ago.

"There now," he said as he concluded, "that's the whole, black business. It is monstrous and incredible, but it is true."

Doctor Plumptree Peterson sat for some time in silence with a very puzzled expression upon his face.

"I never heard of such a thing in my life, never!" he said at last. "You have told me the facts. Now tell me your inferences."

"You can draw your own."

"But I should like to hear yours. You have thought over the matter, and I have not."

"Well, it must be a little vague in detail, but the main points seem to me to be clear enough. This fellow Bellingham, in his Eastern studies, has got hold of some infernal secret by which a mummy—or possibly only this particular mummy—can be temporarily brought to life. He was trying this disgusting business on the night when he fainted. No doubt the sight of the creature moving had shaken his nerve, even though he had expected it. You remember that almost the first words he said were to call out upon himself as a fool. Well, he got more hardened afterwards, and carried the matter through without fainting. The vitality which he could put into it was evidently only a passing thing, for I have seen it continually in its case as dead as this table. He has some elaborate process, I fancy, by which he brings the thing to pass. Having done it, he naturally bethought him that he might use the creature as an agent. It has intelligence and it has strength. For some purpose he took Lee into his confidence; but Lee, like a decent Christian, would have nothing to do with such a business. Then they had a row, and Lee vowed that he would tell his sister of Bellingham's true character. Bellingham's game was to prevent him, and he nearly managed it, by setting this creature of his on his track. He had already tried its powers upon another man—Norton—towards whom he had a grudge. It is the merest chance that he has not two murders upon his soul. Then, when I taxed him with the matter, he had the strongest reasons for wishing to get me out of the way before I could convey my knowledge to anyone else. He got his chance when I went out, for he knew my habits and where I was bound for. I have had a narrow shave, Peterson, and it is mere luck you didn't find me on your doorstep in the morning. I'm not a nervous man as a rule, and I never thought to have the fear of death put upon me as it was to-night."

"My dear boy, you take the matter too seriously," said his companion. "Your nerves are out of order with your work, and you make too much of it. How could such a thing as this stride about the streets of Oxford, even at night, without being seen?"

"It has been seen. There is quite a scare in the town about an escaped ape, as they imagine the creature to be. It is the talk of the place."

"Well, it's a striking chain of events. And yet, my dear fellow, you must allow that each incident in itself is capable of a more natural explanation."

"What! even my adventure of to-night?"

"Certainly. You come out with your nerves all

unstrung, and your head full of this theory of yours. Some gaunt, half-famished tramp steals after you, and seeing you run, is emboldened to pursue you. Your fears and imagination do the rest."

"It won't do, Peterson; it won't do."

"And again, in the instance of your finding the mummy case empty, and then a few moments later with an occupant, you know that it was lamp-light, that the lamp was half turned down, and that you had no special reason to look hard at the case. It is quite possible that you may have overlooked the creature in the first instance."

"No, no; it is out of the question."

"And then Lee may have fallen into the river, and Norton been garrotted. It is certainly a formidable indictment that you have against Bellingham; but if you were to place it before a police magistrate, he would simply laugh in your face."

"I know he would. That is why I mean to take the matter into my own hands."

"Eh?"

"Yes; I feel that a public duty rests upon me, and, besides, I must do it for my own safety, unless I choose to allow myself to be hunted by this beast out of the college, and that would be a little too feeble. I have quite made up my mind what I shall do. And first of all, may I use your paper and pens for an hour?"

"Most certainly. You will find all that you want upon that side-table."

Abercrombie Smith sat down before a sheet of foolscap, and for an hour, and then for a second hour his pen travelled swiftly over it. Page after page was finished and tossed aside while his friend leaned back in his arm-chair, looking across at him with patient curiosity. At last, with an exclamation of satisfaction, Smith sprang to his feet, gathered his papers up into order, and laid the last one upon Peterson's desk.

"Kindly sign this as a witness," he said.

"A witness? Of what?"

" Of my signature, and of the date. The date is the most important. Why, Peterson, my life might hang upon it."

" My dear Smith, you are talking wildly. Let me beg you to go to bed."

" On the contrary, I never spoke so deliberately in my life. And I will promise to go to bed the moment you have signed it."

" But what is it ? "

" It is a statement of all that I have been telling you to-night. I wish you to witness it."

" Certainly," said Peterson, signing his name under that of his companion. " There you are ! But what is the idea ? "

" You will kindly retain it, and produce it in case I am arrested."

" Arrested ? For what ? "

" For murder. It is quite on the cards. I wish to be ready for every event. There is only one course open to me, and I am determined to take it."

" For Heaven's sake, don't do anything rash ! "

" Believe me, it would be far more rash to adopt any other course. I hope that we won't need to bother you, but it will ease my mind to know that you have this statement of my motives. And now I am ready to take your advice and to go to roost, for I want to be at my best in the morning."

Abercrombie Smith was not an entirely pleasant man to have as an enemy. Slow and easy-tempered, he was formidable when driven to action. He brought to every purpose in life the same deliberate resoluteness which had distinguished him as a scientific student. He had laid his studies aside for a day, but he intended that the day should not be wasted. Not a word did he say to his host as to his plans, but by nine o'clock he was well on his way to Oxford.

In the High Street he stopped at Clifford's, the gunmaker's, and bought a heavy revolver, with a box of central-fire cartridges. Six of them he slipped into the chambers, and half-cocking the weapon, placed it in the pocket of his coat. He then made his way to Hastie's rooms, where the big oarsman was lounging over his breakfast, with the *Sporting Times* propped up against the coffee-pot.

"Hullo! What's up?" he asked. "Have some coffee?"

"No, thank you. I want you to come with me, Hastie, and do what I ask you."

"Certainly, my boy."

"And bring a heavy stick with you."

"Hullo!" Hastie stared. "Here's a hunting crop that would fell an ox."

"One other thing. You have a box of amputating knives. Give me the longest of them."

"There you are. You seem to be fairly on the war trail. Anything else?"

"No; that will do." Smith placed the knife inside his coat, and led the way to the quadrangle. "We are neither of us chickens, Hastie," said he. "I think I can do this job alone, but I take you as a precaution. I am going to have a little talk with Bellingham. If I have only him to deal with, I won't, of course, need you. If I shout, however, up you come, and lam out with your whip as hard as you can lick. Do you understand?"

"All right. I'll come if I hear you bellow."

"Stay here, then. I may be a little time, but don't budge until I come down."

"I'm a fixture."

Smith ascended the stairs, opened Bellingham's door and stepped in. Bellingham was seated behind his table, writing. Beside him, among his litter of strange possessions, towered the mummy case, with its sale number 249 still stuck upon its front, and its hideous occupant stiff and stark within it. Smith looked very deliberately round him, closed the door, and then, stepping across to the fireplace, struck a match and set the fire alight. Bellingham sat staring, with amazement and rage upon his bloated face.

"Well, really now, you make yourself at home," he gasped.

Smith sat himself deliberately down, placing his watch upon the table, drew out his pistol, cocked it, and laid it in his lap. Then he took the long amputating knife from his bosom, and threw it down in front of Bellingham.

"Now, then," said he, "just get to work and cut up that mummy."

"Oh, is that it?" said Bellingham with a sneer.

"Yes, that is it. They tell me that the law can't touch you. But I have a law that will set matters straight. If in five minutes you have not set to work, I swear by the God who made me that I will put a bullet through your brain!"

"You would murder me?"

Bellingham had half-risen, and his face was the colour of putty.

"Yes."

"And for what?"

"To stop your mischief. One minute has gone."

"But what have I done?"

"I know and you know."

"This is mere bullying."

"Two minutes are gone."

"But you must give reasons. You are a madman—a dangerous madman. Why should I destroy my own property? It is a valuable mummy."

"You must cut it up, and you must burn it."

"I will do no such thing."

"Four minutes are gone."

Smith took up the pistol and he looked towards Bellingham with an inexorable face. As the second-hand stole round, he raised his hand, and the finger twitched upon the trigger.

"There! there! I'll do it!" screamed Bellingham.

In frantic haste he caught up the knife and hacked at the figure of the mummy, ever glancing round to see the eye and the weapon of his terrible visitor bent upon him. The creature crackled and snapped under every stab of the keen blade. A thick, yellow dust rose up from it. Spices and dried essences rained down upon the floor. Suddenly, with a rending crack, its backbone snapped asunder, and it fell, a brown heap of sprawling limbs, upon the floor.

"Now into the fire!" said Smith.

The flames leaped and roared as the dried and tinder-like debris was piled upon it. The little room was like the stoke-hole of a steamer and the sweat ran down the faces of the two men; but still the one stooped and worked, while the other sat watching him with a set face. A thick, fat smoke oozed out from the fire, and a heavy smell of burned resin and singed hair filled the air. In a quarter of an hour a few charred and brittle sticks were all that was left of Lot No. 249.

"Perhaps that will satisfy you," snarled Bellingham, with hate and fear in his little grey eyes as he glanced back at his tormentor.

"No; I must make a clean sweep of all your materials. We must have no more devil's tricks. In with all these leaves! They may have something to do with it."

"And what now?" asked Bellingham, when the leaves also had been added to the blaze.

"Now the roll of papyrus which you had on the table that night. It is in that drawer, I think."

"No, no," shouted Bellingham. "Don't burn that Why, man, you don't know what you do. It is unique it contains wisdom which is nowhere else to be found.'

"Out with it!"

"But look here, Smith, you can't really mean it. I'l share the knowledge with you. I'll teach you al that is in it. Or, stay, let me only copy it before yoı burn it!"

stepped forward and turned the key in the .. Taking out the yellow, curled roll of paper, he ew it into the fire, and pressed it down with his heel. Bellingham screamed, and grabbed at it; but Smith pushed him back and stood over it until it was reduced to a formless, grey ash.

"Now, Master B.," said he, "I think I have pretty well drawn your teeth. You'll hear from me again, if you return to your old tricks. And now good morning, for I must go back to my studies."

And such is the narrative of Abercrombie Smith as to the singular events which occurred in Old College, Oxford, in the spring of '84. As Bellingham left the university immediately afterwards, and was last heard of in the Soudan, there is no one who can contradict his statement. But the wisdom of men is small, and the ways of Nature are strange, and who shall put a bound to the dark things which may be found by those who seek for them?

J. HABAKUK JEPHSON'S STATEMENT

IN the month of December in the year 1873, the British ship *Dei Gratia* steered into Gibraltar, having in tow the derelict brigantine *Marie Celeste*, which had been picked up in latitude 38° 40′, longitude 17° 15′ W. There were several circumstances in connection with the condition and appearance of this abandoned vessel which excited considerable comment at the time, and aroused a curiosity which has never been satisfied. What these circumstances were was summed up in an able article which appeared in the *Gibraltar Gazette*. The curious can find it in the issue for January 4, 1874, unless my memory deceives me. For the benefit of those, however, who may be unable to refer to the paper in question, I shall subjoin a few extracts which touch upon the leading features of the case.

"We have ourselves," says the anonymous writer in the *Gazette*, "been over the derelict *Marie Celeste*, and have closely questioned the officers of the *Dei Gratia* on every point which might throw light on the affair. They are of opinion that she had been abandoned several days, or perhaps weeks, before being picked up. The official log, which was found in the cabin, states that the vessel sailed from Boston to Lisbon, starting upon October 16. It is, however, most imperfectly kept, and affords little information. There is no reference to rough weather, and, indeed, the state of the vessel's paint and rigging excludes the idea that she was abandoned for any such reason. She is perfectly watertight. No signs of a struggle or of violence are to be detected, and there is absolutely nothing to account for the disappearance of the crew. There are several indications that a lady was present on board, a sewing-machine being found in the cabin and some articles of female attire. These probably belonged to the captain's wife, who is mentioned in the log as having accompanied her husband. As an instance of the mildness of the weather, it may be remarked that a bobbin of silk was found standing upon the sewing-machine, though the least roll of the vessel would have precipitated it to the floor. The boats were intact and slung upon the davits; and the cargo, consisting of tallow and American clocks, was untouched. An old-fashioned sword of curious workmanship was discovered among some lumber in the forecastle, and this weapon is said to exhibit a longitudinal striation on the steel, as if it had been recently wiped. It has been placed in the hands of the police, and submitted to Dr. Monaghan, the analyst, for inspection. The result of his examination has not yet been published. We may remark, in conclusion, that Captain Dalton, of the *Dei Gratia*, an able and intelligent seaman, is of opinion that the *Marie Celeste* may have been abandoned a considerable distance from the spot at which she was picked up, since a powerful current runs up in that latitude from the African coast. He confesses his inability, however, to advance any hypothesis which can reconcile all the facts of the case. In the utter absence of a clue or grain of evidence, it is to be feared that the fate of the crew of the *Marie Celeste* will be added to those numerous mysteries of the deep which will never be solved until the great day when the sea shall give up its dead. If crime has been committed, as is much to be suspected, there is little hope of bringing the perpetrators to justice."

I shall supplement this extract from the *Gibraltar Gazette* by quoting a telegram from Boston, which went the round of the English papers, and represented the total amount of information which had been collected about the *Marie Celeste*. " She was," it said, " a brigantine of 170 tons burden, and belonged to White, Russell & White, wine importers, of this city. Captain J. W. Tibbs was an old servant of the firm, and was a man of known ability and tried probity. He was accompanied by his wife, aged thirty-one, and their youngest child, five years old. The crew consisted of seven hands, including two coloured seamen, and a boy. There were three passengers, one of whom was the well-known Brooklyn specialist on consumption, Dr. Habakuk Jephson, who was a distinguished advocate for Abolition in the early days of the movement, and whose pamphlet, entitled 'Where is thy Brother?' exercised a strong influence on public opinion before the war. The other passengers were Mr. J. Harton, a writer in the employ of the firm, and Mr. Septimius Goring, a half-caste gentleman, from New Orleans. All investigations have failed to throw any light upon the fate of these fourteen human beings. The loss of Dr. Jephson will be felt both in political and scientific circles."

I have here epitomised, for the benefit of the public, all that has been hitherto known concerning the *Marie Celeste* and her crew, for the past ten years have not in any way helped to elucidate the mystery. I have now taken up my pen with the intention of telling all that I know of the ill-fated voyage. I consider that it is a duty which I owe to society, for symptoms which I am familiar with in others lead me to believe that before many months my tongue and hand may be alike incapable of conveying information. Let me remark, as a preface to my narrative, that I am Joseph Habakuk Jephson, Doctor of Medicine of the University of Harvard, and ex-Consulting Physician of the Samaritan Hospital of Brooklyn.

Many will doubtless wonder why I have not proclaimed myself before, and why I have suffered so many conjectures and surmises to pass unchallenged. Could the ends of justice have been served in any way by my revealing the facts in my possession I should unhesitatingly have done so. It seemed to me, however, that there was no possibility of such a result; and when I attempted after the occurrence, to state my case to an English official, I was met with such offensive incredulity that I determined never again to expose myself to the chance of such an indignity. I can excuse the discourtesy of the Liverpool magistrate, however, when I reflect upon the treatment which I received at the hands of my own relatives, who, though they knew my unimpeachable character, listened to my statement with an indulgent smile as if humouring the delusion of a monomaniac. This slur upon my veracity led to a quarrel between myself and John Vanburger, the brother of my wife, and confirmed me in my resolution to let the matter sink into oblivion—a determination which I have only altered through my son's solicitations. In order to make my narrative intelligible, I must run lightly over one or two incidents in my former life which throw light upon subsequent events.

My father, William K. Jephson, was a preacher of the sect called Plymouth Brethren, and was one of the most respected citizens of Lowell. Like most of the other Puritans of New England, he was a determined opponent of slavery, and it was from his lips that I received those lessons which tinged every action of my life. While

I was studying medicine at Harvard University, I had already made a mark as an advanced Abolitionist; and when, after taking my degree, I bought a third share of the practice of Dr. Willis, of Brooklyn, I managed, in spite of my professional duties, to devote a considerable time to the cause which I had at heart, my pamphlet, "Where is thy Brother?" (Swarburgh, Lister & Co., 1859) attracting considerable attention.

When the war broke out I left Brooklyn and accompanied the 113th New York Regiment through the campaign. I was present at the second battle of Bull's Run and at the battle of Gettysburg. Finally, I was severely wounded at Antietam, and would probably have perished on the field had it not been for the kindness of a gentleman named Murray, who had me carried to his house and provided me with every comfort. Thanks to his charity, and to the nursing which I received from his black domestics, I was soon able to get about the plantation with the help of a stick. It was during this period of convalescence that an incident occurred which is closely connected with my story.

Among the most assiduous of the negresses who had watched my couch during my illness there was one old crone who appeared to exert considerable authority over the others. She was exceedingly attentive to me, and I gathered from the few words that passed between us that she had heard of me, and that she was grateful to me for championing her oppressed race.

One day as I was sitting alone in the verandah, basking in the sun, and debating whether I should rejoin Grant's army, I was surprised to see this old creature hobbling towards me. After looking cautiously around to see that we were alone, she fumbled in the front of her dress, and produced a small chamois leather bag which was hung round her neck by a white cord.

"Massa," she said, bending down and croaking the words into my ear, "me die soon. Me very old woman. Not stay long on Massa Murray's plantation."

"You may live a long time yet, Martha," I answered. "You know I am a doctor. If you feel ill let me know about it, and I will try to cure you."

"No wish to live—wish to die. I'm gwine to join the heavenly host." Here she relapsed into one of those half-heathenish rhapsodies in which negroes indulge. "But, massa, me have one thing must leave behind me when I go. No able to take it with me across the Jordan. That one thing very precious, more precious and more holy than all thing else in the world. Me, a poor old black woman, have this because my people, very great people, 'spose they was back in the old country. But you cannot understand this same as black folk could. My fader give it me, and his fader give it him, but now who shall I give it to? Poor Martha hab no child, no relation, nobody. All round I see black man very bad man. Black woman very stupid woman. Nobody worthy of the stone. And so I say, Here is Massa Jephson who write books and fight for coloured folk—he must be a good man, and he shall have it though he is white man, and nebber can know what it mean or where it came from." Here the old woman fumbled in the chamois leather bag and pulled out a flattish black stone with a hole through the middle of it. "Here, take it," she said, pressing it into my hand; "take it. No harm nebber come from anything good. Keep it safe—nebber lose it!" and with a warning gesture the old crone hobbled away in the same cautious way as she had come, looking from side to side to see if we had been observed.

I was more amused than impressed by the old woman's earnestness, and was only prevented from laughing during her oration by the fear of hurting her feelings. When she was gone I took a good look at the stone which she had given me. It was intensely black, of extreme hardness, and oval in shape—just such a flat stone as one would pick up on the seashore if one wished to throw a long way. It was about three inches long, and an inch and a half broad at the middle, but rounded off at the extremities. The most curious part about it was several well-marked ridges which ran in semicircles over its surface, and gave it exactly the appearance of a human ear. Altogether I was rather interested in my new possession and determined to submit it, as a geological specimen to my friend Professor Shroeder of the New York Institute upon the earliest opportunity. In the meantime I thrust it into my pocket, and rising from my chair started off for a short stroll in the shrubbery, dismissing the incident from my mind.

As my wound had nearly healed by this time, I took my leave of Mr. Murray shortly afterwards. The Union armies were everywhere victorious and converging on Richmond, so that my assistance seemed unnecessary, and I returned to Brooklyn. There I resumed my practice, and married the second daughter of Josiah Vanburger, the well-known wood engraver. In the course of a few years I built up a good connection and acquired considerable reputation in the treatment of pulmonary complaints. I still kept the old black stone in my pocket, and frequently told the story of the dramatic way in which I had become possessed of it. I also kept my resolution of showing it to Professor Shroeder, who was much interested both by the anecdote and the specimen. He pronounced it to be a piece of meteoric stone, and drew my attention to the fact that its resemblance to an ear was not accidental, but that it was most carefully worked into that shape. A dozen little anatomical points showed that the worker had been as accurate as he was skilful. "I should not wonder," said the Professor, "if it were broken off from some larger statue, though how such hard material could be so perfectly worked is more than I can understand. If there is a statue to correspond I should like to see it!" So I thought at the time, but I have changed my opinion since.

The next seven or eight years of my life were quiet and uneventful. Summer followed spring, and spring followed winter, without any variation in my duties. As the practice increased I admitted J. S. Jackson as partner, he to have one-fourth of the profits. The continued strain had told upon my constitution, however, and I became at last so unwell that my wife insisted upon my consulting Dr. Kavanagh Smith, who was my colleague at the Samaritan Hospital. That gentleman examined me, and pronounced the apex of my left lung to be in a state of consolidation, recommending me at the same time to go through a course of medical treatment and to take a long sea-voyage.

My own disposition, which is naturally restless, predisposed me strongly in favour of the latter piece of advice, and the matter was clinched by my meeting young Russell, of the firm of White, Russell & White, who offered me a passage in one of his father's ships, the *Marie Celeste*, which was just starting from Boston. "She is a snug little ship," he said, "and Tibbs, the captain, is an excellent fellow. There is nothing like a sailing ship for an invalid." I was very much of the same opinion myself, so I closed with the offer on the spot.

My original plan was that my wife should accompany me on my travels. She has always been a very poor sailor, however, and there were strong family reasons against her exposing herself to any risk at the time, so we determined that she should remain at home. I am not a religious or an effusive man; but oh, thank God for that! As to leaving my practice, I was easily reconciled to it, as Jackson, my partner, was a reliable and hardworking man.

I arrived in Boston on October 12, 1873, and proceeded immediately to the office of the firm in order to thank them for their courtesy. As I was sitting in the counting-house waiting until they should be at liberty to see me, the words *Marie Celeste* suddenly attracted my attention. I looked round and saw a very tall, gaunt man, who was leaning across the polished mahogany counter asking some questions of the clerk at the other side. His face was turned half towards me, and I could see that he had a strong dash of negro blood in him, being probably a quadroon or even nearer akin to the black. His curved aquiline nose and straight lank hair showed the white strain ; but the dark, restless eye, sensuous mouth, and gleaming teeth all told of his African origin. His complexion was of a sickly, unhealthy yellow, and as his face was deeply pitted with small-pox, the general impression was so unfavourable as to be almost revolting. When he spoke, however, it was in a soft, melodious voice, and in well-chosen words, and he was evidently a man of some education.

"I wished to ask a few questions about the *Marie Celeste*," he repeated, leaning across to the clerk. "She sails the day after to-morrow, does she not ?"

"Yes, sir," said the young clerk, awed into unusual politeness by the glimmer of a large diamond in the stranger's shirt front.

"Where is she bound for ?"

"Lisbon."

"How many of a crew ?"

"Seven, sir."

"Passengers ?"

"Yes, two. One of our young gentlemen, and a doctor from New York."

"No gentleman from the South ?" asked the stranger eagerly.

"No, none, sir."

"Is there room for another passenger ?"

"Accommodation, for three more," answered the clerk.

"I'll go," said the quadroon decisively ; "I'll go, I'll engage my passage at once. Put it down, will you—Mr. Septimius Goring, of New Orleans."

The clerk filled up a form and handed it over to the stranger, pointing to a blank space at the bottom. As Mr. Goring stooped over to sign it I was horrified to observe that the fingers of his right hand had been lopped off, and that he was holding the pen between his thumb and the palm. I have seen thousands slain in battle, and assisted at every conceivable surgical operation, but I cannot recall any sight which gave me such a thrill of disgust as that great brown sponge-like hand with the single member protruding from it. He used it skilfully enough, however, for, dashing off his signature, he nodded to the clerk and strolled out of the office just as Mr. White sent out word that he was ready to receive me.

I went down to the *Marie Celeste* that evening, and looked over my berth, which was extremely comfortable considering the small size of the vessel. Mr. Goring, whom I had seen in the morning, was to have the one next mine. Opposite was the captain's cabin and a small berth for Mr. John Harton, a gentleman who was going out in the interests of the firm. These little rooms were arranged on each side of the passage which led from the main-deck to the saloon. The latter was a comfortable room, the panelling tastefully done in oak and mahogany, with a rich Brussels carpet and luxurious settees. I was very much pleased with the accommodation, and also with Tibbs the captain, a bluff, sailor-like fellow, with a loud voice and hearty manner, who welcomed me to the ship with effusion, and insisted upon our splitting a bottle of wine in his cabin. He told me that he intended to take his wife and youngest child with him on the voyage, and that he hoped with good luck to make Lisbon in three weeks. We had a pleasant chat and parted the best of friends, he warning me to make the last of my preparations next morning, as he intended to make a start by the mid-day tide, having now shipped all his cargo. I went back to my hotel, where I found a letter from my wife awaiting me, and, after a refreshing night's sleep, returned to the boat in the morning. From this point I am able to quote from the journal which I kept in order to vary the monotony of the long sea-voyage. If it is somewhat bald in places

I can at least rely upon its accuracy in details, as it was written conscientiously from day to day.

October 16th.—Cast off our warps at half-past two and were towed out into the bay, where the tug left us, and with all sail set we bowled along at about nine knots an hour. I stood upon the poop watching the low land of America sinking gradually upon the horizon until the evening haze hid it from my sight. A single red light, howevcr, continued to blaze balefully behind us, throwing a long track like a trail of blood upon the water, and it is still visible as I write, though reduced to a mere speck. The captain is in a bad humour, for two of his hands disappointed him at the last moment, and he was compelled to ship a couple of negroes who happened to be on the quay. The missing men were steady, reliable fellows, who had been with him several voyages, and their non-appearance puzzled as well as irritated him. Where a crew of seven men have to work a fair-sized ship the loss of two experienced seamen is a serious one, for though the negroes may take a spell at the wheel or swab the decks, they are of little or no use in rough weather. Our cook is also a black man, and Mr. Septimius Goring has a little darkie servant, so that we are rather a piebald community. The accountant, John Harton, promises to be an acquisition, for he is a cheery, amusing young fellow. Strange how little wealth has to do with happiness! He has all the world before him and is seeking his fortune in a far land, yet he is as transparently happy as a man can be. Goring is rich, if I am not mistaken, and so am I; but I know that I have a lung, and Goring has some deeper trouble still, to judge by his features. How poorly do we both contrast with the careless, penniless clerk!

October 17th.—Mrs. Tibbs appeared upon the deck for the first time this morning—a cheerful, energetic woman, with a dear little child just able to walk and prattle. Young Harton pounced on it at once, and carried it away to his cabin, where no doubt he will lay the seeds of future dyspepsia in the child's stomach. Thus medicine doth make cynics of us all ! The weather is still all that could be desired, with a fine fresh breeze from the west-sou'-west. The vessel goes so steadily that you would hardly know that she was moving were it not for the creaking of the cordage, the bellying of the sails, and the long white furrow in our wake. Walked the quarter-deck all morning with the captain, and I think the keen fresh air has already done my breathing good, for the exercise did not fatigue me in any way. Tibbs is a remarkably intelligent man, and we had an interesting argument about Maury's observations on ocean currents, which we terminated by going down into his cabin to consult the original work. There we found Goring, rather to the captain's surprise, as it is not usual for passengers to enter that sanctum unless specially invited. He apologised for his intrusion, however, pleading his ignorance of the usages of ship life ; and the good-natured sailor simply laughed at the incident, begging him to remain and favour us with his company. Goring pointed to the chronometers, the case of which he had opened, and remarked that he had been admiring them. He has evidently some practical knowledge of mathematical instruments, as he told at a glance which was the most trustworthy of the three, and also named their price within a few dollars. He had a discussion with the captain too upon the variation of the compass, and when we came back to the ocean currents he showed a thorough grasp of the subject. Altogether he rather improves upon acquaintance, and is a man of decided culture and refinement. His voice harmonises with his conversation, and both are the very antithesis of his face and figure.

The noonday observation shows that we have run two hundred and twenty miles. Towards evening the breeze freshened up, and the first mate ordered reefs to be taken in the topsails and top-gallant sails in expectation of a windy night. I observe that the barometer has fallen to twenty-nine. I trust our voyage will not be a rough one, as I am a poor sailor, and my health would probably derive more harm than good from a stormy trip, though I have the greatest confidence in the captain's seamanship and in the soundness of the vessel. Played cribbage with Mrs. Tibbs after supper, and Harton gave us a couple of tunes on the violin.

October 18th.—The gloomy prognostications of last night were not fulfilled, as the wind died away again and we are lying now in a long greasy swell, ruffled here, and there by a fleeting catspaw which is insufficient to fill the sails. The air is colder than it was yesterday, and I have put on one of the thick woollen jerseys which my wife knitted for me. Harton came into my cabin in the morning, and we had a cigar together. He says that he remembers having seen Goring in Cleveland, Ohio, in '69. He was, it appears, a mystery then as now, wandering about without any visible employment, and extremely reticent on his own affairs. The man interests me as a psychological study. At breakfast this morning I suddenly had that vague feeling of uneasiness which comes over some people when closely stared at, and, looking quickly up, I met his eyes bent upon me with an intensity which amounted to ferocity, though their expression instantly softened as he made some conventional remark upon the weather. Curiously enough, Harton says that he had a very similar experience yesterday upon deck. I observe that Goring frequently talks to the coloured seamen as he strolls about—a trait which I rather admire, as it is common to find half-breeds ignore their dark strain and treat their black kinsfolk with greater intolerance than a white man would do. His little page is devoted to him, apparently, which speaks well for his treatment of him. Altogether, the man is a curious mixture of incongruous qualities, and unless I am deceived in him will give me food for observation during the voyage.

The captain is grumbling about his chronometers,

which do not register exactly the same time. He says it is the first time that they have ever disagreed. We were unable to get a noonday observation on account of the haze. By dead reckoning, we have done about a hundred and seventy miles in the twenty-four hours. The dark seamen have proved, as the skipper prophesied, to be very inferior hands, but as they can both manage the wheel well they are kept steering, and so leave the more experienced men to work the ship. These details are trivial enough, but a small thing serves as food for gossip aboard ship. The appearance of a whale in the evening caused quite a flutter among us. From its sharp back and forked tail, I should pronounce it to have been a rorqual, or "finner," as they are called by the fishermen.

October 19th.—Wind was cold, so I prudently remained in my cabin all day, only creeping out for dinner. Lying in my bunk I can, without moving, reach my books, pipes, or anything else I may want, which is one advantage of a small apartment. My old wound began to ache a little to-day, probably from the cold. Read *Montaigne's Essays* and nursed myself. Harton came in in the afternoon with Doddy, the captain's child, and the skipper himself followed, so that I held quite a reception.

October 20th and 21st.—Still cold, with a continual drizzle of rain, and I have not been able to leave the cabin. This confinement makes me feel weak and depressed. Goring came in to see me, but his company did not tend to cheer me up much, as he hardly uttered a word, but contented himself with staring at me in a peculiar and rather irritating manner. He then got up and stole out of the cabin without saying anything. I am beginning to suspect that the man is a lunatic. I think I mentioned that his cabin is next to mine. The two are simply divided by a thin wooden partition which is cracked in many places, some of the cracks being so large that I can hardly avoid, as I lie in my bunk, observing his motions in the adjoining room. Without any wish to play the spy, I see him continually stooping over what appears to be a chart and working with a pencil and compasses. I have remarked the interest he displays in matters connected with navigation, but I am surprised that he should take the trouble to work out the course of the ship. However, it is a harmless amusement enough, and no doubt he verifies his results by those of the captain.

I wish the man did not run in my thoughts so much. I had a nightmare on the night of the 20th, in which I thought my bunk was a coffin, that I was laid out in it, and that Goring was endeavouring to nail up the lid, which I was frantically pushing away. Even when I woke up, I could hardly persuade myself that I was not in a coffin. As a medical man, I know that a nightmare is simply a vascular derangement of the cerebral hemispheres, and yet in my weak state I cannot shake off the morbid impression which it produces.[1]

October 22nd.—A fine day, with hardly a cloud in the sky, and a fresh breeze from the sou'-west which wafts us gaily on our way. There has evidently been some heavy weather near us, as there is a tremendous swell on, and the ship lurches until the end of the fore-yard nearly touches the water. Had a refreshing walk up and down the quarter-deck, though I have hardly found my sea-legs yet. Several small birds—chaffinches, I think—perched in the rigging.

4.40 P.M.—While I was on deck this morning I heard a sudden explosion from the direction of my cabin, and, hurrying down, found that I had very nearly met with a serious accident. Goring was cleaning a revolver, it seems, in his cabin, when one of the barrels which he thought was unloaded went off. The ball passed through the side partition and imbedded itself in the bulwarks in the exact place where my head usually rests. I have been under fire too often to magnify trifles, but there is no doubt that if I had been in the bunk it must have killed me. Goring, poor fellow, did not know that I had gone on deck that day, and must therefore have felt terribly frightened. I never saw such emotion in a man's face as when, on rushing out of his cabin with the smoking pistol in his hand, he met me face to face as I came down from deck. Of course, he was profuse in his apologies, though I simply laughed at the incident.

11 P.M.—A misfortune has occurred so unexpected and so horrible that my little escape of the morning dwindles into insignificance. Mrs. Tibbs and her child have disappeared—utterly and entirely disappeared. I can hardly compose myself to write the sad details. About half-past eight Tibbs rushed into my cabin with a very white face and asked me if I had seen his wife. I answered that I had not. He then ran wildly into the saloon and began groping about for any trace of her, while I followed him, endeavouring vainly to persuade him that his fears were ridiculous. We hunted over the ship for an hour and a half without coming on any sign of the missing woman or child. Poor Tibbs lost his voice completely from calling her name. Even the sailors, who are generally stolid enough, were deeply affected by the sight of him as he roamed bareheaded and dishevelled about the deck, searching with feverish anxiety the most impossible places, and returning to them again and again with a piteous pertinacity. The last time she was seen was about seven o'clock, when she took Doddy on to the poop to give him a breath of fresh air before putting him to bed. There was no one there at the time except the black seaman at the wheel, who denies having seen her at all. The whole affair is wrapped in mystery. My own theory is that while Mrs. Tibbs was holding the child and standing near the bulwarks it gave a spring and fell overboard, and that in her convulsive attempt to catch or save it, she followed it. I cannot account for the double disappearance in any other way. It is quite feasible that such a tragedy should be enacted without the knowledge of the man at the wheel, since it was dark

at the time, and the peaked skylights of the saloon screen the greater part of the quarter-deck. Whatever the truth may be it is a terrible catastrophe, and has cast the darkest gloom upon our voyage. The mate has put the ship about, but of course there is not the slightest hope of picking them up. The captain is lying in a state of stupor in his cabin. I gave him a powerful dose of opium in his coffee that for a few hours at least his anguish may be deadened.

October 23rd.—Woke with a vague feeling of heaviness and misfortune, but it was not until a few moments' reflection that I was able to recall our loss of the night before. When I came on deck I saw the poor skipper standing gazing back at the waste of waters behind us which contains everything dear to him upon earth. I attempted to speak to him, but he turned brusquely away, and began pacing the deck with his head sunk upon his breast. Even now, when the truth is so clear, he cannot pass a boat or an unbent sail without peering under it. He looks ten years older than he did yesterday morning. Harton is terribly cut up, for he was fond of little Doddy, and Goring seems sorry too. At least he has shut himself up in his cabin all day, and when I got a casual glance at him his head was resting on his two hands as if in a melancholy reverie. I fear we are about as dismal a crew as ever sailed. How shocked my wife will be to hear of our disaster! The swell has gone down now, and we are doing about eight knots with all sail set and a nice little breeze. Hyson is practically in command of the ship, as Tibbs, though he does his best to bear up and keep a brave front, is incapable of applying himself to serious work.

October 24th.—Is the ship accursed? Was there ever a voyage which began so fairly and which changed so disastrously? Tibbs shot himself through the head during the night. I was awakened about three o'clock in the morning by an explosion, and immediately sprang out of bed and rushed into the captain's cabin to find out the cause, though with a terrible presentiment in my heart. Quickly as I went, Goring went more quickly still, for he was already in the cabin stooping over the dead body of the captain. It was a hideous sight, for the whole front of his face was blown in, and the little room was swimming in blood. The pistol was lying beside him on the floor, just as it had dropped from his hand. He had evidently put it to his mouth before pulling the trigger. Goring and I picked him reverently up and laid him on his bed. The crew had all clustered into his cabin, and the six white men were deeply grieved, for they were old hands who had sailed with him many years. There were dark looks and murmurs among them too, and one of them openly declared that the ship was haunted. Harton helped to lay the poor skipper out, and we did him up in canvas between us. At twelve o'clock the fore-yard was hauled aback, and we committed his body to the deep, Goring reading the Church of England burial service. The breeze has freshened up, and we have done ten knots all day and sometimes twelve. The sooner we reach Lisbon and get away from this accursed ship the better pleased shall I be. I feel as though we were in a floating coffin. Little wonder that the poor sailors are superstitious when I, an educated man, feel it so strongly.

October 25th.—Made a good run all day. Feel listless and depressed.

October 26th.—Goring, Harton, and I had a chat together on deck in the morning. Harton tried to draw Goring out as to his profession, and his object in going to Europe, but the quadroon parried all his questions and gave us no information. Indeed, he seemed to be slightly offended by Harton's pertinacity, and went down into his cabin. I wonder why we should both take such an interest in this man! I suppose it is his striking appearance, coupled with his apparent wealth, which piques our curiosity. Harton has a theory that he is really a detective, that he is after some criminal who has got away to Portugal, and that he chooses this peculiar way of travelling that he may arrive unnoticed and pounce upon his quarry unawares. I think the supposition is rather a far-fetched one, but Harton bases it upon a book which Goring left on deck, and which he picked up and glanced over. It was a sort of scrap-book, it seems, and contained a large number of newspaper cuttings. All these cuttings related to murders which had been committed at various times in the States during the last twenty years or so. The curious thing which Harton observed about them, however, was that they were invariably murders the authors of which had never been brought to justice. They varied in every detail, he says, as to the manner of execution and the social status of the victim, but they uniformly wound up with the same formula that the murderer was still at large, though, of course, the police had every reason to expect his speedy capture. Certainly the incident seems to support Harton's theory, though it may be a mere whim of Goring's, or, as I suggested to Harton, he may be collecting materials for a book which shall outvie De Quincy. In any case it is no business of ours.

October 27th, 28th.—Wind still fair, and we are making good progress. Strange how easily a human unit may drop out of its place and be forgotten! Tibbs is hardly ever mentioned now; Hyson has taken possession of his cabin, and all goes on as before. Were it not for Mrs. Tibbs's sewing-machine upon a side-table we might forget that the unfortunate family had ever existed. Another accident occurred on board to-day, though fortunately not a very serious one. One of our white hands had gone down the afterhold to fetch up a spare coil of rope, when one of the hatches which he had removed came crashing down on the top of him. He saved his life by springing out of the way, but one of his feet was terribly crushed, and he will be of little use for the remainder of the voyage. He attributes the accident to the carelessness of his negro companion, who had helped him to shift the hatches. The latter, however, puts it down to the roll of the ship. Whatever be the cause, it reduces our short-handed crew still further. This run of ill-luck seems to be depressing Harton, for he has lost his usual good spirits and joviality. Goring is the only one who preserves his cheerfulness. I see him still working at his chart in his own cabin. His nautical knowledge would be useful should anything happen to Hyson—which God forbid!

October 29th, 30th.—Still bowling along with a fresh breeze. All quiet and nothing of note to chronicle.

October 31st.—My weak lungs, combined with the exciting episodes of the voyage, have shaken my nervous system so much that the most trivial incident affects me. I can hardly believe that I am the same man who tied the external iliac artery, an operation requiring the nicest precision, under a heavy rifle fire at Antietam. I am as nervous as a child. I was lying half dozing last night about four bells in the middle watch trying in vain to drop into a refreshing sleep. There was no light inside my cabin, but a single ray of moonlight streamed in through the port-hole, throwing a silvery flickering circle upon the door. As I lay I kept my drowsy eyes upon this circle, and was conscious that it was gradually becoming less well-defined as my senses left me, when I was suddenly recalled to full wakefulness by the appearance of a small dark object in the very centre of the luminous disc. I lay quietly and breathlessly watching it. Gradually it grew larger and plainer, and then I perceived that it was a human hand which had been cautiously inserted through the chink of the half-closed door—a hand which, as I observed with a thrill of horror, was not provided with fingers. The door swung cautiously backwards, and Goring's head followed his hand. It appeared in the centre of the moonlight, and was framed as it were in a ghastly uncertain halo, against which his features showed out plainly. It seemed to me that I had never seen such an utterly fiendish and merciless expression upon a human face. His eyes were dilated and glaring, his lips drawn back so as to show his white fangs, and his straight black hair appeared to bristle over his low forehead like the hood of a cobra. The sudden and noiseless apparition had such an effect upon me that I sprang up in bed trembling in every limb, and held out my hand towards my revolver. I was heartily ashamed of my hastiness when he explained the object of his intrusion, as he immediately did in the most courteous language. He had been suffering from toothache, poor fellow! and had come in to beg some laudanum, knowing that I possessed a medicine chest. As to a sinister expression he is never a beauty, and what with my state of nervous tension and the effect of the shifting moonlight it was easy to conjure up something horrible. I gave him twenty drops, and he went off again, with many expressions of gratitude. I can hardly say how much this trivial incident affected me. I have felt unstrung all day.

A week's record of our voyage is here omitted, as nothing eventful occurred during the time, and my log consists merely of a few pages of unimportant gossip.

November 7th.—Harton and I sat on the poop all the morning, for the weather is becoming very warm as we come into southern latitudes. We reckon that we have done two-thirds of our voyage. How glad we shall be to see the green banks of the Tagus, and leave this unlucky ship for ever! I was endeavouring to amuse Harton to-day and to while away the time by telling him some of the experiences of my past life. Among others I related to him how I came into the possession of my black stone, and as a finale I rummaged in the side pocket of my old shooting coat and produced the identical object in question. He and I were bending over it together, I pointing out to him the curious ridges upon its surface, when we were conscious of a shadow falling between us and the sun, and looking round saw Goring standing behind us glaring over our shoulders at the stone. For some reason or other he appeared to be powerfully excited, though he was evidently trying to control himself and to conceal his emotion. He pointed once or twice at my relic with his stubby thumb before he could recover himself sufficiently to ask what it was and how I obtained it—a question put in such a brusque manner that I should have been offended had I not known the man to be an eccentric. I told him the story very much as I had told it to Harton. He listened with the deepest interest and then asked me if I had any idea what the stone was. I said I had not, beyond that it was meteoric. He asked me if I had ever tried its effect upon a negro. I said I had not. "Come," said he, "we'll see what our black friend at the wheel thinks of it." He took the stone in his hand and went across to the sailor, and the two examined it carefully. I could see the man gesticulating and nodding his head excitedly as if making some assertion, while his face betrayed the utmost astonishment, mixed, I think, with some reverence. Goring came across the deck to us presently, still holding the stone in his hand. "He says it is a worthless, useless thing," he said, "and fit only to be chucked overboard," with which he raised his hand and would most certainly have made an end of my relic, had the black sailor behind him not rushed forward and seized him by the wrist. Finding himself secured Goring dropped the stone and turned away with a very bad grace to avoid my angry remonstrances at his breach of faith. The black picked up the stone and handed it to me with a low bow and every sign of profound respect. The whole affair is inexplicable. I am rapidly coming to the conclusion that Goring is a maniac or something very near one. When I compare the effect produced by the stone upon the sailor, however, with the respect shown to Martha on the plantation, and the surprise of Goring on its first production, I cannot but come to the conclusion that I have really got hold of some powerful talisman which appeals to the whole dark race. I must not trust it in Goring's hands again.

November 8th, 9th.—What splendid weather we are having! Beyond one little blow, we have had nothing but fresh breezes the whole voyage. These two days we have made better runs than any hitherto. It is a pretty thing to watch the spray fly up from our prow as it cuts through the waves. The sun shines through it and breaks it up into a number of miniature rainbows —"sun-dogs," the sailors call them. I stood on the fo'c'sle-head for several hours to-day watching the effect, and surrounded by a halo of prismatic colours. The steersman has evidently told the other blacks about my wonderful stone, for I am treated by them all with the greatest respect. Talking about optical phenomena, we had a curious one yesterday evening which was pointed out to me by Hyson. This was the appearance of a triangular well-defined object high up in the heavens to the north of us. He explained that it was exactly like the Peak of Teneriffe as seen from a great distance —the peak was, however, at that moment at least five hundred miles to the south. It may have been a cloud, or it may have been one of those strange reflections of which one reads. The weather is very warm. The mate says that he never knew it so warm in these latitudes. Played chess with Harton in the evening.

November 10th.—It is getting warmer and warmer. Some land birds came and perched in the rigging to-day, though we are still a considerable way from our destination. The heat is so great that we are too lazy to do anything but lounge about the decks and smoke. Goring came over to me to-day and asked me some more questions about my stone; but I answered him rather shortly, for I have not quite forgiven him yet for the cool way in which he attempted to deprive me of it.

November 11th, 12th.—Still making good progress. I had no idea Portugal was ever as hot as this, but no doubt it is cooler on land. Hyson himself seemed surprised at it, and so do the men.

November 13th.—A most extraordinary event has happened, so extraordinary as to be almost inexplicable. Either Hyson has blundered wonderfully, or some magnetic influence has disturbed our instruments. Just about daybreak the watch on the fo'c'sle-head shouted out that he heard the sound of surf ahead, and Hyson thought he saw the loom of land. The ship was put about, and, though no lights were seen, none of us doubted that we had struck the Portuguese coast a little sooner than we had expected. What was our surprise to see the scene which was revealed to us at break of day! As far as we could look on either side was one long line of surf, great, green billows rolling in and breaking into a cloud of foam. But behind the surf what was there! Not the green banks nor the high cliffs of the shores of Portugal, but a great sandy waste which stretched away and away until it blended with the skyline. To right and left, look where you would, there was nothing but yellow sand, heaped in some places into fantastic mounds, some of them several hundred feet high, while in other parts were long stretches as level apparently as a billiard board. Harton and I, who had come on deck together, looked at each other in astonishment, and Harton burst out laughing. Hyson is exceedingly mortified at the occurrence, and protests that the instruments have been tampered with. There is no doubt that this is the mainland of Africa, and that it was really the Peak of Teneriffe which we saw some days ago upon the northern horizon. At the time when we saw the land birds we must have been passing some of the Canary Islands. If we continued on the same course, we are now to the north of Cape Blanco, near the unexplored country which skirts the great Sahara. All we can do is to rectify our instruments as far as possible and start afresh for our destination.

8.30 P.M.—Have been lying in a calm all day. The

coast is now about a mile and a half from us. Hyson has examined the instruments, but cannot find any reason for their extraordinary deviation.

This is the end of my private journal, and I must make the remainder of my statement from memory. There is little chance of my being mistaken about facts, which have seared themselves into my recollection. That very night the storm which had been brewing so long burst over us, and I came to learn whither all those little incidents were tending which I had recorded so aimlessly. Blind fool that I was not to have seen it sooner! I shall tell what occurred as precisely as I can.

I had gone into my cabin about half-past eleven, and was preparing to go to bed, when a tap came at my door. On opening it I saw Goring's little black page, who told me that his master would like to have a word with me on deck. I was rather surprised that he should want me at such a late hour, but I went up without hesitation. I had hardly put my foot on the quarter-deck before I was seized from behind, dragged down upon my back, and a handkerchief slipped round my mouth. I struggled as hard as I could, but a coil of rope was rapidly and firmly wound round me, and I found myself lashed to the davit of one of the boats, utterly powerless to do or say anything, while the point of a knife pressed to my throat warned me to cease my struggles. The night was so dark that I had been unable hitherto to recognize my assailants, but as my eyes became accustomed to the gloom, and the moon broke out through the clouds that obscured it, I made out that I was surrounded by the two negro sailors, the black cook, and my fellow-passenger, Goring. Another man was crouching on the deck at my feet, but he was in the shadow and I could not recognize him.

All this occurred so rapidly that a minute could hardly have elapsed from the time I mounted the companion until I found myself gagged and powerless. It was so sudden that I could scarce bring myself to realize it, or to comprehend what it all meant. I heard the gang round me speaking in short, fierce whispers to each other, and some instinct told me that my life was the question at issue. Goring spoke authoritatively and angrily—the others doggedly and all together, as if disputing his commands. Then they moved away in a body to the opposite side of the deck, where I could still hear them whispering, though they were concealed from my view by the saloon skylights.

All this time the voices of the watch on deck chatting and laughing at the other end of the ship were distinctly audible, and I could see them gathered in a group, little dreaming of the dark doings which were going on within thirty yards of them. Oh! That I could have given them one word of warning, even though I had lost my life in doing it! but it was impossible. The moon was shining fitfully through the scattered clouds, and I could see the silvery gleam of the surge, and beyond it the vast weird desert with its fantastic sand-hills. Glancing down, I saw that the man who had been crouching on the deck was still lying there, and as I gazed at him a flickering ray of moonlight fell full upon his upturned face. Great heaven! even now, when more than twelve years have elapsed, my hand trembles as I write that, in spite of distorted features and projecting eyes, I recognized the face of Harton, the cheery young clerk who had been my companion during the voyage. It needed no medical eye to see that he was quite dead, while the twisted handkerchief round the neck, and the gag in his mouth, showed the silent way in which the hell-hounds had done their work. The clue which explained every event of our voyage came upon me like a flash of light as I gazed on poor Harton's corpse. Much was dark and unexplained, but I felt a great dim perception of the truth.

I heard the striking of a match at the other side of the skylights, and then I saw the tall, gaunt figure of

Goring standing up on the bulwarks and holding in his hands what appeared to be a dark lantern. He lowered this for a moment over the side of the ship, and, to my inexpressible astonishment, I saw it answered instantaneously by a flash among the sand-hills on shore, which came and went so rapidly, that unless I had been following the direction of Goring's gaze, I should never have detected it. Again he lowered the lantern, and again it was answered from the shore. He then stepped down from the bulwarks, and in doing so slipped, making such a noise, that for a moment my heart bounded with the thought that the attention of the watch would be directed to his proceedings. It was a vain hope. The night was calm and the ship motionless, so that no idea of duty kept them vigilant. Hyson, who after the death of Tibbs was in command of both watches, had gone below to snatch a few hours' sleep, and the boatswain, who was left in charge, was standing with the other two men at the foot of the foremast. Powerless, speechless, with the cords cutting into my flesh and the murdered man at my feet, I awaited the next act in the tragedy.

The four ruffians were standing up now at the other side of the deck. The cook was armed with some sort of a cleaver, the others had knives, and Goring had a revolver. They were all leaning against the rail and looking out over the water as if watching for something. I saw one of them grasp another's arm and point as if at some object, and following the direction I made out the loom of a large moving mass making towards the ship. As it emerged from the gloom I saw that it was a great canoe crammed with men and propelled by at least a score of paddles. As it shot under our stern the watch caught sight of it also, and raising a cry hurried aft. They were too late, however. A swarm of gigantic negroes clambered over the quarter, and led by Goring swept down the deck in an irresistible torrent. All opposition was overpowered in a moment, the unarmed watch were knocked over and bound, and the sleepers dragged out of their bunks and secured in the same manner. Hyson made an attempt to defend the narrow passage leading to his cabin, and I heard a scuffle, and his voice shouting for assistance. There was none to assist, however, and he was brought on to the poop with the blood streaming from a deep cut in his forehead. He was gagged like the others, and a council was held upon our fate by the negroes. I saw our black seamen pointing towards me and making some statement, which was received with murmurs of astonishment and incredulity by the savages. One of them then came over to me, and plunging his hand into my pocket took out my black stone and held it up. He then handed it to a man who appeared to be a chief, who examined it as minutely as the light would permit, and muttering a few words passed it on to the warrior beside him, who also scrutinized it and passed it on until it had gone from hand to hand round the whole circle. The chief then said a few words to Goring in the native tongue, on which the quadroon addressed me in English. At this moment I seem to see the scene. The tall masts of the ship with the moonlight streaming down, silvering the yards and bringing the network of cordage into hard relief; the group of dusky warriors leaning on their spears; the dead man at my feet; the line of white-faced prisoners, and in front of me the loathsome half-breed, looking in his white linen and elegant clothes a strange contrast to his associates.

"You will bear me witness," he said in his softest accents, "that I am no party to sparing your life. If it rested with me you would die as these other men are about to do. I have no personal grudge against either you or them, but I have devoted my life to the destruction of the white race, and you are the first that has ever been in my power and has escaped me. You may thank that stone of yours for your life. These poor fellows reverence it, and indeed if it really be what they think it is they have cause. Should it prove when we get ashore that they are mistaken, and that its shape and material is a mere chance, nothing can save your life. In the meantime we wish to treat you well, so if there are any of your possessions which you would like to take with you, you are at liberty to get them." As he finished he gave a sign, and a couple of the negroes unbound me, though without removing the gag. I was led down into the cabin, where I put a few valuables into my pockets, together with a pocket-compass and my journal of the voyage. They then pushed me over the side into a small canoe, which was lying beside the large one, and my guards followed me, and shoving off began paddling for the shore. We had got about a hundred yards or so from the ship when our steersman held up his hand, and the paddlers paused for a moment and listened. Then on the silence of the night I heard a sort of dull, moaning sound, followed by a succession of splashes in the water. That is all I know of the fate of my poor shipmates. Almost immediately afterwards the large canoe followed us, and the deserted ship was left drifting about—a dreary spectre-like hulk. Nothing was taken from her by the savages. The whole fiendish transaction was carried through as decorously and temperately as though it were a religious rite.

The first grey of daylight was visible in the east as we passed through the surge and reached the shore. Leaving half a dozen men with the canoes, the rest of the negroes set off through the sand-hills, leading me with them, but treating me very gently and respectfully. It was difficult walking, as we sank over our ankles into the loose, shifting sand at every step, and I was nearlv dead beat by the time we reached the native village, or town rather, for it was a place of considerable dimensions. The houses were conical structures not unlike bee-hives, and were made of compressed seaweed cemented over with a rude form of mortar, there being neither stick nor stone upon the coast nor anywhere within many hundreds of miles. As we entered the town an enormous crowd of both sexes came swarming out to meet us, beating tom-toms and howling and screaming. On seeing me they redoubled their yells and assumed a threatening attitude, which was instantly quelled by a few words shouted by my escort. A buzz of wonder succeeded the war-cries and yells of the moment before, and the whole dense mass proceeded down the broad central street of the town, having my escort and myself in the centre.

My statement hitherto may seem so strange as to excite doubt in the minds of those who do not know me, but it was the fact which I am now about to relate which caused my own brother-in-law to insult me by disbelief. I can but relate the occurrence in the simplest words, and trust to chance and time to prove their truth. In the centre of this main street there was a large building, formed in the same primitive way as the others, but towering high above them; a stockade of beautifully polished ebony rails was planted all round it, the framework of the door was formed by two magnificent elephant's tusks sunk in the ground on each side and meeting at the top, and the aperture was closed by a screen of native cloth richly embroidered with gold. We made our way to this imposing-looking structure, but on reaching the opening in the stockade, the multitude stopped and squatted down upon their hams, while I was led through into the enclosure by a few of the chiefs and elders of the tribe, Goring accompanying us, and in fact directing the proceedings. On reaching the screen which closed the temple—for such it evidently was—my hat and my shoes were removed, and I was then led in, a venerable old negro leading the way carrying in his hand my stone, which had been taken from my pocket. The building was only lit up by a few long slits in the roof, through which the tropical sun poured, throwing broad golden bars upon the clay floor, alternating with intervals of darkness.

The interior was even larger than one would have imagined from the outside appearance. The walls were hung with native mats, shells, and other ornaments, but the remainder of the great space was quite empty, with the exception of a single object in the centre. This was the figure of a colossal negro, which I at first thought to be some real king or high priest of titanic size, but as I approached it I saw by the way in which the light was reflected from it that it was a statue admirably cut in jet-black stone. I was led up to this idol, for such it seemed to be, and looking at it closer I saw that though it was perfect in every other respect, one of its ears had been broken short off. The grey-haired negro who held my relic mounted upon a small stool, and stretching up his arm fitted Martha's black stone on to the jagged surface on the side of the statue's head. There could not be a doubt that the one had been broken off from the other. The parts dovetailed together so accurately that when the old man removed his hand the ear stuck in its place for a few seconds before dropping into his open palm. The group round me prostrated themselves upon the ground at the sight with a cry of reverence, while the crowd outside, to whom the result was communicated, set up a wild whooping and cheering.

In a moment I found myself converted from a prisoner into a demi-god. I was escorted back through the town in triumph, the people pressing forward to touch my clothing and to gather up the dust on which my foot had trod. One of the largest huts was put at my disposal, and a banquet of every native delicacy was served me. I still felt, however, that I was not a free man, as several spearmen were placed as a guard at the entrance of my hut. All day my mind was occupied with plans of escape, but none seemed in any way feasible. On the one side was the great arid desert stretching away to Timbuctoo, on the other was a sea untraversed by vessels. The more I pondered over the problem the more hopeless did it seem. I little dreamed how near I was to its solution.

Night had fallen, and the clamour of the negroes had died gradually away. I was stretched on the couch of skins which had been provided for me, and was still meditating over my future, when Goring walked stealthily into the hut. My first idea was that he had come to complete his murderous holocaust by making away with me, the last survivor, and I sprang up upon my feet, determined to defend myself to the last. He smiled when he saw the action, and motioned me down again while he seated himself upon the other end of the couch.

"What do you think of me?" was the astonishing question with which he commenced our conversation.

"Think of you!" I almost yelled. "I think you the vilest, most unnatural renegade that ever polluted the earth. If we were away from these black devils of yours I would strangle you with my hands!"

"Don't speak so loud," he said, without the slightest appearance of irritation. "I don't want our chat to be cut short. So you would strangle me, would you!" he went on, with an amused smile. "I suppose I am returning good for evil, for I have come to help you to escape."

"You!" I gasped incredulously.

"Yes, I," he continued. "Oh, there is no credit to me in the matter. I am quite consistent. There is no reason why I should not be perfectly candid with you. I wish to be king over these fellows—not a very high ambition, certainly, but you know what Cæsar said about being first in a village in Gaul. Well, this unlucky stone of yours has not only saved your life, but has turned all their heads so that they think you are come down from heaven, and my influence will be gone until you are out of the way. That is why I am going to help you to escape, since I cannot kill you" —this in the most natural and dulcet voice, as if the desire to do so were a matter of course.

"You would give the world to ask me a few questions,"

he went on, after a pause ; " but you are too proud to do it. Never mind, I'll tell you one or two things, because I want your fellow white men to know them when you go back—if you are lucky enough to get back. About that cursed stone of yours, for instance. These negroes, or at least so the legend goes, were Mahometans originally. While Mahomet himself was still alive, there was a schism among his followers, and the smaller party moved away from Arabia, and eventually crossed Africa. They took away with them, in their exile, a valuable relic of their old faith in the shape of a large piece of the black stone of Mecca. The stone was a meteoric one, as you may have heard, and in its fall upon the earth it broke into two pieces. One of these pieces is still at Mecca. The larger piece was carried away to Barbary, where a skilful worker modelled it into the fashion which you saw to-day. These men are the descendants of the original seceders from Mahomet, and they have brought their relic safely through all their wanderings until they settled in this strange place, where the desert protects them from their enemies."

" And the ear ? " I asked, almost involuntarily.

" Oh, that was the same story over again. Some of the tribe wandered away to the south a few hundred years ago, and one of them, wishing to have good luck for the enterprise, got into the temple at night and carried off one of the ears. There has been a tradition among the negroes ever since that the ear would come back some day. The fellow who carried it was caught by some slaver, no doubt, and that was how it got into America, and so into your hands—and you have had the honour of fulfilling the prophecy."

He paused for a few minutes, resting his head upon his hands, waiting apparently for me to speak. When he looked up again, the whole expression of his face had changed. His features were firm and set, and he changed the air of half-levity with which he had spoken before for one of sternness and almost ferocity.

"I wish you to carry a message back," he said, "to the white race, the great dominating race whom I hate and defy. Tell them that I have battened on their blood for twenty years, that I have slain them until even I became tired of what had once been a joy, that I did this unnoticed and unsuspected in the face of every precaution which their civilization could suggest. There is no satisfaction in revenge when your enemy does not know who has struck him. I am not sorry, therefore, to have you as a messenger. There is no need why I should tell you how this great hate became born in me. See this," and he held up his mutilated hand; "that was done by a white man's knife. My father was white, my mother was a slave. When he died she was sold again, and I, a child then, saw her lashed to death to break her of some of the little airs and graces which her late master had encouraged in her. My young wife, too, oh, my young wife!" a shudder ran through his whole frame. "No matter! I swore my oath, and I kept it. From Maine to Florida, and from Boston to San Francisco, you could track my steps by sudden deaths which baffled the police. I warred against the whole white race as they for centuries had warred against the black one. At last, as I tell you, I sickened of blood. Still, the sight of a white face was abhorrent to me, and I determined to find some bold free black people and to throw in my lot with them, to cultivate their latent powers and to form a nucleus for a great coloured nation. This idea possessed me, and I travelled over the world for two years seeking for what I desired. At last I almost despaired of finding it. There was no hope of regeneration in the slave-dealing Soudanese, the debased Fantee, or the Americanized negroes of Liberia. I was returning from my quest when chance brought me in contact with this magnificent tribe of dwellers in the desert, and I threw in my lot with them. Before doing so, however, my old instinct of revenge prompted me to make one last visit to the United States, and I returned from it in the *Marie Celeste*.

"As to the voyage itself, your intelligence will have told you by this time that, thanks to my manipulation, both compasses and chronometers were entirely untrustworthy. I alone worked out the course with correct instruments of my own, while the steering was done by my black friends under my guidance. I pushed Tibbs's wife overboard. What! You look surprised and shrink away. Surely you had guessed that by this time. I would have shot you that day through the partition, but unfortunately you were not there. I tried again afterwards, but you were awake. I shot Tibbs. I think the idea of suicide was carried out rather neatly. Of course when once we got on the coast the rest was simple. I had bargained that all on board should die; but that stone of yours upset my plans. I also bargained that there should be no plunder. No one can say we are pirates. We have acted from principle, not from any sordid motive."

I listened in amazement to the summary of his crimes which this strange man gave me, all in the quietest and most composed of voices, as though detailing incidents of every-day occurrence. I still seem to see him sitting like a hideous nightmare at the end of my couch, with the single rude lamp flickering over his cadaverous features.

"And now," he continued, "there is no difficulty about your escape. These stupid adopted children of mine will say that you have gone back to heaven from whence you came. The wind blows off the land. I have a boat all ready for you, well stored with provisions and water. I am anxious to be rid of you, so you may rely that nothing is neglected. Rise up and follow me."

I did what he commanded, and he led me through the door of the hut. The guards had either been withdrawn, or Goring had arranged matters with them. We passed unchallenged through the town and across the sandy plain. Once more I heard the roar of the sea, and saw the long white line of the surge. Two figures were standing upon the shore arranging the gear of a small boat. They were the two sailors who had been with us on the voyage.

"See him safely through the surf," said Goring. The two men sprang in and pushed off, pulling me in after them. With mainsail and jib we ran out from the land and passed safely over the bar. Then my two companions without a word of farewell sprang overboard, and I saw their heads like black dots on the white foam as they made their way back to the shore, while I scudded away into the blackness of the night. Looking back I caught my last glimpse of Goring. He was standing upon the summit of a sand-hill, and the rising moon behind him threw his gaunt angular figure into hard relief. He was waving his arms frantically to and fro; it may have been to encourage me on my way, but the gestures seemed to me at the time to be threatening ones, and I have often thought that it was more likely that his old savage instinct had returned when he realized that I was out of his power. Be that as it may, it was the last that I ever saw or ever shall see of Septimius Goring.

There is no need for me to dwell upon my solitary voyage. I steered as well as I could for the Canaries, but was picked up upon the fifth day by the British and African Steam Navigation Company's boat *Monrovia.* Let me take this opportunity of tendering my sincerest thanks to Captain Stornoway and his officers for the great kindness which they showed me from that time till they landed me in Liverpool, where I was enabled to take one of the Guion boats to New York.

From the day on which I found myself once more in the bosom of my family I have said little of what I have undergone. The subject is still an intensely painful one to me, and the little which I have dropped has been discredited. I now put the facts before the they occurred, careless how far they may be , and simply writing them down because my g is growing weaker, and I feel the responsibility of holding my peace longer. I make no vague statement. Turn to your map of Africa. There above Cape Blanco, where the land trends away north and south from the westernmost point of the continent, there it is that Septimius Goring still reigns over his dark subjects, unless retribution has overtaken him ; and there, where the long green ridges run swiftly in to roar and hiss upon the hot yellow sand, it is there that Harton lies with Hyson and the other poor fellows who were done to death in the *Marie Celeste.*

THE GREAT KEINPLATZ EXPERIMENT

OF all the sciences which have puzzled the sons of men, none had such an attraction for the learned Professor von Baumgarten as those which relate to psychology and the ill-defined relations between mind and matter. A celebrated anatomist, a profound chemist, and one of the first physiologists in Europe, it was a relief for him to turn from these subjects and to bring his varied knowledge to bear upon the study of the soul and the mysterious relationship of spirits. At first, when as a young man he began to dip into the secrets of mesmerism, his mind seemed to be wandering in a strange land where all was chaos and darkness, save that here and there some great unexplainable and disconnected fact loomed out in front of him. As the years passed, however, and as the worthy Professor's stock of knowledge increased, for knowledge begets knowledge as money bears interest, much which had seemed strange and unaccountable began to take another shape in his eyes. New trains of reasoning became familiar to him, and he perceived connecting links where all had been incomprehensible and startling. By experiments which extended over twenty years, he obtained a basis of facts upon which it was his ambition to build up a new, exact science which should embrace mesmerism, spiritualism, and all cognate subjects. In this he was much helped by his intimate knowledge of the more intricate parts of animal physiology which treat of nerve currents and the working of the brain; for Alexis von Baumgarten was Regius Professor of Physiology at the University of Keinplatz, and had all the resources of the laboratory to aid him in his profound researches.

Professor von Baumgarten was tall and thin, with a hatchet face and steel-grey eyes, which were singularly bright and penetrating. Much thought had furrowed his forehead and contracted his heavy eyebrows, so that he appeared to wear a perpetual frown, which often misled people as to his character, for though austere he was tender-hearted. He was popular among the students, who would gather round him after his lectures and listen eagerly to his strange theories. Often he would call for volunteers from amongst them in order to conduct some experiment, so that eventually there was hardly a lad in the class who had not, at one time or another, been thrown into a mesmeric trance by his Professor.

Of all these young devotees of science there was none who equalled in enthusiasm Fritz von Hartmann. It had often seemed strange to his fellow-students that wild, reckless Fritz, as dashing a young fellow as ever hailed from the Rhinelands, should devote the time and trouble which he did in reading up abstruse works and in assisting the Professor in his strange experiments. The fact was, however, that Fritz was a knowing and long-headed fellow. Months before he had lost his heart to young Elise, the blue-eyed, yellow-haired daughter of the lecturer. Although he had succeeded in learning from her lips that she was not indifferent to his suit, he had never dared to announce himself to her family as a formal suitor. Hence he would have found it a difficult matter to see his young lady had he not adopted the expedient of making himself useful to the Professor. By this means he frequently was asked to the old man's house, where he willingly submitted to be experimented upon in any way as long as there was a chance of his receiving one bright glance from the eyes of Elise or one touch of her little hand.

Young Fritz von Hartmann was a handsome lad enough. There were broad acres, too, which would descend to him when his father died. To many he would have seemed an eligible suitor; but Madame frowned upon his presence in the house, and lectured the Professor at times on his allowing such a wolf to prowl around their lamb. To tell the truth, Fritz had an evil name in Keinplatz. Never was there a riot or a duel, or any other mischief afoot, but the young Rhinelander figured as a ringleader in it. No one used more free and violent language, no one drank more, no one played cards more habitually, no one was more idle, save in the one solitary subject. No wonder, then, that the good Frau Professorin gathered her Fräulein under her wing, and resented the attentions of such a *mauvais sujet*. As to the worthy lecturer, he was too much engrossed by his strange studies to form an opinion upon the subject one way or the other.

For many years there was one question which had continually obtruded itself upon his thoughts. All his experiments and his theories turned upon a single point. A hundred times a day the Professor asked himself whether it was possible for the human spirit to exist apart from the body for a time and then to return to it once again. When the possibility first suggested itself to him his scientific mind had revolted from it. It clashed too violently with preconceived ideas and the prejudices of his early training. Gradually, however, as he proceeded farther and farther along the pathway of original research, his mind shook off its old fetters and became ready to face any conclusion which could reconcile the facts. There were many things which made him believe that it was possible for mind to exist apart from matter. At last it occurred to him that by a daring and original experiment the question might be definitely decided.

"It is evident," he remarked in his celebrated article upon invisible entities, which appeared in the *Keinplatz wochenliche Medicalschrift* about this time, and which surprised the whole scientific world—"it is evident that under certain conditions the soul or mind does separate itself from the body. In the case of a mesmerised person, the body lies in a cataleptic condition, but the spirit has left it. Perhaps you reply that the soul is there, but in a dormant condition. I answer that this is not so, otherwise how can one account for the condition of clairvoyance, which has fallen into disrepute through the knavery of certain scoundrels, but which can easily be shown to be an undoubted fact. I have been able myself, with a sensitive subject, to obtain an accurate description of what was going on in another room or another house. How can such knowledge be accounted for on any hypothesis save that the soul of the subject has left the body and is wandering through space? For a moment it is recalled by the voice of the operator and says what it has seen, and then wings its way once more through the air. Since the spirit is by its very nature invisible, we cannot see these comings and goings, but we see their effect in the body of the subject, now rigid and inert, now struggling to narrate impressions which could never have come to it by natural means. There is only one way which I can see by which the fact can be demonstrated. Although we in the flesh are unable to see these spirits, yet our own spirits, could we separate them from the body, would be conscious of the presence of others. It is my intention, therefore, shortly to mesmerise one of my pupils. I shall then mesmerise myself in a manner which has become easy to me. After that, if my theory holds good, my spirit will have no difficulty in meeting and communing with the spirit of my pupil, both being separated from the body. I hope to be able to communicate the result of this interesting experiment in an early number of the *Keinplatz wochenliche Medicalschrift.*"

When the good Professor finally fulfilled his promise, and published an account of what occurred, the narrative was so extraordinary that it was received with general incredulity. The tone of some of the papers was so offensive in their comments upon the matter that the angry savant declared that he would never open his mouth again or refer to the subject in any way—a promise which he has faithfully kept. This narrative has been compiled, however, from the most authentic sources, and the events cited in it may be relied upon as substantially correct.

It happened, then, that shortly after the time when Professor von Baumgarten conceived the idea of the above-mentioned experiment, he was walking thoughtfully homewards after a long day in the laboratory, when he met a crowd of roistering students who had just streamed out from a beer-house. At the head of them, half-intoxicated and very noisy, was young Fritz von Hartmann. The Professor would have passed them, but his pupil ran across and intercepted him.

"Heh! my worthy master," he said, taking the old man by the sleeve, and leading him down the road with him. "There is something that I have to say to you, and it is easier for me to say it now, when the good beer is humming in my head, than at another time."

"What is it, then, Fritz?" the physiologist asked, looking at him in mild surprise.

"I hear, mein herr, that you are about to do some wondrous experiment in which you hope to take a man's soul out of his body, and then to put it back again. Is it not so?"

"It is true, Fritz."

"And have you considered, my dear sir, that you may have some difficulty in finding someone on whom to try this? Potztausend! Suppose that the soul went out and would not come back. That would be a bad business. Who is to take the risk?"

"But Fritz," the Professor cried, very much startled by this view of the matter, "I had relied upon your assistance in the attempt. Surely you will not desert me. Consider the honour and glory."

"Consider the fiddlesticks!" the student cried angrily. "Am I to be paid always thus? Did I not stand two hours upon a glass insulator while you poured electricity into my body? Have you not stimulated my phrenic nerves, besides ruining my digestion with a galvanic current round my stomach? Four-and-thirty times you have mesmerised me, and what have I got from all this? Nothing. And now you wish to take my soul out, as you would take the works from a watch. It is more than flesh and blood can stand."

"Dear, dear!" the Professor cried in great distress. "That is very true, Fritz. I never thought of it before. If you can but suggest how I can compensate you, you will find me ready and willing."

"Then listen," said Fritz solemnly. "If you will pledge your word that after this experiment I may have the hand of your daughter, then I am willing to assist you; but if not, I shall have nothing to do with it. These are my only terms."

"And what would my daughter say to this?" the Professor exclaimed, after a pause of astonishment.

"Elise would welcome it," the young man replied. "We have loved each other long."

"Then she shall be yours," the physiologist said with decision, "for you are a good-hearted young man, and one of the best neurotic subjects that I have ever known —that is when you are not under the influence of alcohol. My experiment is to be performed upon the fourth of next month. You will attend at the physiological laboratory at twelve o'clock. It will be a great occasion, Fritz. Von Gruben is coming from Jena, and Hinterstein from Basle. The chief men of science of all South Germany will be there."

"I shall be punctual," the student said briefly; and so the two parted. The Professor plodded homeward, thinking of the great coming event, while the young man staggered along after his noisy companions, with his mind full of the blue-eyed Elise, and of the bargain which he had concluded with her father.

The Professor did not exaggerate when he spoke of the widespread interest excited by his novel psychological experiment. Long before the hour had arrived the room was filled by a galaxy of talent. Besides the celebrities whom he had mentioned, there had come from London the great Professor Lurcher, who had just established his reputation by a remarkable treatise upon cerebral centres. Several great lights of the Spiritualistic body had also come a long distance to be present, as had a Swedenborgian minister, who considered that the proceedings might throw some light upon the doctrines of the Rosy Cross.

There was considerable applause from this eminent assembly upon the appearance of Professor von Baumgarten and his subject upon the platform. The lecturer, in a few well-chosen words, explained what his views were, and how he proposed to test them. "I hold," he said, "that when a person is under the influence of mesmerism, his spirit is for the time released from his body, and I challenge anyone to put forward any other hypothesis which will account for the fact of clairvoyance. I therefore hope that upon mesmerising my young friend here, and then putting myself into a trance, our spirits may be able to commune together, though our bodies lie still and inert. After a time nature will resume her sway, our spirits will return into our respective bodies, and all will be as before. With your kind permission, we shall now proceed to attempt the experiment."

The applause was renewed at this speech, and the audience settled down in expectant silence. With a few rapid passes the Professor mesmerised the young man, who sank back in his chair, pale and rigid. He then took a bright globe of glass from his pocket, and by concentrating his gaze upon it and making a strong mental effort, he succeeded in throwing himself into the same condition. It was a strange and impressive sight to see the old man and the young sitting together in the same cataleptic condition. Whither, then, had their souls fled? That was the question which presented itself to each and every one of the spectators.

Five minutes passed, and then ten, and then fifteen, and then fifteen more, while the Professor and his pupil sat stiff and stark upon the platform. During that time not a sound was heard from the assembled savants, but every eye was bent upon the two pale faces, in search of the first signs of returning consciousness. Nearly an hour had elapsed before the patient watchers were rewarded. A faint flush came back to the cheeks of Professor von Baumgarten. The soul was coming back once more to its earthly tenement. Suddenly he stretched out his long, thin arms, as one awaking from sleep, and rubbing his eyes, stood up from his chair and gazed about him as though he hardly realised where he was. "Tausend Teufel!" he exclaimed, rapping out a tremendous South German oath, to the great astonishment of his audience and to the disgust of the Swedenborgian. "Where the Henker am I then, and what in thunder has occurred? Oh yes, I remember now. One of these nonsensical mesmeric experiments. There is no result this time, for I remember nothing at all since I became unconscious; so you have had all your long journeys for nothing, my learned friends, and a very good joke, too"; at which the Regius Professor of Physiology burst into a roar of laughter and slapped his thigh in a highly indecorous fashion. The audience were so enraged at this unseemly behaviour on the part of their host, that there might have been a considerable disturbance, had it not been for the judicious interference of young Fritz von Hartmann, who had now recovered from his lethargy. Stepping to the front of the platform, the young man apologised for the conduct of his companion. "I am sorry to say," he said, "that he is a harum-scarum sort of fellow, although he appeared so grave at the commencement of this experiment. He is still suffering from mesmeric reaction, and is hardly accountable for his words. As to the experiment itself, I do not consider it to be a failure. It is very possible that our spirits may have been communing in space during this hour; but, unfortunately, our gross bodily memory is distinct from our spirit, and we cannot recall what has occurred. My energies shall now be devoted to devising some means by which spirits may be able to recollect what occurs to them in their free state, and I trust that when I have worked this out, I may have the pleasure of meeting you all once again in this hall, and demonstrating to you the result." This address, coming from so young a student, caused considerable astonishment among the audience, and some were inclined to be offended, thinking that he assumed rather too much importance. The majority, however, looked upon him as a young man of great promise, and many comparisons were made as they left the hall between his dignified conduct and the levity of his professor, who during the above remarks was laughing heartily in a corner, by no means abashed at the failure of the experiment.

Now although all these learned men were filing out of the lecture-room under the impression that they had seen nothing of note, as a matter of fact one of the most wonderful things in the whole history of the world had just occurred before their very eyes. Professor von Baumgarten had been so far correct in his theory that both his spirit and that of his pupil had been, for a time, absent from the body. But here a strange and unforeseen complication had occurred. In their return the spirit of Fritz von Hartmann had entered into the body of Alexis von Baumgarten, and that of Alexis von Baumgarten had taken up its abode in the frame of Fritz von Hartmann. Hence the slang and scurrility which issued from the lips of the serious Professor, and hence also the weighty words and grave statements which fell from the careless student. It was an unprecedented event, yet no one knew of it, least of all those whom it concerned.

The body of the Professor, feeling conscious suddenly of a great dryness about the back of the throat, sallied out into the street, still chuckling to himself over the result of the experiment, for the soul of Fritz within was reckless at the thought of the bride whom he had won so easily. His first impulse was to go up to the house and see her, but on second thoughts he came to the conclusion that it would be best to stay away until Madame Baumgarten should be informed by her husband of the agreement which had been made. He therefore made his way down to the Grüner Mann, which was one of the favourite trysting-places of the wilder students, and ran, boisterously waving his cane in the air, into the little parlour, where sat Spiegel and Müller and half a dozen other boon companions.

"Ha, ha! my boys," he shouted. "I knew I should find you here. Drink up, every one of you, and call for what you like, for I'm going to stand treat to-day."

Had the green man who is depicted upon the signpost of that well-known inn suddenly marched into the room and called for a bottle of wine, the students could not have been more amazed than they were by this unexpected entry of their revered professor. They were so astonished that for a minute or two they glared at him in utter bewilderment without being able to make any reply to his hearty invitation.

"Donner und Blitzen!" shouted the Professor angrily. "What the deuce is the matter with you, then? You sit there like a set of stuck pigs staring at me. What is it then?"

" It is the unexpected honour," stammered Spiegel, who was in the chair.

" Honour—rubbish ! " said the Professor testily. " Do you think that just because I happen to have been exhibiting mesmerism to a parcel of old fossils, I am therefore too proud to associate with dear old friends like you ? Come out of that chair, Spiegel, my boy, for I shall preside now. Beer, or wine, or schnapps, my lads—call for what you like, and put it all down to me."

Never was there such an afternoon in the Grüner Mann. The foaming flagons of lager and the green-necked bottles of Rhenish circulated merrily. By degrees the students lost their shyness in the presence of their Professor. As for him, he shouted, he sang, he roared, he balanced a long tobacco-pipe upon his nose, and offered to run a hundred yards against any member of the company. The Kellner and the barmaid whispered to each other outside the door their astonishment at such proceedings on the part of a Regius Professor of the ancient university of Keinplatz. They had still more to whisper about afterwards, for the learned man cracked the Kellner's crown, and kissed the barmaid behind the kitchen door.

" Gentlemen," said the Professor, standing up, albeit somewhat totteringly, at the end of the table, and balancing his high, old-fashioned wine glass in his bony hand, " I must now explain to you what is the cause of this festivity."

" Hear ! hear ! " roared the students, hammering their beer glasses against the table ; " a speech, a speech !—silence for a speech ! "

" The fact is, my friends," said the Professor, beaming through his spectacles, " I hope very soon to be married."

" Married ! " cried a student, bolder than the others. " Is Madame dead, then ? "

" Madame who ? "

" Why, Madame von Baumgarten, of course."

" Ha, ha ! " laughed the Professor ; " I can see, then, that you know all about my former difficulties. No, she is not dead, but I have reason to believe that she will not oppose my marriage."

"That is very accommodating of her," remarked one of the company.

"In fact," said the Professor, "I hope that she will now be induced to aid me in getting a wife. She and I never took to each other very much; but now I hope all that may be ended, and when I marry she will come and stay with me."

"What a happy family!" exclaimed some wag.

"Yes, indeed; and I hope you will come to my wedding, all of you. I won't mention names, but here is to my little bride!" and the Professor waved his glass in the air.

"Here's to his little bride!" roared the roisterers, with shouts of laughter. "Here's her health. Sie soll leben—Hoch!" And so the fun waxed still more fast and furious, while each young fellow followed the Professor's example, and drank a toast to the girl of his heart.

While all this festivity had been going on at the Grüner Mann, a very different scene had been enacted elsewhere. Young Fritz von Hartmann, with a solemn face and a reserved manner, had, after the experiment, consulted and adjusted some mathematical instruments; after which, with a few peremptory words to the janitor, he had walked out into the street and wended his way slowly in the direction of the house of the Professor. As he walked he saw Von Althaus, the professor of anatomy, in front of him, and, quickening his pace, he overtook him.

"I say, Von Althaus," he exclaimed, tapping him on the sleeve, "you were asking me for some information the other day concerning the middle coat of the cerebral arteries. Now I find——"

"Donnerwetter!" shouted Von Althaus, who was a peppery old fellow. "What the deuce do you mean by your impertinence! I'll have you up before the Academical Senate for this, sir "; with which threat he turned on his heel and hurried away. Von Hartmann was much surprised at this reception. " It's on account of this failure of my experiment," he said to himself, and continued moodily on his way.

Fresh surprises were in store for him, however. He was hurrying along when he was overtaken by two students. These youths, instead of raising their caps or showing any other sign of respect, gave a wild whoop of delight the instant that they saw him, and rushing at him seized him by each arm and commenced dragging him along with them.

" Gott in Himmel ! " roared Von Hartmann. " What is the meaning of this unparalleled insult ? Where are you taking me ? "

" To crack a bottle of wine with us," said the two students. " Come along ! That is an invitation which you have never refused."

" I never heard of such insolence in my life ! " cried Von Hartmann. " Let go my arms ! I shall certainly have you rusticated for this. Let me go, I say ! " and he kicked furiously at his captors.

" Oh, if you choose to turn ill-tempered, you may go where you like," the students said, releasing him. " We can do very well without you."

" I know you. I'll pay you out" said Von Hartmann furiously, and continued in the direction which he imagined to be his own home, much incensed at the two episodes which had occurred to him on the way.

Now, Madame von Baumgarten, who was looking out of the window and wondering why her husband was late for dinner, was considerably astonished to see the young student come stalking down the road. As already remarked, she had a great antipathy to him, and if ever he ventured into the house it was on sufferance, and under the protection of the Professor. Still more astonished was she, therefore, when she beheld him undo the wicket-gate and stride up the garden path with the air of one who is master of the situation. She could hardly believe her eyes, and hastened to the door with all her maternal instincts up in arms. From the upper windows the fair Elise had also observed this daring move upon the part of her lover, and her heart beat quick with mingled pride and consternation.

" Good day, sir," Madame Baumgarten remarked to the intruder, as she stood in gloomy majesty in the open doorway.

" A very fine day indeed, Martha," returned the other. " Now, don't stand there like a statue of Juno, but bustle about and get the dinner ready, for I am wellnigh starved."

" Martha ! Dinner ! " ejaculated the lady, falling back in astonishment.

" Yes, dinner, Martha, dinner ! " howled Von Hartmann, who was becoming irritable. " Is there anything wonderful in that request when a man has been out all day ? I'll wait in the dining-room. Anything will do. Schinken, and sausage, and prunes—any little thing that happens to be about. There you are, standing staring again. Woman, will you or will you not stir your legs ? "

This last address, delivered with a perfect shriek of rage, had the effect of sending good Madame Baumgarten flying along the passage and through the kitchen, where she locked herself up in the scullery and went into violent hysterics. In the meantime Von Hartmann strode into the room and threw himself down upon the sofa in the worst of tempers.

" Elise ! " he shouted. " Confound the girl ! Elise ! "

Thus roughly summoned, the young lady came timidly downstairs and into the presence of her lover. " Dearest ! " she cried, throwing her arms round him, " I know this is all done for my sake ! It is a *ruse* in order to see me."

Von Hartmann's indignation at this fresh attack upon him was so great that he became speechless for a minute from rage, and could only glare and shake his fists, while he struggled in her embrace. When he at last regained his utterance, he indulged in such a bellow of passion that the young lady dropped back, petrified with fear, into an arm-chair.

"Never have I passed such a day in my life," Von Hartmann cried, stamping upon the floor. "My experiment has failed. Von Althaus has insulted me. Two students have dragged me along the public road. My wife nearly faints when I ask her for dinner, and my daughter flies at me and hugs me like a grizzly bear."

"You are ill, dear," the young lady cried. "Your mind is wandering. You have not even kissed me once."

"No, and I don't intend to either," Von Hartmann said with decision. "You ought to be ashamed of yourself. Why don't you go and fetch my slippers, and help your mother to dish the dinner?"

"And is it for this," Elise cried, burying her face in her handkerchief—"is it for this that I have loved you passionately for upwards of ten months? Is it for this that I have braved my mother's wrath? Oh, you have broken my heart; I am sure you have!" and she sobbed hysterically.

"I can't stand much more of this," roared Von Hartmann furiously. "What the deuce does the girl mean? What did I do ten months ago which inspired you with such a particular affection for me? If you are really so very fond, you would do better to run away down and find the Schinken and some bread, instead of talking all this nonsense."

"Oh, my darling!" cried the unhappy maiden, throwing herself into the arms of what she imagined to be her lover, "you do but joke in order to frighten your little Elise."

Now it chanced that at the moment of this unexpected embrace Von Hartmann was still leaning back against the end of the sofa, which, like much German furniture, was in a somewhat rickety condition. It also chanced that beneath this end of the sofa there stood a tank full of water in which the physiologist was conducting certain experiments upon the ova of fish, and which he kept in his drawing-room in order to ensure an equable temperature. The additional weight of the maiden combined with the impetus with which she hurled herself upon him, caused the precarious piece of furniture to give way, and the body of the unfortunate student was hurled backwards into the tank, in which his head and shoulders were firmly wedged, while his lower extremities flapped helplessly about in the air. This was the last straw. Extricating himself with some difficulty from his unpleasant position, Von Hartmann gave an inarticulate yell of fury, and dashing out of the room, in spite of the entreaties of Elise, he seized his hat and rushed off into the town, all dripping and dishevelled, with the intention of seeking in some inn the food and comfort which he could not find at home.

As the spirit of Von Baumgarten encased in the body of Von Hartmann strode down the winding pathway which led down to the little town, brooding angrily over his many wrongs, he became aware that an elderly man was approaching him who appeared to be in an advanced state of intoxication. Von Hartmann waited by the side of the road and watched this individual, who came stumbling along, reeling from one side of the road to the other, and singing a student song in a very husky and drunken voice. At first his interest was merely excited by the fact of seeing a man of so venerable an appearance in such a disgraceful condition, but as he approached nearer, he became convinced that he knew the other well, though he could not recall when or where he had met him. This impression became so strong with him, that when the stranger came abreast of him he stepped in front of him and took a good look at his features.

"Well, sonny," said the drunken man, surveying Von Hartmann and swaying about in front of him, "where the Henker have I seen you before? I know you as well as I know myself. Who the deuce are you?"

"I am Professor von Baumgarten," said the student. "May I ask who you are? I am strangely familiar with your features."

"You should never tell lies, young man," said the other. "You're certainly not the Professor, for he is an ugly, snuffy old chap, and you are a big, broad-shouldered young fellow. As to myself, I am Fritz von Hartmann at your service."

"That you certainly are not," exclaimed the body of Von Hartmann. "You might very well be his father. But hullo, sir, are you aware that you are wearing my studs and my watch-chain?"

"Donnerwetter!" hiccoughed the other. "If those are not the trousers for which my tailor is about to sue me, may I never taste beer again."

Now as Von Hartmann, overwhelmed by the many strange things which had occurred to him that day, passed his hand over his forehead and cast his eyes downwards, he chanced to catch the reflection of his own face in a pool which the rain had left upon the road. To his utter astonishment he perceived that his face was that of a youth, that his dress was that of a fashionable young student, and that in every way he was the antithesis of the grave and scholarly figure in which his mind was wont to dwell. In an instant his active brain ran over the series of events which had occurred and sprang to the conclusion. He fairly reeled under the blow.

"Himmel!" he cried, "I see it all. Our souls are in the wrong bodies. I am you and you are I. My theory is proved—but at what an expense! Is the most scholarly mind in Europe to go about with this frivolous exterior? Oh, the labours of a lifetime are ruined!" and he smote his breast in his despair.

"I say," remarked the real Von Hartmann from the body of the Professor, "I quite see the force of your remarks, but don't go knocking my body about like that.

You received it in excellent condition, but I perceive that you have wet it and bruised it, and spilled snuff over my ruffled shirt-front."

"It matters little," the other said moodily. "Such as we are so must we stay. My theory is triumphantly proved, but the cost is terrible."

"If I thought so," said the spirit of the student, "it would be hard indeed. What could I do with these stiff old limbs, and how could I woo Elise and persuade her that I was not her father? No, thank Heaven, in spite of the beer which has upset me more than ever it could upset my real self, I can see a way out of it."

"How?" gasped the Professor.

"Why, by repeating the experiment. Liberate our souls once more, and the chances are that they will find their way back into their respective bodies."

No drowning man could clutch more eagerly at a straw than did Von Baumgarten's spirit at this suggestion. In feverish haste he dragged his own frame to the side of the road and threw it into a mesmeric trance; he then extracted the crystal ball from the pocket, and managed to bring himself into the same condition.

Some students and peasants who chanced to pass during the next hour were much astonished to see the worthy Professor of Physiology and his favourite student both sitting upon a very muddy bank and both completely insensible. Before the hour was up quite a crowd had assembled, and they were discussing the advisability of sending for an ambulance to convey the pair to hospital, when the learned savant opened his eyes and gazed vacantly around him. For an instant he seemed to forget how he had come there, but next moment he astonished his audience by waving his skinny arms above his head and crying out in a voice of rapture, "Gott sei gedanket! I am myself again. I feel I am!" Nor was the amazement lessened when the student, springing to his feet, burst into the same cry, and the two performed a sort of *pas de joie* in the middle of the road.

For some time after that people had some suspicion of the sanity of both the actors in this strange episode. When the Professor published his experiences in the *Medicalschrift* as he had promised, he was met by an intimation, even from his colleagues, that he would do well to have his mind cared for, and that another such publication would certainly consign him to a madhouse. The student also found by experience that it was wisest to be silent about the matter.

When the worthy lecturer returned home that night he did not receive the cordial welcome which he might have looked for after his strange adventures. On the contrary, he was roundly upbraided by both his female relatives for smelling of drink and tobacco, and also for being absent while a young scapegrace invaded the house and insulted its occupants. It was long before the domestic atmosphere of the lecturer's house resumed its normal quiet, and longer still before the genial face of Von Hartmann was seen beneath its roof. Perseverance, however, conquers every obstacle, and the student eventually succeeded in pacifying the enraged ladies and in establishing himself upon the old footing. He has now no longer any cause to fear the enmity of Madame, for he is Hauptmann von Hartmann of the Emperor's own Uhlans, and his loving wife Elise had already presented him with two little Uhlans as a visible sign and token of her affection.

A LITERARY MOSAIC

FROM my boyhood I have had an intense and overwhelming conviction that my real vocation lay in the direction of literature. I have, however, had a most unaccountable difficulty in getting any responsible person to share my views. It is true that private friends have sometimes, after listening to my effusions, gone the length of remarking, "Really, Smith, that's not half bad!" or, "You take my advice, old boy, and send that to some magazine!" but I have never on these occasions had the moral courage to inform my adviser that the article in question had been sent to well-nigh every publisher in London, and had come back again with a rapidity and precision which spoke well for the efficiency of our postal arrangements.

Had my manuscripts been paper boomerangs they could not have returned with greater accuracy to their unhappy despatcher. Oh, the vileness and utter degradation of the moment when the stale little cylinder of closely written pages, which seemed so fresh and full of promise a few days ago, is handed in by a remorseless postman! And what moral depravity shines through the editor's ridiculous plea of "want of space!" But the subject is a painful one, and a digression from the plain statement of facts which I originally contemplated.

From the age of seventeen to that of three-and-twenty I was a literary volcano in a constant state of eruption. Poems and tales, articles and reviews, nothing came amiss to my pen. From the great sea-serpent to the nebular hypothesis, I was ready to write on anything or everything, and I can safely say that I seldom handled a subject without throwing new lights upon it. Poetry and romance, however, had always the greatest attractions for me. How I have wept over the pathos of my heroines, and laughed at the comicalities of my buffoons! Alas! I could find no one to join me in my appreciation, and solitary admiration for one's self, however genuine, becomes satiating after a time. My father remonstrated with me too on the score of expense and loss of time, so that I was finally compelled to relinquish my dreams of literary independence and to become a clerk in a wholesale mercantile firm connected with the West African trade.

Even when condemned to the prosaic duties which fell to my lot in the office, I continued faithful to my first love. I have introduced pieces of word-painting into the most commonplace business letters which have, I am told, considerably astonished the recipients. My refined sarcasm has made defaulting creditors writhe and wince. Occasionally, like the great Silas Wegg, I would drop into poetry, and so raise the whole tone of the correspondence. Thus what could be more elegant than my rendering of the firm's instructions to the captain of one of their vessels. It ran in this way :—

"From England, Captain, you must steer a
Course directly to Madeira,
Land the casks of salted beef,
Then away to Teneriffe.
Pray be careful, cool, and wary
With the merchants of Canary.
When you leave them make the most
Of the trade-winds to the coast.
Down it you shall sail as far
As the land of Calabar,
And from there you'll onward go
To Bonny and Fernando Po"——

and so on for four pages. The captain, instead of treasuring up this little gem, called at the office next day, and demanded with quite unnecessary warmth what the thing meant, and I was compelled to translate it all back into prose. On this, as on other similar occasions, my employer took me severely to task—for he was, you see, a man entirely devoid of all pretensions to literary taste!

All this, however, is a mere preamble, and leads up to the fact that after ten years or so of drudgery I inherited a legacy which, though small, was sufficient to satisfy my simple wants. Finding myself independent, I rented a quiet house removed from the uproar and bustle of London, and there I settled down with the intention of producing some great work which should single me out from the family of the Smiths, and render my name immortal. To this end I laid in several quires of foolscap, a box of quill pens, and a sixpenny bottle of ink, and having given my housekeeper injunctions to deny me to all visitors, I proceeded to look round for a suitable subject.

I was looking round for some weeks. At the end of that time I found that I had by constant nibbling devoured a large number of the quills, and had spread the ink out to such advantage, what with blots, spills, and abortive commencements, that there appeared to be some everywhere except in the bottle. As to the story itself, however, the facility of my youth had deserted me completely, and my mind remained a complete blank; nor could I, do what I would, excite my sterile imagination to conjure up a single incident or character.

In this strait I determined to devote my leisure to running rapidly through the works of the leading English novelists, from Daniel Defoe to the present day, in the hope of stimulating my latent ideas and of getting a good grasp of the general tendency of literature. For some time past I had avoided opening any work of fiction because one of the greatest faults of my youth had been that I invariably and unconsciously mimicked the style of the last author whom I had happened to read. Now, however, I made up my mind to seek safety in a multitude, and by consulting *all* the English classics to avoid the danger of imitating any one too closely. I had just accomplished the task of reading through the majority of the standard novels at the time when my narrative commences.

It was, then, about twenty minutes to ten on the night of the fourth of June, eighteen hundred and eighty-six, that, after disposing of a pint of beer and a Welsh rarebit for my supper, I seated myself in my arm-chair, cocked my feet upon a stool, and lit my pipe, as was my custom. Both my pulse and my temperature were, as far as I know, normal at the time. I would give the state of the barometer, but that unlucky instrument had experienced an unprecedented fall of forty-two inches—from a nail to the ground—and was not in a reliable condition. We live in a scientific age, and I flatter myself that I move with the times.

Whilst in that comfortable lethargic condition which accompanies both digestion and poisoning by nicotine, I suddenly became aware of the extraordinary fact that my little drawing-room had elongated into a great *salon*, and that my humble table had increased in proportion. Round this colossal mahogany were seated a great number of people who were talking earnestly together, and the surface in front of them was strewn with books and pamphlets. I could not help observing that these persons were dressed in a most extraordinary mixture of costumes, for those at the end nearest to me wore peruke wigs, swords, and all the fashions of two centuries back; those about the centre had tight knee-breeches, high cravats, and heavy bunches of seals; while among those at the far side the majority were dressed in the most modern style, and among them I saw, to my surprise, several eminent men of letters whom I had the honour of knowing. There were two or three women in the company. I should have risen to my feet to greet these unexpected guests, but all power of motion appeared to have deserted me, and I could only lie still and listen to their conversation, which I soon perceived to be all about myself.

"Egad!" exclaimed a rough, weather-beaten man, who was smoking a long churchwarden pipe at my end of the table, "my heart softens for him. Why, gossips, we've been in the same straits ourselves. Gadzooks, never did mother feel more concern for her eldest born than I when Rory Random went out to make his own way in the world."

"Right, Tobias, right!" cried another man, seated at my very elbow. "By my troth, I lost more flesh over poor Robin on his island, than had I the sweating sickness twice told. The tale was well-nigh done when in swaggers my Lord of Rochester—a merry gallant, and one whose word in matters literary might make or mar. 'How now, Defoe,' quoth he, 'hast a tale on hand?' 'Even so, your lordship,' I returned. 'A right merry one, I trust,' quoth he. 'Discourse unto me concerning thy heroine, a comely lass, Dan, or I mistake.' 'Nay,' I replied, 'there is no heroine in the matter.' 'Split not your phrases,' quoth he; 'thou weighest every word like a scald attorney. Speak to me of thy principal female character, be she heroine or no.' 'My lord,' I answered, 'there is no female character.' 'Then out upon thyself and thy book too!' he cried. 'Thou hadst best burn it!'—and so out in great dudgeon, whilst I fell to mourning over my poor romance, which was thus, as it were, sentenced to death before its birth. Yet there are a thousand now who have heard of Robin and his man Friday, to one who has heard of my Lord of Rochester."

"Very true, Defoe," said a genial-looking man in a red waistcoat, who was sitting at the modern end of the table. "But all this won't help our good friend Smith in making a start at his story, which, I believe, was the reason why we assembled."

"The Dickens it is!" stammered a little man beside him, and everybody laughed, especially the genial man, who cried out, "Charley Lamb, Charley Lamb, you'll never alter. You would make a pun if you were hanged for it."

"That would be a case of haltering," returned the other, on which everybody laughed again.

By this time I had begun to dimly realize in my confused brain the enormous honour which had been done me. The greatest masters of fiction in every age of English letters had apparently made a rendezvous beneath my roof, in order to assist me in my difficulties. There were many faces at the table whom I was unable to identify; but when I looked hard at others I often found them to be very familiar to me, whether from paintings or from mere description. Thus between the first two speakers, who had betrayed themselves as Defoe and Smollett, there sat a dark, saturnine, corpulent old man, with harsh prominent features, who I was sure could be none other than the famous author of Gulliver. There were several others of whom I was not so sure, sitting at the other side of the table, but I conjecture that both Fielding and Richardson were among them, and I could swear to the lantern-jaws and cadaverous visage of Lawrence Sterne. Higher up I could see among the crowd the high forehead of Sir Walter Scott, the masculine features of George Eliott, and the flattened nose of Thackeray; while amongst the living I recognised James Payn, Walter Besant, the lady known as "Ouida," Robert Louis Stevenson, and several of lesser note. Never before, probably, had such an assemblage of choice spirits gathered under one roof.

"Well," said Sir Walter Scott, speaking with a very pronounced accent, "ye ken the auld proverb, sirs, 'Ower mony cooks,' or as the Border minstrel sang—

'Black Johnstone wi' his troopers ten
Might mak' the heart turn cauld,
But Johnstone when he's a' alane
Is waur ten thoosand fauld.'

The Johnstones were one of the Redesdale families, second cousins of the Armstrongs, and connected by marriage to——"

"Perhaps, Sir Walter," interrupted Thackeray, "you would take the responsibility off our hands by yourself dictating the commencement of a story to this young literary aspirant."

"Na, na!" cried Sir Walter; "I'll do my share, but there's Chairlie over there as full o' wut as a Radical's full o' treason. He's the laddie to give a cheery opening to it."

Dickens was shaking his head, and apparently about to refuse the honour, when a voice from among the moderns—I could not see who it was for the crowd—said:

"Suppose we begin at the end of the table and work round, anyone contributing a little as the fancy seizes him?"

"Agreed! agreed!" cried the whole company; and every eye was turned on Defoe, who seemed very uneasy, and filled his pipe from a great tobacco-box in front of him.

"Nay, gossips," he said, "there are others more worthy——"

But he was interrupted by loud cries of "No! no!" from the whole table; and Smollett shouted out, "Stand to it, Dan—stand to it! You and I and the Dean here will make three short tacks just to fetch her out of harbour, and then she may drift where she pleases." Thus encouraged, Defoe cleared his throat, and began in this way, talking between the puffs of his pipe:—

"My father was a well-to-do yeoman of Cheshire, named Cyprian Overbeck, but, marrying about the year 1617, he assumed the name of his wife's family, which was Wells; and thus I, their eldest son, was named Cyprian Overbeck Wells. The farm was a very fertile one, and contained some of the best grazing land in those parts, so that my father was enabled to lay by money to the extent of a thousand crowns, which he laid out in an adventure to the Indies with such surprising success that in less than three years it had increased fourfold. Thus encouraged, he bought a part share of the trader, and, fitting her out once more with such commodities as were most in demand (viz. old muskets, hangars and axes, besides glasses, needles, and the like), he placed me on board as supercargo to look after his interests, and dispatched us upon our voyage.

"We had a fair wind as far as Cape de Verde, and there, getting into the north-west trade-winds, made good progress down the African coast. Beyond sighting a Barbary rover once, whereat our mariners were in sad distress, counting themselves already as little better than slaves, we had good luck until we had come within a hundred leagues of the Cape of Good Hope, when the wind veered round to the southward and blew exceeding hard, while the sea rose to such a height that the end of the mainyard dipped into the water, and I heard the master say that though he had been at sea for five-and-thirty years he had never seen the like of it, and that he had little expectation of riding through it. On this I fell to wringing my hands and bewailing myself, until the mast going by the board with a crash, I thought that the ship had struck, and swooned with terror, falling into the scuppers and lying like one dead, which was the saving of me, as will appear in the sequel. For the mariners, giving up all hope of saving the ship, and being in momentary expectation that she would founder, pushed off in the long-boat, whereby I fear that they met the fate which they hoped to avoid, since I have never from that day heard anything of them. For my own part, on recovering from the swoon into which I had fallen, I found that, by the mercy of Providence, the sea had gone down, and that I was alone in the vessel. At which last discovery I was so terror-struck that I could but stand wringing my hands and bewailing my sad fate, until at last taking heart, I fell to comparing my lot with that of my unhappy camerados, on which I became more cheerful, and descending to the cabin, made a meal off such dainties as were in the captain's locker."

Having got so far, Defoe remarked that he thought he had given them a fair start, and handed over the story to Dean Swift, who, after premising that he feared he would find himself as much at sea as Master Cyprian Overbeck Wells, continued in this way :—

" For two days I drifted about in great distress, fearing that there should be a return of the gale, and keeping an eager look-out for my late companions. Upon the third day, towards evening, I observed to my extreme surprise that the ship was under the influence of a very powerful current, which ran to the north-east with such violence that she was carried, now bows on, now stern on, and occasionally drifting sideways like a crab, at a rate which I cannot compute at less than twelve or fifteen knots an hour. For several weeks I was borne away in this manner, until one morning, to my inexpressible joy, I sighted an island upon the starboard quarter. The current would, however, have carried me past it had I not made shift, though single-handed, to set the flying-jib so as to turn her bows, and then clapping on the sprit-sail, studding-sail, and fore-sail, I clewed up the halliards upon the port side, and put the wheel down hard a-star-board, the wind being at the time north-east-half-east."

At the description of this nautical manœuvre I observed that Smollett grinned, and a gentleman who was sitting higher up the table in the uniform of the Royal Navy, and who I guessed to be Captain Marryat, became very uneasy and fidgeted in his seat.

"By this means I got clear of the current and was able to steer within a quarter of a mile of the beach, which indeed I might have approached still nearer by making another tack, but being an excellent swimmer, I deemed it best to leave the vessel, which was almost waterlogged, and to make the best of my way to the shore.

"I had had my doubts hitherto as to whether this new-found country was inhabited or no, but as I approached nearer to it, being on the summit of a great wave, I perceived a number of figures on the beach, engaged apparently in watching me and my vessel. My joy, however, was considerably lessened when on reaching the land I found that the figures consisted of a vast concourse of animals of various sorts who were standing about in groups, and who hurried down to the water's edge to meet me. I had scarce put my foot upon the sand before I was surrounded by an eager crowd of deer, dogs, wild boars, buffaloes, and other creatures, none of whom showed the least fear either of me or of each other, but, on the contrary, were animated by a common feeling of curiosity, as well as, it would appear, by some degree of disgust."

"A second edition," whispered Lawrence Sterne to his neighbour; "Gulliver served up cold."

"Did you speak, sir?" asked the Dean very sternly, having evidently overheard the remark.

"My words were not addressed to you, sir," answered Sterne, looking rather frightened.

"They were none the less insolent," roared the Dean. "Your reverence would fain make a Sentimental Journey of the narrative, I doubt not, and find pathos in a dead donkey—though, faith, no man can blame thee for mourning over thy own kith and kin."

"Better that than to wallow in all the filth of Yahoo-land," returned Sterne warmly, and a quarrel would certainly have ensued but for the interposition of the remainder of the company. As it was, the Dean refused indignantly to have any further hand in the story, and Sterne also stood out of it, remarking with a sneer that he was loth to fit a good blade on to a poor handle. Under these circumstances some further unpleasantness might have occurred had not Smollett rapidly taken up the narrative, continuing it in the third person instead of the first:—

"Our hero, being considerably alarmed at this strange reception, lost little time in plunging into the sea again and regaining his vessel, being convinced that the worst which might befall him from the elements would be as nothing compared to the dangers of this mysterious island. It was as well that he took this course, for before nightfall his ship was overhauled and he himself picked up by a British man-of-war, the *Lightning* (74), then returning from the West Indies, where it had formed part of the fleet under the command of Admiral Benbow. Young Wells, being a likely lad enough, well-spoken and high-spirited, was at once entered on the books as officer's servant, in which capacity he both gained great popularity on account of the freedom of his manners, and found an opportunity for indulging in those practical pleasantries for which he had all his life been famous.

"Among the quartermasters of the *Lightning* there was one named Jedediah Anchorstock, whose appearance was so remarkable that it quickly attracted the attention of our hero. He was a man of about fifty, dark with exposure to the weather, and so tall that as he came along the 'tween decks he had to bend himself nearly double. The most striking peculiarity of this individual was, however, that in his boyhood some evil-minded person had tattooed eyes all over his countenance with such marvellous skill that it was difficult at a short distance to pick out his real ones among so many counterfeits. On this strange personage Master Cyprian determined to exercise his talents for mischief, the more so as he learned that he was extremely superstitious, and also that he had left behind him in Portsmouth a strong-minded spouse of whom he stood in mortal terror. With this object he secured one of the sheep which were kept on board for the officer's table, and pouring a can of rumbo down its throat, reduced it to a state of utter intoxication. He then conveyed it to Anchorstock's berth, and with the assistance of some other imps, as mischievous as himself, dressed it up in a high nightcap and gown, and covered it over with the bedclothes.

" When the quartermaster came down from his watch our hero met him at the door of his berth with an agitated face. 'Mr. Anchorstock,' said he, 'can it be that your wife is on board?' 'Wife!' roared the astonished sailor. 'Ye white-faced swab, what d'ye mean?' 'If she's not here in the ship it must be her ghost,' said Cyprian, shaking his head gloomily. 'In the ship! How in thunder could she get into the ship? Why, master, I believe as how you're weak in the upper works, d'ye see? to as much as think o' such a thing. My Poll is moored head and starn, behind the point at Portsmouth, more'n two thousand mile away.' 'Upon my word,' said our hero, very earnestly, 'I saw a female look out of your cabin not five minutes ago.' 'Ay, ay, Mr. Anchorstock,' joined in several of the conspirators. 'We all saw her—a spanking-looking craft with a dead-light mounted on one side.' 'Sure enough,' said Anchorstock, staggered by this accumulation of evidence, 'my Polly's starboard eye was doused for ever by long Sue Williams of the Hard. But if so be as she be there I must see her, be she ghost or quick'; with which the honest sailor, in much perturbation and trembling in every limb, began to shuffle forward into the cabin, holding the light well in front of him. It chanced, however, that the unhappy sheep, which was quietly engaged in sleeping off the effects of its unusual potations, was awakened by the noise of his approach, and finding herself in such an unusual position, sprang out of bed and rushed furiously for the door, bleating wildly, and rolling about like a brig in a tornado, partly from intoxication and partly from the nightdress which impeded her movements. As Anchorstock saw this extraordinary apparition bearing down upon him, he uttered a yell and fell flat upon his face, convinced that he had to do with a supernatural visitor, the more so as the confederates heightened the effect by a chorus of most ghastly groans and cries. The joke had nearly gone beyond what was originally intended, for the quartermaster lay as one dead, and it was only with the greatest difficulty that he could be brought to his senses. To the end of the voyage he stoutly asserted that he had seen the distant Mrs. Anchorstock, remarking with many oaths that though he was too woundily scared to take much note of the features, there was no mistaking the strong smell of rum which was characteristic of his better half.

"It chanced shortly after this to be the king's birthday, an event which was signalised aboard the *Lightning* by the death of the commander under singular circumstances. This officer, who was a real fair-weather Jack, hardly knowing the ship's keel from her ensign, had obtained his position through parliamentary interest, and used it with such tyranny and cruelty that he was universally execrated. So unpopular was he that when a plot was entered into by the whole crew to punish his misdeeds with death, he had not a single friend among six hundred souls to warn him of his danger. It was the custom on board the king's ships that upon his birthday the entire ship's company should be drawn up upon deck, and that at a signal they should discharge their muskets into the air in honour of his Majesty. On this occasion word had been secretly passed round for every man to slip a slug into his firelock, instead of the blank cartridge provided. On the boatswain blowing his whistle the men mustered upon deck and formed line, whilst the captain, standing well in front of them, delivered a few words to them. 'When I give the word,' he concluded, 'you shall discharge your pieces, and by thunder, if any man is a second before or a second after his fellows I shall trice him up to the weather rigging!' With these words he roared 'Fire!' on which every man levelled his musket straight at his head and pulled the trigger. So accurate was the aim and so short the distance, that more than five hundred bullets struck him simultaneously, blowing away his head and a large portion of his body. There were so many concerned in this matter, and it was so hopeless to trace it to any individual, that the officers were unable to punish anyone for the affair—the more readily as the captain's haughty ways and heartless conduct had made him quite as hateful to them as to the men whom he commanded.

"By his pleasantries and the natural charm of his manners our hero so far won the good wishes of the ship's company that they parted with infinite regret upon their arrival in England. Filial duty, however, urged him to return home and report himself to his father, with which object he posted from Portsmouth to London, intending to proceed thence to Shropshire. As it chanced, however, one of the horses sprained his off foreleg while passing through Chichester, and as no change could be obtained, Cyprian found himself compelled to put up at the Crown and Bull for the night.

"Ods bodikins!" continued Smollett, laughing, "I never could pass a comfortable hostel without stopping and so, with your permission, I'll e'en stop here, and whoever wills may lead friend Cyprian to his further adventures. Do you, Sir Walter, give us a touch of the Wizard of the North."

With these words Smollett produced a pipe, and filling it at Defoe's tobacco-pot, waited patiently for the continuation of the story.

"If I must, I must," remarked the illustrious Scotchman, taking a pinch of snuff; "but I must beg leave to put Mr. Wells back a few hundred years, for of all things I love the true mediæval smack. To proceed then:—

"Our hero being anxious to continue his journey, and learning that it would be some time before any conveyance would be ready, determined to push on alone mounted on his gallant grey steed. Travelling was particularly dangerous at that time, for besides the usual perils which beset wayfarers, the southern parts of England were in a lawless and disturbed state which bordered on insurrection. The young man, however, having loosened his sword in his sheath, so as to be ready for every eventuality, galloped cheerily upon his way, guiding himself to the best of his ability by the light of the rising moon.

"He had not gone far before he realised that the cautions which had been impressed upon him by the landlord, and which he had been inclined to look upon as self-interested advice, were only too well justified. At a spot where the road was particularly rough, and ran across some marshland, he perceived a short distance from him a dark shadow, which his practised eye detected at once as a body of crouching men. Reining up his horse within a few yards of the ambuscade, he wrapped his cloak round his bridle-arm and summoned the party to stand forth.

"'What ho, my masters!' he cried. 'Are beds so scarce, then, that ye must hamper the high road of the king with your bodies? Now, by St. Ursula of Alpuxerra, there be those who might think that birds who fly o' nights were after higher game than the moorhen or the woodcock!'

"'Blades and targets, comrades!' exclaimed a tall powerful man, springing into the centre of the road with several companions, and standing in front of the frightened horse. 'Who is this swashbuckler who summons his Majesty's lieges from their repose? A very soldado, o' truth. Hark ye, sir, or my lord, or thy grace, or whatsoever title your honour's honour may be pleased to approve, thou must curb thy tongue play, or by the seven witches of Gambleside thou may find thyself in but a sorry plight.'

"'I prythee, then, that thou wilt expound to me who and what ye are,' quoth our hero, 'and whether your purpose be such as an honest man may approve of. As to your threats, they turn from my mind as your caitiffly weapons would shiver upon my hauberk from Milan.'

"'Nay, Allen,' interrupted one of the party, addressing him who seemed to be their leader; 'this is a lad of mettle, and such a one as our honest Jack longs for. But we lure not hawks with empty hands. Look ye, sir, there is game afoot which it may need such bold hunters as thyself to follow. Come with us and take a firkin of canary, and we will find better work for that glaive of thine than getting its owner into broil and bloodshed; for, by my troth! Milan or no Milan, if my curtel axe do but ring against that morion of thine it will be an ill day for thy father's son.'

"For a moment our hero hesitated as to whether it would best become his knightly traditions to hurl himself against his enemies, or whether it might not be better to obey their requests. Prudence, mingled with a large share of curiosity, eventually carried the day, and dismounting from his horse, he intimated that he was ready to follow his captors.

"'Spoken like a man!' cried he whom they addressed as Allen. 'Jack Cade will be right glad of such a recruit. Blood and carrion! but thou hast the thews of a young ox; and I swear, by the haft of my sword, that it might have gone ill with some of us hadst thou not listened to reason!'

"'Nay, not so, good Allen—not so,' squeaked a very small man, who had remained in the background while there was any prospect of a fray, but who now came pushing to the front. 'Hadst thou been alone it might indeed have been so, perchance, but an expert swordsman can disarm at pleasure such a one as this young knight. Well I remember in the Palatinate how I clove to the chine even such another—the Baron von Slogstaff. He struck at me, look ye, so; but I, with buckler and blade, did, as one might say, deflect it; and then, countering in carte, I returned in tierce, and so—St. Agnes save us! who comes here?'

"The apparition which frightened the loquacious little man was sufficiently strange to cause a qualm even in the bosom of the knight. Through the darkness there loomed a figure which appeared to be of gigantic size, and a hoarse voice, issuing apparently some distance above the heads of the party, broke roughly on the silence of the night.

"'Now out upon thee, Thomas Allen, and foul be thy fate if thou hast abandoned thy post without good and sufficient cause. By St. Anselm of the Holy Grove, thou hadst best have never been born than rouse my spleen this night. Wherefore is it that you and your men are trailing over the moor like a flock of geese when Michaelmas is near?'

"'Good captain,' said Allen, doffing his bonnet, an example followed by others of the band, 'we have captured a goodly youth who was pricking it along the London road. Methought that some word of thanks were meet reward for such service, rather than taunt or threat.'

"'Nay, take it not to heart, bold Allen,' exclaimed their leader, who was none other than the great Jack Cade himself. 'Thou knowest of old that my temper is somewhat choleric, and my tongue not greased with that unguent which oils the mouths of the lip-serving lords of the land. And you,' he continued, turning suddenly upon our hero, 'are you ready to join the great cause which will make England what it was when the learned Alfred reigned in the land? Zounds, man, speak out, and pick not your phrases.'

"'I am ready to do aught which may become a knight and a gentleman,' said the soldier stoutly.

"'Taxes shall be swept away!' cried Cade excitedly —'the impost and the anpost—the tithe and the hundred-tax. The poor man's salt-box and flour-bin shall be as free as the nobleman's cellar. Ha! what sayest thou?'

"'It is but just,' said our hero.

"'Ay, but they give us such justice as the falcon gives the leveret!' roared the orator. 'Down with them, I say—down with every man of them! Noble and judge, priest and king, down with them all!'

"'Nay,' said Sir Overbeck Wells, drawing himself up to his full height, and laying his hand upon the hilt of his sword, 'there I cannot follow thee, but must rather defy thee as traitor and fainéant, seeing that thou art no true man, but one who would usurp the rights of our master the king, whom may the Virgin protect!'

"At these bold words, and the defiance which they conveyed, the rebels seemed for a moment utterly bewildered; but, encouraged by the hoarse shout of their leader they brandished their weapons and prepared to fall upon the knight, who placed himself in a posture for defence and awaited their attack.

"There now!" cried Sir Walter, rubbing his hands and chuckling, "I've put the chiel in a pretty warm corner, and we'll see which of you moderns can take him oot o't. Ne'er a word more will ye get frae me to help him one way or the other."

"You try your hand, James," cried several voices, and the author in question had got so far as to make an allusion to a solitary horseman who was approaching, when he was interrupted by a tall gentleman a little farther down with a slight stutter and a very nervous manner.

"Excuse me," he said, "but I fancy that I may be able to do something here. Some of my humble productions have been said to excel Sir Walter at his best, and I was undoubtedly stronger all round. I could picture modern society as well as ancient; and as to my plays, why Shakespeare never came near *The Lady of Lyons* for popularity. There is this little thing——" (Here he rummaged among a great pile of papers in front of him). "Ah! that's a report of mine, when I was in India! Here it is. No, this is one of my speeches in the House, and this is my criticism on Tennyson. Didn't I warm him up? I can't find what I wanted, but of course you have read them all—*Rienzi*, and *Harold*, and *The Last of the Barons*. Every schoolboy knows them by heart, as poor Macaulay would have said. Allow me to give you a sample:—

"In spite of the gallant knight's valiant resistance the combat was too unequal to be sustained. His sword was broken by a slash from a brown bill, and he was borne to the ground. He expected immediate death, but such did not seem to be the intention of the ruffians who had captured him. He was placed upon the back of his own charger and borne, bound hand and foot, over the trackless moor, in the fastnesses of which the rebels secreted themselves.

"In the depths of these wilds there stood a stone building which had once been a farmhouse, but having been for some reason abandoned had fallen into ruin, and had now become the headquarters of Cade and his men. A large cow-house near the farm had been utilised as sleeping quarters, and some rough attempts had been made to shield the principal room of the main building from the weather by stopping up the gaping apertures in the walls. In this apartment was spread out a rough meal for the returning rebels, and our hero was thrown, still bound, into an empty outhouse, there to await his fate."

Sir Walter had been listening with the greatest impatience to Bulwer Lytton's narrative, but when it had reached this point he broke in impatiently.

"We want a touch of your own style, man," he said. "The animal-magnetico-electro-hysterical-biological-mysterious sort of story is all your own, but at present you are just a poor copy of myself, and nothing more."

There was a murmur of assent from the company, and Defoe remarked, "Truly, Master Lytton, there is a plaguey resemblance in the style, which may indeed be but a chance, and yet methinks it is sufficiently marked to warrant such words as our friend hath used."

"Perhaps you will think that this is an imitation also," said Lytton bitterly, and leaning back in his chair with a morose countenance, he continued the narrative in this way:—

"Our unfortunate hero had hardly stretched himself upon the straw with which his dungeon was littered, when a secret door opened in the wall and a venerable old man swept majestically into the apartment. The prisoner gazed upon him with astonishment not unmixed with awe, for on his broad brow was printed the seal of much knowledge—such knowledge as it is not granted to a son of man to know. He was clad in a long white robe, crossed and chequered with mystic devices in the Arabic character, while a high scarlet tiara marked with the square and circle enhanced his venerable appearance. 'My son,' he said, turning his piercing and yet dreamy gaze upon Sir Overbeck, 'all things lead to nothing, and nothing is the foundation of all things. Cosmos is impenetrable. Why then should we exist?'

"Astounded at this weighty query, and at the philosophic demeanour of his visitor, our hero made shift to bid him welcome and to demand his name and quality. As the old man answered him his voice rose and fell in musical cadences, like the sighing of the east wind, while an ethereal and aromatic vapour pervaded the apartment.

" 'I am the eternal non-ego,' he answered. 'I am the concentrated negative—the everlasting essence of nothing. You see in me that which existed before the beginning of matter many years before the commencement of time. I am the algebraic *x* which represents the infinite divisibility of a finite particle.'

" Sir Overbeck felt a shudder as though an ice-cold hand had been placed upon his brow. 'What is your message?' he whispered, falling prostrate before his mysterious visitor.

" 'To tell you that the eternities beget chaos, and that the immensities are at the mercy of the divine ananke. Infinitude crouches before a personality. The mercurial essence is the prime mover in spirituality, and the thinker is powerless before the pulsating inanity. The cosmical procession is terminated only by the unknowable and unpronounceable '——

" May I ask, Mr. Smollett, what you find to laugh at?"

" Gadzooks, master," cried Smollett, who had been sniggering for some time back. " It seems to me that there is little danger of anyone venturing to dispute that style with you."

" It's all your own," murmured Sir Walter.

" And very pretty, too," quoth Lawrence Sterne, with a malignant grin. " Pray, sir, what language do you call it?"

Lytton was so enraged at these remarks, and at the favour with which they appeared to be received, that he endeavoured to stutter out some reply, and then, losing control of himself completely, picked up all his loose papers and strode out of the room, dropping pamphlets and speeches at every step. This incident amused the company so much that they laughed for several minutes without cessation. Gradually the sound of their laughter sounded more and more harshly in my ears, the lights on the table grew dim and the company more misty, until they and their symposium vanished away altogether. I was sitting before the embers of what had been a roaring fire, but was now little more than a heap of grey ashes, and the merry laughter of the august company had changed to the recriminations of my wife, who was shaking me violently by the shoulder and exhorting me to choose some more seasonable spot for my slumbers. So ended the wondrous adventures of Master Cyprian Overbeck Wells, but I still live in the hopes that in some future dream the great masters may themselves finish that which they have begun.

PLAYING WITH FIRE

I CANNOT pretend to say what occurred on the 14th of April last at No. 17, Badderly Gardens. Put down in black and white, my surmise might seem too crude, too grotesque, for serious consideration. And yet that something did occur, and that it was of a nature which will leave its mark upon every one of us for the rest of our lives, is as certain as the unanimous testimony of five witnesses can make it. I will not enter into any argument or speculation. I will only give a plain statement, which will be submitted to John Moir, Harvey Deacon, and Mrs. Delamere, and withheld from publication unless they are prepared to corroborate every detail. I cannot obtain the sanction of Paul Le Duc, for he appears to have left the country.

It was John Moir (the well-known senior partner of Moir, Moir, and Sanderson) who had originally turned our attention to occult subjects. He had, like many very hard and practical men of business, a mystic side to his nature, which had led him to the examination, and eventually to the acceptance, of those elusive phenomena which are grouped together with much that is foolish, and much that is fraudulent, under the common heading of spiritualism. His researches, which had begun with an open mind, ended unhappily in dogma, and he became as positive and fanatical as any other bigot. He represented in our little group the body of men who have turned these singular phenomena into a new religion.

Mrs. Delamere, our medium, was his sister, the wife of Delamere, the rising sculptor. Our experience had shown us that to work on these subjects without a medium was as futile as for an astronomer to make observations without a telescope. On the other hand, the introduction of a paid medium was hateful to all of us. Was it not obvious that he or she would feel bound to return some result for money received, and that the temptation to fraud would be an overpowering one? No phenomena could be relied upon which were produced at a guinea an hour. But, fortunately, Moir had discovered that his sister was mediumistic—in other words, that she was a battery of that animal magnetic force which is the only form of energy which is subtle enough to be acted upon from the spiritual plane as well as from our own material one. Of course, when I say this, I do not mean to beg the question; but I am simply indicating the theories upon which we were ourselves, rightly or wrongly, explaining what we saw. The lady came, not altogether with the approval of her husband, and though she never gave indications of any very great psychic force, we were able, at least, to obtain those usual phenomena of message-tilting which are at the same time so puerile and so inexplicable. Every Sunday evening we met in Harvey Deacon's studio at Badderly Gardens, the next house to the corner of Merton Park Road.

Harvey Deacon's imaginative work in art would prepare anyone to find that he was an ardent lover of everything which was *outré* and sensational. A certain picturesqueness in the study of the occult had been the quality which had originally attracted him to it, but his attention was speedily arrested by some of those phenomena to which I have referred, and he was coming rapidly to the conclusion that what he had looked upon as an amusing romance and an after-dinner entertainment was really a very formidable reality. He is a man with a remarkably clear and logical brain—a true descendant of his ancestor, the well-known Scotch professor—and he represented in our small circle the critical element, the man who has no prejudices, is prepared to follow facts as far as he can see them, and refuses to theorise in advance of his data. His caution annoyed Moir as much as the latter's robust faith amused Deacon, but each in his own way was equally keen upon the matter.

And I? What am I to say that I represented? I was not the devotee. I was not the scientific critic. Perhaps the best that I can claim for myself is that I was the dilettante man about town, anxious to be in the swim of every fresh movement, thankful for any new sensation which would take me out of myself and open up fresh possibilities of existence. I am not an enthusiast myself, but I like the company of those who are. Moir's talk, which made me feel as if we had a private pass-key through the door of death, filled me with a vague contentment. The soothing atmosphere of the séance with the darkened lights was delightful to me. In a word, the thing amused me, and so I was there.

It was, as I have said, upon the 14th of April last that the very singular event which I am about to put upon record took place. I was the first of the men to arrive at the studio, but Mrs. Delamere was already there, having had afternoon tea with Mrs. Harvey Deacon. The two ladies and Deacon himself were standing in front of an unfinished picture of his upon the easel. I am not an expert in art, and I have never professed to understand what Harvey Deacon meant by his pictures; but I could see in this instance that it was all very clever and imaginative, fairies and animals and allegorical figures of all sorts. The ladies were loud in their praises, and indeed the colour effect was a remarkable one.

"What do you think of it, Markham?" he asked.

"Well, it's above me," said I. "These beasts—what are they?"

"Mythical monsters, imaginary creatures, heraldic emblems—a sort of weird, bizarre procession of them."

"With a white horse in front!"

"It's not a horse," said he, rather testily—which was surprising, for he was a very good-humoured fellow as a rule, and hardly ever took himself seriously.

"What is it, then?"

"Can't you see the horn in front? It's a unicorn. I told you they were heraldic beasts. Can't you recognize one?"

"Very sorry, Deacon," said I, for he really seemed to be annoyed.

He laughed at his own irritation.

"Excuse me, Markham!" said he; "the fact is that I have had an awful job over the beast. All day I have been painting him in and painting him out, and trying to imagine what a real live, ramping unicorn would look like. At last I got him, as I hoped; so when you failed to recognise it, it took me on the raw."

"Why, of course it's a unicorn," said I, for he was evidently depressed at my obtuseness. "I can see the horn quite plainly, but I never saw a unicorn except beside the Royal Arms, and so I never thought of the creature. And these others are griffins and cockatrices, and dragons of sorts?"

"Yes, I had no difficulty with them. It was the unicorn which bothered me. However, there's an end of it until to-morrow." He turned the picture round upon the easel, and we all chatted about other subjects.

Moir was late that evening, and when he did arrive he brought with him, rather to our surprise, a small, stout Frenchman, whom he introduced as Monsieur Paul Le Duc. I say to our surprise, for we held a theory that any intrusion into our spiritual circle deranged the conditions, and introduced an element of suspicion. We knew that we could trust each other, but all our results were vitiated by the presence of an outsider. However, Moir soon reconciled us to the innovation. Monsieur Paul Le Duc was a famous student of occultism, a seer, a medium, and a mystic. He was travelling in England with a letter of introduction to Moir from the President of the Parisian brothers of the Rosy Cross. What more natural than that he should bring him to our little séance, or that we should feel honoured by his presence?

He was, as I have said, a small, stout man, undistinguished in appearance, with a broad, smooth, clean-shaven face, remarkable only for a pair of large, brown, velvety eyes, staring vaguely out in front of him. He was well dressed, with the manners of a gentleman, and his curious little turns of English speech set the ladies smiling. Mrs. Deacon had a prejudice against our researches and left the room, upon which we lowered the lights, as was our custom, and drew up our chairs to the square mahogany table which stood in the centre of the studio. The light was subdued, but sufficient to allow us to see each other quite plainly. I remember that I could even observe the curious, podgy little square-topped hands which the Frenchman laid upon the table.

"What a fun!" said he. "It is many years since I have sat in this fashion, and it is to me amusing. Madame is medium. Does madame make the trance?"

"Well, hardly that," said Mrs. Delamere. "But I am always conscious of extreme sleepiness."

"It is the first stage. Then you encourage it, and there comes the trance. When the trance comes, then out jumps your little spirit and in jumps another little spirit, and so you have direct talking or writing. You leave your machine to be worked by another. *Hein?* But what have unicorns to do with it?"

Harvey Deacon started in his chair. The Frenchman was moving his head slowly round and staring into the shadows which draped the walls.

"What a fun!" said he. "Always unicorns. Who has been thinking so hard upon a subject so bizarre?"

"This is wonderful!" cried Deacon. "I have been trying to paint one all day. But how could you know it?"

"You have been thinking of them in this room."

"Certainly."

"But thoughts are things, my friend. When you imagine a thing you make a thing. You did not know it, *hein?* But I can see your unicorns because it is not only with my eye that I can see."

"Do you mean to say that I create a thing which has never existed by merely thinking of it?"

"But certainly. It is the fact which lies under all other facts. That is why an evil thought is also a danger."

"They are, I suppose, upon the astral plane?" said Moir.

"Ah, well, these are but words, my friends. They are there—somewhere—everywhere—I cannot tell myself. I see them. I could touch them."

"You could not make *us* see them."

"It is to materialise them. Hold! It is an experiment. But the power is wanting. Let us see what power we have, and then arrange what we shall do. May I place you as I wish?"

"You evidently know a great deal more about it than we do," said Harvey Deacon; "I wish that you would take complete control."

"It may be that the conditions are not good. But we will try what we can do. Madame will sit where she is, I next, and this gentleman beside me. Meester Moir will sit next to madame, because it is well to have blacks and blondes in turn. So! And now with your permission I will turn the lights all out."

"What is the advantage of the dark?" I asked.

"Because the force with which we deal is a vibration of ether and so also is light. We have the wires all for ourselves now—*hein?* You will not be frightened in the darkness, madame? What a fun is such a séance!"

At first the darkness appeared to be absolutely pitchy, but in a few minutes our eyes became so far accustomed to it that we could just make out each other's presence—very dimly and vaguely, it is true. I could see nothing else in the room—only the black loom of the motionless figures. We were all taking the matter much more seriously than we had ever done before.

"You will place your hands in front. It is hopeless that we touch, since we are so few round so large a table. You will compose yourself, madame, and if sleep should come to you you will not fight against it. And now we sit in silence and we expect—*hein?*"

So we sat in silence and expected, staring out into the blackness in front of us. A clock ticked in the passage. A dog barked intermittently far away. Once or twice a cab rattled past in the street, and the gleam of its lamps through the chink in the curtains was a cheerful break in that gloomy vigil. I felt those physical symptoms with which previous séances had made me familiar—the coldness of the feet, the tingling in the hands, the glow of the palms, the feeling of a cold wind upon the back. Strange little shooting pains came in my forearms, especially as it seemed to me in my left one, which was nearest to our visitor—due no doubt to disturbance of the vascular system, but worthy of some attention all the same. At the same time I was conscious of a strained feeling of expectancy which was almost painful. From the rigid, absolute silence of my companions I gathered that their nerves were as tense as my own.

And then suddenly a sound came out of the darkness—a low, sibilant sound, the quick, thin breathing of a woman. Quicker and thinner yet it came, as between clenched teeth, to end in a loud gasp with a dull rustle of cloth.

"What's that? Is all right?" someone asked in the darkness.

"Yes, all is right," said the Frenchman. "It is madame. She is in her trance. Now, gentlemen, if you will wait quiet you will see something, I think, which will interest you much."

Still the ticking in the hall. Still the breathing, deeper and fuller now, from the medium. Still the occasional flash, more welcome than ever, of the passing lights of the hansoms. What a gap we were bridging, the half-raised veil of the eternal on the one side and the cabs of London on the other. The table was throbbing with a mighty pulse. It swayed steadily, rhythmically, with an easy swooping, scooping motion under our fingers. Sharp little raps and cracks came from its substance, file-firing, volley-firing, the sounds of a fagot burning briskly on a frosty night.

"There is much power," said the Frenchman. "See it on the table!"

I had thought it was some delusion of my own, but all could see it now. There was a greenish-yellow phosphorescent light—or I should say a luminous vapour rather than a light—which lay over the surface of the table. It rolled and wreathed and undulated in dim glimmering folds, turning and swirling like clouds of smoke. I could see the white, square-ended hands of the French medium in this baleful light.

"What a fun!" he cried. "It is splendid!"

"Shall we call the alphabet?" asked Moir.

"But no—for we can do much better," said our visitor. "It is but a clumsy thing to tilt the table for every letter of the alphabet, and with such a medium as madame we should do better than that."

"Yes, you will do better," said a voice.

"Who was that? Who spoke? Was that you, Markham?"

"No, I did not speak."

"It was madame who spoke."

"But it was not her voice."

"Is that you, Mrs. Delamere?"

"It is not the medium, but it is the power which uses the organs of the medium," said the strange, deep voice.

"Where is Mrs. Delamere? It will not hurt her, I trust."

"The medium is happy in another plane of existence. She has taken my place, as I have taken hers."

"Who are you?"

"It cannot matter to you who I am. I am one who has lived as you are living, and who has died as you will die."

We heard the creak and grate of a cab pulling up next door. There was an argument about the fare, and the cabman grumbled hoarsely down the street. The green-yellow cloud still swirled faintly over the table, dull elsewhere, but glowing into a dim luminosity in the direction of the medium. It seemed to be piling itself up in front of her. A sense of fear and cold struck into my heart. It seemed to me that lightly and flippantly we had approached the most real and august of sacraments, that communion with the dead of which the fathers of the Church had spoken.

"Don't you think we are going too far? Should we not break up this séance?" I cried.

But the others were all earnest to see the end of it. They laughed at my scruples.

"All the powers are made for use," said Harvey Deacon. "If we *can* do this, we *should* do this. Every new departure of knowledge has been called unlawful in its inception. It is right and proper that we should inquire into the nature of death."

"It is right and proper," said the voice.

"There, what more could you ask?" cried Moir, who was much excited. "Let us have a test. Will you give us a test that you are really there?"

"What test do you demand?"

"Well, now—I have some coins in my pocket. Will you tell me how many?"

"We come back in the hope of teaching and of elevating, and not to guess childish riddles."

"Ha, ha, Meester Moir, you catch it that time," cried

the Frenchman. " But surely this is very good sense what the Control is saying."

" It is a religion, not a game," said the cold, hard voice.

" Exactly—the very view I take of it," cried Moir. " I am sure I am very sorry if I have asked a foolish question. You will not tell me who you are ? "

" What does it matter ? "

" Have you been a spirit long ? "

" Yes."

" How long ? "

" We cannot reckon time as you do. Our conditions are different."

" Are you happy ? "

" Yes."

" You would not wish to come back to life ? "

" No—certainly not."

" Are you busy ? "

" We could not be happy if we were not busy."

" What do you do ? "

" I have said that the conditions are entirely different."

" Can you give us no idea of your work ? "

" We labour for our own improvement and for the advancement of others."

" Do you like coming here to-night ? "

" I am glad to come if I can do any good by coming."

" Then to do good is your object ? "

" It is the object of all life on every plane."

" You see, Markham, that should answer your scruples."

It did, for my doubts had passed and only interest remained.

" Have you pain in your life ? " I asked.

" No ; pain is a thing of the body."

" Have you mental pain ? "

" Yes ; one may always be sad or anxious."

" Do you meet the friends whom you have known on earth ? "

"Some of them."

"Why only some of them?"

"Only those who are sympathetic."

"Do husbands meet wives?"

"Those who have truly loved."

"And the others?"

"They are nothing to each other."

"There must be a spiritual connection?"

"Of course."

"Is what we are doing right?"

"If done in the right spirit."

"What is the wrong spirit?"

"Curiosity and levity."

"May harm come of that?"

"Very serious harm."

"What sort of harm?"

"You may call up forces over which you have no control."

"Evil forces?"

"Undeveloped forces."

"You say they are dangerous. Dangerous to body or mind?"

"Sometimes to both."

There was a pause, and the blackness seemed to grow blacker still, while the yellow-green fog swirled and smoked upon the table.

"Any questions you would like to ask, Moir?" said Harvey Deacon.

"Only this—do you pray in your world?"

"One should pray in every world."

"Why?"

"Because it is the acknowledgment of forces outside ourselves."

"What religion do you hold over there?"

"We differ exactly as you do."

"You have no certain knowledge?"

"We have only faith."

"These questions of religion," said the Frenchman,

" they are of interest to you serious English people, but they are not so much fun. It seems to me that with this power here we might be able to have some great experience—*hein?* Something of which we could talk."

" But nothing could be more interesting than this," said Moir.

" Well, if you think so, that is very well," the Frenchman answered, peevishly. " For my part, it seems to me that I have heard all this before, and that to-night I should weesh to try some experiment with all this force which is given to us. But if you have other questions, then ask them, and when you are finish we can try something more."

But the spell was broken. We asked and asked, but the medium sat silent in her chair. Only her deep, regular breathing showed that she was there. The mist still swirled upon the table.

" You have disturbed the harmony. She will not answer."

" But we have learned already all that she can tell—*hein?* For my part I wish to see something that I have never seen before."

" What then ? "

" You will let me try ? "

" What would you do ? "

" I have said to you that thoughts are things. Now I wish to *prove* it to you, and to show you that which is only a thought. Yes, yes, I can do it and you will see. Now I ask you only to sit still and say nothing, and keep ever your hands quiet upon the table."

The room was blacker and more silent than ever. The same feeling of apprehension which had lain heavily upon me at the beginning of the séance was back at my heart once more. The roots of my hair were tingling.

" It is working ! It is working ! " cried the Frenchman, and there was a crack in his voice as he spoke which told me that he also was strung to his tightest.

The luminous fog drifted slowly off the table, and

wavered and flickered across the room. There in the farther and darkest corner it gathered and glowed, hardening down into a shining core—a strange, shifty, luminous, and yet non-illuminating patch of radiance, bright itself, but throwing no rays into the darkness. It had changed from a greenish-yellow to a dusky sullen red. Then round this centre there coiled a dark, smoky substance, thickening, hardening, growing denser and blacker. And then the light went out, smothered in that which had grown round it.

"It has gone."

"Hush—there's something in the room."

We heard it in the corner where the light had been, something which breathed deeply and fidgeted in the darkness.

"What is it? Le Duc, what have you done?"

"It is all right. No harm will come." The Frenchman's voice was treble with agitation.

"Good heavens, Moir, there's a large animal in the room. Here it is, close by my chair! Go away! Go away!"

It was Harvey Deacon's voice, and then came the sound of a blow upon some hard object. And then . . . And then . . . how can I tell you what happened then?

Some huge thing hurtled against us in the darkness, rearing, stamping, smashing, springing, snorting. The table was splintered. We were scattered in every direction. It clattered and scrambled amongst us, rushing with horrible energy from one corner of the room to another. We were all screaming with fear, grovelling upon our hands and knees to get away from it. Something trod upon my left hand, and I felt the bones splinter under the weight.

"A light! A light!" someone yelled.

"Moir, you have matches, matches!"

"No, I have none. Deacon, where are the matches? For God's sake, the matches!"

"I can't find them. Here, you Frenchman, stop it!"

" It is beyond me. Oh, *mon Dieu*, I cannot stop it. The door! Where is the door?"

My hand, by good luck, lit upon the handle as I groped about in the darkness. The hard-breathing, snorting, rushing creature tore past me and butted with a fearful crash against the oaken partition. The instant that it had passed I turned the handle, and next moment we were all outside, and the door shut behind us. From within came a horrible crashing and rending and stamping.

" What is it? In Heaven's name, what is it?"

" A horse. I saw it when the door opened. But Mrs. Delamere——?"

" We must fetch her out. Come on, Markham; the longer we wait the less we shall like it."

He flung open the door and we rushed in. She was there on the ground amidst the splinters of her chair. We seized her and dragged her swiftly out, and as we gained the door I looked over my shoulder into the darkness. There were two strange eyes glowing at us, a rattle of hoofs, and I had just time to slam the door when there came a crash upon it which split it from top to bottom.

" It's coming through! It's coming!"

" Run, run for your lives!" cried the Frenchman.

Another crash, and something shot through the riven door. It was a long white spike, gleaming in the lamplight. For a moment it shone before us, and then with a snap it disappeared again.

" Quick! Quick! This way!" Harvey Deacon shouted. " Carry her in! Here! Quick!"

We had taken refuge in the dining-room, and shut the heavy oak door. We laid the senseless woman upon the sofa, and as we did so, Moir, the hard man of business, drooped and fainted across the hearthrug. Harvey Deacon was as white as a corpse, jerking and twitching like an epileptic. With a crash we heard the studio door fly to pieces, and the snorting and stamping were in the passage, up and down, up and down, shaking the house with their fury. The Frenchman had sunk his face on his hands, and sobbed like a frightened child.

"What shall we do?" I shook him roughly by the shoulder. "Is a gun any use?"

"No, no. The power will pass. Then it will end."

"You might have killed us all—you unspeakable fool—with your infernal experiments."

"I did not know. How could I tell that it would be frightened? It is mad with terror. It was his fault. He struck it."

Harvey Deacon sprang up. "Good heavens!" he cried.

A terrible scream sounded through the house.

"It's my wife! Here, I'm going out. If it's the Evil One himself I am going out!"

He had thrown open the door and rushed out into the passage. At the end of it, at the foot of the stairs, Mrs. Deacon was lying senseless, struck down by the sight which she had seen. But there was nothing else.

With eyes of horror we looked about us, but all was perfectly quiet and still. I approached the black square of the studio door, expecting with every slow step that some atrocious shape would hurl itself out of it. But nothing came, and all was silent inside the room. Peeping and peering, our hearts in our mouths, we came to the very threshold, and stared into the darkness. There was still no sound, but in one direction there was also no darkness. A luminous, glowing cloud, with an incandescent centre, hovered in the corner of the room. Slowly it dimmed and faded, growing thinner and fainter, until at last the same dense, velvety blackness filled the whole studio. And with the last flickering gleam of that baleful light the Frenchman broke into a shout of joy.

"What a fun!" he cried. "No one is hurt, and only the door broken, and the ladies frightened. But, my friends, we have done what has never been done before."

"And as far as I can help," said Harvey Deacon, "it will certainly never be done again."

And that was what befell on the 14th of April last at No. 17 Badderly Gardens. I began by saying that it would seem too grotesque to dogmatise as to what it was which actually did occur ; but I give my impressions, *our* impressions (since they are corroborated by Harvey Deacon and John Moir), for what they are worth. You may, if it pleases you, imagine that we were the victims of an elaborate and extraordinary hoax. Or you may think with us that we underwent a very real and a very terrible experience. Or perhaps you may know more than we do of such occult matters, and can inform us of some similar occurrence. In this latter case a letter to William Markham, 146M, The Albany, would help to throw a light upon that which is very dark to us.

THE RING OF THOTH

MR. JOHN VANSITTART SMITH, F.R.S., of 147A Gower Street, was a man whose energy of purpose and clearness of thought might have placed him in the very first rank of scientific observers. He was the victim, however, of a universal ambition which prompted him to aim at distinction in many subjects rather than pre-eminence in one. In his early days he had shown an aptitude for zoology and for botany which caused his friends to look upon him as a second Darwin, but when a professorship was almost within his reach he had suddenly discontinued his studies and turned his whole attention to chemistry. Here his researches upon the spectra of the metals had won him his fellowship in the Royal Society ; but again he played the coquette with his subject, and after a year's absence from the laboratory he joined the Oriental Society, and delivered a paper on the Hieroglyphic and Demotic inscriptions of El Kab, thus giving a crowning example both of the versatility and of the inconstancy of his talents.

The most fickle of wooers, however, is apt to be caught at last, and so it was with John Vansittart Smith. The more he burrowed his way into Egyptology the more impressed he became by the vast field which it opened to the inquirer, and by the extreme importance of a subject which promised to throw a light upon the first germs of human civilisation and the origin of the greater part of our arts and sciences. So struck was Mr. Smith that he straightway married an Egyptological young lady who had written upon the sixth dynasty, and having thus secured a sound base of operations he set himself to collect materials for a work which should unite the research of Lepsius and the ingenuity of Champollion. The preparation of this *magnum opus* entailed many hurried visits to the magnificent Egyptian collections of the Louvre, upon the last of which, no longer ago than the middle of last October, he became involved in a most strange and noteworthy adventure.

The trains had been slow and the Channel had been rough, so that the student arrived in Paris in a somewhat befogged and feverish condition. On reaching the Hôtel de France, in the Rue Laffitte, he had thrown himself upon a sofa for a couple of hours, but finding that he was unable to sleep, he determined, in spite of his fatigue, to make his way to the Louvre, settle the point which he had come to decide, and take the evening train back to Dieppe. Having come to his conclusion, he donned his greatcoat, for it was a raw rainy day, and made his way across the Boulevard des Italiens and down the Avenue de l'Opéra. Once in the Louvre he was on familiar ground, and he speedily made his way to the collection of papyri which it was his intention to consult.

The warmest admirers of John Vansittart Smith could hardly claim for him that he was a handsome man. His high-beaked nose and prominent chin had something of the same acute and incisive character which distinguished his intellect. He held his head in a birdlike fashion, and birdlike, too, was the pecking motion with which, in conversation, he threw out his objections and retorts. As he stood, with the high collar of his greatcoat raised to his ears, he might have seen from the reflection in the glass-case before him that his appearance was a singular one. Yet it came upon him as a sudden jar when an English voice behind him exclaimed in very audible tones, "What a queer-looking mortal!"

The student had a large amount of petty vanity in his composition which manifested itself by an ostentatious and overdone disregard of all personal considerations. He straightened his lips and looked rigidly at the roll of papyrus, while his heart filled with bitterness against the whole race of travelling Britons.

"Yes," said another voice, "he really is an extraordinary fellow."

"Do you know," said the first speaker, "one could almost believe that by the continual contemplation of mummies the chap has become half a mummy himself?"

"He has certainly an Egyptian cast of countenance," said the other.

John Vansittart Smith spun round upon his heel with the intention of shaming his countrymen by a corrosive remark or two. To his surprise and relief, the two young fellows who had been conversing had their shoulders turned towards him, and were gazing at one of the Louvre attendants who was polishing some brass-work at the other side of the room.

"Carter will be waiting for us at the Palais Royal," said one tourist to the other, glancing at his watch, and they clattered away, leaving the student to his labours.

"I wonder what these chatterers call an Egyptian cast of countenance," thought John Vansittart Smith, and he moved his position slightly in order to catch a glimpse of the man's face. He started as his eyes fell upon it. It was indeed the very face with which his studies had made him familiar. The regular statuesque features, broad brow, well-rounded chin, and dusky complexion were the exact counterpart of the innumerable statues, mummy-cases, and pictures which adorned the walls of the apartment. The thing was beyond all coincidence. The man must be an Egyptian. The national angularity of the shoulders and narrowness of the hips were alone sufficient to identify him.

John Vansittart Smith shuffled towards the attendant with some intention of addressing him. He was not light of touch in conversation, and found it difficult to strike the happy mean between the brusqueness of the superior and the geniality of the equal. As he came nearer, the man presented his side face to him, but kept his gaze still bent upon his work. Vansittart Smith, fixing his eyes upon the fellow's skin, was conscious of a sudden impression that there was something inhuman and preternatural about its appearance. Over the temple and cheek-bone it was as glazed and as shiny as varnished parchment. There was no suggestion of pores. One could not fancy a drop of moisture upon that arid surface. From brow to chin, however, it was cross-hatched by a million delicate wrinkles, which shot and interlaced as though Nature in some Maori mood had tried how wild and intricate a pattern she could devise.

" Où est la collection de Memphis ? " asked the student, with the awkward air of a man who is devising a question merely for the purpose of opening a conversation.

" C'est là," replied the man brusquely, nodding his head at the other side of the room.

" Vous êtes un Egyptien, n'est-ce pas ? " asked the Englishman.

The attendant looked up and turned his strange dark eyes upon his questioner. They were vitreous, with a misty dry shininess, such as Smith had never seen in a human head before. As he gazed into them he saw some strong emotion gather in their depths, which rose and deepened until it broke into a look of something akin both to horror and to hatred.

" Non, monsieur ; je suis français." The man turned

abruptly and bent low over his polishing. The student gazed at him for a moment in astonishment, and then turning to a chair in a retired corner behind one of the doors he proceeded to make notes of his researches among the papyri. His thoughts, however, refused to return into their natural groove. They would run upon the enigmatical attendant with the sphinx-like face and the parchment skin.

"Where have I seen such eyes?" said Vansittart Smith to himself. "There is something saurian about them, something reptilian. There's the membrana nictitans of the snakes," he mused, bethinking himself of his zoological studies. "It gives a shiny effect. But there was something more here. There was a sense of power, of wisdom—so I read them—and of weariness, utter weariness, and ineffable despair. It may be all imagination, but I never had so strong an impression. By Jove, I must have another look at them!" He rose and paced round the Egyptian rooms, but the man who had excited his curiosity had disappeared.

The student sat down again in his quiet corner, and continued to work at his notes. He had gained the information which he required from the papyri, and it only remained to write it down while it was still fresh in his memory. For a time his pencil travelled rapidly over the paper, but soon the lines became less level, the words more blurred, and finally the pencil tinkled down upon the floor, and the head of the student dropped heavily forward upon his chest. Tired out by his journey, he slept so soundly in his lonely post behind the door that neither the clanking civil guard, nor the footsteps of sightseers, nor even the loud hoarse bell which gives the signal for closing, were sufficient to arouse him.

Twilight deepened into darkness, the bustle from the Rue de Rivoli waxed and then waned, distant Notre Dame clanged out the hour of midnight, and still the dark and lonely figure sat silently in the shadow. It was not until close upon one in the morning that, with a sudden gasp and an intaking of the breath, Vansittart Smith returned to consciousness. For a moment it flashed upon him that he had dropped asleep in his study-chair at home. The moon was shining fitfully through the unshuttered window, however, and as his eye ran along the lines of mummies and the endless array of polished cases, he remembered clearly where he was and how he came there. The student was not a nervous man. He possessed that love of a novel situation which is peculiar to his race. Stretching out his cramped limbs, he looked at his watch, and burst into a chuckle as he observed the hour. The episode would make an admirable anecdote to be introduced into his next paper as a relief to the graver and heavier speculations. He was a little cold, but wide awake and much refreshed. It was no wonder that the guardians had overlooked him, for the door threw its heavy black shadow right across him.

The complete silence was impressive. Neither outside nor inside was there a creak or a murmur. He was alone with the dead men of a dead civilisation. What though the outer city reeked of the garish nineteenth century! In all this chamber there was scarce an article, from the shrivelled ear of wheat to the pigment-box of the painter, which had not held its own against four thousand years. Here was the flotsam and jetsam washed up by the great ocean of time from that far-off empire. From stately Thebes, from lordly Luxor, from the great temples of Heliopolis, from a hundred rifled tombs, these relics had been brought. The student glanced round at the long-silent figures who flickered vaguely up through the gloom, at the busy toilers who were now so restful, and he fell into a reverent and thoughtful mood. An unwonted sense of his own youth and insignificance came over him. Leaning back in his chair, he gazed dreamily down the long vista of rooms, all silvery with the moonshine, which extend through the whole wing of the widespread building. His eyes fell upon the yellow glare of a distant lamp.

John Vansittart Smith sat up on his chair with his nerves all on edge. The light was advancing slowly towards him, pausing from time to time, and then coming jerkily onwards. The bearer moved noiselessly. In the utter silence there was no suspicion of the pat of a footfall. An idea of robbers entered the Englishman's head. He snuggled up farther into the corner. The light was two rooms off. Now it was in the next chamber, and still there was no sound. With something approaching to a thrill of fear the student observed a face, floating in the air as it were, behind the flare of the lamp. The figure was wrapped in shadow, but the light fell full upon the strange, eager face. There was no mistaking the metallic, glistening eyes and the cadaverous skin. It was the attendant with whom he had conversed.

Vansittart Smith's first impulse was to come forward and address him. A few words of explanation would set the matter clear, and lead doubtless to his being conducted to some side-door from which he might make his way to his hotel. As the man entered the chamber, however, there was something so stealthy in his movements, and so furtive in his expression, that the Englishman altered his intention. This was clearly no ordinary official walking the rounds. The fellow wore felt-soled slippers, stepped with a rising chest, and glanced quickly from left to right, while his hurried, gasping breathing thrilled the flame of his lamp. Vansittart Smith crouched silently back into the corner and watched him keenly, convinced that his errand was one of secret and probably sinister import.

There was no hesitation in the other's movements. He stepped lightly and swiftly across to one of the great cases, and, drawing a key from his pocket, he unlocked it. From the upper shelf he pulled down a mummy, which he bore away with him, and laid it with much care and solicitude upon the ground. By it he placed his lamp, and then squatting down beside it in Eastern fashion he began with long, quivering fingers to undo the cerecloths and bandages which girt it round. As the crackling rolls of linen peeled off one after the other, a strong aromatic odour filled the chamber, and fragments of scented wood and of spices pattered down upon the marble floor.

It was clear to John Vansittart Smith that this mummy had never been unswathed before. The operation interested him keenly. He thrilled all over with curiosity, and his bird-like head protruded farther and farther from behind the door. When, however, the last roll had been removed from the four-thousand-year-old head, it was all that he could do to stifle an outcry of amazement. First, a cascade of long, black, glossy tresses poured over the workman's hands and arms. A second turn of the bandage revealed a low, white forehead, with a pair of delicately arched eyebrows. A third uncovered a pair of bright, deeply fringed eyes, and a straight, well-cut nose, while a fourth and last showed a sweet, full, sensitive mouth, and a beautifully curved chin. The whole face was one of extraordinary loveliness, save for the one blemish that in the centre of the forehead there was a single irregular, coffee-coloured splotch. It was a triumph of the embalmer's art. Vansittart Smith's eyes grew larger and larger as he gazed upon it, and he chirruped in his throat with satisfaction.

Its effect upon the Egyptologist was as nothing, however, compared with that which it produced upon the strange attendant. He threw his hands up into the air, burst into a harsh clatter of words, and then, hurling himself down upon the ground beside the mummy, he threw his arms round her, and kissed her repeatedly upon the lips and brow. "Ma petite!" he groaned in French. "Ma pauvre petite!" His voice broke with emotion, and his innumerable wrinkles quivered and writhed, but the student observed in the lamp-light that his shining eyes were still dry and tearless as two beads of steel. For some minutes he lay, with a twitching face, crooning and moaning over the beautiful head. Then he broke into a sudden smile, said some words in an unknown tongue, and sprang to his feet with the vigorous air of one who has braced himself for an effort.

In the centre of the room there was a large, circular case which contained, as the student had frequently remarked, a magnificent collection of early Egyptian rings and precious stones. To this the attendant strode, and, unlocking it, threw it open. On the ledge at the side he placed his lamp, and beside it a small, earthenware jar which he had drawn from his pocket. He then took a handful of rings from the case, and with a most serious and anxious face he proceeded to smear each in turn with some liquid substance from the earthen pot, holding them to the light as he did so. He was clearly disappointed with the first lot, for he threw them petulantly back into the case and drew out some more. One of these, a massive ring with a large crystal set in it, he seized and eagerly tested with the contents of the jar. Instantly he uttered a cry of joy, and threw out his arms in a wild gesture which upset the pot and set the liquid streaming across the floor to the very feet of the Englishman. The attendant drew a red handkerchief from his bosom, and, mopping up the mess, he followed it into the corner, where in a moment he found himself face to face with his observer.

" Excuse me," said John Vansittart Smith, with all imaginable politeness ; " I have been unfortunate enough to fall asleep behind this door."

" And you have been watching me ? " the other asked in English, with a most venomous look on his corpse-like face.

The student was a man of veracity. " I confess," said he, " that I have noticed your movements, and that they have aroused my curiosity and interest in the highest degree."

The man drew a long, flamboyant-bladed knife from his bosom. " You have had a very narrow escape," he said ; " had I seen you ten minutes ago, I should have driven this through your heart. As it is, if you touch me or interfere with me in any way you are a dead man."

"I have no wish to interfere with you," the student answered. "My presence here is entirely accidental. All I ask is that you will have the extreme kindness to show me out through some side-door." He spoke with great suavity, for the man was still pressing the tip of his dagger against the palm of his left hand, as though to assure himself of its sharpness, while his face preserved its malignant expression.

"If I thought——" said he. "But no, perhaps it is as well. What is your name?"

The Englishman gave it.

"Vansittart Smith," the other repeated. "Are you the same Vansittart Smith who gave a paper in London upon El Kab? I saw a report of it. Your knowledge of the subject is contemptible."

"Sir!" cried the Egyptologist.

"Yet it is superior to that of many who make even greater pretensions. The whole keystone of our old life in Egypt was not the inscriptions or monuments of which you make so much, but was our hermetic philosophy and mystic knowledge of which you say little or nothing."

"Our old life!" repeated the scholar, wide-eyed; and then suddenly, "Good God, look at the mummy's face!"

The strange man turned and flashed his light upon the dead woman, uttering a long, doleful cry as he did so. The action of the air had already undone all the art of the embalmer. The skin had fallen away, the eyes had sunk inwards, the discoloured lips had writhed away from the yellow teeth, and the brown mark upon the forehead alone showed that it was indeed the same face which had shown such youth and beauty a few short minutes before.

The man flapped his hands together in grief and horror.

Then mastering himself by a strong effort he turned his hard eyes once more upon the Englishman.

"It does not matter," he said, in a shaking voice. "It does not really matter. I came here to-night with the fixed determination to do something. It is now done. All else is as nothing. I have found my quest. The old curse is broken. I can rejoin her. What matter about her inanimate shell so long as her spirit is awaiting me at the other side of the veil!"

"These are wild words," said Vansittart Smith. He was becoming more and more convinced that he had to do with a madman.

"Time presses, and I must go," continued the other. "The moment is at hand for which I have waited this weary time. But I must show you out first. Come with me."

Taking up the lamp, he turned from the disordered chamber, and led the student swiftly through the long series of the Egyptian, Assyrian, and Persian apartments. At the end of the latter he pushed open a small door let into the wall and descended a winding, stone stair. The Englishman felt the cold, fresh air of the night upon his brow. There was a door opposite him which appeared to communicate with the street. To the right of this another door stood ajar, throwing a spurt of yellow light across the passage. "Come in here!" said the attendant shortly.

Vansittart Smith hesitated. He had hoped that he had come to the end of his adventure. Yet his curiosity was strong within him. He could not leave the matter unsolved, so he followed his strange companion into the lighted chamber.

It was a small room, such as is devoted to a *concierge*. A wood fire sparkled in the grate. At one side stood a truckle bed, and at the other a coarse, wooden chair, with a round table in the centre, which bore the remains of a meal. As the visitor's eye glanced round he could not but remark with an ever-recurring thrill that all the small details of the room were of the most quaint design and antique workmanship. The candlesticks, the vases upon the chimney-piece, the fire-irons, the ornaments upon the walls, were all such as he had been wont to associate with the remote past. The gnarled, heavy-eyed man sat himself down upon the edge of the bed, and motioned his guest into the chair.

"There may be design in this," he said, still speaking excellent English. "It may be decreed that I should leave some account behind as a warning to all rash mortals who would set their wits up against workings of Nature. I leave it with you. Make such use as you will of it. I speak to you now with my feet upon the threshold of the other world.

"I am, as you surmised, an Egyptian—not one of the down-trodden race of slaves who now inhabit the Delta of the Nile, but a survivor of that fiercer and harder people who tamed the Hebrew, drove the Ethiopian back into the southern deserts, and built those mighty works which have been the envy and the wonder of all after generations. It was in the reign of Tuthmosis, sixteen hundred years before the birth of Christ, that I first saw the light. You shrink away from me. Wait, and you will see that I am more to be pitied than to be feared.

"My name was Sosra. My father had been the chief priest of Osiris in the great temple of Abaris, which stood in those days upon the Bubastic branch of the Nile. I was brought up in the temple and was trained in all those mystic arts which are spoken of in your own Bible. I was an apt pupil. Before I was sixteen I had learned all which the wisest priest could teach me. From that time on I studied Nature's secrets for myself, and shared my knowledge with no man.

"Of all the questions which attracted me there were none over which I laboured so long as over those which concern themselves with the nature of life. I probed deeply into the vital principle. The aim of medicine had been to drive away disease when it appeared. It seemed to me that a method might be devised which should so fortify the body as to prevent weakness or death from ever taking hold of it. It is useless that I should recount my researches. You would scarce comprehend them if I did. They were carried out partly upon animals, partly upon slaves, and partly on myself. Suffice it that their result was to furnish me with a substance which, when injected into the blood, would endow the body with strength to resist the effects of time, of violence, or of disease. It would not indeed confer immortality, but its potency would endure for many thousands of years. I used it upon a cat, and afterwards drugged the creature with the most deadly poisons. That cat is alive in Lower Egypt at the present moment. There was nothing of mystery or magic in the matter. It was simply a chemical discovery, which may well be made again.

"Love of life runs high in the young. It seemed to me that I had broken away from all human care now that I had abolished pain and driven death to such a distance. With a light heart I poured the accursed stuff into my veins. Then I looked round for someone whom I could benefit. There was a young priest of Thoth, Parmes by name, who had won my goodwill by his earnest nature and his devotion to his studies. To him I whispered my secret, and at his request I injected him with my elixir. I should now, I reflected, never be without a companion of the same age as myself.

"After this grand discovery I relaxed my studies to some extent, but Parmes continued his with redoubled energy. Every day I could see him working with his flasks and his distiller in the Temple of Thoth, but he said little to me as to the result of his labours. For my own part, I used to walk through the city and look around me with exultation as I reflected that all this was destined to pass away, and that only I should remain. The people would bow to me as they passed me, for the fame of my knowledge had gone abroad.

"There was war at this time, and the Great King had sent down his soldiers to the eastern boundary to drive away the Hyksos. A Governor, too, was sent to Abaris, that he might hold it for the King. I had heard much of the beauty of the daughter of this Governor, but one day as I walked out with Parmes we met her, borne upon the shoulders of her slaves. I was struck with love as with lightning. My heart went out from me. I could have thrown myself beneath the feet of her bearers. This was my woman. Life without her was impossible. I swore by the head of Horus that she should be mine. I swore it to the Priest of Thoth. He turned away from me with a brow which was as black as midnight.

"There is no need to tell you of our wooing. She came to love me even as I loved her. I learned that Parmes had seen her before I did, and had shown her that he, too, loved her, but I could smile at his passion, for I knew that her heart was mine. The white plague had come upon the city and many were stricken, but I laid my hands upon the sick and nursed them without fear or scathe. She marvelled at my daring. Then I told her my secret, and begged her that she would let me use my art upon her.

"'Your flower shall then be unwithered, Atma,' I said. 'Other things may pass away, but you and I, and our great love for each other, shall outlive the tomb of King Chefru.'

"But she was full of timid, maidenly objections. 'Was it right?' she asked, 'was it not a thwarting of the will of the gods? If the great Osiris had wished that our years should be so long, would he not himself have brought it about?'

"With fond and loving words I overcame her doubts, and yet she hesitated. It was a great question, she said. She would think it over for this one night. In the morning I should know of her resolution. Surely one night was not too much to ask. She wished to pray to Isis for help in her decision.

" With a sinking heart and a sad foreboding of evil I left her with her tirewomen. In the morning, when the early sacrifice was over, I hurried to her house. A frightened slave met me upon the steps. Her mistress was ill, she said, very ill. In a frenzy I broke my way through the attendants, and rushed through hall and corridor to my Atma's chamber. She lay upon her couch, her head high upon the pillow, with a pallid face and a glazed eye. On her forehead there blazed a single angry, purple patch. I knew that hell-mark of old. It was the scar of the white plague, the sign-manual of death.

" Why should I speak of that terrible time? For months I was mad, fevered, delirious, and yet I could not die. Never did an Arab thirst after the sweet wells as I longed after death. Could poison or steel have shortened the thread of my existence, I should soon have rejoined my love in the land with the narrow portal. I tried, but it was of no avail. The accursed influence was too strong upon me. One night as I lay upon my couch, weak and weary, Parmes, the priest of Thoth, came to my chamber. He stood in the circle of the lamp-light, and he looked down upon me with eyes which were bright with a mad joy.

" 'Why did you let the maiden die?' he asked; 'why did you not strengthen her as you strengthened me?'

" 'I was too late,' I answered. 'But I had forgot. You also loved her. You are my fellow in misfortune. Is it not terrible to think of the centuries which must pass ere we look upon her again? Fools, fools, that we were to take death to be our enemy!'

" 'You may say that,' he cried with a wild laugh; 'the words come well from your lips. For me they have no meaning.'

" 'What mean you?' I cried, raising myself upon my elbow. 'Surely, friend, this grief has turned your brain.' His face was aflame with joy, and he writhed and shook like one who hath a devil.

"'Do you know whither I go?' he asked.

"'Nay,' I answered, 'I cannot tell.'

"'I go to her,' said he. 'She lies embalmed in the farther tomb by the double palm-tree beyond the city wall.'

"'Why do you go there?' I asked.

"'To die!' he shrieked, 'to die! I am not bound by earthen fetters.'

"'But the elixir is in your blood,' I cried.

"'I can defy it,' said he; 'I have found a stronger principle which will destroy it. It is working in my veins at this moment, and in an hour I shall be a dead man. I shall join her, and you shall remain behind.'

"As I looked upon him I could see that he spoke words of truth. The light in his eye told me that he was indeed beyond the power of the elixir.

"'You will teach me!' I cried.

"'Never!' he answered.

"'I implore you, by the wisdom of Thoth, by the majesty of Anubis!'

"'It is useless,' he said coldly.

"'Then I will find it out,' I cried.

"'You cannot,' he answered; 'it came to me by chance. There is one ingredient which you can never get. Save that which is in the ring of Thoth, none will ever more be made.'

"'In the ring of Thoth!' I repeated, 'where then is the ring of Thoth?'

"'That also you shall never know,' he answered. 'You won her love. Who has won in the end? I leave you to your sordid earth life. My chains are broken. I must go!' He turned upon his heel and fled from the chamber. In the morning came the news that the Priest of Thoth was dead.

"My days after that were spent in study. I must find this subtle poison which was strong enough to undo the elixir. From early dawn to midnight I bent over the test-tube and the furnace. Above all, I collected the papyri and the chemical flasks of the Priest of Thoth. Alas! they taught me little. Here and there some hint or stray expression would raise hope in my bosom, but no good ever came of it. Still, month after month, I struggled on. When my heart grew faint I would make my way to the tomb by the palm-trees. There, standing by the dead casket from which the jewel had been rifled, I would feel her sweet presence, and would whisper to her that I would rejoin her if mortal wit could solve the riddle.

"Parmes had said that his discovery was connected with the ring of Thoth. I had some remembrance of the trinket. It was a large and weighty circlet, made, not of gold, but of a rarer and heavier metal brought from the mines of Mount Harbal. Platinum, you call it. The ring had, I remembered, a hollow crystal set in it, in which some few drops of liquid might be stored. Now, the secret of Parmes could not have to do with the metal alone, for there were many rings of that metal in the Temple. Was it not more likely that he had stored his precious poison within the cavity of the crystal? I had scarce come to this conclusion before, in hunting through his papers, I came upon one which told me that it was indeed so, and that there was still some of the liquid unused.

"But how to find the ring? It was not upon him when he was stripped for the embalmer. Of that I made sure. Neither was it among his private effects. In vain I searched every room that he had entered, every box and vase and chattel that he had owned. I sifted the very sand of the desert in the places where he had been wont to walk; but, do what I would, I could come upon no traces of the ring of Thoth. Yet it may be that my labours would have overcome all obstacles had it not been for a new and unlooked-for misfortune.

"A great war had been waged against the Hyksos, and the Captains of the Great King had been cut off in the desert, with all their bowmen and horsemen. The shepherd tribes were upon us like the locusts in a dry year. From the wilderness of Shur to the great, bitter lake there was blood by day and fire by night. Abaris was the bulwark of Egypt, but we could not keep the savages back. The city fell. The Governor and the soldiers were put to the sword, and I, with many more, was led away into captivity.

"For years and years I tended cattle in the great plains by the Euphrates. My master died, and his son grew old, but I was still as far from death as ever. At last I escaped upon a swift camel, and made my way back to Egypt. The Hyksos had settled in the land which they had conquered, and their own King ruled over the country. Abaris had been torn down, the city had been burned, and of the great Temple there was nothing left save an unsightly mound. Everywhere the tombs had been rifled and the monuments destroyed. Of my Atma's grave no sign was left. It was buried in the sands of the desert, and the palm-trees which marked the spot had long disappeared. The papers of Parmes and the remains of the Temple of Thoth were either destroyed or scattered far and wide over the deserts of Syria. All search after them was vain.

"From that time I gave up all hope of ever finding the ring or discovering the subtle drug. I set myself to live as patiently as might be until the effect of the elixir should wear away. How can you understand how terrible a thing time is, you who have experience only of the narrow course which lies between the cradle and the grave! I know it to my cost, I who have floated down the whole stream of history. I was old when Ilium fell. I was very old when Herodotus came to Memphis. I was bowed down with years when the new gospel came upon earth. Yet you see me much as other men are, with the cursed elixir still sweetening my blood, and guarding me against that which I would court. Now, at last, at last I have come to the end of it!

"I have travelled in all lands and I have dwelt with

all nations. Every tongue is the same to me. I learned them all to help pass the weary time. I need not tell you how slowly they drifted by, the long dawn of modern civilization, the dreary middle years, the dark times of barbarism. They are all behind me now. I have never looked with the eyes of love upon another woman. Atma knows that I have been constant to her.

"It was my custom to read all that the scholars had to say upon Ancient Egypt. I have been in many positions, sometimes affluent, sometimes poor, but I have always found enough to enable me to buy the journals which deal with such matters. Some nine months ago I was in San Francisco, when I read an account of some discoveries made in the neighbourhood of Abaris. My heart leapt into my mouth as I read it. It said that the excavator had busied himself in exploring some tombs recently unearthed. In one there had been found an unopened mummy with an inscription upon the outer case setting forth that it contained the body of the daughter of the Governor of the city in the days of Tuthmosis. It added that on removing the outer case there had been exposed a large platinum ring set with a crystal, which had been laid upon the breast of the embalmed woman. This, then, was where Parmes had hid the ring of Thoth. He might well say that it was safe, for no Egyptian would ever stain his soul by moving even the outer case of a buried friend.

"That very night I set off from San Francisco, and in a few weeks I found myself once more at Abaris, if a few sand-heaps and crumbling walls may retain the name of the great city. I hurried to the Frenchmen who were digging there and asked them for the ring. They replied that both the ring and the mummy had been sent to the Boulak Museum at Cairo. To Boulak I went, but only to be told that Mariette Bey had claimed them and had shipped them to the Louvre. I followed them, and there, at last, in the Egyptian chamber, I came, after close upon four thousand years, upon the remains of my Atma, and upon the ring for which I had sought so long.

"But how was I to lay hands upon them? How was I to have them for my very own? It chanced that the office of attendant was vacant. I went to the Director. I convinced him that I knew much about Egypt. In my eagerness I said too much. He remarked that a Professor's chair would suit me better than a seat in the conciergerie. I knew more, he said, than he did. It was only by blundering, and letting him think that he had over-estimated my knowledge, that I prevailed upon him to let me move the few effects which I have retained into this chamber. It is my first and my last night here.

"Such is my story, Mr. Vansittart Smith. I need not say more to a man of your perception. By a strange chance you have this night looked upon the face of the woman whom I loved in those far-off days. There were many rings with crystals in the case, and I had to test for the platinum to be sure of the one which I wanted. A glance at the crystal has shown me that the liquid is indeed within it, and that I shall at last be able to shake off that accursed health which has been worse to me than the foulest disease. I have nothing more to say to you. I have unburdened myself. You may tell my story or you may withhold it at your pleasure. The choice rests with you. I owe you some amends, for you have had a narrow escape of your life this night. I was a desperate man, and not to be baulked in my purpose. Had I seen you before the thing was done, I might have put it beyond your power to oppose me or to raise an alarm. This is the door. It leads into the Rue de Rivoli. Good night."

The Englishman glanced back. For a moment the lean figure of Sosra the Egyptian stood framed in the narrow doorway. The next the door had slammed, and the heavy rasping of a bolt broke on the silent night.

It was on the second day after his return to London

that Mr. John Vansittart Smith saw the following concise narrative in the Paris correspondence of *The Times* :—

"*Curious Occurrence in the Louvre.*—Yesterday morning a strange discovery was made in the principal Eastern chamber. The *ouvriers* who are employed to clean out the rooms in the morning found one of the attendants lying dead upon the floor with his arms round one of the mummies. So close was his embrace that it was only with the utmost difficulty that they were separated. One of the cases containing valuable rings had been opened and rifled. The authorities are of opinion that the man was bearing away the mummy with some idea of selling it to a private collector, but that he was struck down in the very act by long-standing disease of the heart. It is said that he was a man of uncertain age and eccentric habits, without any living relations to mourn over his dramatic and untimely end."

THE LOS AMIGOS FIASCO

I USED to be the leading practitioner of Los Amigos. Of course, every one has heard of the great electrical generating gear there. The town is widespread, and there are dozens of little townlets and villages all around, which receive their supply from the same centre, so that the works are on a very large scale. The Los Amigos folk say that they are the largest upon earth, but then we claim that for everything in Los Amigos except the gaol and the death-rate. Those are said to be the smallest.

Now, with so fine an electrical supply, it seemed to be a sinful waste of hemp that the Los Amigos criminals should perish in the old-fashioned manner. And then came the news of the electrocutions in the East, and how the results had not after all been so instantaneous as had been hoped. The Western engineers raised their eyebrows when they read of the puny shocks by which these men had perished, and they vowed in Los Amigos that when an irreclaimable came their way he should be dealt handsomely by, and have the run of all the big dynamos.

There should be no reserve, said the engineers, but he should have all that they had got. And what the result of that would be none could predict, save that it must be absolutely blasting and deadly. Never before had a man been so charged with electricity as they would charge him. He was to be smitten by the essence of ten thunderbolts. Some prophesied combustion, and some disintegration and disappearance. They were waiting eagerly to settle the question by actual demonstration, and it was just at that moment that Duncan Warner came that way.

Warner had been wanted by the law, and by nobody else, for many years. Desperado, murderer, train robber and road agent, he was a man beyond the pale of human pity. He had deserved a dozen deaths, and the Los Amigos folk grudged him so gaudy a one as that. He seemed to feel himself to be unworthy of it, for he made two frenzied attempts at escape. He was a powerful, muscular man, with a lion head, tangled black locks, and a sweeping beard which covered his broad chest. When he was tried, there was no finer head in all the crowded court. It's no new thing to find the best face looking from the dock. But his good looks could not balance his bad deeds. His advocate did all he knew, but the cards lay against him, and Duncan Warner was handed over to the mercy of the big Los Amigos dynamos.

I was there at the committee meeting when the matter was discussed. The town council had chosen four experts to look after the arrangements. Three of them were admirable. There was Joseph M'Connor, the very man who had designed the dynamos, and there was Joshua Westmacott, the chairman of the Los Amigos Electrical Supply Company, Limited. Then there was myself as the chief medical man, and lastly an old German of the name of Peter Stulpnagel. The Germans were a strong body at Los Amigos, and they all voted for their man. That was how he got on the committee.

It was said that he had been a wonderful electrician at home, and he was eternally working with wires and insulators and Leyden jars; but, as he never seemed to get any further, or to have any results worth publishing, he came at last to be regarded as a harmless crank, who had made science his hobby. We three practical men smiled when we heard that he had been elected as our colleague, and at the meeting we fixed it all up very nicely among ourselves without much thought of the old fellow who sat with his ears scooped forward in his hands, for he was a trifle hard of hearing, taking no more part in the proceedings than the gentlemen of the press who scribbled their notes on the back benches.

We did not take long to settle it all. In New York a strength of some two thousand volts had been used, and death had not been instantaneous. Evidently their shock had been too weak. Los Amigos should not fall into that error. The charge should be six times greater, and therefore, of course, it would be six times more effective. Nothing could possibly be more logical. The whole concentrated force of the great dynamos should be employed on Duncan Warner.

So we three settled it, and had already risen to break up the meeting, when our silent companion opened his mouth for the first time.

"Gentlemen," said he, "you appear to me to show an extraordinary ignorance upon the subject of electricity. You have not mastered the first principles of its actions upon a human being."

The committee was about to break into an angry reply to this brusque comment, but the chairman of the Electrical Company tapped his forehead to claim its indulgence for the crankiness of the speaker.

"Pray tell us, sir," said he, with an ironical smile, "what is there in our conclusions with which you find fault?"

"With your assumption that a large dose of electricity will merely increase the effect of a small dose. Do you not think it possible that it might have an entirely different result? Do you know anything, by actual experiment, of the effect of such powerful shocks?"

"We know it by analogy," said the chairman pompously. "All drugs increase their effect when they increase their dose; for example—for example——"

"Whisky," said Joseph M'Connor.

"Quite so. Whisky. You see it there."

Peter Stulpnagel smiled and shook his head.

"Your argument is not very good," said he. "When I used to take whisky, I used to find that one glass would excite me, but that six would send me to sleep, which is just the opposite. Now, suppose that electricity were to act in just the opposite way also, what then?"

We three practical men burst out laughing. We had known that our colleague was queer, but we never had thought that he would be as queer as this.

"What then?" repeated Peter Stulpnagel.

"We'll take our chances," said the chairman.

"Pray consider," said Peter, "that workmen who have touched the wires, and who have received shocks of only a few hundred volts, have died instantly. The fact is well known. And yet when a much greater force was used upon a criminal at New York, the man struggled for some little time. Do you not clearly see that the smaller dose is the more deadly?"

"I think, gentlemen, that this discussion has been carried on quite long enough," said the chairman, rising again. "The point, I take it, has already been decided by the majority of the committee, and Duncan Warner shall be electrocuted on Tuesday by the full strength of the Los Amigos dynamos. Is it not so?"

"I agree," said Joseph M'Connor.

"I agree," said I.

"And I protest," said Peter Stulpnagel.

"Then the motion is carried, and your protest will be duly entered in the minutes," said the chairman, and so the sitting was dissolved.

The attendance at the electrocution was a very small one. We four members of the committee were, of course, present with the executioner, who was to act under their orders. The others were the United States Marshal, the governor of the gaol, the chaplain, and three members of the press. The room was a small, brick chamber, forming an out-house to the Central Electrical station. It had been used as a laundry, and had an oven and copper at one side, but no other furniture save a single chair for the condemned man. A metal plate for his feet was placed in front of it, to which ran a thick, insulated wire. Above, another wire depended from the ceiling, which could be connected with a small, metallic rod projecting from a cap which was to be placed upon his head. When this connection was established Duncan Warner's hour was come.

There was a solemn hush as we waited for the coming of the prisoner. The practical engineers looked a little pale, and fidgeted nervously with the wires. Even the hardened Marshal was ill at ease, for a mere hanging was one thing, and this blasting of flesh and blood a very different one. As to the pressmen, their faces were whiter than the sheets which lay before them. The only man who appeared to feel none of the influence of these preparations was the little German crank, who strolled from one to the other with a smile on his lips and mischief in his eyes. More than once he even went so far as to burst into a shout of laughter, until the chaplain sternly rebuked him for his ill-timed levity.

"How can you so far forget yourself, Mr. Stulpnagel," said he, "as to jest in the presence of death?"

But the German was quite unabashed.

"If I were in the presence of death I should not jest," said he, "but since I am not I may do what I choose."

This flippant reply was about to draw another and a sterner reproof from the chaplain, when the door was swung open and two warders entered leading Duncan

Warner between them. He glanced round him with a set face, stepped resolutely forward, and seated himself upon the chair.

"Touch her off!" said he.

It was barbarous to keep him in suspense. The chaplain murmured a few words in his ear, the attendant placed the cap upon his head, and then, while we all held our breath, the wire and the metal were brought in contact.

"Great Scott!" shouted Duncan Warner.

He had bounded in his chair as the frightful shock crashed through his system. But he was not dead. On the contrary, his eyes gleamed far more brightly than they had done before. There was only one change, but it was a singular one. The black had passed from his hair and beard as the shadow passes from a landscape. They were both as white as snow. And yet there was no other sign of decay. His skin was smooth and plump and lustrous as a child's.

The Marshal looked at the committee with a reproachful eye.

"There seems to be some hitch here, gentlemen," said he.

We three practical men looked at each other.

Peter Stulpnagel smiled pensively.

"I think that another one should do it," said I.

Again the connection was made, and again Duncan Warner sprang in his chair and shouted, but, indeed, were it not that he still remained in the chair none of us would have recognised him. His hair and his beard had shredded off in an instant, and the room looked like a barber's shop on a Saturday night. There he sat, his eyes still shining, his skin radiant with the glow of perfect health, but with a scalp as bald as a Dutch cheese, and a chin without so much as a trace of down. He began to revolve one of his arms, slowly and doubtfully at first, but with more confidence as he went on.

"That jint," said he, "has puzzled half the doctors

on the Pacific Slope. It's as good as new, and as limber as a hickory twig."

"You are feeling pretty well?" asked the old German.

"Never better in my life," said Duncan Warner cheerily.

The situation was a painful one. The Marshal glared at the committee. Peter Stulpnagel grinned and rubbed his hands. The engineers scratched their heads. The bald-headed prisoner revolved his arm and looked pleased.

"I think that one more shock——" began the chairman.

"No, sir," said the Marshal; "we've had foolery enough for one morning. We are here for an execution, and an execution we'll have."

"What do you propose?"

"There's a hook handy upon the ceiling. Fetch a rope, and we'll soon set this matter straight."

There was another awkward delay while the warders departed for the cord. Peter Stulpnagel bent over Duncan Warner, and whispered something in his ear. The desperado stared in surprise.

"You don't say?" he asked.

The German nodded.

"What! No ways?"

Peter shook his head, and the two began to laugh as though they shared some huge joke between them.

The rope was brought, and the Marshal himself slipped the noose over the criminal's neck. Then the two warders, the assistant and he swung their victim into the air. For half an hour he hung—a dreadful sight—from the ceiling. Then in solemn silence they lowered him down, and one of the warders went out to order the shell to be brought round. But as he touched ground again what was our amazement when Duncan Warner put his hands up to his neck, loosened the noose, and took a long, deep breath.

"Paul Jefferson's sale is goin' well," he remarked

"I could see the crowd from up yonder," and he nodded at the hook in the ceiling.

"Up with him again!" shouted the Marshal, "we'll get the life out of him somehow."

In an instant the victim was up at the hook once more. They kept him there for an hour, but when he came down he was perfectly garrulous.

"Old man Plunket goes too much to the Arcady Saloon," said he. "Three times he's been there in an hour; and him with a family. Old man Plunket would do well to swear off."

It was monstrous and incredible, but there it was. There was no getting round it. The man was there talking when he ought to have been dead. We all sat staring in amazement, but United States Marshal Carpenter was not a man to be euchred so easily. He motioned the others to one side, so that the prisoner was left standing alone.

"Duncan Warner," said he slowly, "you are here to play your part, and I am here to play mine. Your game is to live if you can, and my game is to carry out the sentence of the law. You've beat us on electricity. I'll give you one there. And you've beat us on hanging, for you seem to thrive on it. But it's my turn to beat you now, for my duty has to be done."

He pulled a six-shooter from his coat as he spoke, and fired all the shots through the body of the prisoner. The room was so filled with smoke that we could see nothing, but when it cleared the prisoner was still standing there, looking down in disgust at the front of his coat.

"Coats must be cheap where you come from," said he. "Thirty dollars it cost me, and look at it now. The six holes in front are bad enough, but four of the balls have passed out, and a pretty fine state the back must be in."

The Marshal's revolver fell from his hand, and he dropped his arms to his sides, a beaten man.

"Maybe some of you gentlemen can tell me what this means," said he, looking helplessly at the committee.

Peter Stulpnagel took a step forward.

"I'll tell you all about it," said he.

"You seem to be the only person who knows anything."

"I *am* the only person who knows anything. I should have warned these gentlemen; but, as they would not listen to me, I have allowed them to learn by experience. What you have done with your electricity is that you have increased the man's vitality until he can defy death for centuries."

"Centuries!"

"Yes, it will take the wear of hundreds of years to exhaust the enormous nervous energy with which you have drenched him. Electricity is life, and you have charged him with it to the utmost. Perhaps in fifty years you might execute him, but I am not sanguine about it."

"Great Scott! What shall I do with him?" cried the unhappy Marshal.

Peter Stulpnagel shrugged his shoulders.

"It seems to me that it does not much matter what you do with him now," said he.

"Maybe we could drain the electricity out of him again. Suppose we hang him up by the heels?"

"No, no, it's out of the question."

"Well, well, he shall do no more mischief in Los Amigos, anyhow," said the Marshal, with decision. "He shall go into the new gaol. The prison will wear him out."

"On the contrary," said Peter Stulpnagel, "I think that it is much more probable that he will wear out the prison."

It was rather a fiasco, and for years we didn't talk more about it than we could help, but it's no secret now, and I thought you might like to jot down the facts in your case-book.

THE SILVER HATCHET

ON the 3rd of December, 1861, Dr. Otto von Hopstein, Regius Professor of Comparative Anatomy of the University of Buda-Pesth, and Curator of the Academical Museum, was foully and brutally murdered within a stone-throw of the entrance to the college quadrangle.

Besides the eminent position of the victim and his popularity amongst both students and towns-folk, there were other circumstances which excited public interest very strongly, and drew general attention throughout Austria and Hungary to this murder. The *Pesther Abendblatt* of the following day had an article upon it, which may still be consulted by the curious, and from which I translate a few passages giving a succinct account of the circumstances under which the crime was committed, and the peculiar features in the case which puzzled the Hungarian police.

"It appears," said that very excellent paper, "that Professor von Hopstein left the University about half-past four in the afternoon, in order to meet the train which is due from Vienna at three minutes after five. He was accompanied by his old and dear friend, Herr Wilhelm Schlessinger, sub-Curator of the Museum and Privat-docent of Chemistry. The object of these two gentlemen in meeting this particular train was to receive the legacy bequeathed by Graf von Schulling to the University of Buda-Pesth. It is well known that this unfortunate nobleman, whose tragic fate is still fresh in the recollection of the public, left his unique collection of mediæval weapons, as well as several priceless black-letter editions, to enrich the already celebrated museum of his Alma Mater. The worthy Professor was too much of an enthusiast in such matters to intrust the reception or care of this valuable legacy to any subordinate, and, with the assistance of Herr Schlessinger, he succeeded in removing the whole collection from the train, and stowing it away in a light cart which had been sent by the University authorities. Most of the books and more fragile articles were packed in cases of pinewood, but many of the weapons were simply done round with straw, so that considerable labor was involved in moving them all. The Professor was so nervous, however, lest any of them should be injured, that he refused to allow any of the railway employés (*Eisenbahndiener*) to assist. Every article was carried across the platform by Herr Schlessinger, and handed to Professor von Hopstein in the cart, who packed it away. When everything was in, the two gentlemen, still faithful to their charge, drove back to the University, the Professor being in excellent spirits, and not a little proud of the physical exertion which he had shown himself capable of. He made some joking allusion to it to Reinmaul, the janitor, who, with his friend Schiffer, a Bohemian Jew, met the cart on its return and unloaded the contents. Leaving his curiosities safe in the store-room, and locking the door, the Professor handed the key to his sub-curator, and, bidding every one good evening, departed in the direction of his lodgings. Schlessinger took a last look to reassure himself that all was right, and also went off, leaving Reinmaul and his friend Schiffer smoking in the janitor's lodge.

"At eleven o'clock, about an hour and a half after Von Hopstein's departure, a soldier of the 14th regiment of Jäger, passing the front of the University on his way to barracks, came upon the lifeless body of the Professor lying a little way from the side of the road. He had fallen upon his face, with both hands stretched out. His head was literally split in two halves by a tremendous blow, which, it is conjectured, must have been struck from behind, there remaining a peaceful smile upon the old man's face, as if he had been still dwelling upon his new archæological acquisition when death had overtaken him. There is no other mark of violence upon the body, except a bruise over the left patella, caused probably by the fall. The most mysterious part of the affair is that the Professor's purse, containing forty-three gulden, and his valuable watch, have been untouched. Robbery cannot, therefore, have been the incentive to the deed, unless the assassins were disturbed before they could complete their work.

"The idea is negatived by the fact that the body must have lain at least an hour before any one discovered it! The whole affair is wrapped in mystery. Dr. Langemann, the eminent medico-jurist, has pronounced that the wound is such as might have been inflicted by a heavy sword-bayonet wielded by a powerful arm. The police are extremely reticent upon the subject, and it is suspected that they are in possession of a clew which may lead to important results."

Thus far the *Pesther Abendblatt*. The researches of the police failed, however, to throw the least glimmer of light upon the matter. There was absolutely no trace of the murderer, nor could any amount of ingenuity invent any reason which could have induced any one to commit the dreadful deed. The deceased Professor was a man so wrapped in his own studies and pursuits that he lived apart from the world, and had certainly never raised the slightest animosity in any human breast. It must have been some fiend, some savage, who loved blood for its own sake, who struck that merciless blow.

Though the officials were unable to come to any conclusions upon the matter, popular suspicion was not long in pitching upon a scapegoat. In the first published accounts of the murder the name of one Schiffer had been mentioned as having remained with the janitor after the Professor's departure. This man was a Jew, and Jews have never been popular in Hungary. A cry was at once raised for Schiffer's arrest; but as there was not the slightest grain of evidence against him, the authorities very properly refused to consent to so arbitrary a proceeding. Reinmaul, who was an old and most respected citizen, declared solemnly that Schiffer was with him until the startled cry of the soldier had caused them both to run out to the scene of the tragedy. No one ever dreamed of implicating Reinmaul in such a matter; but still it was rumored that his ancient and well-known friendship for Schiffer might have induced him to tell a falsehood in order to screen him. Popular feeling ran very high upon the subject, and there seemed a danger of Schiffer's being mobbed in the street, when an incident occurred which threw a very different light upon the matter.

On the morning of the 12th of December, just nine days after the mysterious murder of the Professor, Schiffer, the Bohemian Jew, was found lying in the northwestern corner of the Grand Platz stone dead, and so mutilated that he was hardly recognizable. His head was cloven open in very much the same way as that of Von Hopstein, and his body exhibited numerous deep gashes, as if the murderer had been so carried away and transported with fury that he had continued to hack the lifeless body. Snow had fallen heavily the day before, and was lying at least a foot deep all over the square; some had fallen during the night, too, as was evidenced by a thin layer lying like a winding-sheet over the murdered man. It was hoped at first that this circumstance might assist in giving a clew by enabling the footsteps of the assassin to be traced; but the crime had been committed, unfortunately, in a place much frequented during the day, and there were innumerable tracks in every direction. Besides, the newly-fallen snow had blurred the footsteps to such an extent that it would have been impossible to draw trustworthy evidence from them.

In this case there was exactly the same impenetrable mystery and absence of motive which had characterized the murder of Professor von Hopstein. In the dead man's pocket there was found a note-book containing a considerable sum in gold and several very valuable bills, but no attempt had been made to rifle him. Supposing that any one to whom he had lent money (and this was the first idea which occurred to the police) had taken this means of evading his debt, it was hardly conceivable that he would have left such a valuable spoil untouched. Schiffer lodged with a widow named Gruga, at 49 Marie Theresa Strasse, and the evidence of his landlady and her children showed that he had remained shut up in his room the whole of the preceding day in a state of deep dejection, caused by the suspicion which the populace had fastened upon him. She had heard him go out about eleven o'clock at night for his last and fatal walk, and as he had a latch-key she had gone to bed without waiting for him. His object in choosing such a late hour for a ramble obviously was that he did not consider himself safe if recognized in the streets.

The occurrence of this second murder so shortly after the first threw not only the town of Buda-Pesth, but the whole of Hungary, into a terrible state of excitement and even of terror. Vague dangers seemed to hang over the head of every man. The only parallel to this intense feeling was to be found in our own country at the time of the Williams murders described by De Quincey. There were so many resemblances between the cases of Von Hopstein and of Schiffer that no one could doubt that there existed a connection between the two. The absence of object and of robbery, the utter want of any clew to the assassin, and, lastly, the ghastly nature of the wounds, evidently inflicted by the same or a similar weapon, all pointed in one direction. Things were in this state when the incidents which I am now about to relate occurred, and in order to make them intelligible I must lead up to them from a fresh point of departure.

Otto von Schlegel was a younger son of the old Silesian family of that name. His father had originally destined him for the army, but at the advice of his teachers, who saw the surprising talent of the youth, had sent him to the University of Buda-Pesth to be educated in medicine. Here young Schlegel carried everything before him, and promised to be one of the most brilliant graduates turned out for many a year. Though a hard reader, he was no bookworm, but an active, powerful young fellow, full of animal spirits and vivacity, and extremely popular among his fellow-students.

The New Year examinations were at hand, and Schlegel was working hard—so hard that even the strange murders in the town, and the general excitement in men's minds, failed to turn his thoughts from his studies. Upon Christmas Eve, when every house was illuminated, and the roar of drinking songs came from the Bierkeller in the Student-quartier, he refused the many invitations to roystering suppers which were showered upon him, and went off with his books under his arm to the rooms of Leopold Strauss, to work with him into the small hours of the morning.

Strauss and Schlegel were bosom friends. They were both Silesians, and had known each other from boyhood. Their affection had become proverbial in the University. Strauss was almost as distinguished a student as Schlegel, and there had been many a tough struggle for academic honors between the two fellow-countrymen, which had only served to strengthen their friendship by a bond of mutual respect. Schlegel admired the dogged pluck and never-failing good temper of his old playmate; while the latter considered Schlegel, with his many talents and brilliant versatility, the most accomplished of mortals.

The friends were still working together, the one reading from a volume on anatomy, the other holding a skull and marking off the various parts mentioned in the text, when the deep-toned bell of St. Gregory's church struck the hour of midnight.

"Hark to that!" said Schlegel, snapping up the book and stretching out his long legs towards the cheery fire. "Why, it's Christmas morning, old friend! May it not be the last that we spend together!"

"May we have passed all these confounded examinations before another one comes!" answered Strauss. "But see here, Otto, one bottle of wine will not be amiss. I have laid one up on purpose;" and with a smile on his honest, South German face, he pulled out a long-necked bottle of Rhenish from amongst a pile of books and bones in the corner.

"It is a night to be comfortable indoors," said Otto von Schlegel, looking out at the snowy landscape, "for 'tis bleak and bitter enough outside. Good health, Leopold!"

"*Lebe hoch!*" replied his companion. "It is a comfort indeed to forget sphenoid bones and ethmoid bones, if it be but for a moment. And what is the news of the corps, Otto? Has Graube fought the Swabian?"

"They fight to-morrow," said Von Schlegel. "I fear that our man will lose his beauty, for he is short in the arm. Yet activity and skill may do much for him. They say his hanging guard is perfection."

"And what else is the news amongst the students?" asked Strauss.

"They talk, I believe, of nothing but the murders. But I have worked hard of late, as you know, and hear little of the gossip."

"Have you had time," inquired Strauss, "to look over the books and the weapons which our dear old Professor was so concerned about the very day he met his death? They say they are well worth a visit."

"I saw them to-day," said Schlegel, lighting his pipe. "Reinmaul, the janitor, showed me over the store-room, and I helped to label many of them from the original catalogue of Graf Schulling's museum. As far as we can see, there is but one article missing of all the collection."

"One missing!" exclaimed Strauss. "That would grieve old Von Hopstein's ghost. Is it anything of value?"

"It is described as an antique hatchet, with a head of steel and a handle of chased silver. We have applied to the railway company, and no doubt it will be found."

"I trust so," echoed Strauss; and the conversation drifted into other channels. The fire was burning low and the bottle of Rhenish was empty before the two friends rose from their chairs, and Von Schlegel prepared to depart.

"Ugh! It's a bitter night!" he said, standing on the doorstep and folding his cloak round him. "Why, Leopold, you have your cap on. You are not going out, are you?"

"Yes, I am coming with you," said Strauss, shutting the door behind him. "I feel heavy," he continued, taking his friend's arm, and walking down the street with him. "I think a walk as far as your lodgings, in the crisp, frosty air, is just the thing to set me right."

The two students went down Stephen Strasse together and across Julien Platz, talking on a variety of topics. As they passed the corner of the Grand Platz, however, where Schiffer had been found dead, the conversation turned naturally upon the murder.

"That's where they found him," remarked Von Schlegel, pointing to the fatal spot.

"Perhaps the murderer is near us now," said Strauss. "Let us hasten on."

They both turned to go, when Von Schlegel gave a sudden cry of pain and stooped down.

"Something has cut through my boot!" he cried; and feeling about with his hand in the snow, he pulled out a small, glistening battleaxe, made apparently entirely of metal. It had been lying with the blade turned slightly upwards, so as to cut the foot of the student when he trod upon it.

"The weapon of the murderer!" he ejaculated.

"The silver hatchet from the museum!" cried Strauss in the same breath.

There could be no doubt that it was both the one and the

other. There could not be two such curious weapons, and the character of the wounds was just such as would be inflicted by a similar instrument. The murderer had evidently thrown it aside after committing the dreadful deed, and it had lain concealed in the snow some twenty metres from the spot ever since. It was extraordinary that of all the people who had passed and repassed none had discovered it; but the snow was deep, and it was a little off the beaten track.

"What are we to do with it?" said Von Schlegel, holding it in his hand. He shuddered as he noticed by the light of the moon that the head of it was all dabbled with dark brown stains.

"Take it to the Commissary of Police," suggested Strauss.

"He'll be in bed now. Still, I think you are right. But it is nearly four o'clock. I will wait until morning and take it round before breakfast. Meanwhile, I must carry it with me to my lodgings."

"That is the best plan," said his friend; and the two walked on together talking of the remarkable find which they had made. When they came to Schlegel's door, Strauss said good-by, refusing an invitation to go in, and walked briskly down the street in the direction of his own lodgings.

Schlegel was stooping down putting the key into the lock, when a strange change came over him. He trembled violently, and dropped the key from his quivering fingers. His right hand closed convulsively round the handle of the silver hatchet, and his eye followed the retreating figure of his friend with a vindictive glare. In spite of the coldness of the night the perspiration streamed down his face. For a moment he seemed to struggle with himself, holding his hand up to his throat as if he were suffocating. Then, with crouching body and rapid, noiseless steps, he crept after his late companion.

Strauss was plodding sturdily along through the snow, humming snatches of a student song, and little dreaming of the dark figure which pursued him. At the Grand Platz it was forty yards behind him; at the Julien Platz it was but twenty; in Stephen Strasse it was ten, and gaining on him with panther-like rapidity. Already it was almost within arm's length of the unsuspecting man, and the hatchet glittered coldly in the moonlight, when some slight noise must have reached Strauss's ears, for he faced suddenly round upon his pursuer. He started and uttered an exclamation as his eye met the white, set face, with flashing eyes and clenched teeth, which seemed to be suspended in the air behind him.

"What, Otto!" he exclaimed, recognizing his friend. "Art thou ill? You look pale. Come with me to my— Ah! hold, you madman, hold! Drop that axe! Drop it, I say, or by heaven I'll choke you!"

Von Schlegel had thrown himself upon him with a wild cry and uplifted weapon; but the student was stout-hearted and resolute. He rushed inside the sweep of the hatchet and caught his assailant round the waist, narrowly escaping a blow which would have cloven his head. The two staggered for a moment in a deadly wrestle, Schlegel endeavoring to shorten his weapon; but Strauss with a desperate wrench managed to bring him to the ground, and they rolled together in the snow, Strauss clinging to the other's right arm and shouting frantically for assistance. It was as well that he did so, for Schlegel would certainly have succeeded in freeing his arm had it not been for the arrival of two stalwart gendarmes, attracted by the uproar. Even then the three of them found it difficult to overcome the maniacal strength of Schlegel, and they were utterly unable to wrench the silver hatchet from his grasp. One of the gendarmes, however, had a coil of rope round his waist, with which he rapidly secured the student's arms to his sides. In this way, half pushed, half dragged, he was conveyed, in spite of furious cries and frenzied struggles, to the central police station.

Strauss assisted in coercing his former friend, and accompanied the police to the station; protesting loudly at the same time against any unnecessary violence, and giving it as his opinion that a lunatic asylum would be a more fitting place for the prisoner. The events of the last half-hour had been so sudden and inexplicable that he felt quite dazed himself. What did it all mean? It was certain that his old friend from boyhood had attempted to murder him, and had nearly succeeded. Was Von Schlegel then the murderer of Professor von Hopstein and of the Bohemian Jew? Strauss felt that it was impossible, for the Jew was not even known to him, and the Professor had been his especial favorite. He followed mechanically to the police station, lost in grief and amazement.

Inspector Baumgarten, one of the most energetic and best known of the police officials, was on duty in the absence of the Commissary. He was a wiry, little, active man, quiet and retiring in his habits, but possessed of great sagacity and a vigilance which never relaxed. Now, though he had had a six hours' vigil, he sat as erect as ever, with his pen behind his ear, at his official desk, while his friend, Sub-inspector Winkel, snored in a chair at the side of the stove. Even the inspector's usually immovable features betrayed surprise, however, when the door was flung open and Von Schlegel was dragged in with pale face and disordered clothes, the silver hatchet still grasped firmly in his hand. Still more surprised was he when Strauss and the gendarmes gave their account, which was duly entered in the official register.

"Young man, young man," said Inspector Baumgarten, laying down his pen and fixing his eyes sternly upon the prisoner, "that is pretty work for Christmas morning; why have you done this thing?"

"God knows!" cried Von Schlegel, covering his face with his hands and dropping the hatchet. A change had come over him, his fury and excitement were gone, and he seemed utterly prostrated with grief.

"You have rendered yourself liable to a strong suspicion of having committed the other murders which have disgraced our city."

"No, no, indeed!" said Von Schlegel, earnestly. "God forbid!"

"At least you are guilty of attempting the life of Herr Leopold Strauss."

"The dearest friend I have in the world," groaned the student. "Oh, how could I! How could I!"

"His being your friend makes your crime ten times more heinous," said the inspector, severely. "Remove him for the remainder of the night to the— But steady! Who comes here?"

The door was pushed open, and a man came into the room, so haggard and careworn that he looked more like a ghost than a human being. He tottered as he walked, and had to clutch at the backs of the chairs as he approached the inspector's desk. It was hard to recognize in this miserable-looking object the once cheerful and rubicund sub-curator of the museum and privat-docent of chemistry, Herr Wilhelm Schlessinger. The practiced eye of Baumgarten, however, was not to be baffled by any change.

"Good morning, mein herr," he said; "you are up early. No doubt the reason is that you have heard that one of your students, Von Schlegel, is arrested for attempting the life of Leopold Strauss?"

"No; I have come for myself," said Schlessinger, speaking huskily, and putting his hand up to his throat. "I have come to ease my soul of the weight of a great sin, though, God knows, an unmeditated one. It was I who— But merciful heavens!—there it is—the horrid thing! Oh, that I had never seen it!"

He shrank back in a paroxysm of terror, glaring at the silver hatchet where it lay upon the floor, and pointing at it with his emaciated hand.

"There it lies!" he yelled. "Look at it! It has come to condemn me. See that brown rust on it! Do you know what that is? That is the blood of my dearest, best friend, Professor von Hopstein. I saw it gush over the very handle as I drove the blade through his brain. Mein Gott, I see it now!"

"Sub-inspector Winkel," said Baumgarten, endeavoring to preserve his official austerity, "you will arrest this man, charged on his own confession with the murder of the late Professor. I also deliver into your hands Von Schlegel here, charged with murderous assault upon Herr Strauss. You will also keep this hatchet"—here he picked it from the floor—"which has apparently been used for both crimes."

Wilhelm Schlessinger had been leaning against the table, with a face of ashy paleness. As the inspector ceased speaking, he looked up excitedly.

"What did you say?" he cried. "Von Schlegel attacks Strauss! The two dearest friends in the college! I slay my old master! It is magic, I say; it is a charm! There is a spell upon us! It is—ah, I have it! It is that hatchet—that thrice accursed hatchet!" and he pointed convulsively at the weapon which Inspector Baumgarten still held in his hand.

The inspector smiled contemptuously.

"Restrain yourself, mein herr," he said. "You do but make your case worse by such wild excuses for the wicked deed you confess to. Magic and charms are not known in the legal vocabulary, as my friend Winkel will assure you."

"I know not," remarked his sub-inspector, shrugging his broad shoulders. "There are many strange things in the world. Who knows but that—"

"What!" roared Inspector Baumgarten, furiously. "You would undertake to contradict me! You would set up your opinion! You would be the champion of these accursed murderers! Fool, miserable fool, your hour has come!" and rushing at the astounded Winkel, he dealt a blow at him with the silver hatchet which would certainly have justified his last assertion had it not been that, in his fury, he overlooked the lowness of the rafters above his head. The blade of the hatchet struck one of these, and remained there quivering, while the handle was splintered into a thousand pieces.

"What have I done?" gasped Baumgarten, falling back into his chair. "What have I done?"

"You have proved Herr Schlessinger's words to be correct," said Von Schlegel, stepping forward, for the astonished policemen had let go their grasp of him. "That is what you have done. Against reason, science and everything else though it be, there is a charm at work. There must be! Strauss, old boy, you know I would not, in my right senses, hurt one hair of your head. And you, Schlessinger, we both know you loved the old man who is dead. And you, Inspector Baumgarten, you would not willingly have struck your friend, the sub-inspector?"

"Not for the whole world," groaned the inspector, covering his face with his hands.

"Then is it not clear? But now, thank heaven, the accursed thing is broken, and can never do harm again. But see, what is that?"

Right in the center of the room was lying a thin brown cylinder of parchment. One glance at the fragments of the handle of the weapon showed that it had been hollow. This roll of paper had apparently been hidden away inside the metal case thus formed, having been introduced through a small hole, which had been afterwards soldered up. Von Schlegel opened the document. The writing upon it was almost illegible from age; but as far as they could make out it stood thus, in mediæval German:

"Diese Waffe benutzte Max von Erlichingen um Joanna Bodeck zu ermorden, deshalb beschuldige Ich, Johann Bodeck, mittelst der macht welche mir als mitglied des Concils des rothen Kreuzes verliehan wurde, dieselbe mit dieser unthat. Mag sie anderen denselben schmerz verursachen den sie mir verursacht hat. Mag Jede hand die sie ergreift mit dem blut eines freundes geröthet sein.

" 'Immer übel—niemals gut,
Geröthet mit des freundes blut.' "

Which may be roughly translated:

"This weapon was used by Max von Erlichingen for the murder of Joanna Bodeck. Therefore do I, Johann

Bodeck, accurse it by the power which has been bequeathed to me as one of the Council of the Rosy Cross. May it deal to others the grief which it has dealt to me! May every hand that grasps it be reddened in the blood of a friend!

> " 'Ever evil, never good,
> Reddened with a loved one's blood.' "

There was a dead silence in the room when Von Schlegel had finished spelling out this strange document. As he put it down Strauss laid his hand affectionately upon his arm.

"No such proof is needed by me, old friend," he said. "At the very moment that you struck at me I forgave you in my heart. I well know that if the poor Professor were in the room he would say as much to Herr Wilhelm Schlessinger."

"Gentlemen," remarked the inspector, standing up and resuming his official tones, "this affair, strange as it is, must be treated according to rule and precedent. Sub-inspector Winkel, as your superior officer, I command you to arrest me upon a charge of murderously assaulting you. You will commit me to prison for the night, together with Herr von Schlegel and Herr Wilhelm Schlessinger. We shall take our trial at the coming sitting of the judges. In the meantime take care of that piece of evidence"—pointing to the piece of parchment—"and, while I am away, devote your time and energy to utilizing the clew you have obtained in discovering who it was who slew Herr Schiffer, the Bohemian Jew."

The one missing link in the chain of evidence was soon supplied. On the 28th of December the wife of Reinmaul the janitor, coming into the bedroom after a short absence, found her husband hanging lifeless from a hook in the wall. He had tied a long bolster-case round his neck and stood upon a chair in order to commit the fatal deed. On the table was a note in which he confessed to the murder of

Schiffer the Jew, adding that the deceased had been his oldest friend, and that he had slain him without premeditation, in obedience to some uncontrollable impulse. Remorse and grief, he said, had driven him to self-destruction; and he wound up his confession by commending his soul to the mercy of heaven.

The trial which ensued was one of the strangest which ever occurred in the whole history of jurisprudence. It was in vain that the prosecuting counsel urged the improbability of the explanation offered by the prisoners, and deprecated the introduction of such an element as magic into a nineteenth-century law-court. The chain of facts was too strong, and the prisoners were unanimously acquitted. "This silver hatchet," remarked the judge in his summing up, "has hung untouched upon the wall in the mansion of the Graf von Sculling for nearly two hundred years. The shocking manner in which he met his death at the hands of his favorite house steward is still fresh in your recollection. It has come out in evidence that, a few days before the murder, the steward had overhauled the old weapons and cleaned them. In doing this he must have touched the handle of this hatchet. Immediately afterward he slew his master, whom he had served faithfully for twenty years. The weapon then came, in conformity with the Count's will, to Buda-Pesth, where, at the station, Herr Wilhelm Schlessinger grasped it, and, within two hours, used it against the person of the deceased Professor. The next man whom we find touching it is the janitor Reinmaul, who helped to remove the weapons from the cart to the store-room. At the first opportunity he buried it in the body of his friend Schiffer. We then have the attempted murder of Strauss by Schlegel, and of Winkel by Inspector Baumgarten, all immediately following the taking of the hatchet into the hand. Lastly, comes the providential discovery of the extraordinary document which has been read to you by the clerk of the court. I invite your most careful consideration, gentlemen of the jury, to this chain of facts, knowing that you will find a verdict according to your consciences without fear and without favor."

Perhaps the most interesting piece of evidence to the English reader, though it found few supporters among the Hungarian audience, was that of Dr. Langemann, the eminent medico-jurist, who has written text-books upon metallurgy and toxicology. He said:

"I am not so sure, gentlemen, that there is need to fall back upon necromancy or the black art for an explanation of what has occurred. What I say is merely a hypothesis, without proof of any sort, but in a case so extraordinary every suggestion may be of value. The Rosicrucians, to whom allusion is made in this paper, were the most profound chemists of the early Middle Ages, and included the principal alchemists whose names have descended to us. Much as chemistry has advanced, there are some points in which the ancients were ahead of us, and in none more so than in the manufacture of poisons of subtle and deadly action. This man Bodeck, as one of the elders of the Rosicrucians, possessed, no doubt, the recipe of many such mixtures, some of which, like the *aqua tofana* of the Medicis, would poison by penetrating through the pores of the skin. It is conceivable that the handle of this silver hatchet has been anointed by some preparation which is a diffusible poison, having the effect upon the human body of bringing on sudden and acute attacks of homicidal mania. In such attacks it is well known that the madman's rage is turned against those whom he loved best when sane. I have, as I remarked before, no proof to support me in my theory, and simply put it forward for what it is worth."

With this extract from the speech of the learned and ingenious professor, we may close the account of this famous trial.

The broken pieces of the silver hatchet were thrown into a deep pond, a clever poodle being employed to carry them in his mouth, as no one would touch them for fear some of the infection might still hang about them. The of parchment was preserved in the museum of the ersity. As to Strauss and Schlegel, Winkel and Baumgarten, they continued the best of friends and are so still for all I know to the contrary. Schlessinger became surgeon of a cavalry regiment, and was shot at the battle of Sadowa five years later, while rescuing the wounded under a heavy fire. By his last injunctions his little patrimony was to be sold to erect a marble obelisk over the grave of Professor von Hopstein.

JOHN BARRINGTON COWLES

IT might seem rash of me to say that I ascribe the death of my poor friend, John Barrington Cowles, to any preternatural agency. I am aware that in the present state of public feeling a chain of evidence would require to be strong indeed before the possibility of such a conclusion could be admitted.

I shall therefore merely state the circumstances which led up to this sad event as concisely and as plainly as I can, and leave every reader to draw his own deductions. Perhaps there may be some one who can throw light upon what is dark to me.

I first met Barrington Cowles when I went up to Edinburgh University to take out medical classes there. My landlady in Northumberland Street had a large house, and, being a widow without children, she gained a livelihood by providing accommodation for several students.

Barrington Cowles happened to have taken a bedroom upon the same floor as mine, and when we came to know each other better we shared a small sitting-room, in which we took our meals. In this manner we originated a friendship which was unmarred by the slightest disagreement up to the day of his death.

Cowles' father was the colonel of a Sikh regiment and had remained in India for many years. He allowed his son a handsome income, but seldom gave any other sign of parental affection—writing irregularly and briefly.

My friend, who had himself been born in India, and whose whole disposition was an ardent tropical one, was much hurt by this neglect. His mother was dead, and he had no other relation in the world to supply the blank.

Thus he came in time to concentrate all his affection upon me, and to confide in me in a manner which is rare among men. Even when a stronger and deeper passion came upon him, it never infringed upon the old tenderness between us.

Cowles was a tall, slim young fellow, with an olive, Velasquez-like face, and dark, tender eyes. I have seldom seen a man who was more likely to excite a woman's interest, or to captivate her imagination. His expression was, as a rule, dreamy, and even languid; but if in conversation a subject arose which interested him he would be all animation in a moment. On such occasions his colour would heighten, his eyes gleam, and he could speak with an eloquence which would carry his audience with him.

In spite of these natural advantages he led a solitary life, avoiding female society, and reading with great diligence. He was one of the foremost men of his year, taking the senior medal for anatomy, and the Neil Arnott prize for physics.

How well I can recollect the first time we met her! Often and often I have recalled the circumstances, and tried to remember what the exact impression was which she produced on my mind at the time. After we came to know her my judgment was warped, so that I am curious to recollect what my unbiassed instincts were. It is hard, however, to eliminate the feelings which reason or prejudice afterwards raised in me.

It was at the opening of the Royal Scottish Academy in the spring of 1879. My poor friend was passionately attached to art in every form, and a pleasing chord in music or a delicate effect upon canvas would give exquisite pleasure to his highly-strung nature. We had gone together to see the pictures, and were standing in the grand central *salon*, when I noticed an extremely beautiful woman standing at the other side of the room. In my whole life I have never seen such a classically perfect countenance. It was the real Greek type—the forehead broad, very low, and as white as marble, with a cloudlet of delicate locks wreathing round it, the nose straight and clean cut, the lips inclined to thinness, the chin and lower jaw beautifully rounded off, and yet sufficiently developed to promise unusual strength of character.

But those eyes—those wonderful eyes! If I could but give some faint idea of their varying moods, their steely hardness, their feminine softness, their power of command, their penetrating intensity suddenly melting away into an expression of womanly weakness—but I am speaking now of future impressions!

There was a tall, yellow-haired young man with this lady, whom I at once recognised as a law student with whom I had a slight acquaintance.

Archibald Reeves—for that was his name—was a dashing, handsome young fellow, and had at one time been a ringleader in every university escapade; but of late I had seen little of him, and the report was that he was engaged to be married. His companion was, then, I presumed, his *fiancée*. I seated myself upon the velvet settee in the centre of the room, and furtively watched the couple from behind my catalogue.

The more I looked at her the more her beauty grew upon me. She was somewhat short in stature, it is true; but her figure was perfection, and she bore herself in such a fashion that it was only by actual comparison that one would have known her to be under the medium height.

As I kept my eyes upon them, Reeves was called away for some reason, and the young lady was left alone. Turning her back to the pictures, she passed the time until the return of her escort in taking a deliberate survey of the company, without paying the least heed to the fact that a dozen pair of eyes, attracted by her elegance and beauty, were bent curiously upon her. With one of her hands holding the red silk cord which railed off the pictures, she stood languidly moving her eyes from face to face with as little self-consciousness as if she were looking at the canvas creatures behind her. Suddenly, as I watched her, I saw her gaze become fixed, and, as it were, intense. I followed the direction of her looks, wondering what could have attracted her so strongly.

John Barrington Cowles was standing before a picture—one, I think, by Noel Paton—I know that the subject was a noble and ethereal one. His profile was turned towards us, and never have I seen him to such advantage. I have said that he was a strikingly handsome man, but at that moment he looked absolutely magnificent. It was evident that he had momentarily forgotten his surroundings, and that his whole soul was in sympathy with the picture before him. His eyes sparkled, and a dusky pink shone through his clear olive cheeks. She continued to watch him fixedly, with a look of interest upon her face, until he came out of his reverie with a start, and turned abruptly round, so that his gaze met hers. She glanced away at once, but his eyes remained fixed upon her for some moments. The picture was forgotten already, and his soul had come down to earth once more.

We caught sight of her once or twice before we left, and each time I noticed my friend look after her. He made no remark, however, until we got out into the open air, and were walking arm-in-arm along Princes Street.

"Did you notice that beautiful woman, in the dark dress, with the white fur?" he asked.

"Yes, I saw her," I answered.

"Do you know her?" he asked eagerly. "Have you any idea who she is?"

"I don't know her personally," I replied. "But I have no doubt I could find out all about her, for I believe she is engaged to young Archie Reeves, and he and I have a lot of mutual friends."

"Engaged!" ejaculated Cowles.

"Why, my dear boy," I said, laughing, "you don't mean to say you are so susceptible that the fact that a girl to whom you never spoke in your life is engaged is enough to upset you?"

"Well, not exactly to upset me," he answered, forcing a laugh. "But I don't mind telling you, Armitage, that I never was so taken by any one in my life. It wasn't the mere beauty of the face—though that was perfect enough—but it was the character and the intellect upon it. I hope, if she is engaged, that it is to some man who will be worthy of her."

"Why," I remarked, "you speak quite feelingly. It is a clear case of love at first sight, Jack. However, to put your perturbed spirit at rest, I'll make a point of finding out all about her whenever I meet any fellow who is likely to know."

Barrington Cowles thanked me, and the conversation drifted off into other channels. For several days neither of us made any allusion to the subject, though my companion was perhaps a little more dreamy and distraught than usual. The incident had almost vanished from my remembrance, when one day young Brodie, who is a second cousin of mine, came up to me on the university steps with the face of a bearer of tidings.

"I say," he began, "you know Reeves, don't you?"

"Yes. What of him?"

"His engagement is off."

"Off!" I cried. "Why, I only learned the other day that it was on."

"Oh, yes—it's all off. His brother told me so. Deucedly mean of Reeves, you know, if he has backed out of it, for she was an uncommonly nice girl."

"I've seen her," I said; "but I don't know her name."

"She is a Miss Northcott, and lives with an old aunt of hers in Abercrombie Place. Nobody knows anything about her people, or where she comes from. Anyhow, she is about the most unlucky girl in the world, poor soul!"

"Why unlucky?"

"Well, you know, this was her second engagement," said young Brodie, who had a marvellous knack of knowing everything about everybody. "She was engaged to Prescott—William Prescott, who died. That was a very sad affair. The wedding day was fixed, and the whole thing looked as straight as a die when the smash came."

"What smash?" I asked, with some dim recollection of the circumstances.

"Why, Prescott's death. He came to Abercrombie Place one night, and stayed very late. No one knows exactly when he left, but about one in the morning a fellow who knew him met him walking rapidly in the direction of the Queen's Park. He bade him good night, but Prescott hurried on without heeding him, and that was the last time he was ever seen alive. Three days afterwards his body was found floating in St. Margaret's Loch, under St. Anthony's Chapel. No one could ever understand it, but of course the verdict brought it in as temporary insanity."

"It was very strange," I remarked.

"Yes, and deucedly rough on the poor girl," said Brodie. "Now that this other blow has come it will quite crush her. So gentle and ladylike she is too!"

"You know her personally, then!" I asked.

"Oh, yes, I know her. I have met her several times. I could easily manage that you should be introduced to her."

"Well," I answered, "it's not so much for my own sake as for a friend of mine. However, I don't suppose she will go out much for some little time after this. When she does I will take advantage of your offer."

We shook hands on this, and I thought no more of the matter for some time.

The next incident which I have to relate as bearing at all upon the question of Miss Northcott is an unpleasant one. Yet I must detail it as accurately as possible, since it may throw some light upon the sequel. One cold night, several months after the conversation with my second cousin which I have quoted above, I was walking down one of the lowest streets in the city on my way back from a case which I had been attending. It was very late, and I was picking my way among the dirty loungers who were clustering round the doors of a great gin-palace, when a man staggered out from among them, and held out his hand to me with a drunken leer. The gaslight fell full upon his face, and, to my intense astonishment, I recognised in the degraded creature before me my former acquaintance, young Archibald Reeves, who had once been famous as one of the most dressy and particular men in the whole college. I was so utterly surprised that for a moment I almost doubted the evidence of my own senses; but there was no mistaking those features, which, though bloated with drink, still retained something of their former comeliness. I was determined to rescue him, for one night at least, from the company into which he had fallen.

"Holloa, Reeves!" I said. "Come along with me. I'm going in your direction."

He muttered some incoherent apology for his condition, and took my arm. As I supported him towards his lodgings I could see that he was not only suffering from the effects of a recent debauch, but that a long course of intemperance had affected his nerves and his brain. His hand when I touched it was dry and feverish, and he started from every shadow which fell upon the pavement. He rambled in his speech, too, in a manner which suggested the delirium of disease rather than the talk of a drunkard.

When I got him to his lodgings I partially undressed him and laid him upon his bed. His pulse at this time was very high, and he was evidently extremely feverish. He seemed to have sunk into a doze; and I was about to steal out of the room to warn his landlady of his condition, when he started up and caught me by the sleeve of my coat.

"Don't go!" he cried. "I feel better when you are here. I am safe from her then."

"From her!" I said. "From whom?"

"Her! her!" he answered peevishly. "Ah! you don't know her. She is the devil! Beautiful—beautiful; but the devil!"

"You are feverish and excited," I said. "Try and get a little sleep. You will wake better."

"Sleep!" he groaned. "How am I to sleep when I see her sitting down yonder at the foot of the bed with her great eyes watching and watching hour after hour? I tell you it saps all the strength and manhood out of me. That's what makes me drink. God help me—I'm half drunk now!"

"You are very ill," I said, putting some vinegar to his temples; "and you are delirious. You don't know what you say."

"Yes, I do," he interrupted sharply, looking up at me. "I know very well what I say. I brought it upon myself. It is my own choice. But I couldn't—no, by heaven, I couldn't—accept the alternative. I couldn't keep my faith to her. It was more than man could do."

I sat by the side of the bed, holding one of his burning hands in mine, and wondering over his strange words. He lay still for some time, and then, raising his eyes to me, said in a most plaintive voice—

"Why did she not give me warning sooner? Why did she wait until I had learned to love her so?"

He repeated this question several times, rolling his feverish head from side to side, and then he dropped into a troubled sleep. I crept out of the room, and, having seen that he would be properly cared for, left the house. His words, however, rang in my ears for days afterwards, and assumed a deeper significance when taken with what was to come.

My friend, Barrington Cowles, had been away for his summer holidays, and I had heard nothing of him for several months. When the winter session came on, however, I received a telegram from him, asking me to secure the old rooms in Northumberland Street for him, and telling me the train by which he would arrive. I went down to meet him, and was delighted to find him looking to find him looking wonderfully hearty and well.

"By the way," he said suddenly, that night, as we sat in our chairs by the fire, talking over the events of the holidays, "you have never congratulated me yet!"

"On what, my boy?" I asked.

"What! Do you mean to say you have not heard of my engagement?"

"Engagement! No!" I answered. "However, I am delighted to hear it, and congratulate you with all my heart."

"I wonder it didn't come to your ears," he said. "It was the queerest thing. You remember that girl whom we both admired so much at the Academy?"

"What!" I cried, with a vague feeling of apprehension at my heart. "You don't mean to say that you are engaged to her?"

"I thought you would be suprised," he answered. "When I was staying with an old aunt of mine in Peterhead, in Aberdeenshire, the Northcotts happened to come there on a visit, and as we had mutual friends we soon met. I found out that it was a false alarm about her being engaged, and then—well, you know what it is when you are thrown into the society of such a girl in a place like Peterhead. Not, mind you," he added, "that I consider I did a foolish or hasty thing. I have never regretted it for a moment. The more I know Kate the more I admire her and love her. However, you must be introduced to her, and then you will form your own opinion."

I expressed my pleasure at the prospect, and endeavoured to speak as lightly as I could to Cowles upon the subject, but I felt depressed and anxious at heart. The words of Reeves and the unhappy fate of young Prescott recurred to my recollection, and though I could assign no tangible reason for it, a vague, dim fear and distrust of the woman took possession of me. It may be that this was foolish prejudice and superstition upon my part, and that I involuntarily contorted her future doings and sayings to fit into some half-formed wild theory of my own. This has been suggested to me by others as an explanation of my narrative. They are welcome to their opinion if they can reconcile it with the facts which I have to tell.

I went round with my friend a few days afterwards to call upon Miss Northcott. I remember that, as we went down Abercrombie Place, our attention was attracted by the shrill yelping of a dog—which noise proved eventually to come from the house to which we were bound. We were shown upstairs, where I was introduced to old Mrs. Merton, Miss Northcott's aunt, and to the young lady herself. She looked as beautiful as ever, and I could not wonder at my friend's infatuation. Her face was a little more flushed than usual, and she held in her hand a heavy dog-whip, with which she had been chastising a small Scotch terrier, whose cries we had heard in the street. The poor brute was cringing up against the wall, whining piteously, and evidently completely cowed.

"So Kate," said my friend, after we had taken our seats," "you have been falling out with Carlo again."

"Only a very little quarrel this time," she said, smiling charmingly. "He is a dear, good old fellow, but he needs correction now and then." Then, turning to me, "We all do that, Mr. Armitage, don't we? What a capital thing if, instead of receiving a collective punishment at the end of our lives, we were to have one at once, as the dogs do, when we did anything wicked. It would make us more careful, wouldn't it?"

I acknowledged that it would.

"Supposing that every time a man misbehaved himself a gigantic hand were to seize him, and he were lashed with a whip until he fainted"—she clenched her white fingers as she spoke, and cut out viciously with the dog-whip—"it would do more to keep him good than any number of high-minded theories of morality."

"Why, Kate," said my friend, "you are quite savage to-day."

"No, Jack," she laughed. "I'm only propounding a theory for Mr. Armitage's consideration."

The two began to chat together about some Aberdeenshire reminiscence, and I had time to observe Mrs. Merton, who had remained silent during our short conversation. She was a very strange-looking old lady. What attracted attention most in her appearance was the utter want of colour which she exhibited. Her hair was snow-white, and her face extremely pale. Her lips were bloodless, and even her eyes were of such a light tinge of blue that they hardly relieved the general pallor. Her dress was a grey silk, which harmonised with her general appearance. She had a peculiar expression of countenance, which I was unable at the moment to refer to its proper cause.

She was working at some old-fashioned piece of ornamental needlework, and as she moved her arms her dress gave forth a dry, melancholy rustling, like the sound of leaves in the autumn. There was something mournful and depressing in the sight of her. I moved my chair a little nearer, and asked her how she liked Edinburgh, and whether she had been there long.

When I spoke to her she started and looked up at me with a scared look on her face. Then I saw in a moment what the expression was which I had observed there. It was one of fear—intense and overpowering fear. It was so marked that I could have staked my life on the woman before me having at some period of her life been subjected to some terrible experience or dreadful misfortune.

"Oh, yes, I like it," she said, in a soft, timid voice; "and we have been here long—that is, not very long. We move about a great deal." She spoke with hesitation, as if afraid of committing herself.

"You are a native of Scotland, I presume?" I said.

"No—that is, not entirely. We are not natives of any place. We are cosmopolitan, you know." She glanced round in the direction of Miss Northcott as she spoke, but the two were still chatting together near the window. Then she suddenly bent forward to me, with a look of intense earnestness upon her face, and said—

"Don't talk to me any more, please. She does not like it, and I shall suffer for it afterwards. Please, don't do it."

I was about to ask her the reason for this strange request, but when she saw I was going to address her, she rose and walked slowly out of the room. As she did so I perceived that the lovers had ceased to talk, and that Miss Northcott was looking at me with her keen, grey eyes.

"You must excuse my aunt, Mr. Armitage," she said; "she is old, and easily fatigued. Come over and look at my album."

We spent some time examining the portraits. Miss Northcott's father and mother were apparently ordinary mortals enough, and I could not detect in either of them any traces of the character which showed itself in their daughter's face. There was one old daguerreo-type, however, which arrested my attention. It represented a man of about the age of forty, and strikingly handsome. He was clean shaven, and extraordinary power was expressed upon his prominent lower jaw and firm, straight mouth. His eyes were somewhat deeply set in his head, however, and there was a snake-like flattening at the upper part of his forehead, which detracted from his appearance. I almost involuntarily, when I saw the head, pointed to it, and exclaimed—

"There is your prototype in your family, Miss Northcott."

"Do you think so?" she said. "I am afraid you are paying me a very bad compliment. Uncle Anthony was always considered the black sheep of the family."

"Indeed," I answered; "my remark was an unfortunate one, then."

"Oh, don't mind that," she said; "I always thought myself that he was worth all of them put together. He was an officer in the Forty-first Regiment, and he was killed in action during the Persian War—so he died nobly, at any rate."

"That's the sort of death I should like to die," said

Cowles, his dark eyes flashing, as they would when he was excited; "I often wish I had taken to my father's profession instead of this vile pill-compounding drudgery."

"Come, Jack, you are not going to die any sort of death yet," she said, tenderly taking his hand in hers.

I could not understand the woman. There was such an extraordinary mixture of masculine decision and womanly tenderness about her, with the consciousness of something all her own in the background, that she fairly puzzled me. I hardly knew, therefore, how to answer Cowles when, as we walked down the street together, he asked the comprehensive question—

"Well, what do you think of her?"

"I think she is wonderfully beautiful," I answered guardedly.

"That, of course," he replied irritably. "You knew that before you came!"

"I think she is very clever too," I remarked.

Barrington Cowles walked on for some time, and then he suddenly turned on me with the strange question—

"Do you think she is cruel? Do you think she is the sort of girl who would take a pleasure in inflicting pain?"

"Well, really," I answered, "I have hardly had time to form an opinion."

We then walked on for some time in silence.

"She is an old fool," at length muttered Cowles. "She is mad."

"Who is?" I asked.

"Why, that old woman—that aunt of Kate's—Mrs. Merton, or whatever her name is."

Then I knew that my poor colourless friend had been speaking to Cowles, but he never said anything more as to the nature of her communication.

My companion went to bed early that night, and I sat up a long time by the fire, thinking over all that I had seen and heard. I felt that there was some mystery about the girl—some dark fatality so strange as to defy conjecture. I thought of Prescott's interview with her before their marriage, and the fatal termination of it. I coupled it with poor drunken Reeves' plaintive cry, "Why did she not tell me sooner?" and with the other words he had spoken. Then my mind ran over Mrs. Merton's warning to me, Cowles' reference to her, and even the episode of the whip and the cringing dog.

The whole effect of my recollections was unpleasant to a degree, and yet there was no tangible charge which I could bring against the woman. It would be worse than useless to attempt to warn my friend until I had definitely made up my mind what I was to warn him against. He would treat any charge against her with scorn. What could I do? How could I get at some tangible conclusion as to her character and antecedents? No one in Edinburgh knew them except as recent acquaintances. She was an orphan, and as far as I knew she had never disclosed where her former home had been. Suddenly an idea struck me. Among my father's friends there was a Colonel Joyce, who had served a long time in India upon the staff, and who would be likely to know most of the officers who had been out there since the Mutiny. I sat down at once, and, having trimmed the lamp, proceeded to write a letter to the Colonel. I told him that I was very curious to gain some particulars about a certain Captain Northcott, who had served in the Forty-first Foot, and who had fallen in the Persian War. I described the man as well as I could from my recollection of the daguerreotype, and then, having directed the letter, posted it that very night, after which, feeling that I had done all that could be done, I retired to bed, with a mind too anxious to allow me to sleep.

PART II

I GOT an answer from Leicester, where the Colonel resided, within two days. I have it before me as I write, and copy it verbatim.

"DEAR BOB," it said, "I remember the man well. I was with him at Calcutta, and afterwards at Hyderabad.

He was a curious, solitary sort of mortal; but a gallant soldier enough, for he distinguished himself at Sobraon, and was wounded, if I remember right. He was not popular in his corps—they said he was a pitiless, cold-blooded fellow, with no geniality in him. There was a rumour, too, that he was a devil-worshipper, or something of that sort, and also that he had the evil eye, which, of course, was all nonsense. He had some strange theories, I remember, about the power of the human will and the effects of mind upon matter.

"How are you getting on with your medical studies? Never forget, my boy, that your father's son has every claim upon me, and that if I can serve you in any way I am always at your command.—Ever affectionately yours,

EDWARD JOYCE

"*P.S.*—By the way, Northcott did not fall in action. He was killed after peace was declared in a crazy attempt to get some of the eternal fire from the sunworshippers' temple. There was considerable mystery about his death."

I read this epistle over several times—at first with a feeling of satisfaction, and then with one of disappointment. I had come on some curious information, and yet hardly what I wanted. He was an eccentric man, a devil-worshipper, and rumoured to have the power of the evil eye. I could believe the young lady's eyes, when endowed with that cold, grey shimmer which I had noticed in them once or twice, to be capable of any evil which human eye ever wrought; but still the superstition was an effete one. Was there not more meaning in that sentence which followed—"He had theories of the power of the human will and of the effect of mind upon matter"? I remember having once read a quaint treatise, which I had imagined to be mere charlatanism at the time, of the power of certain human minds, and of effects produced by them at a distance. Was Miss Northcott endowed with some exceptional power of the sort? The idea grew upon me, and very shortly I had evidence which convinced me of the truth of the supposition.

It happened that at the very time when my mind was dwelling upon this subject, I saw a notice in the paper that our town was to be visited by Dr. Messinger, the well-known medium and mesmerist. Messinger was a man whose performance, such as it was, had been again and again pronounced to be genuine by competent judges. He was far above trickery, and had the reputation of being the soundest living authority upon the strange pseudo-sciences of animal magnetism and electro-biology. Determined, therefore, to see what the human will could do, even against all the disadvantages of glaring footlights and a public platform, I took a ticket for the first night of the performance, and went with several student friends.

We had secured one of the side boxes, and did not arrive until after the performance had begun. I had hardly taken my seat before I recognised Barrington Cowles, with his *fiancée* and old Mrs. Merton, sitting in the third or fourth row of the stalls. They caught sight of me at almost the same moment, and we bowed to each other. The first portion of the lecture was somewhat commonplace, the lecturer giving tricks of pure legerdemain, with one or two manifestations of mesmerism, performed upon a subject whom he had brought with him. He gave us an exhibition of clairvoyance too, throwing his subject into a trance, and then demanding particulars as to the movements of absent friends, and the whereabouts of hidden objects, all of which appeared to be answered satisfactorily. I had seen all this before, however. What I wanted to see now was the effect of the lecturer's will when exerted upon some independent member of the audience.

He came round to that as the concluding exhibition in his performance. "I have shown you," he said, "that a mesmerised subject is entirely dominated by the will of the mesmeriser. He loses all power of volition, and his very thoughts are such as are suggested to him by the master-mind. The same end may be attained without any preliminary process. A strong will can, simply by virtue of its strength, take possession of a weaker one, even at a distance, and can regulate the impulses and the actions of the owner of it. If there was one man in the world who had a very much more highly-developed will than any of the rest of the human family, there is no reason why he should not be able to rule over them all, and to reduce his fellow-creatures to the condition of automatons. Happily there is such a dead level of mental power, or rather of mental weakness, among us that such a catastrophe is not likely to occur; but still within our small compass there are variations which produce surprising effects. I shall now single out one of the audience, and endeavour 'by the mere power of will' to compel him to come upon the platform, and do and say what I wish. Let me assure you that there is no collusion, and that the subject whom I may select is at perfect liberty to resent to the uttermost any impulse which I may communicate to him."

With these words the lecturer came to the front of the platform, and glanced over the first few rows of the stalls. No doubt Cowles' dark skin and bright eyes marked him out as a man of a highly nervous temperament, for the mesmerist picked him out in a moment, and fixed his eyes upon him. I saw my friend give a start of surprise, and then settle down in his chair, as if to express his determination not to yield to the influence of the operator. Messinger was not a man whose head denoted any great brain-power, but his gaze was singularly intense and penetrating. Under the influence of it Cowles made one or two spasmodic motions of his hands, as if to grasp the sides of his seat, and then half rose, but only to sink down again, though with an evident effort. I was watching the scene with intense interest, when I happened to catch a glimpse of Miss Northcott's face. She was sitting with her eyes fixed intently upon the mesmerist, and with such an expression of concentrated power upon her features as I have never seen on any other human countenance. Her jaw was firmly set, her lips compressed, and her face as hard as if it were a beautiful sculpture cut out of the whitest marble. Her eyebrows were drawn down, however, and from beneath them her grey eyes seemed to sparkle and gleam with a cold light.

I looked at Cowles again, expecting every moment to see him rise and obey the mesmerist's wishes, when there came from the platform a short, gasping cry as of a man utterly worn out and prostrated by a prolonged struggle. Messinger was leaning against the table, his hand to his forehead, and the perspiration pouring down his face. "I won't go on," he cried, addressing the audience. "There is a stronger will than mine acting against me. You must excuse me for to-night." The man was evidently ill, and utterly unable to proceed, so the curtain was lowered, and the audience dispersed, with many comments upon the lecturer's sudden indisposition.

I waited outside the hall until my friend and the ladies came out. Cowles was laughing over his recent experience.

"He didn't succeed with me, Bob," he cried triumphantly, as he shook my hand. "I think he caught a Tartar that time."

"Yes," said Miss Northcott, "I think that Jack ought to be very proud of his strength of mind; don't you, Mr. Armitage?"

"It took me all my time, though," my friend said seriously. "You can't conceive what a strange feeling I had once or twice. All the strength seemed to have gone out of me—especially just before he collapsed himself."

I walked round with Cowles in order to see the ladies home. He walked in front with Mrs. Merton, and I found myself behind with the young lady. For a minute or so I walked beside her without making any remark, and then I suddenly blurted out, in a manner which must have seemed somewhat brusque to her—

"You did that, Miss Northcott."

"Did what?" she asked sharply.

"Why, mesmerised the mesmeriser—I suppose that is the best way of describing the transaction."

"What a strange idea!" she said, laughing. "You give me credit for a strong will then?"

"Yes," I said. "For a dangerously strong one."

"Why dangerous?" she asked, in a tone of surprise.

"I think," I answered, "that any will which can exercise such power is dangerous—for there is always a chance of its being turned to bad uses."

"You would make me out a very dreadful individual, Mr. Armitage," she said; and then looking up suddenly in my face—"You have never liked me. You are suspicious of me and distrust me, though I have never given you cause."

The accusation was so sudden and so true that I was unable to find any reply to it. She paused for a moment, and then said in a voice which was hard and cold—

"Don't let your prejudice lead you to interfere with me, however, or say anything to your friend, Mr. Cowles, which might lead to a difference between us. You would find that to be very bad policy."

There was something in the way she spoke which gave an indescribable air of a threat to these few words.

"I have no power," I said, "to interfere with your plans for the future. I cannot help, however, from what I have seen and heard, having fears for my friend."

"Fears!" she repeated scornfully. "Pray what have you seen and heard. Something from Mr. Reeves, perhaps—I believe he is another of your friends?"

"He never mentioned your name to me," I answered, truthfully enough. "You will be sorry to hear that he is dying." As I said it we passed by a lighted window, and I glanced down to see what effect my words had upon her. She was laughing—there was no doubt of it; she was laughing quietly to herself. I could see merriment in every feature of her face. I feared and mistrusted the woman from that moment more than ever.

We said little more that night. When we parted she

gave me a quick, warning glance, as if to remind me of what she had said about the danger of interference. Her cautions would have made little difference to me could I have seen my way to benefiting Barrington Cowles by anything which I might say. But what could I say? I might say that her former suitors had been unfortunate. I might say that I believed her to be a cruel-hearted woman. I might say that I considered her to possess wonderful, and almost preternatural powers. What impression would any of these accusations make upon an ardent lover—a man with my friend's enthusiastic temperament? I felt that it would be useless to advance them, so I was silent.

And now I come to the beginning of the end. Hitherto much has been surmise and inference and hearsay. It is my painful task to relate now, as dispassionately and as accurately as I can, what actually occurred under my own notice, and to reduce to writing the events which preceded the death of my friend.

Towards the end of the winter Cowles remarked to me that he intended to marry Miss Northcott as soon as possible—probably some time in the spring. He was, as I have already remarked, fairly well off, and the young lady had some money of her own, so that there was no pecuniary reason for a long engagement. "We are going to take a little house out at Corstorphine," he said, "and we hope to see your face at our table, Bob, as often as you can possibly come." I thanked him, and tried to shake off my apprehensions, and persuade myself that all would yet be well.

It was about three weeks before the time fixed for the marriage, that Cowles remarked to me one evening that he feared he would be late that night. "I have had a note from Kate," he said, "asking me to call about eleven o'clock to-night, which seems rather a late hour, but perhaps she wants to talk over something quietly after old Mrs. Merton retires."

It was not until after my friend's departure that I suddenly recollected the mysterious interview which I had been told of as preceding the suicide of young Prescott. Then I thought of the ravings of poor Reeves, rendered more tragic by the fact that I had heard that very day of his death. What was the meaning of it all? Had this woman some baleful secret to disclose which must be known before her marriage? Was it some reason which forbade her to marry? Or was it some reason which forbade others to marry her? I felt so uneasy that I would have followed Cowles, even at the risk of offending him, and endeavoured to dissuade him from keeping his appointment, but a glance at the clock showed me that I was too late.

I was determined to wait up for his return, so I piled some coals upon the fire and took down a novel from the shelf. My thoughts proved more interesting than the book, however, and I threw it on one side. An indefinable feeling of anxiety and depression weighed upon me. Twelve o'clock came, and then half-past, without any sign of my friend. It was nearly one when I heard a step in the street outside, and then a knocking at the door. I was surprised, as I knew that my friend always carried a key—however, I hurried down and undid the latch. As the door flew open I knew in a moment that my worst apprehensions had been fulfilled. Barrington Cowles was leaning against the railings outside with his face sunk upon his breast, and his whole attitude expressive of the most intense despondency. As he passed in he gave a stagger, and would have fallen had I not thrown my left arm around him. Supporting him with this, and holding the lamp in my other hand, I led him slowly upstairs into our sitting-room. He sank down upon the sofa without a word. Now that I could get a good view of him, I was horrified to see the change which had come over him. His face was deadly pale, and his very lips were bloodless. His cheeks and forehead were clammy, his eyes glazed, and his whole expression altered. He looked like a man who had gone through some terrible ordeal, and was thoroughly unnerved.

"My dear fellow, what is the matter?" I asked, breaking the silence. "Nothing amiss, I trust? Are you unwell?"

"Brandy!" he gasped. "Give me some brandy!"

I took out the decanter, and was about to help him, when he snatched it from me with a trembling hand, and poured out nearly half a tumbler of the spirit. He was usually a most abstemious man, but he took this off at a gulp without adding any water to it. It seemed to do him good, for the colour began to come back to his face, and he leaned upon his elbow.

"My engagement is off, Bob," he said, trying to speak calmly, but with a tremor in his voice which he could not conceal. "It is all over."

"Cheer up!" I answered, trying to encourage him. "Don't get down on your luck. How was it? What was it all about?"

"About?" he groaned, covering his face with his hands. "If I did tell you, Bob, you would not believe it. It is too dreadful—too horrible—unutterably awful and incredible! O Kate, Kate!" and he rocked himself to and fro in his grief; "I pictured you an angel and I find you a——"

"A what?" I asked, for he had paused.

He looked at me with a vacant stare, and then suddenly burst out, waving his arms: "A fiend!" he cried. "A ghoul from the pit! A vampire soul behind a lovely face! Now, God forgive me!" he went on in a lower tone, turning his face to the wall; "I have said more than I should. I have loved her too much to speak of her as she is. I love her too much now."

He lay still for some time, and I had hoped that the brandy had had the effect of sending him to sleep, when he suddenly turned his face towards me.

"Did you ever read of wehr-wolves?" he asked.

I answered that I had.

"There is a story," he said thoughtfully, "in one of Marryat's books, about a beautiful woman who took the form of a wolf at night and devoured her own children. I wonder what put that idea into Marryat's head?"

He pondered for some minutes, and then he cried out for some more brandy. There was a small bottle of laudanum upon the table, and I managed, by insisting upon helping him myself, to mix about half a drachm with the spirits. He drank it off, and sank his head once more upon the pillow. "Anything better than that," he groaned. "Death is better than that. Crime and cruelty; cruelty and crime. Anything is better than that," and so on, with the monotonous refrain, until at last the words became indistinct, his eyelids closed over his weary eyes, and he sank into a profound slumber. I carried him into his bedroom without arousing him; and making a couch for myself out of the chairs, I remained by his side all night.

In the morning Barrington Cowles was in a high fever. For weeks he lingered between life and death. The highest medical skill of Edinburgh was called in, and his vigorous constitution slowly got the better of his disease. I nursed him during this anxious time; but through all his wild delirium and ravings he never let a word escape him which explained the mystery connected with Miss Northcott. Sometimes he spoke of her in the tenderest words and most loving voice. At others he screamed out that she was a fiend, and stretched out his arms, as if to keep her off. Several times he cried that he would not sell his soul for a beautiful face, and then he would moan in a most piteous voice, "But I love her—I love her for all that; I shall never cease to love her."

When he came to himself he was an altered man. His severe illness had emaciated him greatly, but his dark eyes had lost none of their brightness. They shone out with startling brilliancy from under his dark, overhanging brows. His manner was eccentric and variable—sometimes irritable, sometimes recklessly mirthful, but never natural. He would glance about him in a strange, suspicious manner, like one who feared something, and yet hardly knew what it was he dreaded. He never mentioned Miss Northcott's name—never until that fatal evening of which I have now to speak.

In an endeavour to break the current of his thoughts by frequent change of scene, I travelled with him through the highlands of Scotland, and afterwards down the east coast. In one of these peregrinations of ours we visited the Isle of May, an island near the mouth of the Firth of Forth, which, except in the tourist season, is singularly barren and desolate. Beyond the keeper of the lighthouse there are only one or two families of poor fisher-folk, who sustain a precarious existence by their nets, and by the capture of cormorants and solan geese. This grim spot seemed to have such a fascination for Cowles that we engaged a room in one of the fishermen's huts, with the intention of passing a week or two there. I found it very dull, but the loneliness appeared to be a relief to my friend's mind. He lost the look of apprehension which had become habitual to him, and became something like his old self. He would wander round the island all day, looking down from the summit of the great cliffs which gird it round, and watching the long green waves as they came booming in and burst in a shower of spray over the rocks beneath.

One night—I think it was our third or fourth on the island—Barrington Cowles and I went outside the cottage before retiring to rest, to enjoy a little fresh air, for our room was small, and the rough lamp caused an unpleasant odour. How well I remember every little circumstance in connection with that night! It promised to be tempestuous, for the clouds were piling up in the north-west, and the dark wrack was drifting across the face of the moon, throwing alternate belts of light and shade upon the rugged surface of the island and the restless sea beyond.

We were standing talking close by the door of the cottage, and I was thinking to myself that my friend was more cheerful than he had been since his illness, when he gave a sudden, sharp cry, and looking round at him I saw, by the light of the moon, an expression of unutterable horror come over his features. His eyes became fixed and staring, as if riveted upon some approaching object, and he extended his long thin forefinger, which quivered as he pointed.

"Look there!" he cried. "It is she! It is she! You see her there coming down the side of the brae." He gripped me convulsively by the wrist as he spoke. "There she is, coming towards us!"

"Who?" I cried, straining my eyes into the darkness.

"She—Kate—Kate Northcott!" he screamed. "She has come for me. Hold me fast, old friend. Don't let me go!"

"Hold up, old man," I said, clapping him on the shoulder. "Pull yourself together; you are dreaming; there is nothing to fear."

"She is gone!" he cried, with a gasp of relief. "No, by heaven! there she is again, and nearer—coming nearer. She told me she would come for me, and she keeps her word."

"Come into the house," I said. His hand, as I grasped it, was as cold as ice.

"Ah, I knew it!" he shouted. "There she is, waving her arms. She is beckoning to me. It is the signal. I must go. I am coming, Kate; I am coming!"

I threw my arms around him, but he burst from me with superhuman strength, and dashed into the darkness of the night. I followed him, calling to him to stop, but he ran the more swiftly. When the moon shone out between the clouds I could catch a glimpse of his dark figure, running rapidly in a straight line, as if to reach some definite goal. It may have been imagination, but it seemed to me that in the flickering light I could distinguish a vague something in front of him—a shimmering form which eluded his grasp and led him onwards. I saw his outlines stand out hard against the sky behind him as he surmounted the brow of a little hill, then he disappeared, and that was the last ever seen by mortal eye of Barrington Cowles.

The fishermen and I walked round the island all that night with lanterns, and examined every nook and corner without seeing a trace of my poor lost friend. The direction in which he had been running terminated in a rugged line of jagged cliffs overhanging the sea. At one place here the edge was somewhat crumbled, and there appeared marks upon the turf which might have been left by human feet. We lay upon our faces at this spot, and peered with our lanterns over the edge, looking down on the boiling surge two hundred feet below. As we lay there, suddenly, above the beating of the waves and the howling of the wind, there rose a strange wild screech from the abyss below. The fishermen—a naturally superstitious race—averred that it was the sound of a woman's laughter, and I could hardly persuade them to continue the search. For my own part I think it may have been the cry of some sea-fowl startled from its nest by the flash of the lantern. However that may be, I never wish to hear such a sound again.

And now I have come to the end of the painful duty which I have undertaken. I have told as plainly and as accurately as I could the story of the death of John Barrington Cowles, and the train of events which preceded it. I am aware that to others the sad episode seemed commonplace enough. Here is the prosaic account which appeared in the *Scotsman* a couple of days afterwards:—

"*Sad Occurrence on the Isle of May.*—The Isle of May has been the scene of a sad disaster. Mr. John Barrington Cowles, a gentleman well known in University circles as a most distinguished student, and the present holder of the Neil Arnott prize for physics, has been recruiting his health in this quiet retreat. The night before last he suddenly left his friend, Mr. Robert Armitage, and he has not since been heard of. It is almost certain that he has met his death by falling over the cliffs which surround the island. Mr. Cowles' health has been failing for some time, partly from overstudy and partly from worry connected with family affairs. By his death the University loses one of her most promising alumni."

I have nothing more to add to my statement. I have unburdened my mind of all that I know. I can well conceive that many, after weighing all that I have said, will see no ground for an accusation against Miss Northcott. They will say that, because a man of a naturally excitable disposition says and does wild things, and even eventually commits self-murder after a sudden and heavy disappointment, there is no reason why vague charges should be advanced against a young lady. To this, I answer that they are welcome to their opinion. For my own part, I ascribe the death of William Prescott, of Archibald Reeves, and of John Barrington Cowles to this woman with as much confidence as if I had seen her drive a dagger into their hearts.

You ask me, no doubt, what my own theory is which will explain all these strange facts. I have none, or, at best, a dim and vague one. That Miss Northcott possessed extraordinary powers over the minds, and through the minds over the bodies, of others, I am convinced, as well as that her instincts were to use this power for base and cruel purposes. That some even more fiendish and terrible phase of character lay behind this—some horrible trait which it was necessary for her to reveal before marriage—is to be inferred from the experience of her three lovers, while the dreadful nature of the mystery thus revealed can only be surmised from the fact that the very mention of it drove from her those who had loved her so passionately. Their subsequent fate was, in my opinion, the result of her vindictive remembrance of their desertion of her, and that they were forewarned of it at the time was shown by the words of both Reeves and Cowles. Above this, I can say nothing. I lay the facts soberly before the public as they came under my notice. I have never seen Miss Northcott since, nor do I wish to do so. If by the words I have written I can save any one human being from the snare of those bright eyes and that beautiful face, then I can lay down my pen with the assurance that my poor friend has not died altogether in vain.

SELECTING A GHOST

I AM sure that Nature never intended me to be a self-made man. There are times when I can hardly bring myself to realize that twenty years of my life were spent behind the counter of a grocer's shop in the East End of London, and that it was through such an avenue that I reached a wealthy independence and the possession of Goresthorpe Grange. My habits are Conservative, and my tastes refined and aristocratic. I have a soul which spurns the vulgar herd. Our family, the D'Odds, date back to a prehistoric era, as is to be inferred from the fact that their advent into British history is not commented on by any trustworthy historian. Some instinct tells me that the blood of a Crusader runs in my veins. Even now, after the lapse of so many years, such exclamations as "By'r Lady!" rise naturally to my lips, and I feel that, should circumstances require it, I am capable of rising in my stirrups and dealing an infidel a blow—say with a mace—which would considerably astonish him.

Goresthorpe Grange is a feudal mansion—or so it was termed in the advertisement which originally brought it under my notice. Its right to this adjective had a most remarkable effect upon its price, and the advantages gained may possibly be more sentimental than real. Still, it is soothing to me to know that I have slits in my staircase through which I can discharge arrows; and there is a sense of power in the fact of possessing a complicated apparatus by means of which I am enabled to pour molten lead upon the head of the casual visitor. These things chime in with my peculiar humor, and I do not grudge to pay for them. I am proud of my battlements and of the circular uncovered sewer which girds me round. I am proud of my portcullis and donjon and keep. There is but one thing wanting to round off the mediævalism of my abode, and to render it symmetrically and completely antique. Goresthorpe Grange is not provided with a ghost.

Any man with old-fashioned tastes and ideas as to how such establishments should be conducted, would have been disappointed at the omission. In my case it was particularly unfortunate. From my childhood I had been an earnest student of the supernatural, and a firm believer in it. I have revelled in ghostly literature until there is hardly a tale bearing upon the subject which I have not perused. I learned the German language for the sole purpose of mastering a book upon demonology. When an infant I have secreted myself in dark rooms in the hope of seeing some of those bogies with which my nurse used to threaten me; and the same feeling is as strong in me now as then. It was a proud moment when I felt that a ghost was one of the luxuries which my money might command.

It is true that there was no mention of an apparition in the advertisement. On reviewing the mildewed walls, however, and the shadowy corridors, I had taken it for granted that there was such a thing on the premises. As the presence of a kennel presupposes that of a dog, so I imagined that it was impossible that such desirable quarters should be untenanted by one or more restless shades. Good heavens, what can the noble family from whom I purchased it have been doing during these hundreds of years! Was there no member of it spirited enough to make away with his sweetheart, or take some other steps calculated to establish a hereditary spectre? Even now I can hardly write with patience upon the subject.

For a long time I hoped against hope. Never did rat squeak behind the wainscot, or rain drip upon the attic floor, without a wild thrill shooting through me as I thought that at last I had come upon traces of some unquiet soul. I felt no touch of fear upon these occasions. If it occurred in the night-time, I would send Mrs. D'Odd—who is a strong-minded woman—to investigate the matter, while I covered up my head with the bedclothes and indulged in an ecstasy of expectation. Alas, the result was always the same! The suspicious sound would be traced to some cause so absurdly natural and commonplace that the most fervid imagination could not clothe it with any of the glamour of romance.

I might have reconciled myself to this state of things, had it not been for Jorrocks of Havistock Farm. Jorrocks is a coarse, burly, matter-of-fact fellow, whom I only happened to know through the accidental circumstance of his fields adjoining my demesne. Yet this man, though utterly devoid of all appreciation of archæological unities, is in possession of a well-authenticated and undeniable spectre. Its existence only dates back, I believe, to the reign of the Second George, when a young lady cut her throat upon hearing of the death of her lover at the battle of Dettingen. Still, even that gives the house an air of respectability, especially when coupled with blood stains upon the floor. Jorrocks is densely unconscious of his good fortune; and his language when he reverts to the apparition is painful to listen to. He little dreams how I covet every one of those moans and nocturnal wails which he describes with unnecessary objurgation. Things are indeed coming to a pretty pass when democratic spectres are allowed to desert the landed proprietors and annul every social distinction by taking refuge in the houses of the great unrecognized.

I have a large amount of perseverance. Nothing else could have raised me into my rightful sphere, considering the uncongenial atmosphere in which I spent the earlier part of my life. I felt now that a ghost must be secured, but how to set about securing one was more than either Mrs. D'Odd or myself was able to determine. My reading taught me that such phenomena are usually the outcome of crime. What crime was to be done, then, and who was to do it? A wild idea entered my mind that Watkins, the house-steward, might be prevailed upon—for a consideration—to immolate himself or someone else in the interests of the establishment. I put the matter to him in a half-jesting manner; but it did not seem to strike him in a favorable light. The other servants sympathized with him in his opinion—at least, I cannot account in any other way for their having left the house in a body the same afternoon.

"My dear," Mrs. D'Odd remarked to me one day after dinner, as I sat moodily sipping a cup of sack—I love the good old names—"my dear, that odious ghost of Jorrocks' has been gibbering again."

"Let it gibber!" I answered, recklessly.

Mrs. D'Odd struck a few chords on her virginal and looked thoughtfully into the fire.

"I'll tell you what it is, Argentine," she said at last, using the pet name which we usually substituted for Silas, "we must have a ghost sent down from London."

"How can you be so idiotic, Matilda?" I remarked, severely. "Who could get us such a thing?"

"My cousin, Jack Brocket, could," she answered, confidently.

Now, this cousin of Matilda's was rather a sore subject between us. He was a rakish, clever young fellow, who had tried his hand at many things, but wanted perseverance to succeed at any. He was, at that time, in chambers in London, professing to be a general agent, and really living, to a great extent, upon his wits. Matilda managed so that most of our business should pass through his hands, which certainly saved me a great deal of trouble; but I found that Jack's commission was generally considerably larger than all the other items of the bill put together. It was this fact which made me feel inclined to rebel against any further negotiations with the young gentleman.

"O yes, he could," insisted Mrs. D., seeing the look of disapprobation upon my face. "You remember how well he managed that business about the crest?"

"It was only a resuscitation of the old family coat-of-arms, my dear," I protested.

Matilda smiled in an irritating manner. "There was a resuscitation of the family portraits, too, dear," she remarked. "You must allow that Jack selected them very judiciously."

I thought of the long line of faces which adorned the walls of my banqueting-hall, from the burly Norman robber, through every gradation of casque, plume, and ruff, to the sombre Chesterfieldian individual who appears to have staggered against a pillar in his agony at the return of a maiden MS. which he grips convulsively in his right hand. I was fain to confess that in that instance he had done his work well, and that it was only fair to give him an order—with the usual commission—for a family spectre, should such a thing be attainable.

It is one of my maxims to act promptly when once my mind is made up. Noon of the next day found me ascending the spiral stone staircase which leads to Mr. Brocket's chambers, and admiring the succession of arrows and fingers upon the whitewashed wall, all indicating the direction of that gentleman's sanctum. As it happened, artificial aids of the sort were entirely unnecessary, as an animated flat-dance overhead could proceed from no other quarter, though it was replaced by a deathly silence as I groped my way up the stair. The door was opened by a youth evidently astounded at the appearance of a client, and I was ushered into the presence of my young friend, who was writing furiously in a large ledger—upside down, as I afterward discovered.

After the first greetings, I plunged into business at once.

"Look here, Jack," I said, "I want you to get me a spirit, if you can."

"Spirits you mean!" shouted my wife's cousin, plunging his hand into the waste-paper basket and producing a bottle with the celerity of a conjuring trick. "Let's have a drink!"

I held up my hand as a mute appeal against such a proceeding so early in the day; but on lowering it again I found that I had almost involuntarily closed my fingers round the tumbler which my adviser had pressed upon me. I drank the contents hastily off, lest anyone should come in upon us and set me down as a toper. After all there was something very amusing about the young fellow's eccentricities.

"Not spirits," I explained, smilingly; "an apparition—a ghost. If such a thing is to be had, I should be very willing to negotiate."

"A ghost for Goresthorpe Grange?" inquired Mr. Brocket, with as much coolness as if I had asked for a drawing-room suite.

"Quite so," I answered.

"Easiest thing in the world," said my companion, filling up my glass again in spite of my remonstrance. "Let us see!" Here he took down a large red note-book, with all the letters of the alphabet in a fringe down the edge. "A ghost you said, didn't you? That's G. G—gems—gimlets—gas-pipes—gauntlets—guns—galleys. Ah, here we are. Ghosts. Volume nine, section six, page forty-one. Excuse me!" And Jack ran up a ladder and began rummaging among a pile of ledgers on a high shelf. I felt half inclined to empty my glass into the spittoon when his back was turned; but on second thoughts I disposed of it in a legitimate way.

"Here it is!" cried my London agent, jumping off the ladder with a crash, and depositing an enormous volume of manuscript upon the table. "I have all these things tabulated, so that I may lay my hands upon them in a moment. It's all right—it's quite weak" (here he filled our glasses again). "What were we looking up, again?"

"Ghosts," I suggested.

"Of course; page 41. Here we are. 'J. H. Fowler & Son, Dunkel Street, suppliers of mediums to the nobility and gentry; charms sold—love philtres—mummies—horoscopes cast.' Nothing in your line there, I suppose.

I shook my head despondently.

"'Frederick Tabb,'" continued my wife's cousin, "'sole channel of communication between the living and the dead. Proprietor of the spirits of Byron, Kirke White, Grimaldi, Tom Cribb, and Inigo Jones.' That's about the figure!"

"Nothing romantic enough there," I objected. "Good heavens! Fancy a ghost with a black eye and a handkerchief tied round its waist, or turning summersaults, and saying, 'How are you to-morrow?'" The very idea made me so warm that I emptied my glass and filled it again.

"Here is another," said my companion, "'Christopher McCarthy; bi-weekly séances—attended by all the eminent spirits of ancient and modern times. Nativities—charms—abracadabras, messages from the dead.' He might be able to help us. However, I shall have a hunt round myself to-morrow, and see some of these fellows. I know their haunts, and it's odd if I can't pick up something cheap. So there's an end of business," he concluded, hurling the ledger into the corner, "and now we'll have something to drink."

We had several things to drink—so many that my inventive faculties were dulled next morning, and I had some little difficulty in explaining to Mrs. D'Odd why it was that I hung my boots and spectacles upon a peg along with my other garments before retiring to rest. The new hopes excited by the confident manner in which my agent had undertaken the commission, caused me to rise superior to alcoholic reaction, and I paced about the rambling corridors and old-fashioned rooms, picturing to myself the appearance of my expected acquisition, and deciding what part of the building would harmonize best with its presence. After much consideration, I pitched upon the banqueting-hall as being, on the whole, most suitable for its reception. It was a long low room, hung round with valuable tapestry and interesting relics of the old family to whom it had belonged. Coats of mail and implements of war glimmered fitfully as the light of the fire played over them, and the wind crept under the door, moving the hangings to and fro with a ghastly rustling. At one end there was the raised dais, on which in ancient times the host and his guests used to spread their table, while a descent of a couple of steps led to the lower part of the hall, where the vassals and retainers held wassail. The floor was uncovered by any sort of carpet, but a layer of rushes had been scattered over it by my direction. In the whole room there was nothing to remind one of the nineteenth century; except, indeed, my own solid silver plate, stamped with the resuscitated family arms, which was laid out upon an oak table in the centre. This, I determined, should be the haunted room, supposing my wife's cousin to succeed in his negotiation with the spirit-mongers. There was nothing for it now but to wait patiently until I heard some news of the result of his inquiries.

A letter came in the course of a few days, which, if it was short, was at least encouraging. It was scribbled in pencil on the back of a playbill, and sealed apparently with a tobacco-stopper. "Am on the track," it said. "Nothing of the sort to be had from any professional spiritualist, but picked up a fellow in a pub yesterday who says he can manage it for you. Will send him down unless you wire to the contrary. Abrahams is his name, and he has done one or two of these jobs before." The letter wound up with some incoherent allusions to a check, and was signed by my affectionate cousin, John Brocket.

I need hardly say that I did not wire, but awaited the arrival of Mr. Abrahams with all impatience. In spite of my belief in the supernatural, I could scarcely credit the fact that any mortal could have such a command over the spirit-world as to deal in them and barter them against mere earthly gold. Still, I had Jack's word for it that such a trade existed; and here was a gentleman with a Judaical name ready to demonstrate it by proof positive. How vulgar and commonplace Jorrocks' eighteenth-century ghost would appear should I succeed in securing a real mediæval apparition! I almost thought that one had been sent down in advance, for, as I walked round the moat that night before retiring to rest, I came upon a dark figure engaged in surveying the machinery of my portcullis and drawbridge. His start of surprise, however, and the manner in which he hurried off into the darkness, speedily convinced me of his earthly origin, and I put him down as some admirer of one of my female retainers mourning over the muddy Hellespont which divided him from his love. Whoever he may have been, he disappeared and did not return, though I loitered about for some time in the hope of catching a glimpse of him and exercising my feudal rights upon his person.

Jack Brocket was as good as his word. The shades of another evening were beginning to darken round Goresthorpe Grange, when a peal at the outer bell, and the sound of a fly pulling up, announced the arrival of Mr. Abrahams. I hurried down to meet him, half expecting to see a choice assortment of ghosts crowding in at his rear. Instead, however, of being the sallow-faced, melancholy-eyed man that I had pictured to myself, the ghost-dealer was a sturdy little podgy fellow, with a pair of wonderfully keen sparkling eyes and a mouth which was constantly stretched in a good-humored, if somewhat artificial, grin. His sole stock-in-trade seemed to consist of a small leather bag jealously locked and strapped, which emitted a metallic chink upon being placed on the stone flags of the hall.

"And 'ow are you, sir?" he asked, wringing my hand with the utmost effusion. "And the missus, 'ow is she? And all the others—'ow's all their 'ealth?"

I intimated that we were all as well as could reasonably be expected, but Mr. Abrahams happened to catch a glimpse of Mrs. D'Odd in the distance, and at once plunged at her with another string of inquiries as to her health, delivered so volubly and with such an intense earnestness, that I half expected to see him terminate his cross-examination by feeling her pulse and demanding a sight of her tongue. All this time his little eyes rolled round and round, shifting perpetually from the floor to the ceiling, and from the ceiling to the walls, taking in apparently every article of furniture in a single comprehensive glance.

Having satisfied himself that neither of us was in a pathological condition, Mr. Abrahams suffered me to lead him upstairs, where a repast had been laid out for him to which he did ample justice. The mysterious little bag he carried along with him, and deposited it under his chair during the meal. It was not until the table had been cleared and we were left together that he broached the matter on which he had come down.

"I hunderstand," he remarked, puffing at a trichinopoly, "that you want my 'elp in fitting up this 'ere 'ouse with a happarition."

I acknowledged the correctness of his surmise, while mentally wondering at those restless eyes of his, which still danced about the room as if he were making an inventory of the contents.

"And you won't find a better man for the job, though I says it as shouldn't," continued my companion. "Wot did I say to the young gent wot spoke to me in the bar of the Lame Dog? 'Can you do it?' says he. 'Try me,' says I, 'me and my bag. Just try me.' I couldn't say fairer than that."

My respect for Jack Brocket's business capacities began to go up very considerably. He certainly seemed to have managed the matter wonderfully well. "You don't mean to say that you carry ghosts about in bags?" I remarked, with diffidence.

Mr. Abrahams smiled a smile of superior knowledge. "You wait," he said; "give me the right place and the right hour, with a little of the essence of Lucoptolycus"—here he produced a small bottle from his waistcoat pocket—"and you won't find no ghost that I ain't up to. You'll see them yourself, and pick your own, and I can't say fairer than that."

As all Mr. Abrahams' protestations of fairness were accompanied by a cunning leer and a wink from one or other of his wicked little eyes, the impression of candor was somewhat weakened.

"When are you going to do it?" I asked, reverentially.

"Ten minutes to one in the morning," said Mr. Abrahams, with decision. "Some says midnight, but I says ten to one, when there ain't such a crowd, and you can pick your own ghost. And now," he continued, rising to his feet, "suppose you trot me round the premises, and let me see where you wants it; for there's some places as attracts 'em, and some as they won't hear of—not if there was no other place in the world."

Mr. Abrahams inspected our corridors and chambers with a most critical and observant eye, fingering the old tapestry with the air of a connoisseur, and remarking in an undertone that it would "match uncommon nice." It was not until he reached the banqueting-hall, however, which I had myself picked out, that his admiration reached the pitch of enthusiasm. "'Ere's the place!" he shouted, dancing, bag in hand, round the table on which my plate was lying, and looking not unlike some quaint little goblin himself. "'Ere's the place; we won't get nothin' to beat this! A fine room—noble, solid, none of your electro-plate trash! That's the way as things ought to be done, sir. Plenty of room for 'em to glide here. Send up some brandy and the box of weeds; I'll sit here by the fire and do the preliminaries, which is more trouble than you'd think; for them ghosts carries on hawful at times, before they finds out who they've got to deal with. If you was in the room they'd tear you to pieces as like as not. You leave me alone to tackle them, and at half-past twelve come in, and I lay they'll be quiet enough by then."

Mr. Abrahams' request struck me as a reasonable one, so I left him with his feet upon the mantelpiece, and his chair in front of the fire, fortifying himself with stimulants against his refractory visitors. From the room beneath, in which I sat with Mrs. D'Odd, I could hear that, after sitting for some time, he rose up and paced about the hall with quick impatient steps. We then heard him try the lock of the door, and afterward drag some heavy article of furniture in the direction of the window, on which, apparently, he mounted, for I heard the creaking of the rusty hinges as the diamond-paned casement folded backward, and I knew it to be situated several feet above the little man's reach. Mrs. D'Odd says that she could distinguish his voice speaking in low and rapid whispers after this, but that may have been her imagination. I confess that I began to feel more impressed than I had deemed it possible to be. There was something awesome in the thought of the solitary mortal standing by the open window and summoning in from the gloom outside the spirits of the nether world. It was with a trepidation which I could hardly disguise from Matilda that I observed that the clock was pointing to half-past twelve, and that the time had come for me to share the vigil of my visitor.

He was sitting in his old position when I entered, and there were no signs of the mysterious movements which I had overheard, though his chubby face was flushed as with recent exertion.

"Are you succeeding all right?" I asked as I came in, putting on as careless an air as possible, but glancing involuntarily round the room to see if we were alone.

"Only your help is needed to complete the matter," said Mr. Abrahams, in a solemn voice. "You shall sit by me and partake of the essence of Lucoptolycus, which removes the scales from our earthly eyes. Whatever you may chance to see, speak not and make no movement, lest you break the spell." His manner was subdued, and his usual cockney vulgarity had entirely disappeared. I took the chair which he indicated, and awaited the result.

My companion cleared the rushes from the floor in our neighborhood, and, going down upon his hands and knees, described a half-circle with chalk, which enclosed the fireplace and ourselves. Round the edge of this half-circle he drew several hieroglyphics, not unlike the signs of the zodiac. He then stood up and uttered a long invocation, delivered so rapidly that it sounded like a single gigantic word in some uncouth guttural language. Having finished this prayer, if prayer it was, he pulled out the small bottle which he had produced before, and poured a couple of teaspoonfuls of clear transparent fluid into a phial, which he handed to me with an intimation that I should drink it.

The liquid had a faintly sweet odor, not unlike the aroma of certain sorts of apples. I hesitated a moment before applying it to my lips, but an impatient gesture from my companion overcame my scruples, and I tossed it off. The taste was not unpleasant; and, as it gave rise to no immediate effects, I leaned back in my chair and composed myself for what was to come. Mr. Abrahams seated himself beside me, and I felt that he was watching my face from time to time, while repeating some more of the invocations in which he had indulged before.

A sense of delicious warmth and langour began gradually to steal over me, partly, perhaps, from the heat of the fire, and partly from some unexplained cause. An uncontrollable impulse to sleep weighed down my eyelids, while at the same time my brain worked actively, and a hundred beautiful and pleasing ideas flitted through it. So utterly lethargic did I feel that, though I was aware that my companion put his hand over the region of my heart, as if to feel how it were beating, I did not attempt to prevent him, nor did I even ask him for the reason of his action. Everything in the room appeared to be reeling slowly round in a drowsy dance, of which I was the centre. The great elk's head at the far end wagged solemnly backward and forward, while the massive salvers on the tables performed cotillons with the claret-cooler and the épergne. My head fell upon my breast from sheer heaviness, and I should have become unconscious had I not been recalled to myself by the opening of the door at the other end of the hall.

This door led on to the raised dais, which, as I have

mentioned, the heads of the house used to reserve for their own use. As it swung slowly back upon its hinges, I sat up in my chair, clutching at the arms, and staring with a horrified glare at the dark passage outside. Something was coming down it—something unformed and intangible, but still a *something*. Dim and shadowy, I saw it flit across the threshold, while a blast of ice-cold air swept down the room, which seemed to blow through me, chilling my very heart. I was aware of the mysterious presence, and then I heard it speak in a voice like the sighing of an east wind among pine-trees on the banks of a desolate sea.

It said: "I am the invisible nonentity. I have affinities and am subtle. I am electric, magnetic, and spiritualistic. I am the great ethereal sigh-heaver. I kill dogs. Mortal, wilt thou choose me?"

I was about to speak, but the words seemed to be choked in my throat; and, before I could get them out, the shadow flitted across the hall and vanished in the darkness at the other side, while a long-drawn melancholy sigh quivered through the apartment.

I turned my eyes toward the door once more, and beheld, to my astonishment, a very small old woman, who hobbled along the corridor and into the hall. She passed backward and forward several times, and then, crouching down at the very edge of the circle upon the floor, she disclosed a face the horrible malignity of which shall never be banished from my recollection. Every foul passion appeared to have left its mark upon that hideous countenance.

"Ha! ha!" she screamed, holding out her wizened hands like the talons of an unclean bird. "You see what I am. I am the fiendish old woman. I wear snuff-colored silks. My curse descends on people. Sir Walter was partial to me. Shall I be thine, mortal?"

I endeavored to shake my head in horror; on which she aimed a blow at me with her crutch, and vanished with an eldritch scream.

By this time my eyes turned naturally toward the open door, and I was hardly surprised to see a man walk in of tall and noble stature. His face was deadly pale, but was surmounted by a fringe of dark hair which fell in ringlets down his back. A short pointed beard covered his chin. He was dressed in loose-fitting clothes, made apparently of yellow satin, and a large white ruff surrounded his neck. He paced across the room with slow and majestic strides. Then turning, he addressed me in a sweet, exquisitely modulated voice.

"I am the cavalier," he remarked. "I pierce and am pierced. Here is my rapier. I clink steel. This is a blood stain over my heart. I can emit hollow groans. I am patronized by many old Conservative families. I am the original manor-house apparition. I work alone, or in company with shrieking damsels."

He bent his head courteously, as though awaiting my reply, but the same choking sensation prevented me from speaking; and, with a deep bow, he disappeared.

He had hardly gone before a feeling of intense horror stole over me, and I was aware of the presence of a ghastly creature in the room, of dim outlines and uncertain proportions. One moment it seemed to pervade the entire apartment, while at another it would become invisible, but always leaving behind it a distinct consciousness of its presence. Its voice, when it spoke, was quavering and gusty. It said: "I am the leaver of footsteps and the spiller of gouts of blood. I tramp upon corridors. Charles Dickens has alluded to me. I make strange and disagreeable noises. I snatch letters and place invisible hands on people's wrists. I am cheerful. I burst into peals of hideous laughter. Shall I do one now?" I raised my hand in a deprecating way, but too late to prevent one discordant outbreak which echoed through the room. Before I could lower it the apparition was gone.

I turned my head toward the door in time to see a man come hastily and stealthily into the chamber. He was a sunburnt powerfully built fellow, with ear-rings in his ears and a Barcelona handkerchief tied loosely round his neck. His head was bent upon his chest, and his whole aspect was that of one afflicted by intolerable remorse. He paced rapidly backward and forward like a caged tiger, and I observed that a drawn knife glittered in one of his hands, while he grasped what appeared to be a piece of parchment in the other. His voice, when he spoke, was deep and sonorous. He said, "I am a murderer. I am a ruffian. I crouch when I walk. I step noiselessly. I know something of the Spanish Main. I can do the lost treasure business. I have charts. Am able-bodied and a good walker. Capable of haunting a large park." He looked toward me beseechingly, but before I could make a sign I was paralyzed by the horrible sight which appeared at the door.

It was a very tall man, if, indeed, it might be called a man, for the gaunt bones were protruding through the corroding flesh, and the features were of a leaden hue. A winding-sheet was wrapped round the figure, and formed a hood over the head, from under the shadow of which two fiendish eyes, deep set in their grisly sockets, blazed and sparkled like red-hot coals. The lower jaw and fallen upon the breast, disclosing a withered, shrivelled tongue and two lines of black and jagged fangs. I shuddered and drew back as this fearful apparition advanced to the edge of the circle.

"I am the American blood-curdler," it said, in a voice which seemed to come in a hollow murmur from the earth beneath it. "None other is genuine. I am the embodiment of Edgar Allan Poe. I am circumstantial and horrible. I am a low-caste spirit-subduing spectre. Observe my blood and my bones. I am grisly and nauseous. No depending on artificial aid. Work with grave-clothes, a coffin-lid, and a galvanic battery. Turn hair white in a night." The creature stretched out its fleshless arms to me as if in entreaty, but I shook my head; and it vanished, leaving a low, sickening, repulsive odor behind it. I sank back in my chair, so overcome by terror and disgust that I would have very willingly resigned myself to dispensing with a ghost altogether, could I have been sure that this was the last of the hideous procession.

A faint sound of trailing garments warned me that it was not so. I looked up, and beheld a white figure emerging from the corridor into the light. As it stepped across the threshold I saw that it was that of a young and beautiful woman dressed in the fashion of a bygone day. Her hands were clasped in front of her, and her pale proud face bore traces of passion and of suffering. She crossed the hall with a gentle sound, like the rustling of autumn leaves, and then, turning her lovely and unutterably sad eyes upon me, she said,

"I am the plaintive and sentimental, the beautiful and ill-used. I have been forsaken and betrayed. I shriek in the night-time and glide down passages. My antecedents are highly respectable and generally aristocratic. My tastes are æsthetic. Old oak furniture like this would do, with a few more coats of mail and plenty of tapestry. Will you not take me?"

Her voice died away in a beautiful cadence as she concluded, and she held out her hands as if in supplication. I am always sensitive to female influences. Besides, what would Jorrocks's ghost be to this? Could anything be in better taste? Would I not be exposing myself to the chance of injuring my nervous system by interviews with such creatures as my last visitor, unless I decided at once? She gave me a seraphic smile, as if she knew what was passing in my mind. That smile settled the matter. "She will do!" I cried; "I choose this one;" and as, in my enthusiasm, I took a step toward her I passed over the magic circle which had girdled me round.

"Argentine, we have been robbed!"

I had an indistinct consciousness of these words being spoken, or rather screamed, in my ear a great number of times without my being able to grasp their meaning. A violent throbbing in my head seemed to adapt itself to their rhythm, and I closed my eyes to the lullaby of "Robbed, robbed, robbed." A vigorous shake caused me to open them again, however, and the sight of Mrs. D'Odd in the scantiest of costumes and most furious of tempers was sufficiently impressive to recall all my scattered thoughts, and make me realize that I was lying on my back on the floor, with my head among the ashes which had fallen from last night's fire, and a small glass phial in my hand.

I staggered to my feet, but felt so weak and giddy that I was compelled to fall back into a chair. As my brain became clearer, stimulated by the exclamations of Matilda, I began gradually to recollect the events of the night. There was the door through which my supernatural visitors had filed. There was the circle of chalk with the hieroglyphics round the edge. There was the cigar-box and brandy-bottle which had been honored by the attentions of Mr. Abrahams. But the seer himself—where was he? and what was this open window with a rope running out of it? And where, O where, was the pride of Goresthorpe Grange, the glorious plate which was to have been the delectation of generations of D'Odds? And why was Mrs. D. standing in the gray light of dawn, wringing her hands and repeating her monotonous refrain? It was only very gradually that my misty brain took these things in, and grasped the connection between them.

Reader, I have never seen Mr. Abrahams since; I have never seen the plate stamped with the resuscitated family crest; hardest of all, I have never caught a glimpse of the melancholy spectra with the trailing garments, nor do I expect that I ever shall. In fact my night's experiences have cured me of my mania for the supernatural, and quite reconciled me to inhabiting the humdrum nineteenth-century edifice on the outskirts of London which Mrs. D. has long had in her mind's eye.

As to the explanation of all that occurred—that is a matter which is open to several surmises. That Mr. Abrahams, the ghost-hunter, was identical with Jemmy

Wilson, *alias* the Nottingham crackster, is considered more than probable at Scotland Yard, and certainly the description of that remarkable burglar tallied very well with the appearance of my visitor. The small bag which I have described was picked up in a neighboring field next day, and found to contain a choice assortment of jemmies and centrebits. Footmarks deeply imprinted in the mud on either side of the moat showed that an accomplice from below had received the sack of precious metals which had been let down through the open window. No doubt the pair of scoundrels, while looking round for a job, had overheard Jack Brocket's indiscreet inquiries, and promptly availed themselves of the tempting opening.

And now as to my less substantial visitors, and the curious grotesque vision which I had enjoyed—am I to lay it down to any real power over occult matters possessed by my Nottingham friend? For a long time I was doubtful upon the point, and eventually endeavored to solve it by consulting a well-known analyst and medical man, sending him the few drops of the so-called essence of Lucoptolycus which remained in my phial. I append the letter which I received from him, only too happy to have the opportunity of winding up my little narrative by the weighty words of a man of learning:

"ARUNDEL STREET.

"DEAR SIR: Your very singular case has interested me extremely. The bottle which you sent contained a strong solution of chloral, and the quantity which you describe yourself as having swallowed must have amounted to at least eighty grains of the pure hydrate. This would of course have reduced you to a partial state of insensibility, gradually going on to complete coma. In this semi-unconscious state of chloralism it is not unusual for circumstantial and *bizarre* visions to present themselves—more especially to individuals unaccustomed to the use of the drug. You tell me in your note that your mind was saturated with ghostly literature, and that you had long taken a morbid interest in classifying and recalling the various forms in which apparitions have been said to appear. You must also remember that you were expecting to see something of that very nature, and that your nervous system was worked up to an unnatural state of tension. Under the circumstances, I think that, far from the sequel being an astonishing one, it would have been very surprising indeed to any one versed in narcotics had you not experienced some such effects.—I remain, dear sir, sincerely yours,

"T. E. STUBE, M.D.

"ARGENTINE D'ODD, ESQ.
"THE ELMS, BRIXTON."

THE AMERICAN'S TALE

"IT air strange, it air," he was saying as I opened the door of the room where our social little semi-literary society met; "but I could tell you queerer things than that 'ere—almighty queer things. You can't learn everything out of books, sirs, nohow. You see it ain't the men as can string English together and as has had good eddications as finds themselves in the queer places I've been in. They're mostly rough men, sirs, as can scarce speak aright, far less tell with pen and ink the things they've seen; but if they could they'd make some of your European's har riz with astonishment. They would, sirs, you bet!"

His name was Jefferson Adams, I believe; I know his initials were J. A., for you may see them yet deeply whittled on the right-hand upper panel of our smoking-room door. He left us this legacy, and also some artistic patterns done in tobacco juice upon our Turkey carpet; but beyond these reminiscences our American storyteller has vanished from our ken. He gleamed across our ordinary quiet conviviality like some brilliant meteor, and then was lost in the outer darkness. That night, however, our Nevada friend was in full swing; and I quietly lit my pipe and dropped into the nearest chair, anxious not to interrupt his story.

"Mind you," he continued, "I hain't got no grudge against your men of science. I likes and respects a chap as can match every beast and plant, from a huckleberry to a grizzly with a jaw-breakin' name; but if you wants real interestin' facts, something a bit juicy, you go to your whalers and your frontiersmen, and your scouts and Hudson Bay men, chaps who mostly can scarce sign their names."

There was a pause here, as Mr. Jefferson Adams produced a long cheroot and lit it. We preserved a strict silence in the room, for we had already learned that on the slightest interruption our Yankee drew himself into his shell again. He glanced round with a self-satisfied smile as he remarked our expectant looks, and continued through a halo of smoke,

"Now which of you gentlemen has ever been in Arizona? None, I'll warrant. And of all English or Americans as can put pen to paper, how many has been in Arizona? Precious few, I calc'late. I've been there, sirs, lived there for years; and when I think of what I've seen there, why, I can scarce get myself to believe it now.

"Ah, there's a country! I was one of Walker's filibusters, as they chose to call us; and after we'd busted up, and the chief was shot, some of us made tracks and located down there. A reg'lar English and American colony, we was, with our wives and children, and all complete. I reckon there's some of the old folk there yet, and that they hain't forgotten what I'm agoing to tell you. No, I warrant they hain't, never on this side of the grave, sirs.

"I was talking about the country, though; and I guess I could astonish you considerable if I spoke of nothing else. To think of such a land being built for a few 'Greasers' and half-breeds! It's a misusing of the gifts of Providence, that's what I calls it. Grass as hung over a chap's head as he rode through it, and trees so thick that you couldn't catch a glimpse of blue sky for leagues and leagues, and orchids like umbrellas! Maybe some on you has seen a plant as they calls the 'fly-catcher,' in some parts of the States?"

"Dionaea muscipula," murmured Dawson, our scientific man *par excellence.*

"Ah, 'Die near a municipal,' that's him! You'll see a fly stand on that 'ere plant, and then you'll see the two sides of a leaf snap up together and catch it between them, and grind it up and mash it to bits, for all the world like some great sea squid with its beak; and hours after, if you open the leaf, you'll see the body lying half-digested, and in bits. Well, I've seen those flytraps in Arizona with leaves eight and ten feet long, and thorns or teeth a foot or more; why, they could—But darn it, I'm going too fast!

"It's about the death of Joe Hawkins I was going to tell you; 'bout as queer a thing, I reckon, as ever you heard tell on. There wasn't nobody in Montana as didn't know of Joe Hawkins—'Alabama' Joe, as he was called there. A reg'lar out and outer, he was, 'bout the darndest skunk as ever man clapt eyes on. He was a good chap enough, mind ye, as long as you stroked him the right way; but rile him anyhow, and he were worse nor a wild-cat. I've seen him empty his six-shooter into a crowd as chanced to jostle him agoing into Simpson's bar when there was a dance on; and he bowied Tom Hooper 'cause he spilt his liquor over his weskit by mistake. No, he didn't stick at murder, Joe didn't; and he weren't a man to be trusted further nor you could see him.

"Now at the time I tell on, when Joe Hawkins was swaggerin' about the town and layin' down the law with his shootin'-irons, there was an Englishman there of the name of Scott—Tom Scott, if I rec'lects aright. This chap Scott was a thorough Britisher (beggin' the present company's pardon), and yet he didn't freeze much to the British set there, or they didn't freeze much to him. He was a quiet simple man, Scott was—rather too quiet for a rough set like that; sneakin' they called him, but he weren't that. He kept hisself mostly apart, an' didn't interfere with nobody so long as he were left alone. Some said as how he'd been kinder ill-treated at home—been a Chartist, or something of that sort, and had to up stick and run; but he never spoke of it hisself, an' never complained. Bad luck or good, that chap kept a stiff lip on him.

"This chap Scott was a sort o' butt among the men about Montana, for he was so quiet an' simple-like. There was no party either to take up his grievances; for, as I've been saying, the Britishers hardly counted him one of them, and many a rough joke they played on him. He never cut up rough, but was polite to all hisself. I think the boys got to think he hadn't much grit in him till he showed 'em their mistake.

'It was in Simpson's bar as the row got up, an' that led to the queer thing I was going to tell you of. Alabama Joe and one or two other rowdies were dead on the Britishers in those days, and they spoke their opinions pretty free, though I warned them as there'd be an almighty muss. That partic'lar night Joe was nigh half drunk, an' he swaggered about the town with his six-shooter, lookin' out for a quarrel. Then he turned into the bar where he know'd he'd find some o' the English as ready for one as he was hisself. Sure enough, there was half a dozen lounging about, an' Tom Scott standin' alone before the stove. Joe sat down by the table, and put his revolver and bowie down in front of him. 'Them's my arguments, Jeff,' he says to me, 'if any white-livered Britisher dares give me the lie.' I tried to stop him, sirs; but he weren't a man as you could easily turn, an' he began to speak in a way as no chap could stand. Why, even a 'Greaser' would flare up if you said as much of Greaserland! There was a commotion at the bar, an' every man laid his hands on his wepin's; but afore they could draw we heard a quiet voice from the stove: 'Say your prayers, Joe Hawkins; for, by Heaven, you're a dead man!' Joe turned, round and looked like grabbin' at his iron; but it weren't no manner of use. Tom Scott was standing up, covering him with his Derringer; a smile on his white face, but the very devil shining in his eye. 'It ain't that the old country has used me over-well,' he says, 'but no man shall speak agin it afore me, and live.' For a second or two I could see his finger tighten round the trigger, an' then he gave a laugh, an' threw the pistol on the floor. 'No,' he says, 'I can't shoot a half-drunk man. Take your dirty life, Joe, an' use it better nor you have done. You've been nearer the grave this night than you will be agin until your time comes. You'd best make tracks now, I guess. Nay, never look black at me, man; I'm not afeard at your shootin'-iron. A bully's nigh always a coward.' And he swung contemptuously round, and relit his half-smoked pipe from the stove; while Alabama slunk out o' the bar, with the laughs of the Britishers ringing in his ears. I saw his face as he passed me, and on it I saw murder, sirs—murder, as plain as ever I seed anything in my life.

"I stayed in the bar after the row, and watched Tom Scott as he shook hands with the men about. It seemed kinder queer to me to see him smilin' and cheerful-like; for I knew Joe's bloodthirsty mind, and that the Englishman had small chance of ever seeing the morning. He lived in an out-of-the-way sort of place, you see, clean off the trail, and had to pass through the Flytrap Gulch to get to it. This here gulch was a marshy gloomy place, lonely enough during the day even; for it were always a creepy sort o' thing to see the great eight- and ten-foot leaves snapping up if aught touched them; but at night there were never a soul near. Some parts of the marsh, too, were soft and deep, and a body thrown in would be gone by the morning. I could see Alabama Joe crouchin' under the leaves of the great Flytrap in the darkest part of the gulch, with a scowl on his face and a revolver in his hand; I could see it, sirs, as plain as with my two eyes.

"'Bout midnight Simpson shuts up his bar, so out we had to go. Tom Scott started off for his three-mile walk at a slashing pace. I just dropped him a hint as he passed me, for I kinder liked the chap. 'Keep your Derringer loose in your belt, sir,' I says, 'for you might chance to need it.' He looked round at me with his quiet smile, and then I lost sight of him in the gloom. I never thought to see him again. He'd hardly gone afore Simpson comes up to me and says, 'There'll be a nice job in the Flytrap Gulch to-night, Jeff; the boys say that Hawkins started half an hour ago to wait for Scott and shoot him on sight. I calc'late the coroner 'll be wanted to-morrow.'

"What passed in the gulch that night? It were a question as were asked pretty free next morning. A half-breed was in Ferguson's store after daybreak, and he said as he'd chanced to be near the gulch 'bout one in the morning. It warn't easy to get at his story, he seemed so uncommon scared; but he told us, at last, as he'd heard the fearfulest screams in the stillness of the night. There weren't no shots, he said, but scream after scream, kinder muffled, like a man with a serapé over his head, an' in mortal pain. Abner Brandon and me, and a few more, was in the store at the time; so we mounted and rode out to Scott's house, passing through the gulch on the way. There weren't nothing partic'lar to be seen there—no blood nor marks of a fight, nor nothing; and when we gets up to Scott's house, out he comes to meet us as fresh as a lark. 'Hullo, Jeff!' says he, 'no need for the pistols after all. Come in an' have a cocktail, boys.' 'Did ye see or hear nothing as ye came home last night?' says I. 'No,' says he; 'all was quiet enough. An owl kinder moaning in the Flytrap Gulch—that was all. Come, jump off and have a glass.' 'Thank ye,' said Abner. So off we gets, and Tom Scott rode into the settlement with us when we went back.

"An allfired commotion was on in Main-street as we rode into it. The 'Merican party seemed to have gone clean crazed. Albama Joe was gone, not a darned particle of him left. Since he went out to the gulch nary eye had seen him. As we got off our horses there was a considerable crowd in front of Simpson's, and some ugly looks at

Tom Scott, I can tell you. There was a clickin' of pistols, and I saw as Scott had his hand in his bosom too. There weren't a single English face about. 'Stand aside, Jeff Adams,' says Zebb Humphrey, as great a scoundrel as ever lived, 'you hain't got no hand in this game. Say, boys, are we, free Americans, to be murdered by any darned Britisher?' It was the quickest thing as ever I seed. There was a rush an' a crack; Zebb was down, with Scott's ball in his thigh, and Scott hisself was on the ground with a dozen men holding him. It weren't no use struggling, so he lay quiet. They seemed a bit uncertain what to do with him at first, but then one of Alabama's special chums put them up to it. 'Joe's gone,' he said; 'nothing ain't surer nor that, an' there lies the man as killed him. Some on you knows as Joe went on business to the gulch last night; he never came back. That 'ere Britisher passed through after he'd gone; they'd had a row, screams is heard 'mong the great flytraps. I say agin he has played poor Joe some o' his sneakin' tricks, an' thrown him into the swamp. It ain't no wonder as the body is gone. But air we to stan' by and see English murderin' our own chums? I guess not. Let Judge Lynch try him, that's what I say.' 'Lynch him!' shouted a hundred angry voices—for all the rag-tag an' bobtail o' the settlement was round us by this time. 'Here, boys, fetch a rope, and swing him up. Up with him over Simpson's door!' 'See here though,' says another, coming forrards; 'let's hang him by the great flytrap in the gulch. Let Joe see as he's revenged, if so be as he's buried 'bout theer.' There was a shout for this, an' away they went, with Scott tied on his mustang in the middle, and a mounted guard, with cocked revolvers, round him; for we knew as there was a score or so Britishers about, as didn't seem to recognise Judge Lynch, and was dead on a free fight.

"I went out with them, my heart bleedin' for Scott, though he didn't seem a cent put out, he didn't. He were game to the backbone. Seems kinder queer, sirs, hangin' a man to a flytrap; but our'n were a reg'lar tree, and the leaves like a brace of boats with a hinge between 'em and thorns at the bottom.

"We passed down the gulch to the place where the great one grows, and there we seed it with the leaves, some open, some shut. But we seed something worse nor that. Standin' round the tree was some thirty men, Britishers all, an' armed to the teeth. They was waitin' for us evidently, an' had a businesslike look about 'em, as if they'd come for something and meant to have it. There was the raw material there for about as warm a scrimmidge as ever I seed. As we rode up, a great red-bearded Scotchman—Cameron were his name—stood out afore the rest, his revolver cocked in his hand. 'See here, boys,' he says, 'you've got no call to hurt a hair of that man's head. You hain't proved as Joe is dead yet; and if you had, you hain't proved as Scott killed him. Anyhow, it were in self-defence; for you all know as he was lying in wait for Scott, to shoot him on sight; so I say agin, you hain't got no call to hurt that man; and what's more, I've got thirty six-barrelled arguments against your doin' it.' 'It's an interestin' pint, and worth arguin' out,' said the man as was Alabama Joe's special chum. There was a clickin' of pistols, and a loosenin' of knives, and the two parties began to draw up to one another, an' it looked like a rise in the mortality of Montana. Scott was standing behind with a pistol at his ear if he stirred, lookin' quiet and composed as having no money on the table, when sudden he gives a start an' a shout as rang in our ears like a trumpet. 'Joe!' he cried, 'Joe! Look at him! In the flytrap!' We all turned an' looked where he was pointin'. Jerusalem! I think we won't get that picter out of our minds agin. One of the great leaves of the flytrap, that had been shut and touchin' the ground as it lay, was slowly rolling back upon its hinges. There, lying like a child in its cradle, was Alabama Joe in the hollow of the leaf. The great thorns had been slowly driven through his heart as it shut upon him. We could see as he'd tried to cut his way out, for there was a slit in the thick fleshy leaf, an' his bowie was in his hand; but it had smothered him first. He'd lain down on it likely to keep the damp off while he were awaitin' for Scott, and it had closed on him as you've seen your little hothouse ones do on a fly; an' there he were as we found him, torn and crushed into pulp by the great jagged teeth of the man-eatin' plant. There, sirs, I think you'll own as that's a curious story."

"And what became of Scott?" asked Jack Sinclair.

"Why, we carried him back on our shoulders, we did, to Simpson's bar, and he stood us liquors round. Made a speech too—a darned fine speech—from the counter. Somethin' about the British lion an' the 'Merican eagle walkin' arm in arm for ever an' a day. And now, sirs, that yarn was long, and my cheroot's out, so I reckon I'll make tracks afore it's later"; and with a "Good-night!" he left the room.

"A most extraordinary narrative!" said Dawson. "Who would have thought a Dionaea had such power!"

"Deuced rum yarn!" said young Sinclair.

"Evidently a matter-of-fact truthful man," said the doctor.

"Or the most original liar that ever lived," said I.

I wonder which he was.

A CATALOG OF SELECTED

DOVER BOOKS

IN ALL FIELDS OF INTEREST

A CATALOG OF SELECTED DOVER BOOKS IN ALL FIELDS OF INTEREST

ALICE'S ADVENTURES IN WONDERLAND, Lewis Carroll. Beloved classic about a little girl lost in a topsy-turvy land and her encounters with the White Rabbit, March Hare, Mad Hatter, Cheshire Cat, and other delightfully improbable characters. 42 illustrations by Sir John Tenniel. 96pp. 5³⁄₁₆ x 8¼. 0-486-27543-4

AMERICA'S LIGHTHOUSES: An Illustrated History, Francis Ross Holland. Profusely illustrated fact-filled survey of American lighthouses since 1716. Over 200 stations — East, Gulf, and West coasts, Great Lakes, Hawaii, Alaska, Puerto Rico, the Virgin Islands, and the Mississippi and St. Lawrence Rivers. 240pp. 8 x 10¾. 0-486-25576-X

AN ENCYCLOPEDIA OF THE VIOLIN, Alberto Bachmann. Translated by Frederick H. Martens. Introduction by Eugene Ysaye. First published in 1925, this renowned reference remains unsurpassed as a source of essential information, from construction and evolution to repertoire and technique. Includes a glossary and 73 illustrations. 496pp. 6⅛ x 9¼. 0-486-46618-3

ANIMALS: 1,419 Copyright-Free Illustrations of Mammals, Birds, Fish, Insects, etc., Selected by Jim Harter. Selected for its visual impact and ease of use, this outstanding collection of wood engravings presents over 1,000 species of animals in extremely lifelike poses. Includes mammals, birds, reptiles, amphibians, fish, insects, and other invertebrates. 284pp. 9 x 12. 0-486-23766-4

THE ANNALS, Tacitus. Translated by Alfred John Church and William Jackson Brodribb. This vital chronicle of Imperial Rome, written by the era's great historian, spans A.D. 14-68 and paints incisive psychological portraits of major figures, from Tiberius to Nero. 416pp. 5³⁄₁₆ x 8¼. 0-486-45236-0

ANTIGONE, Sophocles. Filled with passionate speeches and sensitive probing of moral and philosophical issues, this powerful and often-performed Greek drama reveals the grim fate that befalls the children of Oedipus. Footnotes. 64pp. 5³⁄₁₆ x 8 ¼. 0-486-27804-2

ART DECO DECORATIVE PATTERNS IN FULL COLOR, Christian Stoll. Reprinted from a rare 1910 portfolio, 160 sensuous and exotic images depict a breathtaking array of florals, geometrics, and abstracts — all elegant in their stark simplicity. 64pp. 8⅜ x 11. 0-486-44862-2

THE ARTHUR RACKHAM TREASURY: 86 Full-Color Illustrations, Arthur Rackham. Selected and Edited by Jeff A. Menges. A stunning treasury of 86 full-page plates span the famed English artist's career, from *Rip Van Winkle* (1905) to masterworks such as *Undine, A Midsummer Night's Dream,* and *Wind in the Willows* (1939). 96pp. 8⅜ x 11. 0-486-44685-9

THE AUTHENTIC GILBERT & SULLIVAN SONGBOOK, W. S. Gilbert and A. S. Sullivan. The most comprehensive collection available, this songbook includes selections from every one of Gilbert and Sullivan's light operas. Ninety-two numbers are presented uncut and unedited, and in their original keys. 410pp. 9 x 12. 0-486-23482-7

THE AWAKENING, Kate Chopin. First published in 1899, this controversial novel of a New Orleans wife's search for love outside a stifling marriage shocked readers. Today, it remains a first-rate narrative with superb characterization. New introductory Note. 128pp. 5³⁄₁₆ x 8¼. 0-486-27786-0

BASIC DRAWING, Louis Priscilla. Beginning with perspective, this commonsense manual progresses to the figure in movement, light and shade, anatomy, drapery, composition, trees and landscape, and outdoor sketching. Black-and-white illustrations throughout. 128pp. 8⅜ x 11. 0-486-45815-6

A CHRISTMAS CAROL, Charles Dickens. This engrossing tale relates Ebenezer Scrooge's ghostly journeys through Christmases past, present, and future and his ultimate transformation from a harsh and grasping old miser to a charitable and compassionate human being. 80pp. 5$\frac{3}{16}$ x 8$\frac{1}{4}$. 0-486-26865-9

COMMON SENSE, Thomas Paine. First published in January of 1776, this highly influential landmark document clearly and persuasively argued for American separation from Great Britain and paved the way for the Declaration of Independence. 64pp. 5$\frac{3}{16}$ x 8$\frac{1}{4}$. 0-486-29602-4

THE COMPLETE SHORT STORIES OF OSCAR WILDE, Oscar Wilde. Complete texts of "The Happy Prince and Other Tales," "A House of Pomegranates," "Lord Arthur Savile's Crime and Other Stories," "Poems in Prose," and "The Portrait of Mr. W. H." 208pp. 5$\frac{3}{16}$ x 8$\frac{1}{4}$. 0-486-45216-6

COMPLETE SONNETS, William Shakespeare. Over 150 exquisite poems deal with love, friendship, the tyranny of time, beauty's evanescence, death, and other themes in language of remarkable power, precision, and beauty. Glossary of archaic terms. 80pp. 5$\frac{3}{16}$ x 8$\frac{1}{4}$. 0-486-26686-9

THE COUNT OF MONTE CRISTO: Abridged Edition, Alexandre Dumas. Falsely accused of treason, Edmond Dantès is imprisoned in the bleak Chateau d'If. After a hair-raising escape, he launches an elaborate plot to extract a bitter revenge against those who betrayed him. 448pp. 5$\frac{3}{16}$ x 8$\frac{1}{4}$. 0-486-45643-9

CRAFTSMAN BUNGALOWS: Designs from the Pacific Northwest, Yoho & Merritt. This reprint of a rare catalog, showcasing the charming simplicity and cozy style of Craftsman bungalows, is filled with photos of completed homes, plus floor plans and estimated costs. An indispensable resource for architects, historians, and illustrators. 112pp. 10 x 7. 0-486-46875-5

CRAFTSMAN BUNGALOWS: 59 Homes from "The Craftsman," Edited by Gustav Stickley. Best and most attractive designs from Arts and Crafts Movement publication — 1903–1916 — includes sketches, photographs of homes, floor plans, descriptive text. 128pp. 8$\frac{1}{4}$ x 11. 0-486-25829-7

CRIME AND PUNISHMENT, Fyodor Dostoyevsky. Translated by Constance Garnett. Supreme masterpiece tells the story of Raskolnikov, a student tormented by his own thoughts after he murders an old woman. Overwhelmed by guilt and terror, he confesses and goes to prison. 480pp. 5$\frac{3}{16}$ x 8$\frac{1}{4}$. 0-486-41587-2

THE DECLARATION OF INDEPENDENCE AND OTHER GREAT DOCUMENTS OF AMERICAN HISTORY: 1775-1865, Edited by John Grafton. Thirteen compelling and influential documents: Henry's "Give Me Liberty or Give Me Death," Declaration of Independence, The Constitution, Washington's First Inaugural Address, The Monroe Doctrine, The Emancipation Proclamation, Gettysburg Address, more. 64pp. 5$\frac{3}{16}$ x 8$\frac{1}{4}$. 0-486-41124-9

THE DESERT AND THE SOWN: Travels in Palestine and Syria, Gertrude Bell. "The female Lawrence of Arabia," Gertrude Bell wrote captivating, perceptive accounts of her travels in the Middle East. This intriguing narrative, accompanied by 160 photos, traces her 1905 sojourn in Lebanon, Syria, and Palestine. 368pp. 5$\frac{3}{8}$ x 8$\frac{1}{2}$. 0-486-46876-3

A DOLL'S HOUSE, Henrik Ibsen. Ibsen's best-known play displays his genius for realistic prose drama. An expression of women's rights, the play climaxes when the central character, Nora, rejects a smothering marriage and life in "a doll's house." 80pp. 5$\frac{3}{16}$ x 8$\frac{1}{4}$. 0-486-27062-9

DOOMED SHIPS: Great Ocean Liner Disasters, William H. Miller, Jr. Nearly 200 photographs, many from private collections, highlight tales of some of the vessels whose pleasure cruises ended in catastrophe: the *Morro Castle, Normandie, Andrea Doria, Europa,* and many others. 128pp. 8⅞ x 11¾. 0-486-45366-9

THE DORÉ BIBLE ILLUSTRATIONS, Gustave Doré. Detailed plates from the Bible: the Creation scenes, Adam and Eve, horrifying visions of the Flood, the battle sequences with their monumental crowds, depictions of the life of Jesus, 241 plates in all. 241pp. 9 x 12. 0-486-23004-X

DRAWING DRAPERY FROM HEAD TO TOE, Cliff Young. Expert guidance on how to draw shirts, pants, skirts, gloves, hats, and coats on the human figure, including folds in relation to the body, pull and crush, action folds, creases, more. Over 200 drawings. 48pp. 8¼ x 11. 0-486-45591-2

DUBLINERS, James Joyce. A fine and accessible introduction to the work of one of the 20th century's most influential writers, this collection features 15 tales, including a masterpiece of the short-story genre, "The Dead." 160pp. 5³⁄₁₆ x 8¼. 0-486-26870-5

EASY-TO-MAKE POP-UPS, Joan Irvine. Illustrated by Barbara Reid. Dozens of wonderful ideas for three-dimensional paper fun — from holiday greeting cards with moving parts to a pop-up menagerie. Easy-to-follow, illustrated instructions for more than 30 projects. 299 black-and-white illustrations. 96pp. 8⅜ x 11. 0-486-44622-0

EASY-TO-MAKE STORYBOOK DOLLS: A "Novel" Approach to Cloth Dollmaking, Sherralyn St. Clair. Favorite fictional characters come alive in this unique beginner's dollmaking guide. Includes patterns for Pollyanna, Dorothy from *The Wonderful Wizard of Oz,* Mary of *The Secret Garden,* plus easy-to-follow instructions, 263 black-and-white illustrations, and an 8-page color insert. 112pp. 8¼ x 11. 0-486-47360-0

EINSTEIN'S ESSAYS IN SCIENCE, Albert Einstein. Speeches and essays in accessible, everyday language profile influential physicists such as Niels Bohr and Isaac Newton. They also explore areas of physics to which the author made major contributions. 128pp. 5 x 8. 0-486-47011-3

EL DORADO: Further Adventures of the Scarlet Pimpernel, Baroness Orczy. A popular sequel to *The Scarlet Pimpernel,* this suspenseful story recounts the Pimpernel's attempts to rescue the Dauphin from imprisonment during the French Revolution. An irresistible blend of intrigue, period detail, and vibrant characterizations. 352pp. 5³⁄₁₆ x 8¼. 0-486-44026-5

ELEGANT SMALL HOMES OF THE TWENTIES: 99 Designs from a Competition, Chicago Tribune. Nearly 100 designs for five- and six-room houses feature New England and Southern colonials, Normandy cottages, stately Italianate dwellings, and other fascinating snapshots of American domestic architecture of the 1920s. 112pp. 9 x 12. 0-486-46910-7

THE ELEMENTS OF STYLE: The Original Edition, William Strunk, Jr. This is the book that generations of writers have relied upon for timeless advice on grammar, diction, syntax, and other essentials. In concise terms, it identifies the principal requirements of proper style and common errors. 64pp. 5⅜ x 8½. 0-486-44798-7

THE ELUSIVE PIMPERNEL, Baroness Orczy. Robespierre's revolutionaries find their wicked schemes thwarted by the heroic Pimpernel — Sir Percival Blakeney. In this thrilling sequel, Chauvelin devises a plot to eliminate the Pimpernel and his wife. 272pp. 5³⁄₁₆ x 8¼. 0-486-45464-9

HEART OF DARKNESS, Joseph Conrad. Dark allegory of a journey up the Congo River and the narrator's encounter with the mysterious Mr. Kurtz. Masterly blend of adventure, character study, psychological penetration. For many, Conrad's finest, most enigmatic story. 80pp. 5 3/16 x 8¼. 0-486-26464-5

HENSON AT THE NORTH POLE, Matthew A. Henson. This thrilling memoir by the heroic African-American who was Peary's companion through two decades of Arctic exploration recounts a tale of danger, courage, and determination. "Fascinating and exciting." — *Commonweal.* 128pp. 5⅜ x 8½. 0-486-45472-X

HISTORIC COSTUMES AND HOW TO MAKE THEM, Mary Fernald and E. Shenton. Practical, informative guidebook shows how to create everything from short tunics worn by Saxon men in the fifth century to a lady's bustle dress of the late 1800s. 81 illustrations. 176pp. 5⅜ x 8½. 0-486-44906-8

THE HOUND OF THE BASKERVILLES, Arthur Conan Doyle. A deadly curse in the form of a legendary ferocious beast continues to claim its victims from the Baskerville family until Holmes and Watson intervene. Often called the best detective story ever written. 128pp. 5 3/16 x 8¼. 0-486-28214-7

THE HOUSE BEHIND THE CEDARS, Charles W. Chesnutt. Originally published in 1900, this groundbreaking novel by a distinguished African-American author recounts the drama of a brother and sister who "pass for white" during the dangerous days of Reconstruction. 208pp. 5⅜ x 8½. 0-486-46144-0

THE HUMAN FIGURE IN MOTION, Eadweard Muybridge. The 4,789 photographs in this definitive selection show the human figure — models almost all undraped — engaged in over 160 different types of action: running, climbing stairs, etc. 390pp. 7⅞ x 10⅝. 0-486-20204-6

THE IMPORTANCE OF BEING EARNEST, Oscar Wilde. Wilde's witty and buoyant comedy of manners, filled with some of literature's most famous epigrams, reprinted from an authoritative British edition. Considered Wilde's most perfect work. 64pp. 5 3/16 x 8¼. 0-486-26478-5

THE INFERNO, Dante Alighieri. Translated and with notes by Henry Wadsworth Longfellow. The first stop on Dante's famous journey from Hell to Purgatory to Paradise, this 14th-century allegorical poem blends vivid and shocking imagery with graceful lyricism. Translated by the beloved 19th-century poet, Henry Wadsworth Longfellow. 256pp. 5 3/16 x 8¼. 0-486-44288-8

JANE EYRE, Charlotte Brontë. Written in 1847, *Jane Eyre* tells the tale of an orphan girl's progress from the custody of cruel relatives to an oppressive boarding school and its culmination in a troubled career as a governess. 448pp. 5 3/16 x 8¼. 0-486-42449-9

JAPANESE WOODBLOCK FLOWER PRINTS, Tanigami Kônan. Extraordinary collection of Japanese woodblock prints by a well-known artist features 120 plates in brilliant color. Realistic images from a rare edition include daffodils, tulips, and other familiar and unusual flowers. 128pp. 11 x 8¼. 0-486-46442-3

JEWELRY MAKING AND DESIGN, Augustus F. Rose and Antonio Cirino. Professional secrets of jewelry making are revealed in a thorough, practical guide. Over 200 illustrations. 306pp. 5⅜ x 8½. 0-486-21750-7

JULIUS CAESAR, William Shakespeare. Great tragedy based on Plutarch's account of the lives of Brutus, Julius Caesar and Mark Antony. Evil plotting, ringing oratory, high tragedy with Shakespeare's incomparable insight, dramatic power. Explanatory footnotes. 96pp. 5 3/16 x 8¼. 0-486-26876-4

THE JUNGLE, Upton Sinclair. 1906 bestseller shockingly reveals intolerable labor practices and working conditions in the Chicago stockyards as it tells the grim story of a Slavic family that emigrates to America full of optimism but soon faces despair. 320pp. 5³⁄₁₆ x 8¼. 0-486-41923-1

THE KINGDOM OF GOD IS WITHIN YOU, Leo Tolstoy. The soul-searching book that inspired Gandhi to embrace the concept of passive resistance, Tolstoy's 1894 polemic clearly outlines a radical, well-reasoned revision of traditional Christian thinking. 352pp. 5³⁄₁₆ x 8¼. 0-486-45138-0

THE LADY OR THE TIGER?: and Other Logic Puzzles, Raymond M. Smullyan. Created by a renowned puzzle master, these whimsically themed challenges involve paradoxes about probability, time, and change; metapuzzles; and self-referentiality. Nineteen chapters advance in difficulty from relatively simple to highly complex. 1982 edition. 240pp. 5⅜ x 8½. 0-486-47027-X

LEAVES OF GRASS: The Original 1855 Edition, Walt Whitman. Whitman's immortal collection includes some of the greatest poems of modern times, including his masterpiece, "Song of Myself." Shattering standard conventions, it stands as an unabashed celebration of body and nature. 128pp. 5³⁄₁₆ x 8¼. 0-486-45676-5

LES MISÉRABLES, Victor Hugo. Translated by Charles E. Wilbour. Abridged by James K. Robinson. A convict's heroic struggle for justice and redemption plays out against a fiery backdrop of the Napoleonic wars. This edition features the excellent original translation and a sensitive abridgment. 304pp. 6⅛ x 9¼. 0-486-45789-3

LILITH: A Romance, George MacDonald. In this novel by the father of fantasy literature, a man travels through time to meet Adam and Eve and to explore humanity's fall from grace and ultimate redemption. 240pp. 5⅜ x 8½. 0-486-46818-6

THE LOST LANGUAGE OF SYMBOLISM, Harold Bayley. This remarkable book reveals the hidden meaning behind familiar images and words, from the origins of Santa Claus to the fleur-de-lys, drawing from mythology, folklore, religious texts, and fairy tales. 1,418 illustrations. 784pp. 5⅜ x 8½. 0-486-44787-1

MACBETH, William Shakespeare. A Scottish nobleman murders the king in order to succeed to the throne. Tortured by his conscience and fearful of discovery, he becomes tangled in a web of treachery and deceit that ultimately spells his doom. 96pp. 5³⁄₁₆ x 8¼. 0-486-27802-6

MAKING AUTHENTIC CRAFTSMAN FURNITURE: Instructions and Plans for 62 Projects, Gustav Stickley. Make authentic reproductions of handsome, functional, durable furniture: tables, chairs, wall cabinets, desks, a hall tree, and more. Construction plans with drawings, schematics, dimensions, and lumber specs reprinted from 1900s *The Craftsman* magazine. 128pp. 8⅛ x 11. 0-486-25000-8

MATHEMATICS FOR THE NONMATHEMATICIAN, Morris Kline. Erudite and entertaining overview follows development of mathematics from ancient Greeks to present. Topics include logic and mathematics, the fundamental concept, differential calculus, probability theory, much more. Exercises and problems. 641pp. 5⅜ x 8½. 0-486-24823-2

MEMOIRS OF AN ARABIAN PRINCESS FROM ZANZIBAR, Emily Ruete. This 19th-century autobiography offers a rare inside look at the society surrounding a sultan's palace. A real-life princess in exile recalls her vanished world of harems, slave trading, and court intrigues. 288pp. 5⅜ x 8½. 0-486-47121-7

ONE OF OURS, Willa Cather. The Pulitzer Prize–winning novel about a young Nebraskan looking for something to believe in. Alienated from his parents, rejected by his wife, he finds his destiny on the bloody battlefields of World War I. 352pp. 5³⁄₁₆ x 8¼. 0-486-45599-8

ORIGAMI YOU CAN USE: 27 Practical Projects, Rick Beech. Origami models can be more than decorative, and this unique volume shows how! The 27 practical projects include a CD case, frame, napkin ring, and dish. Easy instructions feature 400 two-color illustrations. 96pp. 8¼ x 11. 0-486-47057-1

OTHELLO, William Shakespeare. Towering tragedy tells the story of a Moorish general who earns the enmity of his ensign Iago when he passes him over for a promotion. Masterly portrait of an archvillain. Explanatory footnotes. 112pp. 5³⁄₁₆ x 8¼. 0-486-29097-2

PARADISE LOST, John Milton. Notes by John A. Himes. First published in 1667, *Paradise Lost* ranks among the greatest of English literature's epic poems. It's a sublime retelling of Adam and Eve's fall from grace and expulsion from Eden. Notes by John A. Himes. 480pp. 5³⁄₁₆ x 8¼. 0-486-44287-X

PASSING, Nella Larsen. Married to a successful physician and prominently ensconced in society, Irene Redfield leads a charmed existence — until a chance encounter with a childhood friend who has been "passing for white." 112pp. 5⅜ x 8½. 0-486-43713-2

PERSPECTIVE DRAWING FOR BEGINNERS, Len A. Doust. Doust carefully explains the roles of lines, boxes, and circles, and shows how visualizing shapes and forms can be used in accurate depictions of perspective. One of the most concise introductions available. 33 illustrations. 64pp. 5⅜ x 8½. 0-486-45149-6

PERSPECTIVE MADE EASY, Ernest R. Norling. Perspective is easy; yet, surprisingly few artists know the simple rules that make it so. Remedy that situation with this simple, step-by-step book, the first devoted entirely to the topic. 256 illustrations. 224pp. 5⅜ x 8½. 0-486-40473-0

THE PICTURE OF DORIAN GRAY, Oscar Wilde. Celebrated novel involves a handsome young Londoner who sinks into a life of depravity. His body retains perfect youth and vigor while his recent portrait reflects the ravages of his crime and sensuality. 176pp. 5³⁄₁₆ x 8¼. 0-486-27807-7

PRIDE AND PREJUDICE, Jane Austen. One of the most universally loved and admired English novels, an effervescent tale of rural romance transformed by Jane Austen's art into a witty, shrewdly observed satire of English country life. 272pp. 5³⁄₁₆ x 8¼. 0-486-28473-5

THE PRINCE, Niccolò Machiavelli. Classic, Renaissance-era guide to acquiring and maintaining political power. Today, nearly 500 years after it was written, this calculating prescription for autocratic rule continues to be much read and studied. 80pp. 5³⁄₁₆ x 8¼. 0-486-27274-5

QUICK SKETCHING, Carl Cheek. A perfect introduction to the technique of "quick sketching." Drawing upon an artist's immediate emotional responses, this is an extremely effective means of capturing the essential form and features of a subject. More than 100 black-and-white illustrations throughout. 48pp. 11 x 8¼. 0-486-46608-6

RANCH LIFE AND THE HUNTING TRAIL, Theodore Roosevelt. Illustrated by Frederic Remington. Beautifully illustrated by Remington, Roosevelt's celebration of the Old West recounts his adventures in the Dakota Badlands of the 1880s, from roundups to Indian encounters to hunting bighorn sheep. 208pp. 6¼ x 9¼. 0-486-47340-6

SMALL HOUSES OF THE FORTIES: With Illustrations and Floor Plans, Harold E. Group. 56 floor plans and elevations of houses that originally cost less than $15,000 to build. Recommended by financial institutions of the era, they range from Colonials to Cape Cods. 144pp. 8⅜ x 11. 0-486-45598-X

SOME CHINESE GHOSTS, Lafcadio Hearn. Rooted in ancient Chinese legends, these richly atmospheric supernatural tales are recounted by an expert in Oriental lore. Their originality, power, and literary charm will captivate readers of all ages. 96pp. 5⅜ x 8½. 0-486-46306-0

SONGS FOR THE OPEN ROAD: Poems of Travel and Adventure, Edited by The American Poetry & Literacy Project. More than 80 poems by 50 American and British masters celebrate real and metaphorical journeys. Poems by Whitman, Byron, Millay, Sandburg, Langston Hughes, Emily Dickinson, Robert Frost, Shelley, Tennyson, Yeats, many others. Note. 80pp. 5 3/16 x 8¼. 0-486-40646-6

SPOON RIVER ANTHOLOGY, Edgar Lee Masters. An American poetry classic, in which former citizens of a mythical midwestern town speak touchingly from the grave of the thwarted hopes and dreams of their lives. 144pp. 5 3/16 x 8¼. 0-486-27275-3

STAR LORE: Myths, Legends, and Facts, William Tyler Olcott. Captivating retellings of the origins and histories of ancient star groups include Pegasus, Ursa Major, Pleiades, signs of the zodiac, and other constellations. "Classic." — *Sky & Telescope.* 58 illustrations. 544pp. 5⅜ x 8½. 0-486-43581-4

THE STRANGE CASE OF DR. JEKYLL AND MR. HYDE, Robert Louis Stevenson. This intriguing novel, both fantasy thriller and moral allegory, depicts the struggle of two opposing personalities — one essentially good, the other evil — for the soul of one man. 64pp. 5 3/16 x 8¼. 0-486-26688-5

SURVIVAL HANDBOOK: The Official U.S. Army Guide, Department of the Army. This special edition of the Army field manual is geared toward civilians. An essential companion for campers and all lovers of the outdoors, it constitutes the most authoritative wilderness guide. 288pp. 5 3/16 x 8¼. 0-486-46184-X

A TALE OF TWO CITIES, Charles Dickens. Against the backdrop of the French Revolution, Dickens unfolds his masterpiece of drama, adventure, and romance about a man falsely accused of treason. Excitement and derring-do in the shadow of the guillotine. 304pp. 5 3/16 x 8¼. 0-486-40651-2

TEN PLAYS, Anton Chekhov. *The Sea Gull, Uncle Vanya, The Three Sisters, The Cherry Orchard,* and *Ivanov,* plus 5 one-act comedies: *The Anniversary, An Unwilling Martyr, The Wedding, The Bear,* and *The Proposal.* 336pp. 5 3/16 x 8¼. 0-486-46560-8

THE FLYING INN, G. K. Chesterton. Hilarious romp in which pub owner Humphrey Hump and friend take to the road in a donkey cart filled with rum and cheese, inveighing against Prohibition and other "oppressive forms of modernity." 320pp. 5⅜ x 8½. 0-486-41910-X

THIRTY YEARS THAT SHOOK PHYSICS: The Story of Quantum Theory, George Gamow. Lucid, accessible introduction to the influential theory of energy and matter features careful explanations of Dirac's anti-particles, Bohr's model of the atom, and much more. Numerous drawings. 1966 edition. 240pp. 5⅜ x 8½. 0-486-24895-X

TREASURE ISLAND, Robert Louis Stevenson. Classic adventure story of a perilous sea journey, a mutiny led by the infamous Long John Silver, and a lethal scramble for buried treasure — seen through the eyes of cabin boy Jim Hawkins. 160pp. 5 3/16 x 8¼. 0-486-27559-0

THE TRIAL, Franz Kafka. Translated by David Wyllie. From its gripping first sentence onward, this novel exemplifies the term "Kafkaesque." Its darkly humorous narrative recounts a bank clerk's entrapment in a bureaucratic maze, based on an undisclosed charge. 176pp. 5³⁄₁₆ x 8¼. 0-486-47061-X

THE TURN OF THE SCREW, Henry James. Gripping ghost story by great novelist depicts the sinister transformation of 2 innocent children into flagrant liars and hypocrites. An elegantly told tale of unspoken horror and psychological terror. 96pp. 5³⁄₁₆ x 8¼. 0-486-26684-2

UP FROM SLAVERY, Booker T. Washington. Washington (1856-1915) rose to become the most influential spokesman for African-Americans of his day. In this eloquently written book, he describes events in a remarkable life that began in bondage and culminated in worldwide recognition. 160pp. 5³⁄₁₆ x 8¼. 0-486-28738-6

VICTORIAN HOUSE DESIGNS IN AUTHENTIC FULL COLOR: 75 Plates from the "Scientific American – Architects and Builders Edition," 1885-1894, Edited by Blanche Cirker. Exquisitely detailed, exceptionally handsome designs for an enormous variety of attractive city dwellings, spacious suburban and country homes, charming "cottages" and other structures — all accompanied by perspective views and floor plans. 80pp. 9¼ x 12¼. 0-486-29438-2

VILLETTE, Charlotte Brontë. Acclaimed by Virginia Woolf as "Brontë's finest novel," this moving psychological study features a remarkably modern heroine who abandons her native England for a new life as a schoolteacher in Belgium. 480pp. 5³⁄₁₆ x 8¼. 0-486-45557-2

THE VOYAGE OUT, Virginia Woolf. A moving depiction of the thrills and confusion of youth, Woolf's acclaimed first novel traces a shipboard journey to South America for a captivating exploration of a woman's growing self-awareness. 288pp. 5³⁄₁₆ x 8¼. 0-486-45005-8

WALDEN; OR, LIFE IN THE WOODS, Henry David Thoreau. Accounts of Thoreau's daily life on the shores of Walden Pond outside Concord, Massachusetts, are interwoven with musings on the virtues of self-reliance and individual freedom, on society, government, and other topics. 224pp. 5³⁄₁₆ x 8¼. 0-486-28495-6

WILD PILGRIMAGE: A Novel in Woodcuts, Lynd Ward. Through startling engravings shaded in black and red, Ward wordlessly tells the story of a man trapped in an industrial world, struggling between the grim reality around him and the fantasies his imagination creates. 112pp. 6⅛ x 9¼. 0-486-46583-7

WILLY POGÁNY REDISCOVERED, Willy Pogány. Selected and Edited by Jeff A. Menges. More than 100 color and black-and-white Art Nouveau–style illustrations from fairy tales and adventure stories include scenes from Wagner's "Ring" cycle, *The Rime of the Ancient Mariner, Gulliver's Travels,* and *Faust.* 144pp. 8⅜ x 11. 0-486-47046-6

WOOLLY THOUGHTS: Unlock Your Creative Genius with Modular Knitting, Pat Ashforth and Steve Plummer. Here's the revolutionary way to knit — easy, fun, and foolproof! Beginners and experienced knitters need only master a single stitch to create their own designs with patchwork squares. More than 100 illustrations. 128pp. 6½ x 9¼. 0-486-46084-3

WUTHERING HEIGHTS, Emily Brontë. Somber tale of consuming passions and vengeance — played out amid the lonely English moors — recounts the turbulent and tempestuous love story of Cathy and Heathcliff. Poignant and compelling. 256pp. 5³⁄₁₆ x 8¼. 0-486-29256-8